LPGA
Minus One

A Novel

By LEE JORGENSON

This effort is dedicated to the talented women of the LPGA

CHAPTER ONE

Congratulations Golfers. Amazon.Com has stepped up to the plate and revitalized the game for you up here. Safeco Insurance used to sponsor an LPGA annual tournament every September in Seattle at Meridian Valley Country Club. But regrettably, due to unforeseen circumstances, and some better offers, that went away in 1999. Now, just as the women's game is as vibrant as it has ever been, we are going to have another preeminent event on the ladies' calendar. And it will be played at the venerable Chambers Bay Golf Complex in University Place, host of the USGA's United States Open Golf Championship in 2015.

This tournament is contracted to be held on the second weekend in July 2019 and will continue for the next five years in that time slot. The total five-year purse is rumored to surpass the ten-million-dollar mark in prize money. Not to mention it will be held at an optimum time of the summer in the beautiful northwest climate, and on a world class course. Again, congratulations to the LPGA and Amazon for their hard work in putting the Pacific Northwest back on the (Inter)National Women's Golfing Map.

Two guys met in a bar. This sounds like the start of a joke. Its' not. Stuart Melman walked up to the bar at Vincenzo's on the south Seattle end of Highway 99, recoiled slightly at the dank smell of stale booze, and asked the barkeep for Vincent DeGrazzi.

"He's waitin' for you over there, kid," she pointed and told him.

"Good morning, sir," Stuart said upon approaching the far back corner booth, and offering his hand.

The two men, one much older and one much younger endured a perfunctory handshake, and Vincent DeGrazzi told his guest to sit down. Melman was still relatively green in the ways of the world. But he was reasonably intelligent, articulate, and in addition to possessing some basic street smarts and computer skills, he had devised a plan. He was determined to see if his plan had any legs, so he had sucked up his courage, and scheduled a mid-morning meeting in this infamous pit of vipers with the man himself. That made his young heart race. He was nervous as a dirt farmer with no rain coming soon.

"Thank you so much for taking this meeting, sir," Stuart said by way of an ice breaker.

"You ain't a flatfoot, are you?" DeGrazzi growled at him. "You look just like a rookie cop."

"Not a chance," Stuart replied immediately.

"Good, then you won't mind spending a minute in the restroom with my associate here."

One of Vincent's goons appeared and motioned Stuart to follow him. He led them into the men's room and locked the door. "Take your jacket off, and rest your hands on the sink counter," that command was followed by patting Stuart down thoroughly for a wire or a weapon.

Stuart complied readily, which helped this unpleasant little task go quickly enough. "He's clean, boss," the thug informed Vincent upon escorting Stuart back into the dimly lit bar. Stuart's eyes started to adjust, but he was still squinting a bit.

"Would you like something to drink?" Vincent asked.

"Coffee, please."

Then, from Vincent, "What can I do for you today, Mr. Melman?"

DeGrazzi was an old pro, a grizzled veteran by most standards. He had operated his restaurant and bar for twenty-five years, and also specialized in prostitution, bookmaking, and running numbers on the side. He was usually happy to discuss anything else that might come along and turn a buck. Whether it was a legal or illegal proposition. Better illegal actually, no taxes to pay. In his world he was a respected man, and he had eluded the long arm of the law in the south end of Seattle for over thirty years now. His local underworld connections were well established, and he considered himself to be very good at what he did.

As the bartender appeared with mugs of coffee, Stuart said "I have an opportunity for you to consider, sir."

"What kind of an opportunity?" And you can call me Vincent."

"Yes sir, Vincent. I think it could be a very lucrative opportunity," Stuart said hopefully.

"Go on."

"Well, there's an LPGA golf tournament coming here in July. It's going to be held at Chambers Bay Golf Club right near us in Tacoma. I went to high school with this girl who's a big LPGA star now. I think she would be fairly easy to snatch, and we could ransom her for some big money."

"Why are you sayin' we?" Vincent asked curiously.

"Because I'm a computer guy. I could organize things, but this would need some professional people to pull off."

"Oh, so you could be like the brains of the outfit, and I would take all of the risks, eh?"

"No sir, it's not like that at all. I have studied this situation in depth. This girl is a workaholic. It's common knowledge about her habitually staying out on the driving range until almost dark. There's usually no one around by the time she leaves the course. It would be so easy to get to her. She is a big name on tour now, and she's the sweetheart of Washington golf. If we grabbed her, we could make a fortune." Stuart was nervous enough that his coffee tasted like chalk dust, but he was making his spiel to the best of his ability.

"You dumb little shit. You come in here and waste my time. Don't you know a ransom gig is the hardest thing to manage in the trades anymore? It's virtually impossible to pull off with all of the technology the cops have nowadays. Plus, if she is so smokin' hot, you know she will bring down an incredible amount of heat on anything like this. And I mean some big-time pushback." DeGrazzi stared at Stuart Melman with hard eyes, eyes like onyx stones.

"I know that sir, but she would also be worth ten to twelve million bucks easy. She has money, her people are well off, and the LPGA would probably want to help. Hell, look at the resources the tournament sponsor Amazon has, they would no doubt pitch in too. Plus, I could work the computer side. We would never even have to talk to the cops or the feds. We contact her banker from an untraceable source, he gets the cash together, passes it off, and we are set."

"The banker does the transfer? And lower your voice, would you?"

"Sorry, sorry," Stuart said, and resumed talking in a near whisper. "No, the banker reference was just a figure of speech. He rounds up the payoff to whoever makes the drop. I have a couple of ideas about that too."

"I'll bet you do," Vincent said with a snort.

"There's a house in down in Pierce County I have access to. It would be a perfect spot to hide her out," Stuart said, continuing to warm to his task. "It is semi-isolated, sits on the water, and has a basement to stash her in. If we keep her for a week or two, the tension and effort to buy her back would be phrenic. We could do this, because it's a plan that has a lot of potential, but you are smart. You are a pro, and you and your people know how to make this kind of thing happen." Stuart was a computer guy, but it was becoming obvious he had some born salesman in him.

"I never seen you before, well maybe once or twice in my bar, and you come in here and tell me how smart I am, how easy this would be, and talking all about my people. Are you crazy or something?" The last person who had gotten his wires crossed with Vincent had barely lived to regret it, and then left town in the dark of night.

"Mr. DeGrazzi, I have watched your operation for over a year now. And let me tell you how smart you are: You run a clean place. You keep a lot of working girls around, and you keep them happy and busy. You have a great staff of people surrounding you. A guy could come in here, meet someone and have a great time. I mean hook up good, and with no questions asked. Now then, you look at these dumb jerks, one hundred thirty-nine of them to be exact, who just got busted last fall because they were stupid enough to go online and solicit a hooker on an undercover police website. Sight unseen, they went online, thought they had a secure connection with someone they had never met, someone they had no experience with, and put their butts out there in front of God and everyone. So, what happened? They got busted like chumps! And some of them were big time, high profile dudes, who were all over the news. Tell me then who is smarter, you, who has been running this place and making good money at it for twenty-five years, or a bunch of horny idiots in Bellevue?"

"Well, you got a point there, kid. They was pretty damn dumb."

"Mr. DeGrazzi, I urge you to just think about it. That don't cost anything, and it could prove to be very profitable. I am also in a position to contribute by supplying the technology we would need, a safe house, and some of the operational support. Do us a favor, and just think about it for a few days. We could grab Miss Preppy Pants easy, and she could turn into a big payday. I would do anything you asked of me."

"You know what? This girl dump on you in high school or something like that? You sound like this is kinda personal."

"Are you kidding me? It would take the Yakima Mafia to get into that girl's pants. She has three tough brothers, and her dad must have half a dozen hombres working on his property. If you messed up, they could off you, bury your body out on the back forty somewhere, and no one would be the wiser. She probably doesn't even remember me anyway."

"What do you know about the Yakima Mafia?"

"Nothing, really nothing, sir. It was just a manner of speaking."

"Are you a fag or somethin'?"

"No way, why do you ask?"

"Well, stop sayin' shit like phrenic and manner of speaking. My people don't talk like that. And never, ever say or use the word Mafia around me. I run a legitimate business here."

"Yes sir. I mean no sir, I mean yes sir," Stuart stammered.

"You know kid, if I ever did get involved in something like this, my people are professionals, period. You get that right? If you did anything that looked funny, or something went wrong, they would make dogfood out of you."

"Yes sir, I know this is serious business. That's why I would never attempt something of this magnitude without your expertise."

"So, you just might have something here kid. Of course, I would have to talk to some people and see if there was any interest, capiche?"

"Yes sir. Here, take a business card, my cell numbers on it. I look forward to hearing from you."

"Sure kid, yeah, yeah. Hey, you say you is a computer guy?"

"Yes sir."

Chrissy Jensen was excited at the news of the Amazon Tournament. A Washington native, she grew up in the Yakima Valley. Yakima is a fertile and developing region in the central area of the state, which grows extensive yields of tree fruit, vegetables, berries, nuts, world class hops, and is now emerging as a highly desirable wine growing terroir.

The Jensen family breeds/sells/trades/races thoroughbred horses and also has over a hundred acres of peaches under cultivation on their two hundred acre spread in the valley. Chrissy's tight-knit family consists of parents Bob and Ginny, three brothers, grand folk, and numerous in-laws. Chrissy is the third child of the four siblings, and keeping up with three brothers, she couldn't help but develop into a world class tomboy. Now twenty-seven years old and graduated from the University of Washington with a degree in Psychology, she enjoyed a full ride scholarship to the U as a member of the Women's Golf Team, and is in her fourth full year of competition on the LPGA Tour.

Tall, graceful, attractive, and smart, she possesses the good looks that most men and some women will pause to look twice at, but she is also mentally as tough as nails. Her long blond hair is usually pulled back in a flowing pony tail. For more formal events, it is nicely curled and cascades down over the top of her shoulders. Her hazel brown eyes aren't afraid to look directly at you, and a wide friendly smile lights up her face most of the time. A face so fetching, it looks as sweet and refreshing as one of those ripe peaches from her family's orchard might taste. Her eyes dominate, twinkling nicely when she is happy, and can definitely light up a room. But when she is in a tournament and its game time, they can be absolutely smoldering. Especially if she has on a darker shade of eye liner, and her putts aren't dropping.

Spending time breaking high-strung horses helped her develop great balance, strength in her hands and forearms, and made her tough and fearless. During summer harvest, helping her dad and brothers haul heavy crates of tree fruit, itchy with peach fuzz, made her wiry strong, but also created a work ethic in her that is second to none.

Chrissy's mom is an avid golfer and one of the lower ladies' handicaps at their course. She and her daughter would sneak away every chance they got during the long, hot summer days to tee it up at Yakima Valley Country Club. Chrissy was beating her single digit handicap mom regularly by her freshman year in high school, and was already winning junior tournaments in the central region of Washington by then. She became the first female member of her family to receive an athletic scholarship, and soon enough there were three Jensens attending college. Her older brother Will went to Washington State University in Pullman on a basketball scholarship, and was studying in the business college. He would become Chrissy's Agent/Business Manager after graduation. Little bro Bobby was two years behind her, and had also opted for WSU. However, he was on more of a non-scholarship partying program. This would actually prove useful in his chosen career, because he took up looping as his big sister's caddy. What else do you do with a degree in Recreation Management from WSU?

Chrissy needed a year to survive LPGA Qualifying School after college, but now has six professional tournament wins under her belt, including one major, and is in the top five in tour earnings for the current year. This has also brought her no shortage of endorsement opportunities, and another parallel income well into six-figure altitude.

Chrissy is a student of the game of golf, loves the often-colorful pioneers who preceded her and arduously laid such a substantial foundation for today's players. Babe Zaharias, Kathy Whitworth, Judy Rankin, Nancy Lopez, Anika Sorenstam, Lorena Ochoa, and also their male counterparts: Bobby Jones, Walter Hagan, Slammin' Sammy Snead, Arnie, Jack, Tiger, to name a few. But she is especially enthralled with Mr. Ben Hogan--this little giant of a man who achieved so much through his tenacious personal philosophy of outworking everyone. Chrissy could see no other way to approach the game.

Wouldn't your God-given talents only be enhanced by intensive practice and a little self-sacrifice? Therefore, she has developed a reputation for logging long hours on the range and then more time on her short game. And, it is pretty obvious that all the hard work is paying some substantial dividends.

With all Chrissy has going on, how could her life get any better? She is hot; the media, her sponsors, her bankers, her downhome family, her alma mater, and her fans all love her. As close as she is to family/friends/fans, as much as she loved life as a kid growing up back on the ranch, and then her great experiences at the University of Washington and on the LPGA Tour, it seems like it is in her DNA to get back home and win this big-time new golf tournament.

CHAPTER TWO

Stuart left Vincent in his Bar/Restaurant's informal business office and began the twenty-minute drive back home. He lived in a three-bedroom townhouse with two roommates. His partner in crime, Chester Lincoln, and his fiancée, Monica Brown. Chet was sitting on their couch waiting for a report when Stuart walked in the front door.

"How'd it go?"

"Pretty well. He might be interested, but said he wants to think about it for a couple of days. You wouldn't believe what happened."

"Tell me."

Stuart sat down opposite Chet and began an incredible yarn.

"I gave him a business card as I was leaving, so he would have my number, and he asked me for some help with his computer. I wanted to know what kind of problem he was having, and he said his regular tech guy was away and he needed a copy of some stuff from his confidential files."

"You're kidding me."

"No way. So, I told him I had a wireless printer in my car, and I would be happy to help him out. He takes me back into his office and pulls this laptop out of a locked drawer in his desk. There was an old lady working in the office who had the access codes, so I booted it up, and began to sync our machines. He got a phone call, and while he was talking, I texted his ID and password to my other phone, then went to the TeamSpy Website, downloaded a Quick Support App with Sessions Codes. It only took another minute to activate the App, and now we have access to all his private information.

"Dude, you better be really careful! You are freaking me out."

"I know, I know. I buried the App, and you could never recall it without the retrieval codes. They won't even know there is anything in there. He already warned me he would have to off anyone who might let his stuff get into the wrong hands. I assured him his information was safe with me."

"You are seriously crazy."

"I know, but don't you think it'll be good to have something like this to hold over his head? I mean, if we ever did do any business. I am sure he would try to screw us, but this way we can keep him honest. He causes any problems, we could RICO his butt."

"Yeah sure. But you be careful." Chet was more conservative than Stuart. Although they had known each other for almost five years now, Chet was going to be the support guy in any activities they got involved with. He was pretty savvy for his twenty-seven years. Athletic, a certified water sports enthusiast with an AA degree from South Seattle Community College, he sold real estate on the south end of Seattle, enjoyed cruising in his BMW 320i, and was pretty confident of his future. He was doing what most twenty-something bachelors do, e.g., work, eat, sleep, party, and not necessarily in that order. But he was also approachable with any reasonable scams that had the possibility of some easy money and adventure.

"I will be very careful," Stuart said. "Let me go download his stuff right now. Then I can deactivate the program, rebury it in his archives, and he will be none the wiser. He is computer illiterate anyway."

"Okay. But don't keep his password and Wi-Fi info around either. And didn't you say he had a computer guy?"

"Yeah, apparently his regular guy Dimitri is away on some kind of business."

"Jeez, he even sounds dangerous. Like he is a Russian thug or something."

"Trust me, I will be careful."

"I gotta go to work. I'm showing a couple of houses this afternoon, and then teaching a scuba diving class at the Y at four. If this guy wants to move forward, we need to get going. I put a tentative hold on that waterfront rental listing, but it's only good for another week."

"I get it. We just have to wait until he calls back. Where is Monica?"

"She went out to run some errands. Said she'd be back in an hour or so."

Stuart nodded as he exited the living room, went into the master bedroom and turned on his PC.

Vincent had an early lunch in the same back booth of the bar, and then got ready to depart for his afternoon golf match. He played at Oakridge Golf Club in Lakewood, which was thirty minutes away and on the south side of Tacoma, Washington.

There was nothing too fancy about Oakridge. It was a combo public/private course, but it was casual, and Vincent liked that. People respected his group and gave them plenty of space and seclusion when they wanted it. He hated the stodgier private clubs like Emerald Golf and Country Club or Redwood Grove Golf Club. They were so formal, the people were mostly older retired professionals, the Club dues were expensive, and the members were so cliquey.

Oakridge was cool, and it was user-friendly for him. If the guys wanted to curse a little or tell a few stories in the bar after a round, no problem. Even if they brought a few of the working girls around now and then, no problem. Vincent ensured it wasn't a problem by making a serious donation to the Employees Christmas Fund every year. He was Oakridge's largest benefactor, and therefore, Vincent was a major player at the club. He was treated with deference and veneration. People called him Mr. DeGrazzi. His golf cart was always ready for him, loaded with his clubs, and sitting in front of the pro shop an hour before he was scheduled to tee off. His gin and tonic was icy cold and waiting on the bar as soon as he walked in after a round. He was greeted courteously by name wherever he went. A connected guy craves respect, and Vincent felt loved and appreciated at Oakridge.

Today he was playing with his usual foursome. Mickey DeAngelo, Ronnie "the Barber" Barbieri, and Tommy "the T" Thurston. These were the only guys Vincent trusted, had known forever, and done major business with over the years. The boys called themselves "The Guapos," which translates roughly into "The Elegant Scoundrels."

They are all getting into early middle age and aren't quite the golfers they used to be. But they are experienced players, serious gamblers, and aren't out there to break any course records anyway. No one at Oakridge has more fun than the Guapos. Besides, it's all about keeping in touch, enjoying the friendship they have shared over the years, and of course, if a little business should come up, so much the better.

Mickey DeAngelo is another connected guy who's the group's best player. He owns a twelve handicap and is the most fun-loving Guapo. He is a Union Rep affiliated with the construction trades in King and Pierce Counties. Just what his exact job description is, no one is quite sure. But Mickey tells some great stories and is a first-rate drinking buddy. Rumor has it he knows all about where Jimmy Hoffa was cremated.

Ronnie Barbieri is just the opposite of Mickey. He is the straight man. Serious, conservative, and extremely well groomed. If he isn't at the barbershop once a week, everyone knows he's a sick man. Therefore, his shortish hair is never messed up or out of place, and he doesn't have bad hair days. He had also given an extremely close shave, sic, with the straight razor to a guy one time. Hence, for these two reasons they call him "the Barber." Ronnie is a CPA and Financial Advisor to people who have special administrative needs. He is meticulous in what he does, he has to be. Many people depend on him to launder their money efficiently. He plays to a fifteen. Some people think he is too analytical about his game, too stiff--but that is just his personal and professional style.

Tommy Thurston is an operator. An independent operator. He takes care of things that need tending to for some folks. All his contract work is very confidential and booked on referral only. He has taken jobs from industrial arson and extortion, to occasionally helping people disappear. He is an ex-marine, and totally self-employed, but he seldom finds himself with more time on his hands than he cares for. Tommy plays to a fourteen handicap and wins his fair share of money from the boys. He is fearless and at his best when facing a clinching putt of six feet, with all the money on the line. Tommy is the longest hitter of the four fellas.

Vincent DeGrazzi, of course, owns and operates his bar and Italian restaurant, pours an honest drink, runs numbers on the south end of King County, and is an unofficial bookie in the neighborhood for major sporting events. He also runs a sizeable stable of working girls out of his bar. To accommodate the girls, he purchased two nondescript motels near the bar, which feature convenient hourly or half day rates. Everyone enjoys this arrangement. The girls feel safe and like his protection. The customers feel secure, and frequently are regulars. The south end cops are treated generously, and the whole operation is just a money maker for Vincent. A real cash cow. As it is a regular bar and restaurant and not a strip joint, he isn't subjected to the constant harassment of the Vice Squad. He plays to a fourteen handicap, is happy to get out three times a week with his pals, and as he turns fifty, is for the most part satisfied with what he has accomplished in life. He isn't a big-time mobster, but he is connected, and has created a comfortable lifestyle with three grown kids, an adorable wife, a spacious home in the suburbs, and a steady income. If anything, he is probably somewhat bored with his ongoing routine.

Our boys teed off, on a sunny but cool late spring afternoon. Monday is usually a major maintenance day on most golf courses. But since it was a regular playing day for Vincent and the boys, and with the respect they generate, Oakridge is happy to move any primary maintenance that doesn't get finished on Monday morning back a day. Even though Tuesday is Ladies Day.

"Are you guys going to be able to stick around for a drink after golf?" Vincent inquired on the first tee box. "I might have something for us."

"Sure, sure," they responded. No one had anything urgent planned on a Monday afternoon.

Their game went well today. The guys liked to play skins, because it was exciting, and didn't kill someone who had a blowup hole or two. This way they could also keep legitimate handicaps for more formal club-wide tournaments.

Vincent made a couple of long birdie putts on the par three holes. He ended up winning ten carry over skins, and his second birdie on the back nine won all of the presses and the side action. He won around six hundred bucks and was feeling pretty expansive and flush. The boys repaired to the bar.

Drinks were served, and Vinnie (he was Vinnie with these guys) said, "so this kid comes to see me this morning."

"Yeah?"

Vinnie lowered his voice and looked around both ways. No one was too close or paying any noticeable attention to them. No one dared. "He wants to work with us, and grab one of the LPGA players in two months at the Chambers Bay LPGA tournament. He thinks she could go for around twelve mil."

"Who was dis kid?" asked Mickey.

"I don't know him. I seen him around my bar a few times with his girlfriend, and she is a knockout, but he is definitely a civilian."

"We doing business with civilians now?"

"Hell no. He had a good idea is all I'm sayin'. And he's smart. He done some work on my computer. He is a computer guy."

"You let somebody off of the street work on your computer?" Ronnie asked, and his accountant radar lit up immediately.

"Aw, I just axked him to print some stuff for me with his wireless printer. He wanted to hook the laptop to our system, and I wouldn't let him. Don't even think about it, I told him. He said printers just print, you know, they don't retain no information, but

I still made him print my stuff out on his wireless. Phoenix wants their quarterly update is all, and Dimitri is away for a little while longer." Vincent seemed very comfortable and unthreatened with Stuart's assistance.

"You gave some clown access to your second books? Are you crazy?" said Ronnie.

"Don't get all paranoid on me. This is a good kid. He is smart, and very respectful. He wants to do business with us, and he had a good idea. He printed out some damn papers, that's all."

"Yeah, well you be careful. I have computer guys if you need anyone. These young guys can come in and put a virus in your computer, and you are screwed. You can't trust anyone anymore. So, what is his big idea?"

"Ah, this guy is okay, you'll see. It's about the Amazon golf tournament at Chambers Bay in July. He knows one of the LPGA players from his high school days over in Yakima. She is a big star now. Chrissy Jensen, if you know the name. She is a workaholic. Out on the practice range 'til dark almost every night. We wait until everyone is gone and grab her. This Stuart guy wants to rent a safe house over on the peninsula, right on the water. We hold her for a week or two without contacting anyone. Let everyone get all nervous as hell, and then this guy gets in touch with her banker real untraceable like. We don't even talk to the Feds. The hell with them. We give them two or three days to raise the dough, then we arrange a drop off, let the kid grab the money, then we bone him, and pick up twelve million bucks. Whatta ya think? It could be our last big heist. Then we retire and move to Palm Desert and play golf nine months a year."

Tommy the T who was the ops guy in the group spoke up. "Kidnapping is always risky. This sounds easy, but it would bring major heat. Grabbing and holding her is nothing compared to the exchange for the ransom money. It's a big payday, but also could be major trouble. We don't want to spend our golden years in McNeil Island State Pen or someplace like that."

"Yeah well," Vincent responded. "We make a plan and let Vassily and Dimitri handle it. We let the schmuck pick up the cash drop, and if he makes it, we heist the dough like I said, and get rid of the kid. Then we pay off the Russians, and split the rest. This is some serious money we're talking about. I could sell my joint and retire, Ronnie. Just think about it will you guys? We can talk again on Wednesday. Sleep on it for a few days, eh?" and with that, the casual business meeting was officially over.

"You lucky little turkey," Mickey DeAngelo said to his old pal Vinnie DeGrazzi. "Who you been takin' puttin' lessons from? You ain't never made two long putts like that in your life. Let alone in one damn round. You on steroids?"

"Relax, let me buy you a drink. Don't take it personal that you got your ass whipped by a tremendous athlete who is a lot better lookin' than you."

Vincent caught the bartender's eye and motioned to her for another round, and the drinking, table talk, and the jockeying began. After an hour, the gentlemen left for home or wherever, and all of them agreed to be back on Wednesday. Same time, same place.

CHAPTER THREE

Chrissy was in Singapore at the last Asian Tournament of the early LPGA season, and she found the foreign cultures fascinating. As a matter of fact, the hustle and bustle of the world-class, international cities captivated her: Jakarta, Bangkok, Seoul, Shanghai, Taipei. And who wouldn't be amazed by the congestion and chaos of the almost infinite density of humanity--walking, riding bicycles, scooters, buses and juxtaposed with the shiny, new Mercedes sedans careening around them. The gleaming glass and metal, high rise-urban centers, the luxurious hillside mansions, the squalid shantytowns, the adorable children.

Chrissy would have preferred staying in the midst of these glamorous, exotic cities, absorbing more of the indigenous cuisines, cultures, and acquisition opportunities. But transportation back and forth to the golf courses would have presented logistical problems. They were far enough away, and traffic was such that she was obliged to stay at the lodging (usually luxurious, or close to it) provided by her tournament hosts. There was so much going on around said tournaments (pro-am festivities, practice time, practice rounds, tourney rounds, sponsored dinners, etc.), staying off-site would have seriously compromised her professional routine.

But being housed with the other players allowed all of them time to bond a little closer. And there was never a shortage of side trips: educational, cultural, recreational, shopping, and social events if you were interested. There was always a whirlwind of activity going on.

After the Indonesia swing, it was back to the states and a few weeks off. Then she would start to work on peaking her game for the new Chambers Bay/Amazon tournament. While the Asian stops were interesting, and the purses were good, they entailed a lot of travel time. This was often tiring, and the Asian girls were tough enough to beat back in the US. But here, you were playing them on their own turf. Definitely a challenge.

The Guapos were at Oakridge for their Wednesday game. Spring weather in the Puget Sound region that day was its usual unpredictable self. Cool and sunny one minute, then windy, cloudy, and sprinkling the next. But as long as the rain wasn't pelting down, they couldn't care less. Such is the power and almost magic appeal for the game of golf with some people.

Mickey had the hot hand for the day and was happy to let his pals understand this would be the new norm going forward. Of course, that brought forth a chorus of derision. But he was soon to have their money in his pocket, and he couldn't help but poke them about it all afternoon.

Halfway through drinks in the clubhouse, Vincent inquired after anyone's thoughts of last Monday's conversation. He was for investigating this opportunity thoroughly, as he could smell a worthwhile payday in it. But it would take some convincing to enlist his pals. He must proceed with patience and guile. He actually wished he had not put the opportunity on the table to all of them. But then again, it was good to get the group's input. He trusted them implicitly, and if he couldn't convince anyone of the potential in his scheme, then it was up to them to dissuade him from getting involved.

Ronnie spoke up first. "This is a very serious matter here. Sure, the payoff could be good. But there are so many risks. From an operational standpoint, grabbing someone is no sweat. Even holding someone is not a big problem. The issue is always transferring the ransom dough."

"In the first place," Vincent opened his end of the conversation, "we would not have any active part of this job. If we had a couple of the Russians grab her, and sit on her, so be it union. Get it? Russians/Sobeit Union?"

"Har, har," was the response.

"This is no joking matter, Vincent. How long have those guys worked for you?" Mickey wanted to know. "Can they be trusted with something big like this?"

"They been with me for three years now. I ain't never had no trouble whatever. And they pick up all my number's money, which is in cash, and promote the games every week. I think they would be excited to take on something bigger like this. They is very smart."

"Almost too smart to be trusted. You know what I mean?" commented the Barber.

A couple of guys came in and sat down next to the boys' table. Rather than make a scene, they got their drinks transferred to traveling cups and went out to Vincent's black Cadillac Escalade.

When they were settled in, Vincent continued on. "For one thing, we would be dealing with state cops more than the Feds. Secondly, if we was to get involved, we let the kid do the dirty work for half a share, and we set it up to grab all of the dough anyway. Thirdly, if things did go wrong, we get the Russians out of here, and over the border into Canada. I don't think they give a damn anyway, they are doing so much business up there as it is. And we let computer boy take the fall."

"Well, you know the little sucker would squawk like a chicken hawk if the cops got their hands on him," said Ronnie.

"Not if his family or his girlfriend was at risk, or he was to disappear," replied Vincent. "Listen, why don't we just sit down and talk to him. No strings attached. Pick his little pea brain and see if we can move on it or not. Probably not, but it don't cost nothin' to talk. How about tomorrow at my place? I'll buy lunch."

"We're good with that," Tommy replied for the group. "About time you bought something."

Stuart Melman's phone rang around five that evening. A friend was calling him from a burner cell phone.

"This is your old buddy. Come for lunch at my place tomorrow at one o'clock."

"Yes sir, I will be delighted to see you again."

"Fuck you. Don't be late."

"No sir."

Stuart clicked off the phone and turned to his girlfriend Monica. "Hey, I've got a meeting with him tomorrow at one."

"No kidding, I didn't know if they would bite or not," Monica replied.

"Well, they must think there is some potential. Or they wouldn't be wasting their time."

"Do you think we should we hook up your mini ProCam for the meeting?"

"Nah, I don't want to screw anything up too soon. Let's get them signed on first," Stuart said.

"Yeah, you're probably right. But we should go over the plan. I'm off tonight, and we can get you prepped up for your meeting."

"Sure, good idea. You want to go out and eat or stay in?" Stuart was always ready to go out.

"Let's go to Ziggy's. We can grab a pizza and have a few beers while we talk. I'll check with Chester and see if he is available." There's nothing to eat at the house anyway, Monica thought.

"Cool. How about seven?"

Stuart had it for Monica. They met at her place of business over a year ago, and it didn't take long for him to ask her out. When she had her hair up in a topknot and smiled her frisky little smile at him, he went to the moon. Monica was tough. Not mean tough, just feisty. Heck, she was a professional bartender. At twenty-nine she was a little older than Stuart, and was raised in a military family. She and her brother had lived all over the US. The world actually. As a military brat, she thought of herself as rootless, and was somewhat cynical about her life to date. But the travel and experiences she had gained over time had widened her horizons and contributed greatly to the hardened tenacity she was so proud of in herself.

Her father retired from the United States Army as a Sergeant First Class and died of tuberculous two years later. There was talk that exposure to Agent Orange during two tours of duty in Vietnam had damaged his lungs, but nothing had been confirmed on that front by the Veterans Administration. And they moved so very slowly on any type of claim, Monica had given up trying to deal with them.

She actually wondered what the twenty-five years her father had spent in the military had accomplished. Other than dragging his family all over the world, what was the benefit? Her father was a patriot, and she respected that. Monica, on the other hand, was a pragmatist. She was close to her mom, however, and when this gambol of theirs was over, a visit to the Philippines would be in the works. It might not be a bad place to chill for a while.

Her dad was an American citizen, born and raised a proud NY Mets fan from the borough of Queens, and her mom was a native of the Philippines. They met while he was on temporary assignment at Subic Bay as a military advisor. Her parents had been married for thirty years. But after her dad passed, Monica's mom moved back to Manilla and her birth family, leaving her son and daughter on their own in the US. Monica's brother joined the Army and followed in his father's footsteps. Monica wouldn't have joined the military on a bet, so after her father had mustered out of the service at Joint Base Lewis/McCord in Tacoma, Washington, Monica stayed on in the area and decided to called it home.

She had inherited her father's height, and willowy body type, standing five foot nine, and sturdy, but not bulky. Nicely proportioned would be an appropriate description, with her mom's straight, dark hair, widely spaced brown eyes, high cheek bones, and the muted olive skin typical of a biracial child. Her eyes were her defining feature. They were animated and immediately attracted your attention. Then you enjoyed the rest of her as a secondary pleasure. Her face had a beauty mark high on the outside of her right cheek. She had a mischievous smile, which was just disinterested enough to keep the barflies in her insanely busy bar from getting overly friendly or chummy. She walked jauntily and was a working supervisor at the bustling Emerald Queen Casino in Tulalip, Washington, a Tacoma suburb. After working the six p.m. to two a.m. shift for the last two years, dealing with drunks or losers in the casino, and having had her ass grabbed or being hit on more times than she cared to remember, she was ready for an opportunity to scam some real cash. To make a life for herself. Embracing her mother's strong Philippine personality and her father's military discipline, she decided she was willing to take the risks involved in abetting a major crime if it would turn into a big-time payday. Plus, she trusted Stuart's street smarts, his computer/tech skills, and Chet's multi-faceted talents implicitly. She and Stuart had been a couple for a year now, and Chet had been their buddy and roomie throughout.

The three partners in crime settled into Ziggy's, their favorite dive tavern, and ordered a round of PBRs. While Vincent had his lifelong friends, Chet and Stuart had also gotten to be about as tight as possible for two twenty-something white guys. They met in their first classes together at South Seattle Community College four and a half years ago, and had roomed together for three years now.

"I can't believe we are actually doing this," Monica said.

Chet chimed in, "No kidding. This is gnarly, but it is just a meeting. We aren't really doing anything yet. If this thing goes, we could make a killing. But we have to be really careful, too. These guys are nothing to screw around with. That was brilliant getting access to the old man's laptop. Did you download his stuff?"

"Yeah, I got it all on a flash drive. I haven't had time to really dig into it yet. But there has got to be some good stuff on there."

"Whatever it is, we have to get enough on these monkeys to keep them off of our backs. I'm sure they are going to try and stick it to us when the time comes," Chet observed.

"Yeah, you're right about that," Stuart replied. "I just want them to get used to seeing me with my laptop. Then we can plant a bug or a mini cam in it later. Like you say, get enough on them, and then if they try anything, we got some live ammo to fire back with."

"Don't ever trust them with anything," Monica said. "These are not good people. Vincent DeGrazzi comes into the casino now and then, and even our security guys back off of him."

"So, how much are you going to tell them tomorrow?" Chet wanted to know.

"Just the basics. First of all, if they want to do this, we've got to rent the waterfront house in Gig Harbor. Then we buy week-long passes to the tournament, including a Class C Clubhouse parking pass. Vincent's guys show up every day at Chambers Bay and get to know the place. Probably, drive a Lincoln Town Car like they are chauffeurs. Hopefully, Chrissy is doing good in the tournament. After Friday or Saturday's round, they grab her when she is staying late to practice. She comes out of the clubhouse to her car, almost everyone is already gone, and she is alone. I saw her do exactly the same thing last year in Portland, at the LPGA tourney down there at Edgewood.

"Vincent's guys grab her and take her to the house, carefully! Then we hold her for a week, and everyone will be going crazy. Finally, we call her banker on a burner phone. Tell 'em that we want twelve million bucks in unmarked hundred-dollar bills. We don't even talk to the cops. Just the banker. I will set up online ghost accounts, and we give them our commands. No chance for the cops to negotiate or trace anything. They won't like that at all. We give 'em maybe two or three days to get up the money. No tracking devices, no dyes, nothing funny, or Chrissy gets it. She will be totally freaked out by then anyway. Every one of her people will be frantic."

"Whatta ya mean Chrissy gets it?" Monica asked. "I don't like the way you are talking Stuart, and I won't be a part of anything like that."

"That's just an idle threat, babe. I would never hurt anyone like her."

Chet chimed in, trying to change the subject, "We should make a YouTube of Chrissy, and they can see how badly she wants to get out of there."

Stuart got back on task and continued detailing his plan. "Then, we put a couple of crab pots out somewhere around Fox Island. We tell the banker to wrap the money in plastic garbage sacks, at the last minute we tell them where the crab pots are located. They go hoist them up, tie the money to the pots, drop 'em back in and then beat it. This is the best part. We dive out to the crab pots, grab the money, and scuba out of there. Split the dough and take off. The cops and probably the FBI are sitting there all night watching the pots, waiting for someone to pull them up, and we are long gone."

"Dude," Chet said, "first of all, do you know how much money a million bucks in one hundred-dollar bills weighs? Secondly, you know the FBI is going to be on this like rain on Seattle in January."

"Well, I hadn't gotten far enough to weigh the money out yet, and I agree with you, everyone will be on this big time. All I'm sayin' is, we negotiate with the bankers. Not the cops or the FBI."

"The cash will weigh just over twenty-two pounds per million," Chet said. "Twenty-two times twelve, equals two hundred sixty-four pounds."

"Hot dang, that is a lot."

"Yeah, but the good news is that dead weight drops by one-third under water."

"So, if we split it into two bags that would be one hundred thirty-two pounds each, less one-third for the underwater weight? How much is that?"

"About eighty-eight pounds,"

"Well, that's doable."

"We collect the bags, and drop one off for them, and split with our half."

"What about us?" Chet wanted to know. "Are you going to tell them you have partners?"

"I don't think so just yet. The less they know the better. I can tell them I am going to do the computer stuff, and they grab Chrissy, and hold her at the house. When we get to the underwater work, that we have someone who will go down with one of their guys. If any of them need lessons, they will have almost two months to get certified. You can even do that maybe. I will tell them there are lessons available at the YMCA. If they don't want to dive, then I will go down with you."

"I don't necessarily want to be underwater fighting those currents with some stupid rookie. Think they will go for just you and me picking up the cash?"

"I don't know. It depends on if their guys have any diving experience. Hey, why don't you go down with their rookie, and see if he might have an accident down there. Then we just pick up the dough and split with all of it."

"Great idea, Stuart," Chet replied sarcastically. "That would be like murder one on me, eh? Not to mention the guy would be a fucking mobster. That ain't gonna happen, bro. We should set it up that we handle the money though. Because if they get their hands on it first, we will never see a damn dime. These guys would kill their sister for twelve million bucks."

"Yeah, I know they would. But don't forget about the thumb drive with Vincent's financial records on it either."

"That's true. As long as we don't get wasted over a thumb drive. I think it is really important that we agree on a plan for exchanging the money. Something that covers our butts. Or these guys are going to try and rip us."

"I agree. That's why I like the crab pot plan."

"Well, let's see what they have to say. Don't commit to anything until you talk to me."

"I won't. I need another beer, dude. I am starting to freak out."

CHAPTER FOUR

Stuart showed up at ten minutes to one the next day and was told to wait at the bar. "You be sure your tats are well covered," Monica told him while he was dressing. "Those guys are old school; they won't like your ink."

The Guapos were already seated in the back room, which doubled as a private meeting space/poker parlor, and Vincent wanted a few words with them before sitting down with anyone.

"Listen guys, I been thinkin' about this, and I believe we need to hear what this kid has to say. If he has a good idea, then we could maybe run with it. If not, fuhgeddaboudit. The Russians make me nervous. I think Ronnie is right about trusting them around this kind of money." Vincent liked the way he had moved the negotiation to a reactionary level, rather than just a simple informational exchange.

"You been thinkin', eh?" said Mickey. "That must be exhausting."

Ronnie the Barber sat stone-faced. He thought Vincent was crazy to get involved with any high-level risk at this point in his career. He certainly wasn't remotely interested in participating in the fun, and he knew from experience that the more talk that went on about this kind of thing, the more reasonable and doable it sounded. At best, a professional challenge, and these guys all considered themselves to be experienced pros. But he would wait to weigh in at the right time.

Mickey was also skeptical, and didn't want to get involved at all.

I will be the quiet one, Tommy thought, non-committal at this point, but still willing to listen.

Vincent went out to the bar, found Stuart, had Dimitri shake him down, and returned into the back room with young Mr. Melman. Stuart felt like he was appearing before the Supreme Court Justices in their entirety. He was dressed in Nordstrom blue jeans, a long sleeve blue dress shirt, black loafers, and a light weight, black leather jacket. Not exactly a power outfit, but dressy enough to show respect to Vincent and the Guapos.

"This my new friend Stuart. What you say is your last name again?" The Guapos nodded sternly. "So, Stuart," Vincent continued, "why don't youse tell us a little about yourself."

"Well gentlemen, thank you for being here. I am honored. My last name is Melman by the way. I grew up in Yakima, Washington. My father sold farm equipment, my mother worked part-time in town, various type stuff of no importance. They divorced when I was a senior in high school, and I don't see my mom too much since she remarried and moved to Kansas. My dad died in an automobile crash four years ago. I have one older brother who is in the Army, currently serving a tour of the middle east." Stuart had a sip of the water that was at his table setting. At the pause in the conversation, Vincent took the opportunity to announce that he had ordered Italian for everyone. What a surprise, eh? Just a nice little two-hour luncheon befitting his guests.

Stuart plodded on. "After graduating high school, I moved to the Puget Sound area to continue my education, and studied computers at South Seattle Community College. Got an AA Degree, then went to work in the computer industry on several jobs. Two years ago, I started my own tech consulting business here in the South King County/Tacoma area. My girlfriend lives with me in Puyallup, and she works at the Emerald Queen Casino. That's about it."

"So now you want to be a little preppy mobster? Is that your new schtick?" asked the T.

"Not necessarily, sir. I just know this girl from high school and had a plan on how to make some serious money off her. So, I came and discussed the idea with Mr. DeGrazzi, that's all."

"This is not an idea like you decided to bet on the Super Bowl, and came and talked to Mr. DeGrazzi about it, sonny boy. This is some very serious shit here. You are talking about multiple felonies, district attorneys, time in the state penitentiary if things so wrong. Do you get that? This is not some stupid computer game, where you lose, and you get up and walk away from the TV. You unnerstand?" Ronnie the Barber was laying into Stuart.

"Yes sir. I realize all that. I just thought it was a great opportunity, with a chance for an incredible payout. That is why I wanted to discuss it with a professional like Mr. DeGrazzi."

Ronnie continued on. "You just thought it was a great opportunity, huh? Can you say FBI you little putz? Do you realize the kind of heat that police detectives, the FBI regional office and our state politicians, and the media will bring down on something like this? And you think you will just grab her and hold her for a week or two. Like you are holding a damn sack of potatoes from Costco? You don't have a freaking clue what you are getting yourself into. You are a rank fucking amateur, with absolutely no experience-- a computer nerd at that. You are going to end up being someone's bitch in prison, and I am washing my hands of this half-baked plan right now." With that said, Ronnie the Barber rose from the table, threw his napkin down, picked up his brief case, and stormed out of the room.

The remaining Guapos were somewhat taken aback by his vitriolic outburst. Vinnie, Tommy and Mickey all looked at each other a little sheepishly. Vinnie finally broke the ice. "Let me go call for lunch," he said rising, and left the room. Tommy and Mickey both had a sip of Barolo red wine and stared with venom at Vincent's boy. Stuart felt like guzzling the whole bottle.

"The real key here," Mickey said, "is this better be a flawless plan, kid."

Luncheon came in a wave. Mostaccioli to start, insalata greens with Italian dressing, followed by linguini puttanesca for an entree, fresh cannoli for dessert. More red wine flowed. That seemed to lighten the mood a bit.

"You play golf kid?" someone asked.

"I play the game," Stuart responded, "but I don't play enough to be any good."

"How you know so much about the LPGA then?"

"My ex-girlfriend loved to play golf, and she got me into it. We went to about six LPGA tournaments, here on the west coast. I am amazed at how accessible the players are. I just thought it would be easy to make some dough off of it without hurting anyone."

"So, you don't think ripping someone off for twelve million bucks would be hurting them?"

"Not if they could afford it. Besides, Chrissy Jensen could probably make twelve million bucks off of writing a book about it when everything was over with."

"Okay, let's go into some detail here," suggested Vincent. "If this thing is even feasible, we have lots of time to do some research and planning. Stuart, in your LPGA tournament visits, what have you seen for security?"

"Well, Mr. DeGrazzi, there seems to be lots of law enforcement personnel around during the daytime's official rounds. But I haven't seen much presence off of the actual course, or around the perimeter areas. I have not seen any extensive exterior security cameras or police presence at all. If there are cops, it is on the course, and around the players on the course. They don't seem to be as concerned once the players are on their own. Plus, if there was an immediate problem, we wouldn't have to go through with the snatch anyway. The location is right here in our backyard, so there wouldn't be any travel expenses. The only initial cost would be the rental of the waterfront holding property, and I am willing to personally underwrite that part of the operation."

"Maybe we could have Sully with Associated Security check out some stuff for us," Mickey offered. "He does a lot of industrial work for me here in Washington."

"Be careful who you are talking to," Tommy cautioned. "Something like this would have to pretty much stay with the people in this room."

"I know this guy good, and he could give me professional info without me raising any suspicions."

"Just be careful is all I am saying."

"Where is this house you want to rent kid?" Tommy asked.

"It's a big, secluded home on the water on the north east side of Gig Harbor. Hardly no neighbors around most of the time. It has four bedrooms, with a sealed basement, and a boathouse, and leases out as a summer rental. It would be a perfect place to hole up. Put the girl in the basement, maintain her for a week, and we're done."

"Now for the sixty-four-thousand-dollar question," asked Mickey. "How you gonna get away with twelve million bucks? That's a lotta dough." He would have said both "literally and figuratively," if he had that kind of vocabulary.

"Gentlemen, you may have a lot better idea than I do, because you are the pros here. But I thought the best way to transfer the cash is to do it underwater."

"Under friggin' water?" The T was amused, if not outright shocked. "How does that happen kid?"

"Well sir, a million bucks in hundred-dollar bills weighs just over twenty-two pounds. Twenty-two times twelve is two hundred sixty-four pounds. I would put out a couple of crab pots around the tip of Defiance Point, just off of the Tacoma waterfront. We have them go pull up the crab pots. The cash is split into two industrial trash bags, tied up real tight. They would weigh one hundred thirty-two pounds each. They tie a bag of cash to each crab pot, and drop 'em back in. When the bags of cash are submerged, they lose one third of their weight. Then, while the cops and the Feds are watching the crab pots for a pickup, we are waiting under water with scuba gear at the spot, to retrieve the cash. We scuba back under the cover of the boathouse in Gig Harbor, split the cash, and go. We can drop the girl off somewhere remote, and that's it."

"Whoa, whoa, whoa there!" Vincent came up out of his chair. "Did I hear you say split up the money? Like in a fifty-fifty split?"

"That seems fair to me," said Stuart.

"How many guys you see at this table?"

"Four."

"Well, that seems like at least a four-way split to me."

"That can be negotiated later, sir. What do you think of the underwater plan?"

"Do you dive?" Tommy asked.

"Yes, I do. I would be perfectly comfortable going out with one of your people to bring back the cash."

"We will have to think about that. It is definitely an original idea."

"It is a great idea. Because the cops won't know where the drop is going to be until the very last minute. By the time we tell 'em, and the drop is made, they won't have time to get people under water. We grab it and go, before they can react. If they even figure out what is going on."

"So, let me think this all through," Vincent said. "You gonna rent the house. We would need to check that out first. Then we gonna snatch the babe and keep her in the house for a week or so. Then you gonna communicate with her banker by computer or burner phone. You gonna arrange the drop, dive down, and pick it up. Then we split four ways and let her go. That's about it, eh?"

"Basically, yeah."

"Alright, kid. Let us think about it for another day or two. We will get back to you."

"Good enough. Just let me know in time to lease the house. I should wrap that up in a week or so."

"I will call you this weekend," Vincent said. "Don't leave town."

Stuart continued talking. "If I might make a suggestion gentleman, there is an LPGA tournament down in Orange County, California next weekend. Maybe a couple of you could go down there, and check it out? It would be fun, and give you a personal look at the logistics of a live tournament in the bargain."

"Not a bad idea, kid. We'll talk about it. In the meantime, you need to be very careful about dealing with this rental house. They can trace stuff like that very easily if it ain't done right."

"Yes sir, I am aware of that. I have fake ID, and I would go in disguise to an Easy Loan checking outlet and buy a money order with cash. I will handle all of the paperwork by computer and mail in the deposit. The realtor would never even see me. Plus, when we lose the girl, we dump her back in Tacoma somewhere. She won't have ever laid eyes on the place, and the cops will never even see the house either. If we keep her blindfolded going in and out, she won't have a clue where she was."

"Okay, kid. But you be careful. And don't do anything before you talk to us." Stuart bided his time throughout the rest of the meal. The Guapos mostly talked about golf, sports in general and Seattle sports in particular. Finally, like a schoolboy being excused by his teacher, Stuart was sent from the table. He rose to make his exit, but not before thanking Vincent for his lunch, and surreptitiously slipping a twenty-dollar bill under his dessert plate as a tip. The meal actually was delicious, and with all of the Italian wine being served at midday like this, he had a bit of a buzz going. Good thing Vincent served cups of espresso along with the cannoli. Stuart ambled out of Vincenzo's into the bright afternoon sunlight and back to his silver Honda Accord. His brain was spinning.

His generosity at leaving a gratuity, however, did not go unnoticed by Vincent.

Vinnie looked around at his two buddies. "Anyone want to go to LA next weekend?"

"I'm out," said Mickey DeAngelo.

"Out for LA," asked Vinnie. "Or out for good?"

"I'm out for good. I just don't want to get involved."

"Tommy?"

"Well, Vinnie, I can't promise anything, but I will go to LA with you."

"Great. I'll check it out and call you."

That works for me, Vinnie thought after everyone had dispersed. I would rather only have one partner anyway. But the kid doesn't necessarily need to know that.

"Doris," Vincent grunted as he walked into his inner office,

"Yes, Mr. DeGrazzi?"

"Book two round trip, business class tickets into Orange County Airport for me and Tommy Thurston, will you? Leaving next Thursday afternoon, and back Sunday evening."

"Yes sir."

"Thanks."

Vincent made a couple more calls, packed it in for the day, and departed for his happy home.

CHAPTER FIVE

"Hi hon, how was your day?" Vincent's wife Angela asked.

"Very interesting. Had a long luncheon with the boys. I've got to go to Southern California next weekend though."

"Can I go?"

"Sorry babe, it's a business trip."

"Come on, Vinnie. It's been a long winter. I need to get out of here, too."

"I know, I know. How about the weekend after that we go to Vegas or something? This time it's a business trip. Just me and Tommy."

"You promise?"

"Sure babe. We ain't been to Vegas in a long time. We can stay at Caesar's Palace and take in a couple of shows. You check it out for us."

"Okay."

The week flew by, and Tommy met Vinnie at the bar, where Vinnie had one of his guys ready to drive them up to Sea-Tac Airport. The tournament was scheduled at beautiful Pelican Hill Golf Course in Newport Beach, giving Pelican a chance to not only host a certified event, but also to show off their semi new $10 million-dollar (plus) course and clubhouse upgrade. So how do two wise guys wile away a weekend in posh Newport Beach, California? Enter a bridge tournament? Take a tour of the University of California Irvine? Go to a stamp collector's convention? Nah.

"My pal Carlo is hooking us up," Vinnie told Tommy.

"How's that?"

"We got a limo waitin' for us at the airport with a couple of Carlo's best girls, and two adjoining suites reserved at the Newport Beach Hyatt Regency. Tomorrow we got a box at the Del Mar Race Track, with Carlo's guy's tip sheet for the races. He reserved a car for us at the hotel. Then he got us two full weekend passes to the 18th Green Champions Club for the Tournament."

"Jeez, who is this guy?"

"He is an old buddy of mine from Seattle. We made our bones together on a couple of jobs up here, then he went down south and got big in the garbage business. I done him a few favors over the years."

"We gonna see him while we are down there?"

"Yeah, we supposed to go over to his house for drinks on Friday night. Maybe we eat there or go out, I dunno."

"Sounds like a great weekend, Vinnie."

"You bet."

Their flight down the coast was silky smooth, except Vincent (who wasn't crazy about flying anyway), thought the descent into John Wayne Airport was a little tight. Orange County's Airport as late as the early 1960s, was no more than a small, private plane landing strip located out in the middle of some inland bean fields.

As the southland grew, the tiny airstrip was converted into an international transportation facility. But the rest of the bean fields also evolved into major commercial and residential developments. Vincent was absolutely correct in observing how their tight landing approach over major urban congestion made for an interesting--if disconcerting and steep--descent. But the boys had already had a couple of drinks by the time their Alaska jet arrived at John Wayne Airport, and this helped settle the V's nerves. This proper lubrication was, of course, a major benefit of business class travel.

Life got even better after they landed, and their limo driver loaded them up. Two long-legged California beauties welcomed them into the luxury stretch vehicle. Where there was more French Champagne on ice waiting for them.

"Hi ladies," Vinnie said, and gave the buxom young beauty seated next to him a perfunctory fist bump.

"Driver, can you take us on a spin down to Laguna Beach so we can relax after our flight, then back to the hotel?"

"Yes sir."

"Would you two ladies care to join us for dinner later on?" Vinnie asked.

"Oh sure. Carlo told us we should stick around and tuck you two into bed at the end of the night," said Vinnie's new girlfriend.

In spite of the afternoon's traffic, everyone enjoyed the ride. The sun was beginning its descent over the Pacific, and the vast waters were seemingly dappled with millions of diamonds that danced merrily in the setting sunbeams for everyone's pleasure. The Champagne was cold, and the girls were more than friendly. Who gave a toot about a little traffic? And speaking of toot, Carlo had even supplied a couple grams of that for their pleasure. The girls seemed to especially enjoy Carlo's generosity.

After the limo tour, both couples freshened up in their separate suites, did some horizontal frolicking, took a snuggle break, and awoke with an appetite. About eight o'clock, it was off to Il Barone for dinner.

And what a dinner it was! The tasting menu was six courses, accompanied by Italy's finest specimens from her golden vineyards, concluding with a bottle of aged Moscato dessert wine, and a platter of pastries with such a flourish of spun sugar sculptural toppings, it turned heads throughout the dining room. Their table was hovered over by the Maître d' and Sommelier. The obvious fact that two fifty-year-old gentlemen were dining with two young ladies, who were half their age, however creepy it might appear to some, wasn't even acknowledged in a sophisticated restaurant like Il Barone.

Vincent winked at Tommy and picked up the check. It was an evening to remember, and the group poured back into their waiting limo. Our guys were more than a little tipsy, and the two young ladies both had the giggles. Back at the hotel, Vinnie was up to the task one more time. Tommy, unfortunately, had overindulged, and was helped out of his shirt and slacks, and smartly tucked into bed by his paramour. He was asleep instantly. So his friend kissed him lightly on the forehead and walked next door to Vincent's suite. She looked so seductive in her hip hugging pink panties that Vincent invited her to join them and get comfortable in his king-sized bed.

Vinnie's phone rang at exactly nine a.m. as requested. "Ugh," he answered after fumbling over the girls to answer the phone. "Send up some coffee, willya?" It took a minute for him to realize he was talking to a recorded voice, where upon he hung up and called the hotel operator.

"This is Mr. DeGrazzi in Suite 319. Can you please send up a pot of coffee and some Danish ASAP?"

He walked through the adjoining door in his boxer shorts into Tommy's well-appointed salon and rousted him out of a sound sleep. "Wake up, lover boy, time to rise and shine. I've got some coffee on the way."

Tommy rolled over and grimaced sheepishly. "What time is it?" he wanted to know.

"Time to get out of bed, and go have some more fun," Vincent told him.

"Did we go to a wedding chapel last night? I dreamed that Lisa and I got married."

"No, we didn't. But I can ask her if you want me to. She spent the night next door with us."

"You dog. What a broad, though. Makes me want to be twenty-five again."

"Good idea. I'll see if Carlo can turn the clock back for you."

"Thanks, partner."

After picking up their black Land Rover SUV, they invited the girls to go with them to the races. "Sorry guys, we're already booked." Vincent and Tommy reluctantly kissed them good-bye, and headed off down the Pacific Coast Highway again. This time for Del Mar and the race track. It was another glorious Southern

California day, as the morning inversion layer of clouds was just burning off. "You wanna stop in Corona del Mar for some breakfast, or wait until we get to the track to eat?" Vincent asked.

"Shoot, I'm still full from dinner last night. I could sure use a beer though."

Vincent pulled over in Corona del Mar for beers instead of breakfast. He hit a drive-through liquor store and purchased a six-pack of sixteen-ounce Budweiser's to go. No one could see them drinking through their tinted glass windows anyway.

"Next stop, the PONIES," he shouted to a completely hung-over Tommy Thurston.

Tommy downed a couple of brews, and between that and the coffee, he was starting to feel a little better. It was a pleasant two-and-a-half-hour drive back down the coast, with more spectacular views of some of Southern California's premier surfing beaches, and the vast ocean as a backdrop. Vincent and Tommy the T cruised into Del Mar's valet parking around twelve thirty.

The guys headed up to the Paddock Tavern on the fourth floor of the historic old track for a light lunch. Del Mar Racetrack was founded by Bing Crosby and some of his Hollywood cronies in the golden era of Tinseltown. The small coastal town of Del Mar is the epitome of Southern California cool, and the aging race track is blessed with crisp ocean air, panoramic views, and balmy late spring weather. "Now more than ever" was the track's self-promoting, current marketing slogan, and the guys were lucky that there was this special week-long run of late spring racing available to them.

Vincent pulled out the tout sheet Carlo had given one of the hookers to give him. "I like to start slow," Vincent told Tommy, "but there is a star here by the sixth race, so I guess that is the baby to lay it down."

Following their tip sheet, the boys bet a hundred bucks to win on each of the first five races, and hit on two of them. They were already up a thousand bucks each by the time the sixth race rolled around.

"I'm going to lay it all back down," Tommy told Vincent.

"Let's do it," Vincent said.

"This nag is holding at thirteen-to-one, so the odds will probably drop a good deal when we bet. Let's wait until the last minute to lay down." The horse, a three-year-old named Monkeyaround, ended up going off at seven-to-one.

"Bet him to win," was Vincent's plan.

The guys went up to adjacent pari-mutuel windows and made their bets. The odds immediately dropped, but no problem. It was racing time, and their bets were already in.

The distance was a mile and a quarter thoroughbred claimer, and Monkeyaround broke strong out of the gate. He was in the second racing slot, and held the rail well coming around the first three turns. Kicking it up a gear at the start of the backstretch, he cruised in for the win by a full length.

The boys, of course, rooted him around the oval all the way. They were hooting and hollering like Navy cadets at their first football game.

"What a nag!" Tommy said as they counted their money, some fourteen thousand bucks between them. "We should buy him, just for the hell of it."

They dallied around for a bit at the track but decided to head back to the hotel and relax at the pool before going to Carlo's for cocktails. "Maybe we can crash for half an hour," Tommy said, still fighting off his alcohol demons.

"Why not?"

"We should just give the dough to Carlo tonight," Tommy reasoned. "Hell, it was all his picks anyway."

"Ah, he won't take any of it," Vincent replied.

With that, they retrieved the Range Rover from Valet, and headed north on Pacific Coast Highway. "These California drivers sure act crazy," Vincent turned and said to Tommy. "You'd think they was all on the way to get laid for the first time."

"No kidding. If one more sucker cuts us off doing ninety-five miles an hour, we should just cap his sorry ass!"

"I think they call that road rage, my man."

"I got some road rage for 'em."

"Calm down, pal."

Tommy and Vincent were poolside, when Vincent's cell phone rang. "Hey Vinnie, this is Carlo. How were the races?"

"Jeez Carlo, we made a killing, thanks to you. We are picking up the tab for dinner tonight, that's for sure."

"Awesome, my friend. The wife is expecting you and your friend at seven for cocktails. Then we can go out."

"What's the address?"

"We are in the third high-rise on Lido Park Drive. It's called the Lido Park Villas. It faces west, and we're in condo number 12B."

"Great. See you at seven. Thanks for everything, we are having a great time."

While Lido Isle is a bit of an older folk's demographic in the Newport Beach communities, Carlo liked it because he had a tremendous view of the ocean from the twelfth floor. He could also keep his forty-foot Kettenburg sailing yacht moored directly behind the condo. If it was earlier, they could have taken a spin out in the harbor.

"Nice place, Carlo." Vincent gave his friend a warm hug and introduced Tommy Thurston.

"Thanks, Vinnie old boy. Waste Inc. has been very good to me."

"I can see that. Thanks for the tip sheet today. Your pony killed it in the sixth race."

"Good. I hope you bet a ton of money."

"We did okay. So, does your company own the whole county here?"

"Nah. Just the coastal cities from Seal Beach down to Dana Point, including Costa Mesa and Santa Ana. It's a pretty profitable territory, and we've owned it since the late eighties."

"Bet that cost some ching."

"Well that, and it's about knowing the right people."

Carlo's trophy wife Gina eased into the living room with a pitcher of booze and four chilled and garnished stemmed glasses.

"Carlo likes vodka martinis. I hope that's good with you guys," she purred.

"Fantastic," the boys chimed, although Tommy would have preferred a Bloody Mary.

"Our amigos went down to Del Mar today," Carlo told Gina. "They like my handicapper."

"Most of your pals do, honey," Gina replied.

The old and new friends made small talk and ended up going out to the back deck facing east to watch the moonrise. The roomy lanai looked directly out over the harbor, and it was most relaxing to watch the sleek boats bob easily at their moorings to the gentle lap of the inner bay currents.

When everyone was caught up on small talk, Carlo inquired as to dinner. "We could do old school and go to the Crab Cooker on the Peninsula. It's funky but has been there for decades. The locals love it. Or, there is a restaurant we both like a lot called Sol. It's kind of hip, upscale Baja food. I have a reservation at both places. Take your pick."

Vincent looked at Tommy, who gave him a noncommittal shrug. Vincent asked Carlo if there was a steak house in town. "We just had ethnic last night, and we got seafood coming out of our ears in the Northwest. How about we take youse out for a nice steak dinner."

"Sure, sure," Carlo replied. "There is a Fleming's right in Fashion Island. I know the Maître d', let me call him. That okay with you, Gina?"

Gina was hoping for Sol, but nodded agreeably. "Sure, Carlo, that's fine."

A couple of crisp hundred-dollar bills for Carlo's connection helped grease the skids, and soon the foursome was seated at a sumptuously padded booth. The boys were flush with found money, and there would be no expenses spared on tonight's dinner.

"So, what brings you to town, Vinnie?" Carlo asked.

"Actually, Tommy has some family business, so we thought we might as well come down and make a weekend of it. Take in the sights, watch the ladies tee it up. That sort of thing."

The captain stopped by and took their orders. He communicated with the sommelier, who arrived with some suggestions.

Vincent had some suggestions of his own. "Let's start off with a bottle of Dom. Then would you please open a bottle of the 1989 Chateau Margaux? And we would like to follow that with a bottle of the 2008 Richebourg, Grand Cru."

"If I may make a suggestion sir," the captain said, "you may possibly wish to start with the Richebourg. It is just a little lighter that the Margaux, and that would give the older bottle a chance to clear its head properly, so to speak."

"That would be acceptable," Vincent replied. The value of the wine came to a little over fifteen hundred dollars. Like a loyal soldier, Tommy didn't flinch at Vincent's extravagance.

"Good choices, Vincent. Thanks to the ponies, this is going to be a great dinner."

And it was. Their thick rib eye steaks cut like butter and were ultra-flavorful but unbelievably tender. Gina had the miso-marinated Chilean Sea Bass and loved it. The wine was superb!

As dinner wound down, our guys again thanked Carlo and his wife for their thoughtfulness. "I hope the limo driver knew what he was doing yesterday," Carlo remarked with a twinkle in his eyes.

"He couldn't have been more professional and attentive," Vincent assured him. "I would like to have his number actually; in case we need him again. Also, why don't you let us reimburse you. You don't need to be supporting all of our habits."

"What are friends for?" Carlo retorted.

"Well, I would still like his number."

"Done. I'll text it to you. Have fun tomorrow. It's supposed to be unseasonable warm out."

So, after their twenty-five-hundred-dollar dinner, (three thousand-dollar meal actually, with a healthy tip), the friends parted, and Vinnie and Tommy were still relatively flush. "If you can break away, we could go out in the boat early Sunday before you leave for the airport," Carlo offered.

"Let's see how everything goes," Vincent replied. "That would be great." Tommy looked nervous, as he got severely seasick. But he held his tongue.

"Call me, and be careful driving. Or would you just prefer to take an Uber?"

"No, I'm okay. I'll be careful. We're only a couple of miles away, and it's still early."

"Don't take any chances. These Newport Beach cops are brutal."

"What's up for tomorrow?" Tommy inquired on the way back to the Hyatt Regency.

"Well, we should go over to the golf course and check that out, eh?"

"Yeah, that's what we're here for."

"Let's get to the course about noon. It's only a couple miles from the hotel. Carlo got us a full ride Clubhouse pass, which also gives us parking access, including the players lot."

"Let's definitely park in there, that should be our base."

"Right on. We could sleep in, and go down to the pool for a while in the morning before we leave."

"See you around nine

CHAPTER SIX

The boys had a morning dip in the spacious Regency pool and headed to the course just before noon. According to the Orange County Register's morning sports page update, Chrissy Jensen was holding down fourth place, and sitting three shots back. It looked like it was going to be a tight tournament, and her scheduled tee time was one seventeen in the afternoon.

"That's perfect timing. We get to the players parking lot, check that out, then we can follow Miss Chrissy around for a bit. Get to know her." Smelling more potential found money, Vincent was all business this morning.

While most of the gallery was being bussed in from satellite parking lots over by Newport's Back Bay area, Vincent and Tommy cruised through the herd of volunteers who helped direct and control the traffic flow. The guys, with their Capital C parking permit dangling from the Land Rover's rearview mirror, were motioned on into the player's personal lot. And while arriving a little late, they still found adequate parking toward the back of that private, roped-off area.

A golf tournament, like any major sporting event, is preceded by anticipation. Whether it is a kickoff, tip-off, first pitch, or hockey face-off, the excitement of the action is usually building and palpable before game time. And the more so, of course, the bigger the event. Golf has essentially the same anticipation; however, it is spread out over a four-day period. Professional golfers need to perform with precision, under often extreme pressure, for four consecutive days to achieve their trophies and game checks, and said excitement peaks as the weekend progresses. Obviously, depending on who is leading the tournament, and by how much. Sunday's golf fans often hang onto every shot, especially if it is a tightly contested, major event.

In professional golf, there are no teammates between the ropes to aid, assist, cover for, encourage, or motivate. There are no time outs. It is just the golfer and their caddy, slogging down the well-groomed fairways. Golf also differs in its approach from the big four sporting leagues who rely on boisterous fans, especially on the home field, to help propel their team to victory. Ideally, golf fans maintain a dignified silence for each and every shot or putt a golfer makes. The simple click of a camera shutter at a critical moment can be a distraction that undoes four days of hard work and effort, and can drive a professional golfer into apoplexy.

If ever there was a home field advantage for golfers, it was back in the days of Arnold Palmer and his Army, a.k.a. Arnie's Army, where a large and vocal contingent of the gallery strongly supported their hero.

This may have been the most significant era of the game of professional golf, as it ushered in live national television coverage of the game and brought it into living rooms across the USA. That raised the bar of payoff money to today's multimillion-dollar levels, and it effectively delivered the game to the masses.

Arnold Palmer virtually owned golf in America in the 1960s, until Jack Nicklaus blew onto the scene, and their classic rivalry began. And Jack certainly felt the wrath of Arnie's Army as he emerged as a fearless, gifted challenger.

But golf fans since those days tend to show their support and appreciation in a much more subdued manner. While in the other major sports, the fans are creating mayhem, and directly trying to influence the ongoing action, golf fans quietly watch and appreciate the activity after the fact, from a variety of perches around the course.

Furthermore, while most major league sports figures have signed contracts, which may or may not have incentive performance clauses, those athletes will still collect their paychecks, win or lose. Rain or shine. Not so for the long-suffering golfer. Having a bad day usually translates into a bad week, which can equal less money, less endorsements, worse tee times, and usually, an early exit for the week. Or in the worst-case scenario, even failure to maintain one's LPGA/PGA Tour Card at the end of the year. In other words, like no other sport, golfers earn their keep day after day, week after week, and year after year. And to even get into the major tours and tournaments takes incredible skill, hard work, perseverance, mental toughness and often times exceptional luck or a fortuitous break.

As can be expected, in an ongoing four-day event, the action and suspense build to a climax on the last day of the tournament, which is on a Sunday unless extreme weather interferes. So, as Vincent and Tommy strolled on to the premises of the luxurious Pelican Hill Golf & Country Club around twelve thirty on Saturday afternoon, the action was in full progress, but with that polite restraint known only to golf. Things hadn't reached the quiet fervor and heightened crowds that are reserved for the final round.

The guys were headed for the pro shop, but took their time getting along. They had some work to do and were busy checking out the players' parking lot. There was an admin trailer with a stenciled sign indicating this was headquarters for the Director of Transportation. There was a similarly designated golf cart parked in front of the trailer. But the guys could see no evidence of any security cameras attached to the trailer, in the lot, at the entry gate or around the area's perimeter.

Vincent stopped at the portable shade tent at the lot's entrance, where a young woman was controlling the comings and goings of the area. "We are meeting friends for a drink after the tournament today," Vincent said. "How late are you open here? We won't get locked in, will we?"

"Oh, no sir," the attractive, young California co-ed in her UCLA t-shirt replied. "This gate is manned until five p.m. By then pretty much everyone is gone, and whoever is left in the lot can just exit at will."

"What about the guys in the trailer?" Tommy asked.

"They are usually gone by the early afternoon, and mostly deal with rental cars and transportation issues for the players. That's pretty much under control after the first day of the tournament."

"We're just being careful," Vincent said. "We would hate to get locked up in here for the night with someone as pretty as you."

The young woman flashed Vincent a quizzical look. "Sorry guys, I leave at three today." What a couple of weirdos, she thought to herself.

"Just kidding," Vincent replied, and began walking away.

Tommy followed along, and Vincent told him, "I think she wants me."

"In your dreams, assbite." Tommy was amused by Vincent's chutzpah. "Do you just want to jump everything you see today?"

"I tell you it must be those dang yoga pants."

The guys continued on toward the clubhouse. The huge, posh clubhouse.

"Jesus, Tommy, look at this joint. A bunch of rich dudes playing some golf here, eh?"

"No kidding, Vinnie. This place looks like the Taj Mahal."

"Well, I'm only seeing four cameras on the front of the building, and they look like they are mostly pointed at the driveway and the entry way."

"Let's take a few pictures with our phones, and we can check it out in more detail later."

"I think we can shoot from this angle, and not get into actual range of the cameras."

After scouting the front of the building, the boys climbed up the extended stairway into the main entrance of the clubhouse, and still looking around, they headed for the pro shop. The clubhouse was as well-appointed inside as it had appeared sumptuous outside. They passed a security guard who was posted at the exit of the ladies' locker room. "That's where the women come and go from, before they head out," Vincent said quietly to Tommy.

"Yeah, I see that. Let's go to the pro shop. I need a new big dog, but I haven't made up my mind yet."

"I know what you mean," Vincent replied, "there are so many choices now. I have always liked Callaway though. I hear their new Epic driver is awesome."

After a leisurely look around the shop, the guys meandered out the front door, and down the steps to the promotional area, where many booths offered knickknacks, freebies, and come-ons to get you onto their email lists.

"Let's go up to the Sky Booth. We can get some snacks and grab a beer."

"Good idea, T. I want to relax a little if we are going to follow this dame around for nine holes. Maybe there will be some hotties up there."

"Maybe," Tommy replied. My buddy the freakin' horndog, he thought to himself.

Vincent and Tommy showed their badges and began the healthy climb up to their huge, private reception area. Once upstairs, they couldn't help but marvel at the deluxe layout. There was a well-stocked wet bar to the left on the entry side of the spacious canopied tent, replete with a bartender in some type of a dinner jacket, adorned with epaulets on his shoulders. He appeared to have everything your heart might desire from champagne to custom drinks with umbrellas or imported olives in them.

On the other side of the large canopied area was a bruncheon buffet. If it wasn't sumptuous, it was certainly, as the LPGA ladies would say: Delish! It even included an omelet station with a toqued-up chef standing at attention. There was dinner theater style seating for a hundred or so people between the bar and the buffet, and facing the eighteenth green was bleacher seating for another couple hundred people.

"Hey, this is airtight, huh? That Carlo is really taking care of us down here."

"No kidding, man. I think I am going to have me a stiff one."

"Ditto."

"Hey fella, how about a Bloody Mary?" Vincent was dressed in black: polo shirt, slacks, Italian loafers, aviator sunglasses. Even his Augusta National golf tournament hat, was entirely black, except for the small gold Master's logo directly above the bill of the cap. Tommy was also in black, but his shirt had some white piping around the neck and collar. He had on his favorite Oakridge Golf hat, also black. So what if it had a few sweat stains around the brim? It was his lucky hat.

"Make it two, my man," Tommy chimed in.

"What is your preference of vodka, gentlemen?" the suave bartender asked.

Tommy looked quizzically at Vincent, and shrugged. "Smirnoff is fine for me," he replied.

"Sorry sir," the bartender replied archly. "This is a premium bar only. We have Stolichnaya, Absolut, Grey Goose or Beluga Noble."

"Well, la-di-da," Vincent crooned. "I'll have the Grey Goose," thinking to himself how he would like to have a couple of his boys insert a real Canadian Honker's squawky beak in this guy's ear--the one with the loopy gold earring in it.

"Me too," said Tommy. The bartender was overcome with bored condescension and poured them both a short shot of vodka.

Vincent immediately took issue and barked at the barman to "put some damn booze in that, willya?"

"Sorry sir, that is a standard pour."

One of the two security personnel from the main entrance sidled over to the bar. "Is there a problem, James?" he asked the bartender.

"Not on my end," James replied. "You may want to ask Tony Soprano and his buddy here."

Vincent did have the appearance of an Italian Goombah in his all black outfit, made starker by the fact that he was among Southern California's finest, and this was a place where black outfits in springtime were more appropriate for funerals. Also, this being early June, unseasonably warm and a women's tournament, the lovelies were out in their filmy, spring pastel finery, or hot-colored athletic wear. And this made the two pale, Northwestern guys with the dark sunglasses and blackout casual wear all the more noticeable in a negative way.

Still, Vincent was a man who commanded respect in his own arena. He didn't take any crap off any swishy bartender or rent-a-cop security guard. And, he had his Glock 42 strapped to his ankle if it should be needed. He removed his sunglasses and returned the steady gaze of the big security guard.

"No, no problem partner. We was just ordering a drink from tutti-frutti here. No problem at all." He turned and gave the bartender a death glare, as if to say, would you like to step outside sonny? The barman ignored him, garnished their drinks with Castelvetrano olives and a spear of fresh rosemary.

"Hey," Tommy blurted out. "I don't want none of that crap in my drink. Don't you got no celery?"

With a dour look on his face, the bartender looked at his security guard as if to say, can you please lose these morons for me?

"Sir, I am going to have to ask you both to calm down," the big security guard said. "We won't be having any trouble here. Do you understand me?"

"Sure, bud. No trouble at all. Just give us our drinks, and we will go get something to eat," Vincent said as he picked up his Bloody Mary, removed the stalk of rosemary, and dropped it on James's bar top, making a puddled mess.

The hospitality suite was starting to fill up, and the bouncer wasn't going to allow any problems so early in the day. As a rule, this kind of duty was a piece of cake for him. Rarely, if ever, were there any hassles in the sky box.

Tommy grabbed his drink and also dumped his rosemary twig. The boys stiffed the bartender's tip jar and headed over to the buffet layout.

"We should try to keep a low profile," Tommy whispered to his pal.

"Yeah, I know that. Just tell that pillow-biter not to get wise, eh?"

"Settle down. Let's go get something to eat."

Seattle's finest wandered through the maze of tables in the dining area on their way to the omelet station, and Vinnie noticed several very attractive women who were holding hands with their heads intimately close together. They seemed to be engaged in deep, personal conversation, and neither of the women appeared to be wearing a brassiere. He nudged Tommy and whispered "nip alert."

"How can I help you, sir?" the young sauté chef said to Vinnie.

"Gimme me a cheese omelet, willya?" the V asked him. He could feel the eyes of the security guard on the back of his head.

"What is your preference of cheeses?" the omelet man asked.

"Jesus H. Christ, buddy! Can you just put some damn cheese in it? I don't care what kind of cheese it is." Why is this guy talking to me with a lisp anyway, Vinnie wondered?

"You don't have to curse at me sir," omelet man replied with a smile, as he looked over toward the security guard. Vinnie noticed the direction of his gaze and stepped sideways to block the security guard's line of sight.

"I'll have the same thing," Tommy told their chef, and nudged Vinnie over towards the buffet layout.

"Let's get something while we are waiting." Tommy could readily see the need to get Vincent calmed down before they got themselves bounced out of the sky box, and he felt like that was maybe a blink or two away.

The guys continued on to the buffet line. "What the hell is this crap?" Vinnie said to Tommy when they were bellied up to the refrigerated food station. People were congregated around the area, and they too began to stare.

Tommy looked down and saw about a dozen different types of fresh fruit. There were light and healthy yogurt sauces for the fruit in half a dozen tantalizing colors and textures. Fresh tofu was offered, both marinated and grilled, and a delicious kale and kumquat salad, plus organic condiments for the salad, with a cruet of honey mustard raspberry vinaigrette standing by. Then too many mini pastries, muffins, and croissants to count, all piled artistically into a rounded mound of goodness.

"What the hell is wrong with this place?" Vinnie demanded of Tommy. People were definitely gawking now, but Vinnie was oblivious. He just wanted some bacon to go with his eggs, and he wasn't going to get it.

"Gentlemen, your plates are ready," omelet man gushed at our boys, and they went over to pick up.

"I made them with blueberry cream cheese and honey-infused goat cheese. I hope you like them." He handed Vincent a plate and winked at him.

Vinnie gave him a nasty sneer, took his plate, and began to look for a place to sit. The room had filled up considerably in the last half hour. But Vinnie saw an eight-top table with only a couple of somewhat attractive young women sitting there alone. He led Tommy over, and as politely as he could, Vincent bent forward, smiled, and asked if they might sit down.

One of the women jerked her chin at the middle of the table. "Beat it buddy. Can't you see this is a rainbow table?"

Vincent looked around, turned to his left and peered outside. "I don't see no rainbow, sister."

"This is an LGBTQ table only, so get lost."

"Is that part of the LPGA? We've got a pass here," Vincent replied, flashing his credentials at the women.

"Would you beat it, you jerk, before I call security?"

Dang it, thought Tommy, here we go again.

"What is the matter with these screwed-up people?" Vincent muttered to Tommy. He looked up and the security guard was seriously eyeballing them now. Vincent squinted over at another four-top table with a couple of striking matrons sitting there demurely noshing on their fruit and yogurt. When Vincent made eye contact and jerked his head up, asking in effect, you got any room over there? the women quickly looked away.

As he didn't care to be called a jerk-off again this early in the day, he and Tommy went over to the bleacher section to sit down and eat their specially prepared, fancy boy omelets.

"Let's get outta this toilet, Tommy. My food tastes like shit, I can't eat this stuff. My dog wouldn't eat some kinda crap with honey-infused cheese in it."

"Yeah, let's go. Chrissy is about ready to tee off anyway."

The guys extended a cordial good day to the bartender and security guard. Actually, half the heads in the hospitality suite swiveled and followed their exit. "We'll be back," Vincent grunted, and they headed down to the first tee box.

"Ladies and Gentlemen, will you please give a warm Southern California welcome to Ms. Chrissy Jensen. Chrissy is from Yakima, Washington, and played her collegiate golf at the University of Washington up in Seattle. She has won six titles on the LPGA tour, and her first major at the ANA Inspirational Tournament at Mission Hills last year." There was loud applause following her introduction. Chrissy, looking lovely in a luscious, sea mist colored skirt, fitted top, and a white oversized visor, teed up her ball, and put on her game face in preparation for today's round.

Chrissy's tee shot flew straight and long down the fairway, and her threesome was off. She was playing with one of the tour's many young Asian stars and an older journeywoman player who had managed to work herself into today's third-to-last pairing. Chrissy was friendly but noncommittal with the Asian players, who were usually all business between the ropes. The older tour player might be a problem, as she was very slow and methodical. As long as they didn't get put on the clock, Chrissy was okay with her.

Being an American woman, and also from out west, Chrissy was very popular on the left coast of the women's tour, and her group had collected the largest gallery of the day so far. They were all off like a herd of turtles, and Chrissy would be waiting to hit last, as her drive was a good twenty yards further down the fairway than either of her playing partners. Chrissy's gallery aggressively scrambled for position and the best spectating windows.

Vincent and Tommy took off down the right side of the first hole with the other spectators, and Vincent immediately felt jostled and put off of his game by the multitude of Chrissy fans. We should be walking inside of the ropes, he thought to himself. And here he and his buddy were, stumping along like any other jackass in America. He considered calling Carlo for an upgrade for tomorrow, but then it occurred to him that it was probably wise to keep a little lower profile than strolling down the fairway, inside the ropes behind the young golf star he was plotting to kidnap.

So he and Tommy trooped on. The further they went, the more annoyed Vincent became. Not only were they being jostled around, but when they finally got to most of the greens, the crowd was such that they could hardly see anything anyway. Sure, Vincent was all of five foot ten, but every one of these California cheeseballs seemed to tower over him, blocking his view. He was getting annoyed at all the standing around. And then there was the matter of his black outfit in the hot afternoon sun, which seemed to be gaining temperature by the minute. He had rivulets of sweat running down his forehead, his neck, his back, the vertical chasm located below the back of his belt. Just about everywhere.

After six holes, Vincent turned to Tommy and said, 'Let's get the hell outta here."

"Where you wanna go?"

"Wherever."

"I don't think we should go back to the Sky Box just yet. You're gonna kill somebody up there."

"We should go find a beer vendor and a TV in a covered area, and we can watch the tournament on a big screen in the shade."

"That sounds like a plan to me. I think I saw just the place back there. Come on."

The boys turned around and began the long trudge back toward the tournament's commercial area. Of course, by now they were at the furthest point away from the first tee box that they could possibly get.

"Hey," Tommy said. "Let's just go into the main bar, and watch it in there. The clubhouse has got to be air conditioned, eh?"

"Now you're talking," Vinnie replied, and gave Tommy a playful shove.

Suddenly Vincent felt light-headed. He was perspiring like a marathon runner in the heat of July. And the next thing Tommy knew, Vinnie was down on one knee, then he keeled over onto his side with his eyes open, but they were staring blankly into space. Tommy was shocked and dumb struck to see his buddy on the ground. As the crowd surged forward to get close enough to watch the ladies' putt out, an adjacent crowd gathered around the fallen Vincent.

The next thing Tommy knew, a large woman, weighing approximately fourteen stones, which is roughly equal to two hundred pounds, took charge of the situation.

"Someone call emergency services now," she shouted out, and then a real crowd began to gather. Even the three lady golfers looked down at Vincent as they passed by on their way to the seventh tee box. "I am a registered nurse," the oversized woman said loudly. Rousing himself a bit, Tommy felt the crowd staring, but he bent and poured a healthy dribble of water on Vinnie's face to try and refresh him.

As if on cue, the registered nurse screamed at Tommy to stand down, then dropped onto her knees. She looked like an Olympic style wrestler going in for the pin to win a match. Yes, the nurse was overweight, although you wouldn't necessarily say she was unattractive, except for the large mole on her chin. And God knows she had a good heart to jump into action like she did. But, as a working health care specialist, she was committed to saving Vincent's life, or at least keeping him going until the medics arrived.

The nurse rolled Vincent over on his back, crawled in closer, took his pulse, and prepared to administer artificial respiration. She tilted his head back, pinched his nose off, and was moving in toward his face with her pudgy lips parted, pursed, and ready to perform.

The water Tommy poured on Vincent seemed to revive him. And when the nurse was about six inches from his face and ready to begin mouth-to-mouth, Vincent's eyes suddenly focused, and grew as big as saucers. He was disoriented, attempting to clear his head, and this bear of a woman was coming at him. A woman he had never seen in his life! And she was almost on top of him. He could see her tongue, smell her scent, and it scared him. He looked up at the black mole on her chin and shouted out, "what the hell?" Vincent instinctively jerked upward, trying to throw his medical intervenor off of him. He inadvertently banged heads with the nurse, essentially butting her on the bridge of her nose and right between the eyes with his forehead. She was knocked out cold, and sank like a sack of rocks on top of Vincent. She was dead weight, unconscious, bleeding, and sprawled all over Vinnie--who was fighting like a tiger cat to get out from under her.

Vincent finally rolled the woman over, freed himself, and grabbed his fallen golf cap. He got up just as the tournament medical staff arrived in an extended golf cart with a big red cross taped to the side. They immediately rushed to the aid of the stricken woman.

"Let's get outta here," Vincent fumed at Tommy. In the confusion, the boys filtered back through the crowd--who were now focused on the downed woman--and high tailed it back for the clubhouse.

"What in the hell happened back there?" Tommy asked.

"I just got a little overheated is all. Who was that big leg mofo on top of me? That was a terrifying sight to wake up to!"

"She was going to apply some mouth-to-mouth to revive you," Tommy said. He was trying really hard to stifle his laughter.

"Holy shit! That right there could have put me in my damn grave."

"She was just trying to help," Tommy offered.

"Can we please just go the clubhouse, cool off, and get a beer," Vincent said.

"Sure," Tommy responded, and they continued the long trek back.

"How long was I out?" Vincent asked.

"Not long at all, maybe ten minutes max. I poured some water on your head. I think it helped revive you."

"That was weird. Nothing like that has ever happened to me before."

"Maybe you should get a checkup when you get home."

"I probably will. I'll feel a lot better when I get a cold beer down me."

"You know, maybe you should try wearing some of these microfiber shirts. They wick the perspiration off of you when it is hot, or act as insulation if it is cold. And they are so comfortable. You would never have overheated if you had one of these babies on."

Vincent looked at Tommy out of the corner of his eye. Microfiber? Are you seriously kidding me? We are walking down the fairway here, I could have died, or been suffocated by the corpulent one, and you want to talk about microfiber?

The guys made it back to the clubhouse, grabbed a couple of seats at the bar, and Vincent excused himself to go to the restroom and freshen up. Not only was he still overheated from their long walk, but he had detritus all over his back from nearly being pinned for the count on the grass.

Tommy ordered a bloody beer and smiled nicely at the nubile young lady sitting next to him. As she was on the last legs of her umbrella drink, Tommy offered to buy her another.

"Oh, thanks so much. You from around here?" she asked.

"No, no. We just came down from Seattle for the tournament. I go by Tommy."

"Pleased to meet ya, Tommy, my name is Georgina. Thanks for the drink. I hear it rains a lot up there."

"Not really as much as people think. We get by."

"What do you do for a living?"

"I'm a private investigator."

"No kidding, how exciting. Isn't that kind of dangerous?"

"Well, it is if you don't know what you are doing. But if you can take care of yourself, it's usually no problem."

Tommy and Georgina continued chatting, and Tommy was starting to think they had quite a bit in common. He liked the fact that she was an excellent conversationalist, and she liked a man who could take care of himself. He felt like he was already rounding first base. For her part, Georgina had big brown eyes, and one of those slightly shaggy, precision-bob fashion cuts. She was wearing a miniskirt, medium height pumps, and seemed to be very friendly.

Vincent went into the men's locker room and found a clear glass ewer of raspberry/mint flavored water in the foyer. He drank three glasses straight down. A cold shower looked pretty inviting, but as he had nothing to change into, he grabbed a face towel, soaked it in cold water, and wrapped it around his neck. He got another one, and soaked it good, then went over and lay down on one of the changing benches, with the towel over his face. He felt the crown of his head and discovered a small to medium sized lump forming where he had head butted the registered nurse. Damn it, he thought.

After ten minutes Vincent was beginning to feel normal again. He stirred himself upright, had the locker room attendant brush off his back side, dropped a twenty-dollar bill onto the old man's tip plate, and headed out to the bar.

"Whattaya got on tap there, Mac?" he asked the barkeep.

"Here is our beverage menu, sir."

Although Seattle is famous for bringing the micro beer culture to American suds drinkers, and Vincent owned a bar, he just wasn't a fan. "You got any Budweiser?"

"Only in the can, sir."

"Well, I will have one of those, and if they are twelve-ouncers, bring me two."

The tournament was on three different sixty-inch, high-def flat screen TVs, and according to them, Chrissy wasn't doing too well. She was even par for the day, and getting off the tee well enough, but kept striking her second shots off to the right and couldn't buy a putt. The tournament leaders had picked up three shots on her for the day so far.

Vincent had been back at the bar for about twenty minutes, and finally he turned to Tommy and said, "she is taking it back too far inside and pushing her approach shots. She is blocking herself out."

"Huh?" Tommy replied. He was engrossed in conversation with Georgina, and oblivious to what was happening on TV. "Georgina, this is my pal Vincent, he's from Seattle too."

Georgina leaned forward, looked around Tommy and gave Vincent a warm smile. "Nice to meet ya, welcome to Newport Beach," she said in her husky, sexy voice. Vincent looked down and saw Georgina's left hand on Tommy's thigh. Her right hand was playing with the hair on Tommy's burly right forearm.

Tommy leaned over to Vincent and whispered in his ear. "Give me the car keys willya? Georgina and I are going to go out and get a little fresh air."

Georgina was already halfway off of her bar stool when suddenly a tall, ruddy looking fellow with an Australian flag on the front of his T-shirt, and a headful of electric red hair bellied up to the bar. He slapped Georgina soundly on the back, knocking her straight down onto her bar stool. "Howya doin', Georgie old boy?" he asked.

Tommy spun around and snarled at the Aussie. "Get your hands off my girlfriend, pal," he warned the redheaded dude.

"Girlfriend?" the Aussie roared, "that ain't no girl mate, it's a bloke. Ain't you, Georgie porgy boy? Yeah, I met her three days ago. She took me out to the car, and I got me hand down her knickers, and she had a little peckerwood down there. Didn't ya, Georgie girl?"

Tommy looked at Georgina who had turned a modest shade of blush. She turned back to him, and said "oh, what does it even matter?" Vincent was about to fall off his barstool, he was laughing so hard.

Tommy turned back to the young woman he was ready to have some serious back seat car time with only a few minutes ago.

"Get outta here," Tommy spit out at Georgina. Her head turned aside with a look of indignation. But she turned back to Tommy, and said "I need some cab fare." He threw a hundred-dollar bill at her, and reiterated, "now beat it." The bartender was staring at them and began to approach.

She snatched up the money and turned back to the Aussie. "You rotten prick," she told him, "why don't you go to hell." She picked up her handbag, slung it over her shoulder, and walked--sashayed? -- out of the bar with her head held high.

"Jesus, I sure owe you, buddy," Tommy said to the Aussie.

"No problem, mate. She's very good, ain't she? And cute as a bug's ear," he said sitting down by Tommy.

"No kidding. Let me buy you a drink, eh?"

"For sure."

Tommy motioned to the bartender and said, "get him whatever he wants."

The Aussie's booming voice was calming down, and he ordered a gold margarita, with a Corona chaser. Again, the entire bar was looking over in Vincent and Tommy's direction.

Vincent was still laughing hard enough that his eyes were watering. The Aussie was drinking like his insides were on fire, and Tommy was feeling everyone's stares.

"Can we get the damnation outta here, and go to a real bar?" Tommy asked.

"Hey, you two ever been to Blackie's?" asked the Aussie.

"What is Blackie's?"

"It's a great dive bar for surfers in old Newport, right down by the pier, and there are no trannies."

"Let's go," said Tommy. He looked over at Vincent.

"Okay," Vinnie replied. "The way Chrissy is playing today. she'll be here practicing until dark. We can come back."

Vincent extracted his wad, tossed a C-note on the bar to cover their drinks, and off they went.

CHAPTER SEVEN

Blackie's is to old Newport what Swannie's is to Pioneer Square, Seattle; the Tides Tavern is to Gig Harbor, Washington; Olvera Street is to LA; Hussong's is to Tijuana; Rip's Tequila Bar is to Cabo San Lucas. You get the picture. An authentic dive with history and panache.

And the place was in classic form on a warm, sunny Saturday afternoon. The front doors were propped open, letting the balmy seafront air waft in and out, and people were milling about. Mostly guys in Bermuda shorts, T-shirts or Hawaiian shirts and flip flops. Some were half blasted, some weren't. Inside, there were dead peanut shells all over the floor, and the walls and most of the ceiling were covered with license plates, tin beer promo signs, surfing murals, posters of famous surfer dudes or women with large breasts, old Dick Dale concert placards, used surf and boogie boards, diving goggles, snorkels, more diving gear, palm fronds, and a couple of huge stuffed bill fish. Obviously, state-of-the-art nautical, road house decor.

The fellas sauntered in, found an empty booth with grungy, cracked Naugahyde seats, and sat down. The aging booths ran down the south wall of the bar. The sit-down bar was on your left as you walked in, and there were a couple of pool tables filling the rear portion of the joint. Vinnie and Tommy immediately felt comfortable and ordered a couple of twenty-ounce drafts of Budweiser from their aging, surfer-chick cocktail waitress. The tall Aussie elected to stay with a margarita and Corona chaser.

"Ain't this place great?" asked the Aussie.

Vinnie and Tommy both were thinking it was either feast or famine, the Ritz or the ghetto around this Newport Beach place. But they felt a lot more comfortable here, than they did in the Pelican Hill sky box.

"Yeah, this place is funky," they both agreed, but any real appreciation from two Seattle goombahs for the SoCal surfer culture was going to be a stretch. "At least it's a lot better than hanging out with those clowns at the golf tournament."

"Or that freako in the bar," Tommy said.

"Ah, she was just attracted to your microfiber shirt," Vincent goaded him.

"You two blokes need to lighten up is all," the Aussie told them. "Go buy some Bermuda shorts and a colorful jersey. Get some runners. Lose the black. You look like somebody from the Jersey Mafia," the Aussie told them. "Then you'll fit right in. The LPGA is the most awesome sporting event in the world right now. I have come all the way from Sydney to try and pick up a loop with one of these sheilas."

"You want to be a caddy?" Vincent asked incredulously.

"No kidding. That would be the flocking cheese, mate. I mean these gals are some of the best pound-for-pound athletes in the world. Take Lori Thomas, for example. She hits the ball off of the tee almost two hundred eighty-five yards on average. She weighs maybe a hundred forty-some pounds. Now Doug Jones from the PGA tour, he averages three hundred fourteen yards, and he is sixty pounds heavier than she is and four inches taller. She would give him a tussle, mate, if they ever had a match, and she teed off from the women's tees."

"Yeah, but those people over there at the tournament are a bunch of stiffs. Most of them are major constipated," Vincent carped.

"Ah, that's the way it is at a lot of tournaments, men's or women's. But look at all of the fans out there at the match this weekend. Wasn't that great? People, all kinds of people, love the LPGA. It is the most approachable organization in Professional Sports. I mean, you can get a personal tweet from Commissioner

Wilson--from the bloody Commissioner himself! Or autographs from all of the players, as well as their social media posts. And these women, man, they hit the ball and hit it straight and far. Plus, a lot of them are pretty easy on the eyeballs, if you get my drift."

"They are actually going to start up an LPGA tournament in Seattle in July," Tommy put in.

"That's fantastic mate. I'll come up there and see you guys, maybe one of you can put me up for the week, eh? I'll tell you another thing; these gals work their tails off. You look in the conditioning trailer and it is always full. And then, no matter how hard they play, and no matter how well they do, their purses are only about twenty percent of the men's. Twenty damn percent. You talk about a glass ceiling! And they have still managed to donate millions of bucks to charity, developing Junior Golf programs, and golf scholarships. It just don't seem right."

"Okay, okay, calm down. It's all about the TV ratings," said Vincent. "The men get better ratings."

"Yeah, well I'll bet you if Augusta National held a Women's Masters tournament and broadcast it on prime-time TV, had an eleven-million-dollar purse, and had all of the talking heads there yakking away, the women would get some pretty big ratings too. It is very annoying. I don't think the boys can handle the competition."

"Maybe they just need to have their own Tiger Woods type superstar emerge, and they would start to get the ratings," Tommy said.

"Yeah, well if that happened, the guys would probably just say she was not very feminine and continue to ignore them. I mean, yeah, the men hit it farther, but five-to-one in prize money? It ain't right. I'm just saying. These women are a whole helluva lot better than they are getting paid."

As far as women's libbers or social tolerance, the Aussie was talking to deaf ears in Vincent and Tommy, but they had certainly seen enough today to have to agree with him to some extent.

"Hey, I have a thought," said Vincent. "Maybe they should do some crossover, co-ed type stuff. Kind of combine the two tours and host some male/female tournaments. I know they have a lot of couples' stuff going on at our club all the time. Ain't that right. Tommy?"

"Yeah, sure Vinnie, it's very popular," Tommy replied. "But it's a fact: guys just watch more televised sports than women do, and that's why the men have better purses. Hey, remember Billie Jean King and Bobby Riggs on TV for that big men versus women's tennis match? That was something, eh? Everybody was watching that one."

"That's what I'm talking about," Vincent said.

"I'll tell you what else," the Aussie groused. "Some of these big corporations should get their heads out of their arses and step up to the plate. There is huge money to be made right here in fashion, cosmetics, jewelry, health care, hospitality, retail, the food and grocery industries, professional services, pharmaceuticals, entertainment, and transportation, to name a few. The right people just need to commit is all. I mean, look at the venue this week. It's beautiful, the weather is perfect, the golf is awesome-- it's a total package. It could sell. I think if the purses were bigger, more people would watch. It is all about the bucks. That, and I need to be caddying is all."

"Forget caddying man, you should be working for the LPGA Marketing Department, or the Newport Beach Chamber of Commerce," Vincent said.

Their waitress came, and everyone reordered, except Vinnie. "Just water for me, please. I'm the DD."

The guys shot the breeze for a spell. How long had the Aussie been here? A little over a year. What were his chances of getting a loop? Getting better. How did he like America? Awesome, especially Southern California, etc. How can you have a better time on a sunny Saturday afternoon at the beach than to be drinking with an Aussie? It's the accent probably.

Vincent's cell phone rang. "Let me get this." He listened for a minute and finally said "so what if the bar refer box is out? Get some damn bus tubs and fill them up with ice, transfer the bottled beer, and get through the night. Then schedule the refrigeration guy first thing in the morning. Why do you bother me with this kind of petty crap?" Vincent hung up his phone with an annoyed expression on his face.

"Trouble in paradise?" Tommy asked.

"The usual stupid junk," Vincent replied.

"You own a bar?" the Aussie asked.

"It's a bar and restaurant actually," Vincent replied.

"That's awesome, mate. Where is it?"

"South end of Seattle."

"What kind of restaurant is it?"

"I don't want to talk about it. I'm on vacation here."

Vincent gave Tommy the look. "It's about time we hit the road, eh?"

He glanced over at the Aussie, "We got some business to tend to. You want a ride back to the tournament?"

"Cheerio. By the way, do you think I might be able to touch you blokes for a couple of quid? I'll get it back to you as soon as I get my first loop."

"How you gonna do that?"

"Well, I could post it to you at your restaurant." The Aussie had seen Vincent's stash and was hoping for some charity.

Vincent was still flush from the race track. He retrieved his bankroll and peeled off a couple of hundred-dollar bills. "Here," he said, and tossed them across the table at the Aussie.

"Goodonya, mate. You're no wanker."

"Fuhgeddaboudit," Vincent replied.

The Aussie had the two bills in hand and looked over at Tommy. If anyone at the table owed anything, it was surely Tommy.

Tommy got the look. He dug out a couple more C-notes and eased them across the table.

"Rippin' good, mate. Cheers. Just let me get a traveler for the road. We can hang out back at the tournament, and then go do dinner." One more margarita he signaled to their waitress.

"We'll give you a ride back buddy, but no go for dinner. We're busy." The Aussie got his drink, and Tommy dropped a hundred-dollar bill on the table. "Let's go," he said.

Back at Pelican Hill, Vincent let his new best friend off in front of the clubhouse.

"G'day, mates, and thanks," the Aussie said, and ambled up the stairs.

Vincent drove around for a few minutes to create some space between them and their new drinking buddy, eventually making his way back to the players lot. Parking spaces were easy to find now that the place was three-quarters empty.

Chrissy finished her round for the day at one under par. One under par is a decent round, but nothing that is going to gain any ground on the leaders. "I am going to stay around and hit some balls," Chrissy told Bobby.

"Do you want me to hang with you?" he replied.

"Nah, you've been here all day. You should go see what Will is doing. I will catch up with you guys at the hotel for a bite to eat. Or if you go out, I will just stay in and order from room service. I've got to get these irons straightened out, and then go putt for a while. I probably won't be back until about seven or so."

"Okay, here are the car keys. I'll see you in the morning. What time do you want to get to the course?"

"Tee off is around twelve thirty, so we should probably get here by nine thirty."

"Got it, see you in the coffee shop at quarter to. I'll get a ride back to the hotel with one of the guys."

"Don't stay out too late, will you? We've got a big day tomorrow." Chrissy was well aware of the foibles of the caddy crowd Bobby loved to hang and party with.

"Okay, mom," he replied laughingly, and waved goodbye as he started to back pedal off.

"Mom? You think I am your mom? I would have put you up for adoption years ago if I was your mother!"

Bobby ignored Chrissy's retort and ambled off, happy to be done with what had turned out to be a frustrating day.

So, Chrissy was pounding away on the driving range when our guys showed back up. She had a swing coach, but not on a regular basis. Like Ben Hogan, she believed in digging her game out of the dirt. But on a semiannual basis, she would meet with her old college coach for a tune-up. In the meantime, hitting three or four hundred balls after a round was her daily routine.

The sun was beginning its descent as the guys sat down, so it would probably be no more than another hour of waiting around. They took a seat in the near corner of the bleachers and tried to be inconspicuous. Pretty soon, Tommy wanted another beer, and got up to make a run up to the bar. "Watch out for that damn Aussie, I don't want him hanging around us all night, eh?"

"Got it. You want another beer?"

"Sure."

Said Aussie had gotten his own beer from the bar and parked himself on a bench outside of the Ladies' Locker Room. He thought if he might impress even one late exiting golfer with his work ethic, it would be worthwhile. He planned to hang around for a bit and hand out his business card. The ladies' tour was pretty famous for changing caddies like people change underwear, and he wanted in on the action. So, he finished his beer, popped a breath mint in his mouth, and sat down to wait.

Out of the corner of his eye he saw Tommy slide into the lounge. What are those two wankers up to now? he asked himself.

Tommy bought two beers in clear plastic cups and headed back to the practice range. The Aussie got up and followed him at a discrete distance. Tommy climbed up the steps to the range grandstand, balancing the beers carefully, and turned left for his bleacher seat.

The tall Aussie walked around to the far side of the bleachers. He climbed up the stairs on his side and peered through the mesh screening at the top of the foot ramp without rounding the corner onto the front aisleway. Vincent and Tommy were sitting drinking beer. Tommy was pecking at his cell phone, and Vincent was absent-mindedly watching Chrissy Jensen hit ball after ball. There were two other young people up in the stands, and Chrissy was the only person left on the driving range. The young people were deep in conversation, and looked like a newbie couple who just wanted to be alone and have some face time.

The Aussie wondered what the devil are these two chaps so interested in out here? He waited around for a few minutes, which was just when Chrissy stowed her eight iron and picked up her golf bag.

A professional golfer's bag can be pretty heavy. Especially a large, leather monogrammed tour style bag, which has just about one of everything a player might ever need. But no problem, Chrissy hoisted the bag onto her shoulder like it was nothing and walked off of the range. "She's a fit one," the Aussie muttered as he descended back down the stairs. He stood in the shadow of the far side of the bleachers and watched Chrissy stop at the putting green. She put down her bag, took out her wand, dropped a couple of Pro-Vs on the grass, and began to stroke some putts.

Tommy and Vincent were about fifty yards behind Chrissy. They paused for a moment and then headed on up to the bar. The Aussie let them pass, then angled around way behind them through the concessions area and emerged back out in front of the clubhouse.

He walked across the street and straight back to his rental sedan, got in, sat down and stuck the key into the ignition slot. There were three cars left in the player's lot. His sedan, Vincent's black Range Rover, and a Volvo station wagon. He recognized Vincent and Tommy's car, and concluded that the other one must be Chrissy's. Man, this place is almost deserted he thought, as he started his car and drove away.

Vincent and Tommy exited the bar/clubhouse and proceeded to their Rover. They got in and waited. Chrissy's Volvo station had been parked just about in the middle of the lot, as was Vincent's

Range Rover. The two cars were about fifty feet apart. It was deep into dusk, but not dark yet. Significantly, there were no official personnel around, and just two vehicles left in the lot.

As Chrissy finally approached and stowed her gear, she seemed to glance over at the Rover, then she started her car, backed out and drove away. Vinnie looked at Tommy, and Tommy back looked at his pal. "Piece of cake," Vinnie said.

As an operational specialist, and with the caper they had in mind, Tommy was on board. "I cannot disagree with you," he replied.

"There was an ad in the program for Mama's Italian food over in Fashion Island. Let's go get a bowl of pasta and do a little shopping. I want to buy something nice for Angela."

"No problem," said Tommy.

The guys headed down the Coast Highway for the huge, upscale shopping mall. They saw Angela's favorite salon, a Tiffany's jewelry store, and proceeded to go in. Vincent took his time and picked out a flashy nineteen-hundred-dollar tennis bracelet for his wife. Tommy saw an Adidas storefront, and the boys continued on in and bought golf shorts, polo type shirts, and walking shoes.

They found Mama's Italian Restaurant and headed for the bar. The pasta was excellent, the house wine was good, and the people watching was fun. "Some kind of dames they got in this town, eh?" Tommy mused. Vincent concurred, and was actually hoping to run into the two working girls they had entertained on Thursday evening. No luck there.

"What time you wanna go back tomorrow?" Vincent threw out. "We should see how our girl does. If nothing is happening, we can always go back to Carlo's place for a drink before we leave town."

"Sounds good to me," Tommy responded. "Let's get there around one, one thirty."

CHAPTER EIGHT

Chrissy got back to her suite in the Newport Hills Marriott Hotel and got ready to hit the shower. She threw her catchall bag at the corner of the bedroom in tired frustration after her long day, but in a good way. She felt like she had worked the bugs out of her irons, and her putts were dropping again. Now it was time to forget about the game of golf and relax.

She checked messages and was happy to hear that her mom and dad were flying in for the final round of the tournament tomorrow. Will had met friends for dinner, and Bobby was out and about. She called room service and ordered a grilled chicken breast and vegetables, with a green salad, and a piece of carrot cake. Desserts had been a weakness since her days back in Yakima, what with all of the fresh fruit available to her family and her grandma's pie-baking talents. As she was a lite drinker, it also helped with her sugar fix.

Flipping on the TV, she checked the cable stations for a movie. What a glamorous life I lead, she thought. World famous, and here I sit alone in my hotel room on a Saturday night, getting ready to eat from room service, so I can watch a movie by myself.

A knock came at the door twenty-five minutes later, and she opened it to: "Room service, ma'am," and a burly young waiter.

"Come on in," she said stepping aside. Ma'am? Chrissy thought, not at all comfortable with the waiter's matronly address. Maybe he should stick around for a couple of hours, and I will show him some ma'am.

But that was not in the cards. Instead, she thanked the young dude, tipped him a twenty-dollar bill from her wallet cash, and sat down to eat. She was starving, and feeling a bit reflective. It is high time I took a little break, she thought. I am getting a little lonely, cranky, and am annoyed with Will for going out to dinner without me. Bobby, she didn't care so much about. She was with him almost all day, every day, and he was still a bit young for much mature dinner conversation. Brother Will however, was her right-hand man, and she wanted and needed to have good communication with him. There was so much going on in her everyday career while she was out on the golf course, and she insisted on hearing from her business manager on a frequent basis about the money side of things. She grabbed her cell phone and dialed his number. He didn't pick up, so she hung up, then left a text message for them to meet for breakfast at eight fifteen in the hotel coffee shop.

There was nothing left to do but finish a surprisingly good dinner, then kick back and start channel surfing. She had a book started, and a couple of women's magazines, but there was nothing better than mindlessly channel surfing after a long day. Wow. The golf channel was showing the *Greatest Game Ever Played* and it had only started fifteen minutes ago. She propped herself up on two fluffy pillows in the middle of the king-sized bed and settled in to watch Shia LaBoeuf play his vintage role of Francis Ouimet overcoming the greatest possible odds, and taking down the reigning British world champion, Harry Vardon, in that early 1913 United States Open Championship.

Ouimet's victory over Vardon, an almost unbelievable tale of David slaying Goliath, is capable of producing incredible inspiration. For the average golfer, it is the awareness that anything is possible. During the tense final match of the movie and the Championship, it was as if by divine intervention, Ouimet had an angel perched on his shoulder. Who was nonstop calming his nerves, steeling his mind, and helping his shots fly straight. To a professional such as Chrissy Jensen, who was in a similarly difficult situation in her current tournament, it could possibly have been the very best movie ever made for her to stumble upon.

She had seen it enough times to know a lot of the dialogue by heart. But the emotional impact was never lost on her. Don't quit, never give up. Never, ever.

By the end of the movie, tears of happiness misted in her eyes for the game of golf in America, and for Francis Ouimet, the humble, courageous hardscrabble boy/hero, who triumphed under such intense pressure. She loved the gallantry displayed by Harry Vardon, and the grace he was able to demonstrate in defeat. But the main concept of the movie was the indomitable spirit of Francis Ouimet, and his belief not only that he should be out there on the course, but that he could/would triumph. And triumph in the face of impossible odds. Then there was the pluck of his diminutive, wonder boy caddie, Eddie.

Chrissy got up, sighed, stretched, and did some ab crunches and push-ups, and then went into the bathroom to begin her evening's ablutions. She took off her Seattle Seahawks tee shirt, and admired her upper body in the mirror. Cocking her arms and playfully flexing her biceps, she decided then and there that she was going to win the tournament tomorrow.

She brushed her hair, her teeth, cleansed her face, put on moisturizer, and went back into the bedroom suite. It was getting late, but she felt centered. In five minutes, at precisely eleven twenty-two p.m., she was curled up, clutched a pillow to her stomach, and fell fast asleep.

Seven fifteen a.m. rolled around, and Chrissy stirred and yawned. She was a sound sleeper, and as she roused herself, she felt good. Excellent, in fact. After brushing her teeth and washing up, she came back in and did some morning stretches. Then it was down to the hotel's workout room for fifteen minutes with the jump rope to get her heart going, head back up in the elevator, take a shower, start putting on makeup and get her outfit together for the day.

At eight ten, she strolled into the coffee shop, grabbed an Orange County Register and a Wall Street Journal off of the hostess stand, and sat herself at a back booth. She turned away from her fellow patrons for some privacy and opened the Register to the sports page.

Will came in a couple minutes later, as Chrissy was looking up the third-round standings. "Morning, Sis."

"Morning, William," she responded. Will looked at her out of the corner of his eye, checking to see if something was up. There was usually some kind of an issue when she called him William.

Chrissy was always interested in the standings during the tournament to see what was going on in the fickle game known as professional golf, and she meticulously poured over the results of the previous three days of competition. Some of her friends had aspired to greatness and were in the top twenty. Some had floundered and were not going to see much of a check. Several had not even made the cut. This being the women's tour, menstruation can always be a factor for some of the gals. Often some of them wished they could blame their problems on their menstrual cycles.

"I'm seven strokes back, but I am going to win this thing," Chrissy declared to Will.

"Awesome, Sis. That would kick some butt. How was your night?"

"It was great, since you deserted me. I seduced the room service waiter, we drank a quart of tequila, watched some porn and I went to sleep around three a.m. Slept great though, and the tequila is still kicked in."

"Ha, ha. Sorry to leave you. These two old fraternity brothers have been bugging me to meet them for dinner. It was all the way up in Santa Monica, so I had to take off pretty early to try and beat traffic."

"You can never beat traffic in LA, don't you know that?"

"I just drove up the Coast Highway. Before dinner we went to muscle beach in Venice. I gotta show you the pics. That place is a nuthouse. You wouldn't believe what a bunch of characters are out there. Here, look at this." Will proceeded to flip through some shots of a near naked guy playing Mozart on a grand piano on the promenade, while someone else was juggling live gerbils in the foreground, accompanied by bongos and a tambourine. Tourists were weaving in and out of the picture in throngs. And then there was muscle beach and the skateboard park.

"Wow," Chrissy said. "Looks like an interesting place."

"Here are some of the muscle guys. They must own a steroid factory somewhere, they are huge," and he ran through some more shots for her. "Then at the skateboard park, with all of the kids zooming around on their boards, a lady was doing all of the drops and runs in a wheelchair! It was amazing, but enough of that. How was your night?""

"Oh, I got back around seven thirty, ordered room service, and watched a movie. A pretty quiet night all in all. How is business?"

"Great. I talked at length with the Vitamin Water people yesterday. They want to sign you up on a two-year deal. National commercials three times a year, with a spot in a super bowl package."

"That would be cool. Wanna go to the Super Bowl with me?"

"Sure, Sis. Let's go. They want to take over the Pure Silk slot on your collar, too. I told them that was worth at least a hundred grand a year. They said they would work it into the package, and they would take care of you. It's a good thing you are a Washington resident; if you lived in California, state income taxes would be killing you. Federal taxes are stiff enough."

"I know. Thanks for helping with all of this stuff. At least we have the good problem of having to pay taxes. With your help, it lets me focus on my game more."

"Well, the more you concentrate--the better you do, and the better the endorsement offers are. We should start thinking about getting a foundation set up for you."

Chrissy ordered some fruit, rye toast, and three scrambled eggs with coffee. That would hold her over pretty well until after the tournament, except for a few energy bars. She would have plenty of time to start digesting her breakfast before teeing off. Get the blood flow out of her belly, and back in her brain where it belonged.

"Anything else?' she asked Will, just as Bobby dragged himself over to the booth.

"Morning sunshine," Will greeted him.

"Ugh," he responded.

"Dang it, Bobby--I asked you to keep it to a dull roar last night," Chrissy remarked irritably.

"Jeez, Sis. I go out and beat streets for a scoop for you, and that is the thanks I get! Wait until you hear this one."

"What?"

"Heather Layton is rumored to be preggo."

"You are kidding me."

"Nope. No wonder she has missed the last three cuts."

"Everyone thought she was enjoying a little slump is all. So, who is the lucky guy?"

"Yeah, word is still out on that one."

"She has been with that David dude for about a year. It's got to be him."

"But I thought they broke up a couple of months ago."

Chrissy pondered the situation for a moment and shook her head sadly. Unwed motherhood was certainly not in her long-range plan, and she felt for the popular Heather who had worked so hard to get here, only to jeopardize it all with a growing personal issue.

"Are you ready to win this thing today?" Chrissy said to her little brother. "We are going to kick some butt out there."

"Right on Sissy, let's do it." Bobby checked the time on his phone, and he opted for the breakfast buffet rather than wait on ordering something from the menu.

All three Jensens took off in the Volvo and arrived at Pelican Hill at nine fifteen. Bobby grabbed Chrissy's golf clubs and headed for the range, and after checking her tee time, she went out to begin warming up. She loved a leisurely start-up routine. Take it slow, methodically let her ingrained swing mechanics fall into place. Within half an hour, high arcing parabolas were flying crisply off the face of her irons onto the green expanse of the driving range.

Next, she would head over to the conditioning tent and get a ten-minute Shiatsu massage. Not enough to bliss herself out, but enough to remove any kinks and contusions. Then it was over to the short game range, hit some pitch shots, bump a few, tune up her chipping, and practice getting out of the sand.

By now, she was in her concentration mode and getting psyched up. That focus and the rhythm that professional golfers achieve is nothing short of amazing. The pace of their shots is consistent, the execution is flawless and timeless. It is almost like they are transported out of their bodies and are watching themselves deliberately execute shot after shot.

The crowd was growing around the practice facilities, including the range, the putting green, and the short game practice area. But the players mostly had their game faces on. This was the time for warming up, and it was nice to be social, but not overly chatty or distracted.

Bobby watched Chrissy closely, and he liked what he saw. First of all, looks like she worked out the flaw in her iron shots last evening, and her short game had looked spot-on to him earlier this morning. Now it was over to the putting green, and then she would finish up back on the big range with the driver. But best of all, he liked the edge in her attitude and facial expression. She was ready. Bobby was back from his first duties of the morning, that of getting a pin sheet, formulating today's strategy and double-checking some of the closer pin placements. He and Chrissy would review that information before they went out.

Chrissy continued to feel good. She knew she was four groups back from the leaders, and seven strokes behind Belinda Jones, who was a three-time winner on tour and a very steady, if unspectacular, player. Of the remaining twelve players ahead of her: six were Asian women, there was a rookie from Canada, four were Americans girls, and the last competitor was her old friend Kandy Carter. She and Kandy were in the same pairing, had played against each other in college, and loved the competition. It was the UDub against ASU all over again, and this was the kind of head-to-head contest that made each of them play better and harder not only against each other, but the field at large as well.

The last member of their threesome was one of the Asian girls. I say "girl", because this young lady had just barely turned twenty-one and was as slender as a sapling tree. She must be wiry as hell, Chrissy thought, to hit the ball as far as she does. But then again, she has that fabulous flexibility of youth, that some of the LPGA women were just beginning to lose a bit as they advanced into old age in their late twenties.

Chrissy couldn't have been happier with her pairing and was scheduled off at twelve forty-seven. She left the putting green and went back over to the driving range to begin warming up her metal clubs. Boom, boom, boom. The ball was jumping off everything from her Titleist 917 driver on down. She threw in a few irons and wrapped up hitting lob wedges ridiculously close to the fifty-yard flag. Bobby returned, and they retired to the players tent, where he shared his course info with her, and she picked up an official scorecard.

"It is really important for us to get off to a good start, Bobby. If we are going to catch the leaders, we have got to get out of the box early and strong. And if we get lucky, someone might falter ahead of us."

"Right on, Sis. The flags are reasonable today, we should have a shot at it. You warmed up great. You feeling good?"

"I feel incredible."

"Okay, see you on the tee box." Bobby went off to the nearest SaniCan before the game got under way. "He is still young and parties too much," Chrissy told herself, "but when the bell rings, he is all business. I like that."

Vincent and Tommy enjoyed a leisurely morning at the Hyatt Regency pool, and around eleven thirty they started getting ready to head over to the golf course.

"I wanna call Carlo, and tell him we may stop by this afternoon," Vinnie said.

"This is Carlo speaking."

"Hi pal, It's Vinnie. You gonna be around later on?"

"What time?"

"Oh, probably around three or four. We are going over to the golf course now and thought we might stop by for a cocktail before we head to the airport."

"Well, call before you come over. We are already out on the boat with friends, and I'm not sure what time we will be in. We may just stay out on the bay for cocktail hour."

"Okay buddy. If I don't see you before we go, thanks again for everything. I owe you."

"Nonsense, happy I was here for you. Have a great day."

The boys had lunch at the hotel coffee shop before they left. They were packed up and ready to go but didn't want to rely on the buffet in the Pelican Hill hospitality suite for any sustenance.

"You got any tofu burgers?" Vincent asked their waitress in jest. She gave him a funny look, but he did get a healthy guffaw out of Tommy, who appreciated his inside joke. They opted for more traditional loaded cheeseburgers.

Looking at the two Seattle imports in Sunday's light of day, you couldn't be sure if they didn't look better in yesterday's black outfits, than in their newly minted Cali cool duds. The Bermuda shorts still had that shine of newness on them, not to mention the store-bought creases and folds from sitting on a shelf. The shirts were too loud for middle-aged guys; their tennis shoes were spanking new and still flawlessly white. The guys hadn't purchased athletic socks, so they were wearing black, silky, high top numbers, which accentuated their dorkiness and the whiteness of their untanned legs. About all they needed now was a camera around one of their necks, brown bag lunches, and some kind of tacky fedora hats to look like complete turkeys.

But again, in Vinnie's world, one reason he was such a cool dude was because no one dared to suggest otherwise. No matter what he was wearing.

Getting to the course was no problem. They again bypassed all of the congestion points with their VIP parking pass and cruised into the players lot. Said lot was crammed today, on the last day of the tournament, but they were able to find a space on the very back row. Then it was up to the sky box. Vinnie wasn't about to take the chance of having another heat stroke, or of running into the corpulent woman who had risked life and limb coming to his aid yesterday.

Fortunately for the guys, there was plenty of cold beer in a large cooler box to take the strain off of the bartenders. Vinnie and Tommy helped themselves to some snacks, grabbed beers, and dawdled over to the bleachers to watch the early foursomes begin dribbling in.

Vinnie's bartender buddy wasn't here today, and he wasn't sure if security recognized him. He also cut a wide swath around the rainbow table. But the guys were able to snag two of the few remaining seats in the grandstand, and settled down in the warm afternoon sun to watch and wait for the leaders to come in. It was a beautiful setting and quite a treat for a couple of web-footed Seattle guys who had endured a long, cold, grey, and wet winter together.

The crowd at the first tee was twice the size of Saturday's showing, and Chrissy was given a very warm welcome. She didn't disappoint, and pounded the ball a smooth two-eighty down the middle of the first fairway. Her irons appeared to be very well straightened out when she telegraphed a nine iron one hundred fifty-eight yards to the green, and ran a six-footer into the cup for an opening birdie.

"Center cut, baby," Bobby cooed. And they were off to the second hole.

Chrissy continued her early success. She bombed the fairways and greens, and was hot with the short stick. Like in the book about Zen putting, she literally could see the line of her putts on the slick, Sunday afternoon surfaces, and as she trusted in her line, boom--she had them dropping left and right.

After seven holes, Chrissy had made four birdies and three pars. And by the turn, she stood at five under. "You need to stay focused," Bobby told her. "We haven't won a dang thing yet."

Whereupon she promptly birdied the four hundred twenty-foot par four tenth hole. "That's what I'm talking about," Bobby said, and gave her a wink.

Kandy Carter was two under for the day, and the Asian girl was even par, having seemingly melted under Chrissy's vicious onslaught. Belinda, the leader out of the clubhouse, was three under par for the day and stood at ten under, which was also a great start to her round. With her torrid front side, and the tenth hole, Chrissy had gained six shots, shot an even thirty, and sat at nine under. She had by passed ten of the players who had started ahead of her and was still feeling it. She was in the zone.

While they weren't playing together, Belinda Jones could certainly hear the roars from Chrissy's large gallery. And after every roar, which wouldn't seem to quit, she seemed to get a little tighter. Belinda could also see the on-course scoreboards and knew Chrissy was closing hard on her lead.

Chrissy cooled off for two holes, then bombed a three hundred-seven-yard drive on the par five downhill, thirteenth hole. She followed that shot by ripping a two hundred thirty-seven yard screaming three-wood to the front of the green. The gallery erupted! And Belinda, who was lined up over the ball on the eighth green, jerked her putt six feet past the hole and missed the come backer for a bogey.

The tournament was now tied. And of course, Chrissy's chip to the left middle of the green rolled cleanly up and into the cup for an eagle three, and a two-stroke lead. Another ear-splitting roar from the crowd, and the tournament was for all intents and purposes, was over and done with.

To keep the pressure on, Chrissy birdied two of the remaining five holes to come in at ten under par for the day. Francis Ouimet was dancing a jig up there in golf heaven! Vincent DeGrazzi leaned over in his bleacher seat, glanced at Tommy Thurston, and whispered, "Hell, that girl is worth twenty million." Tommy and

Vincent looked down at the standing gallery around the eighteenth green. They saw the Aussie jumping around and knew he would give his left testicle to be carrying Chrissy Jensen's bag right now. Stuart, Monica, and Chet Lincoln were watching the tournament in their Puyallup, Washington townhouse and slapped their hands together in a high five. Many of them, actually.

When Chrissy rolled into the eighteenth green, the roar of the crowd was deafening and nonstop. She putted out and stood politely and tipped her visor to the crowd. The scene was truly electric. Finally, her brother Will and her mom and dad came out between the ropes to give her a hug, and Will and Bobby led her away to the scorer's tent.

She followed her brothers back through the ropes, chatting with her mom, and holding a four-stroke lead. Her opponents had four holes left to play. But no one was going to catch her today. It was one of the greatest final day rounds in LPGA history. Ten strokes under par and overcoming a significant deficit to win the tournament going away. Amazing.

The impact of her round hadn't quite dawned on her yet. She finished her scoring table duties and retired to the player's lounge to catch her breath. The Golf Channel people were standing by for an interview. But they wouldn't chat until the last two threesomes had come in, and the tournament was officially over. Soon Chrissy was back out on the putting green, trying to stay loose and relaxed should a sudden death playoff improbably occur.

Finally, the wait was over. She returned to the eighteenth green for the awards ceremony and a roar from the assembled crowd. She smiled a beautiful, broad, beaming smile into the cameras and began the exit interview. Her whole persona was lit up by the amazing comeback, her supportive fans, and the brilliance of the sparkling late afternoon California sunshine.

"I felt great today," she shared with her attentive female interviewer. "We got off to an awesome start and just took it one shot at a time. The crowd was fantastic throughout and gave me a huge edge out there. I couldn't have done it without them. I would also like to thank my family who were here for me today.

My mom and dad, brother Will who is my manager, little bro Bobby who caddies for me, and my oldest brother Chas who was with us in spirit. Thanks also go the LPGA for organizing such a great tournament, to all of the hundreds of volunteers out here who make it happen, and Pelican Hill for hosting this event. The course was in tremendous shape." Finally, Chrissy caved a bit and began to get a little teary. Immediately, she was engulfed by the family. And instead of crying Bobby got them all jumping up and down and dancing for joy.

The Golf Channel's lead story on their Golf Central program that evening was, and had to be: *Another Star is Born!*

CHAPTER NINE

The immediate Jensen family, plus Bob Jensen's brother and his wife had a reservation at the exclusive Five Crowns Restaurant in Corona Del Mar, and everyone waited patiently for the two hours it took Chrissy to wrap up her official and media obligations, collect her gear, bid her adieus, sign some autographs, check her gazillion phone messages and head off for her family celebration.

The Five Crowns is a prime rib restaurant under the Lawry's umbrella of premium beef houses. It's an Olde English style fine dining establishment and is housed in an antique Tudor mansion in the heart of CDM. It has been around seemingly longer than Southern California Edison, and Maître d' Tommy Brennley had the Jensen's private dining room staffed and mise en place.

Chrissy was ready for an adult beverage. She was drained from the emotions of winning and the responsibilities that accompanies, but she was still on a substantial high from her spectacular round. She felt like this is how she had always dreamed it would be. A round of golf so almost perfect, it seemed to be effortless. And then a celebration with her entire (except for Charlie) family.

The Jensen's settled in, and took care of the first order of business, which was ordering drinks and several bottles of premium wine. "Please make sure there is a bottle of Rombauer Chardonnay on the table for me," Chrissy asked Will before retiring to powder her nose. When the drinks came and Chrissy returned, Bob Jensen rose and commanded the floor. "On behalf of Ginny and myself, and no matter how many times we get to make this speech," he said, "it is still a thrill and an honor to congratulate

Chrissy on another tremendous victory. As a matter of fact, this is without doubt the greatest win yet. Congratulations, Chrissy." And with that, the family raised their glasses, clinked all around, and began to enjoy the festivities.

Chrissy stood, lifted her tumbler of Rombauer, and playfully thanked her brothers for deserting her the previously evening. "Without Will and Bobby's self-indulgent neglect, this win would never have happened," she teased. "I was surfing around for something to watch on TV feeling very sad and alone, alienated actually," and she related the story of the inspirational movie she found on the tellie, and what a motivating factor it had been for her today.

"Here, here," someone toasted.

Will stood up and on behalf of himself and Bobby, thanked Chrissy for recognizing their considerable contributions to today's victory. There were catcalls over that, and the family goodwill was now flowing in waves. A magnitude of life altering joy that not enough people ever get to experience.

"Have you rented a place for us all yet?" Chrissy asked Will about the Amazon Tournament.

"Yep. I reserved a five thousand square foot home right in University Village as soon as I heard about the tournament. It sleeps sixteen people, so we should be all set with lodging for everyone, then have plenty of room to entertain as well. And best of all, Nike is mostly comping us. It is one of the corporate lodgings they bought when the US Open was at Chambers Bay, and they use it as a retreat and VRBO now. All we have to pay for is utilities and cleaning."

"Great job son," Bob Jensen spoke approvingly to Will. "I think half of Yakima is going to be there. What do you need from us before we leave tomorrow?"

"Oh, don't worry about anything, dad," Chrissy said. "We've got this. Just come and enjoy yourself."

Soon Tommy Brennley, a miserable hacker of a golfer, but a huge fan nonetheless, presented a selection of complimentary appetizers to the party, and as they ordered dinner, the private room now smelled wonderful, the wine and appetizers tasted equally scrumptious, and the evening was lifting off nicely.

Tommy and Vincent filed out of the hospitality suite with the rest of the day's elite crowd. They had watched Chrissy's interviews on the big screen TV's and were as pumped as everyone else at her incredible comeback win.

"What a broad," Vincent said. "I am amazed she didn't shoot a fifty-nine, and then go swim to Catalina Island or something. She was on some kind of a roll."

"You got that right," Tommy agreed. "Tremendous athlete, and she is so unassuming too."

"We got to talk this thing through. If we was to move on this, we got to be really careful to do it absolutely right." In spite of the obvious risks in abducting a tour player, Vincent seemed close to being star struck by the excitement of the whole Chrissy/LPGA scene.

"I hear that. Let's talk about it on the plane."

The guys fought traffic to the airport, dropped the rental car, took their luggage inside, found a pre-security restroom and changed out of their casual wear and into more appropriate northwestern clothing before checking their luggage. Vincent had already stowed his revolver, and soon enough they had checked in, were through security and sitting in a hospitality lounge by their gate waiting to board.

"Some kinda wild weekend, eh?" Vincent mused.

"Yeah, it sure was," Tommy replied. Both of the fellas were still dazzled by the whole sequence of events they had just experienced. Especially, as they were confirmed golfers, the amazing performance of Chrissy Jensen that afternoon, but all of the other action as well; from the working girls to the horse races, to fine dining and hanging with Carlo and Gina.

They both had their heads together and spoke quietly. "I would never want anything bad to happen to that girl," Tommy said. "She's special."

"You are so right," Vincent replied. "The worst would be for her to be out of action for a few weeks or so. I would see to it that no one ever laid a hand on her other than that."

"I'm glad to hear you say that my friend."

"But I been thinkin'. I mean, you and I both saw how easy it would be to snatch her. If there was an opportunity like we had last evening, she would be so easy to get to. Then we stash her for a week, the hard part is getting the money out clean."

"Yeah, the first part would be easy."

"I'm thinking we keep things going forward on a smaller scale. You and I grab the girl. We drop her off at the house. I want one of my guys there watching her, not the Russians, I don't trust them. We get that Stuart kid and his girlfriend over there to help out. The guys trade off, twelve-hour shifts, and the girl goes into the basement twice a day to feed her, and make sure she is okay. You know what I mean?" Vincent was on a roll now.

"Okay," Tommy said.

"I mean, we could grab her so easy, if we had the same set up as we had Saturday night. We could get to her and get out of there pronto. That could be the biggest no-brainer scam I ever seen. The broad was all alone. We throw her on the floor of the back seat, put a blanket over her, and we are gone. And that is all we have to do. The other three hold her, we negotiate the deal, we let Stuart grab the cash and take all the risks, and we're done. Whadda ya think?"

"I know what you are saying, but I think we should drop the deal down to ten million bucks. Twelve million sounds greedy. And if I do this, all I am in for, is helping you snatch the girl. I ain't involved with any of the other stuff, but I still get a cut. Capiche?"

"Capiche."

"If anything happened to that girl, if anything went wrong, I don't want nothin' to do with it."

"That's the beauty of the whole thing. Ain't nothin' gonna happen. We grab her, we hold her, we ransom her. Boom, we're done."

"You aren't worried about the FBI or anything?"

"Well, what are they going to have to go on? If there is a chance of any problems, we shut down. No deal. If we can get her clean, we take her, and bring her to the house. How they gonna know where to look? No, the only problems would be in the money exchange, and we let the kid handle that. We let him take all of the chances."

"Okay. I'm in for what I said I was in for," Tommy declared.

"Me too. I'm in. I will call the kid tomorrow and have a sit down wid him."

Their boarding call came over the PA system, and Vincent and Tommy queued up for departure. Rarely has anyone had as wild a weekend in Newport Beach as these two guys, and still left for home with a healthy wad of cash in their pockets.

"Wow, this thing is going to go," Stuart gushed at Monica and Chet. "Vincent left me a phone message, and he wants to have a meeting tomorrow. I think he wants to buy in."

"Damn," was about all Chet could muster.

Monica was her usual stoic self. She was conservative and cynical to a fault by her nature.

"He wants you to come with me, babe."

"Me?" she asked. "I'm shocked."

"That's what he said. Here listen to the message."

"How does he even know anything about me?"

"All he knows is that I have a girlfriend. Maybe he just wants to check you out."

"I guess we will find out tomorrow. What time does he want us?"

"He said to be at the bar at eleven."

At eleven o'clock sharp Monica and Stuart rolled into Vincenzo's Italian Bar and Restaurante on Highway 99 and asked for the proprietor.

Monica was a trifle nervous, and subsequently was compulsively fiddling around with her cuticles and kept tapping her finger tips together. But she looked great. Tall, darkly attractive in jeans, a black turtleneck and black ankle high boots, she was wearing Vincent's favorite color. Her hair was in a more subdued do than the top knot Stuart preferred, but it looked current and sexy. He had already forewarned her of a possible pat down.

Stuart wore his usual casual collegiate/geek clothes and was more excited than distressed. He ushered Monica back to Vincent's private booth area, where Vincent stood, greeted them and invited them into the back room. Once in there, Vincent had his guy go over them with a wand and asked both of them to deposit their phones with him. He took Monica's over the shoulder sling bag for good measure. "Don't worry, it's safe with me," he told her. She gave him the look, a.k.a., it better be buddy.

Vincent unobtrusively sized Monica up, and liked what he saw. He fancied himself an expert judge of people, especially on first impressions. This was a skill he had developed from his many years of interacting with the public and his various and sundry business dealings. He trusted his instincts implicitly.

"So, how was Orange County and the tournament?" Stuart asked.

"It was good kid," Vincent replied. "Warm and sunny, we had lots to do, and then the tournament was great. Some comeback huh?"

"No kidding. I think her market value about quadrupled overnight."

"My associate and I was talkin' about that on the way home last night. We want to dial it down a bit. Go for ten mil, and not appear to be greedy, then split that two ways. Half for you, half for my people. We want to keep the operation smaller and tighter. Less problems that way. You will have rented the house, and we will make the snatch. Once we drop her off, we are out of there, so if you screw up the rental, or there are any problems, they will come down on you. I will provide one of my guys to help out, and you and Monica need to be there for the rest of the security team. Once we've got her, and we will bring her in blindfolded, she stays locked in the cellar. You and my guy will alternate taking twelve-hour shifts sitting around upstairs, and Monica goes into the cellar to feed her twice a day. One of youse must always be with Monica when she goes down in. You will wear ski masks at all times, so there is no possible chance of any recognition by her. Monica is her liaison in case she needs anything. Here's five hundred bucks. Get her a change of clothes, underwear, toothpaste, that kinda stuff. But don't leave nothin' extra laying around down there, it must be very spartan. I think there is a bed, and a small bath, she will need a towel, all of that. If she wants to behave and co-operate, we take it easy on her. If she tries anything cute, we will need to keep her restrained. We will be nice to her, but we still have to maintain control of the situation. Monica, if she has any requests, and they are reasonable, take care of it."

"Once we have her for a week, we can start to make our demands, but we need to be extremely careful how we deal with their contacts. There will be an incredible amount of heat on this thing. One stupid move, and you are in big trouble. Do you understand me? The FBI is absolutely no one to screw around with. When they come up with the dough, have you figured out how to manage the drop?"

"We are working on that, sir. If we place our crab pots somewhere around the eastern end of Fox Island we can already be underwater, and as soon as the cash comes down, it is ours, and we are gone. We think it might be a good idea to take the money to a different location, rather than come back to the rental with it. If they put any sensors in with the cash, we won't be able to scan anything until we get ashore, and we wouldn't want to lead anyone back to the house. Also, I have something here you might be interested in."

"What is it?"

"It's a book by Jeffrey Toobin called *American Heiress*. It is about Patty Hearst and her kidnapping back in the seventies by the Symbionese Liberation Army. It is a great example of how hard it is for the FBI to track down anyone who has been abducted. I especially like your idea to keep our thing small, so we have less chance of anything leaking or getting out of hand. Definitely the hard part is getting away with the cash. That is what we are working on now."

"Okay, let's meet once a week until the tournament, and you call me if anything comes up," Vincent told them.

"I will, and here is another burner phone for you. I have the number, and I programmed my burner phone number in it for you. We should not use our regular cell phones under any circumstances, they are too easy to track."

"Got it. See you later, I'm going golfing."

CHAPTER TEN

Bobby and Chrissy walked off the eighteenth hole at Alabama's famous Shoal Creek Golf Course the next Sunday afternoon, and both of them were ready to hit the road. Chrissy went to the scorer's tent and completed her obligations. Then she made it to the media tent to rehash her crappy (sic) week with the tour reporters. She could readily see the indifference her twenty-fourth place finish had produced, and was happy to be out of the press tent as quickly as possible. The scribes were equally disappointed, sorry she didn't have a better story for them. Finally, she spent a half hour signing autographs. Her fans were excited to see her, appreciated the time she spent with them, couldn't have cared less what place she finished in, and raised Chrissy's spirits instantly. Bobby went to the beer garden, and that raised his spirits just as quickly.

"What a crappy tournament partner," Chrissy offered when they reunited at the car, and headed for the airport. "I never got it going."

"Ah, it was probably the heat and humidity and a little letdown after last weekend, sis. You can't win 'em all."

"Yeah, but it is embarrassing. What were we, tied for twenty fourth?"

"Hey, we are off for a week and a half. Let's go recharge and get ready to kick some butt in Seattle. Where are you going?"

"I'm meeting a friend in Miami for six days of beach time, a few rounds of casual golf, and a little clubbing. Then I'm going up to

New York City to meet some people Will has lined up. After that, I'll start working my way towards Wisconsin. What about you?"

"I'm going to Cabo for a week, then I will meet you in Wisconsin. Who are you hanging with in Miami? You going to South Beach?"

"Steve Reed. Remember him? Played wide receiver for the Seahawks for three years, now he's with the Chicago Bears. He's a super nice guy, and a great golfer. We're staying at Gloria Estefan's hotel in South Beach."

"Try and have some fun without me."

"I'll do my best. Have a good time in Mexico. Be safe."

"Tata."

Chrissy was so looking forward to a few days of down time. Steve was exactly her age, and a superb physical specimen. As an NFL wide receiver, he was a lithe and graceful six feet one inches tall, was no stranger to a bench press, carried about three percent body fat on him, and possessed the physical presence and steady confidence of a professional athlete. Chrissy was Steve's female counterpart in every respect: tanned, toned, tough, and bubbling with excitement for her R & R with him. Chrissy felt like they had been together enough, that this downtime would flow nicely without any early relationship awkwardness. All she had left to do, was get Will to line up a couple of tee times at Coral Gables or Doral golf clubs, and they would be all set. She was excited to be with a man for the week, and take a break from all the estrogen on the tour. It also occurred to her that she was about to have some recreational golf in her future. Hmmm, I wonder what that is like anymore? she thought.

Tommy and Vincent hung around after their golf game that Wednesday afternoon. They had some loose ends to tie up.

"The kid locked up the house lease, and I went over there yesterday with him to look around. It is somewhat secluded, and it's right on the water. It has a three-car garage, so we can stash the town car there after the job until we move it back out. The basement is pretty big, and it don't have no windows, so it is perfect for our needs. There is even a dock and a boathouse."

"Good, good."

"You got the car ready?"

"Yeah, I told Jerry Arno we wanted to rent one of his black Lincolns for about four days. Cash. He said no problem."

"We need to get some masks and/or disguises. Nothing too serious, but something to throw anyone off a little bit. You better get a hoodie sweatshirt so they can't see you too good. I'm reading the FBI has got incredible image tracking systems now. They can pick someone out of a crowd just by the shape of their head or your walking gait if they can get you on film. We also need to change out the license plates."

"Yeah, if they even have any cameras near us."

"You got your guns ready?"

"Oh yeah, my handguns are locked and loaded."

"You met the kid's girlfriend?"

"Yeah, she's okay. She is a big girl, and tends bar over at the Emerald Queen, so she knows how to handle some shit when it comes along. I think she will do just fine and is the perfect person to play nursemaid for our guest. She is going to get all the little stuff that will be needed, change of clothes, miscellaneous junk, and get some food in the place. I already give her five bills."

"Okay then, I think I will spend some time over at Chambers Bay. Get to know the layout really good."

"Yeah, I gotta meet with the kid again, and find out specifically what his plan is to get the money out of there."

"Let me know what you hear."

"See you later."

"The Executive and Operating Committees of the first annual Chambers Bay Ladies Professional Golf Association annual tournament is hereby called to order." Mr. Mac Tenderson, Vice Commissioner of the LPGA lightly tapped his gavel on its round, maplewood sound block, called the session to order and launched the final committee meeting before the start of the tournament.

"We are so excited to be here at this handsome, world class golf course, and the time has finally arrived to begin winding up our preparations. I personally played the course yesterday, and can honestly say I have never seen such a spectacular layout. There is a water view from each and every hole, the course is challenging and in excellent condition, and this is going to be a sensational tournament." He turned to his left, smiled broadly, introduced his first lieutenant, Ms. Cynthia Summers, and turned the floor over to her. Present at the meeting, and in no special order were: Ms. Summers, Chief of LPGA Tour Operations; Charles Preston, Special Assistant to LPGA Commissioner Richard Wilson; Anthony Palmer, Tournament Director; Brita Smith, LPGA Liaison to the Players; Brian Hougsland, Television and Media Production Director; Carmen Ayala, VP of Marketing, and representing tournament sponsor Amazon Corporation, liaised with our LPGA Director of Marketing Penny Brown; Paula Olsen, Head Rules Official; Sheila Weathersby, Director and Co-Ordinator of Volunteers; Alexander Herron, General Manager of the Chambers Bay Golf Complex; Jasper Thomas, Pierce County Commissioner/County Parks Specialist; Kathy Turner, Supervisor, Pierce County Parks and Recreation; Val Kingsley, Chambers Bay Head Golf Professional; Randy McKenna, CBay Golf Course Superintendent; in additional to these executives, there were representatives from the areas of: Communications, Technology, Grounds, Boundaries and Maintenance, Sanitation and Hydration systems, Facilities Co-ordination, Merchandise, Concessions, Transportation, Security, Signage, Licensing, the Pierce County Legal Offices, an LPGA Agronomist, the Sub Contractors Co-Ordinator, and local sports writers from the Tacoma News Tribune, the Bellevue Reporter, and the Seattle Times.

It was a heavily weighted project committee, and this last organizational meetup would take all day. They would go department by department, making sure everyone knew everyone, was able to communicate effectively, and finally, to make sure that all bases were completely covered. Fortunately, this was not the first rodeo for the majority of the meeting's attendees, but still, everyone wanted to make sure every i was dotted and t crossed for this premier Northwest LPGA event.

Cynthia, who was seated on the dais, with executives on each side of her, accepted the microphone from Mac, and after welcoming everyone and talking for a few minutes about the significance of the tournament to everyone connected to the LPGA, she introduced Carmen Ayala, Amazon's Corporate Rep.

"We would like to thank you and Amazon profusely, because without your efforts, of course, none of us would be assembled here today. Also, let us assure you we are committed to producing the finest tournament possible with our A level Communications Team and Commentators, and that we will also work at achieving maximum exposure for Amazon. We will need you to meet with our Broadcast Production Team, as you are invited into the TV booth for some promo shots and candid dialogue. Also, if you would like to include any other Amazon officials, don't hesitate to let us know." And Cynthia continued, "at this time, let me launch our meeting by turning the floor over to Carmen who has some very exciting news for us this morning. Carmen?"

Ms. Ayala stood from her seat on the dais, took the hand mic from Cynthia, circled around the dais, and began to walk back and forth across the front of the conference room as she addressed the crowd. Carmen was a comely woman nearing her mid-thirties, with traditional Latina features: medium height, black hair, flashing brown eyes, flawless olive skin, and in her case, a made for TV marketing personality. She was wearing an attractive floral print sleeveless frock, three-inch-high heels, and flashed her wide, money-making smile at the room. Raising the mic, her presentation began: "Thank you, Cynthia, it is a distinct pleasure to be here this morning. On behalf of Amazon.Com, we are honored to be the title sponsor of this inaugural event and also to help bring professional golf back to our region. I do indeed have very special news, and am happy to share it with you now. As a means of incorporating some of the luminary figures of the Northwest sporting world into contact with this tournament and elevating the image and exposure of our event to not only our immediate region, but the nation as a whole, and since the LPGA is such an international organization, a worldwide audience, I am elated to be able to announce to you that on Friday we have a special celebrity starter for the ladies. None other than one of the most venerated Northwestern golfers of all time, Mr. Freddie Carson, will be doing the official honors." Applause echoed within the room.

"That is not all ladies and gentlemen. Saturday your celebrity starters will be Ms. Sue Wild, ten-time WNBA All-Star guard for our own Seattle Storm professional basketball team, teaming up with perhaps the most iconic athlete ever to play ball in Seattle, Mr. Ken Graham Jr." This time the room erupted at Carmen's update. Sue Wild is very well loved, and Kenny Graham, ex slugging star of the Seattle Mariners, is truly Seattle's own favorite son.

When the applause died down a little Carmen continued. "Ladies and gentlemen, to round out the final spot in our daily starters, I am delighted, no completely overjoyed, to announce that we have come to an agreement, with the Super Bowl winning quarterback of the Seattle Seahawks, Mr. Russell Williams, to mingle, and do a portion of the introductions on Sunday." This last piece of hot news brought the crowd to their feet in a standing ovation that lasted for half a minute.

Finally, Carmen held up her hand to quiet everyone. "Not only will they be involved as starters, but will be attending the official tournament launch dinner on Tuesday evening, as well as staying around for a couple of hours after they perform their starting duties on the weekend in a hospitality booth to interact with our tournament fans." More applause, and Cynthia Summers couldn't help but think to herself what a spectacular event this was going to be. Freddie, Sue, Kenny Jr. and Russell, that should sell a few tickets, eh? It brought a director's smile to her handsome face with it's expensive and tasteful maquillage.

Carmen Ayala continued on. "I would like to turn the microphone over to a young woman who needs little if any introduction. Ms. Penny Brown, Director of Marketing for the LPGA, please come on up and give us some more details about the events and activities we have planned for you this tournament week. Penny…"

"Thank you, Carmen," Penny began, as she walked up to the front of the meeting room and took the mic from Carmen's outstretched hand. "First of all, let me say on behalf of all the entire LPGA staff, we are grateful for this opportunity to work with one of the world's greatest companies which has evolved from Seattle, Washington's own market culture. We have a number of activities you should be aware of, and I will begin by introducing the newest member of our Marketing Team, Mr. Alton Walker, late of Queensland, Australia. Alton has been involved with the LPGA for the last year as an unofficial representative, present at tournaments to casually interact with our fans, get some grassroots input from them, and favor us all with his charming Aussie accent. In his time with us, Alton has demonstrated a singular passion and support of the LPGA, along with showcasing some brilliant marketing and promotional ideas, and has now worked himself into a permanent position on our staff. This is his first official event, so please offer Alton your congratulations and support. Alton, please stand and take a bow. Alton Walker stood six feet two inches, but with a kinky mop of afro like red hair that extended another three inches, it ultimately measured him to be more like six foot five inches tall. In his dark suit and tie, he looked like a neon red and black exclamation point that had been inverted.

"Alton's initial duties with us, will be managing Monday's Pro-Am golf tournament. I am happy to announce that we are completely sold out for that event, at five thousand dollars a pop. We have some popular local talent coming in for the barbeque dinner and awards banquet following the golf tournament. Rumor has it that tremendous local music scene favorite Mackenzie and his band will be performing, but that is only hearsay at this time. We will update everyone when we lock up the final arrangements." Penny went on to outline the activities from Tuesday thru Sunday.

The presentations followed throughout the day. Brian Hougsland, event Media Manager commented on the great weather being expected for the weekend, the celebrities who would be in attendance, and plenty of technical information on the number and location of cameras and commentators he would have on the course. "This will present some outstanding photo ops not only for the LPGA, but also for Chambers Bay, and our television audience," he said. Mr. Ralph Dexter quickly reviewed Event Security. "We have partnered with the Tacoma Police Department, and they will have an average of one dozen uniformed police personnel on the Golf Course throughout the event. They will be escorting some of the bigger name players around the individual links and will be stationed at critical positions by the finishing holes and grandstands from eight am to the end of play each day. We will have the usual civilian perimeter security in place, and for the week we have contracted with a local company owned by Mr. Bennie Lanza. His organization's primary responsibility will be to prevent any gate crashing or illegal access to the course. His group will also maintain vehicular traffic flow as efficiently as possible in and around the grounds. On behalf of Puget Sound Event Management, please stand up and take a bow, Mr. Lanza." Her presentations droned on, and the assembled functionaries voted to take a short half hour lunch break in order to keep the agenda moving along. Finally, nearing five o'clock, the last but not least topic of the day was covered by Sanitation and Hydration. Mountain fresh spring bottled water provided by Evian, will be available throughout the grounds at a nominal price. Sani Cans will be provided at four different locations, and will be serviced nightly. Of course, access to restricted restrooms in the clubhouse for the executives assembled here today will be available. When it became readily apparent that everyone's bodily functions were going to be well taken care of, Cynthia Summers terminated the meeting, and invited everyone next door for refreshments.

Upon adjournment, the sliding doors partitioning off the adjoining social suite slid open, and the more relaxed portion of the afternoon began. As golfers are rarely shy to approach a watering hole, an immediate line queued up at both of the full-service beverage stations in the room, and the hospitality hour was under way. There was a splendid buffet available with an assortment of crudité, antipasto, as well as charcuterie, fresh and smoked northwestern seafood, selected cheeses, dipping sauces and a fresh fruit display for dessert.

The thirsty managers and directors were happy to get to work on that first drink, but it was also a fertile environment to schmooze with many of the powers that be in the LPGA for the junior members of the organization, and an opportunity to meet some of the next generation for the senior execs.

For one, Mr. Alton Walker was in his element. He was still ecstatic over his very recent promotion, and there were also any number of attractive, upwardly mobile, single young women in the room. Not to mention almost everyone from the organization with the exception of the Commissioner himself. As the new person on the block, Alton was prepared to mingle and make himself available to each and every person on the premises, both professionally and socially. He proceeded to introduce himself about, being particularly careful to knock their socks off with his fetching Aussie accent and charming colloquialisms. He seemed to be able to turn his native charm off and on at will.

Carmen Ayala approached and introduced herself. "I look forward to working with you this week Mr. Walker," she purred.

"Pleased to meet you, mum," Alton came back at her. "That is quite a lineup you announced up there today."

"It is amazing the support that is intrinsic from within the community for this golf tournament. And it certainly doesn't hurt to have Amazon open a few doors for us."

"We are going to have a smashing time of it, aren't we?"

"Yes indeed. Hope to see you around this week." Carmen winked at him, and moved on. Alton watched her turn and move away. What a beautiful sheila he thought to himself.

Cynthia Saunders was deep in conversation with Mac Tenderson, but as Alton moved by, she paused for a moment, and stuck out her hand in greeting. "It's Cynthia. So nice to see you again, and have you officially on staff. Have you met Mac Tenderson?"

"Allo, Mr. Tenderson, so nice to meet yew," Alton said, laying on the cockney as heavily as he dared.

"Please call me Mac, and welcome aboard."

"Thank you, Mr. Mac. It is hard for me to express how jolly good it is to be here."

They made small talk for several minutes, and Alton continued to circulate. He had spoken the absolute truth to Mac Tenderson. In the last year since first arriving in the United States with the express intent of working in some capacity for the LPGA, he had been willing to do anything to get his foot in the door. Even caddying. Now here he was, seemingly mere months later, rubbing elbows with the crème. "It's a bloody miracle," he said to himself, rather too loud apparently, as his immediate supervisor, Ms. Penny Brown sidled up. "What's a bloody miracle Alton?" She smiled sweetly up at him, "us redheads have to stick together you know."

"Me new job, mum. Can I buy you a bit of grog?"

"Everything is comped tonight, Alton, but I'd be delighted to join you."

"I know it is, mum, I'm just trying to suck up with me new boss a bit."

"No need, Mr. Walker. Let's go get a cocktail."

"Shall we go out on the porch and enjoy some of this beautiful evening?" Alton returned pleasantly. "By the way, you look lovely this evening, and you spoke very well today."

"Thank you, sir." Penny was pleased with both compliments, and looked forward to taking Alton under her wing as he launched his LPGA career.

And so it went for the next couple of hours. Most of the crowd was younger, and the mingling was fun for everyone. For some, it was renewing old times or acquaintances. For others, it was making new friends and contacts. Everyone wanted to shake the right hands, and the LPGA staffers tended to congregate with their own, as did the outside contractors. The contractors were more interested in a couple of free drinks and an early dinner, while the staffers were definitely organization oriented. They were billeted together in adjoining Tacoma hotels for the next week. They would be sharing many meals, duties, responsibilities, and down times throughout, so they might as well have some fun, and get to know each other. But this was without doubt the easy part of things. As soon as the Tournament approached and the players started arriving, it would be all business.

It goes without saying that a good time was had by all at the hospitality portion of the day's agenda. That is if you were still young, beautiful and had secured a position working in your dream field. And hey, the players weren't even due in for a few more days.

CHAPTER ELEVEN

Monica and Stuart stopped on the way home at Harry Canary's, an upscale bistro near their place. They parked, went in, got settled in a corner, and ordered a beer for Stuart and a glass of pinot grigio for Monica.

"Jeez Stuart, I didn't know I was going to be so involved with this thing," she said, and gave him a sideways look.

"That guy is full of surprises. Today was the first time he said anything at all about you. And now he wants you in from the get go. Your first impression must have been great. You okay with everything?"

Monica was mulling some options around in her mind. She thought about tending bar for another twenty years, or maybe go and deal cards in the casino instead. She certain wasn't going to be a damn food waitress at her age, or I could go join the Army. Not! Well hell, if we can pull this deal off, I can leave all of those crappy options behind me.

"I'm still trying to wrap my head around it, and I have some conflicts right now. But I think I am okay going forward as long as we clearly define the nature of our relationship with Vincent in this thing. Also, and this is a big one. If anyone gets hurt, I am out of there. I will walk away immediately if any of that kind of stuff goes down. I am not going to be a part of any personal violence. Period."

"What other kind of conflicts?" Stuart asked quietly.

"Well, I wasn't brought up to go around kidnapping people. But if no one gets hurt, and we can get out clean with the money, then I'm in. And I want an equal cut with you and Chet."

"I feel the same way, and I will let Vincent know that. He told me the other day when he came back from California what a classy girl he thought Chrissy was. So, I don't think he wants any more trouble than we do. As far as the cuts go, it's an equal split, three ways, after expenses."

"How about you? He wants you in the house twenty-four seven, too."

"Yeah, I know. I had no clue about that either. I think he just wants us fully bought in. You know, committed and implicated. Which I am okay with, but I think you are going to have to quit your job now, so as not to raise any suspicions when the time comes." Stuart thought of his father trying to sell broken down tractors and harvesters to struggling farmers. Remembered his mother serving sodas and malts to snotty high school kids at the counter of the local drug store. Thought of being on the lower rungs of the high school social ladder. No freaking problem with Chrissy Jensen remembering me, he thought. She didn't even know I was alive. So, I could take Monica back to Yakima and we could live in a modular home, or I could stay here and keep fixing old people's computers for the next twenty years and go crazy. Or, I could be flush for once in my life. For the rest of my life if I played my cards right. No kidding, I am willing to go for it. He was glad Monica was in too.

"I'm all in," he looked at her evenly, their eyes met, and he said it slowly, like he had put a great deal of thought behind his words.

"Yeah, me too Frankie. You just better be on top of your computer, so we don't have any problems."

"If I didn't think we could do it, I would have bailed a long time ago. And don't call me by my real name. It just might slip out at the wrong time somewhere."

"Sorry, sorry. Can I still call you Frankie in our bedroom?" she asked, and reached up casually and gave his nipple a playful tweak. "What are we going to do with all of that money anyway," she whispered in his ear?

Stuart reached over and moved her hand back down to his leg. "We spend it nice and slow. Chet and I have a plan to launder it.

We should sit down and put our heads together now that this thing is happening so quickly. After everything comes down, you will need to think about flying to Manila for a while. Get out of here, go spend some time with your mom. We would meet you there in a couple of weeks. Maybe we buy a restaurant or a small hotel or something. Retire in style, you know. Have you got your passport all squared away and current?"

"Yep. I would love to spend some time with my mom. And I want to hear all about your plan."

"We can sit down and talk with Chet as soon as possible. But basically, we are going to sail out in Chet's new boat while you are already in the Philippines. Once we get there, it's you and me, and Chet is on his own. In the meantime, we need to get everything out of the townhouse by next week. All of our personal stuff. The furniture is all rented, so it stays."

"Okay, I'll give my notice at the casino tomorrow, and start packing."

"Don't raise any suspicions. Maybe ask them for a leave or something. Tell 'em you have a family issue."

"I have a family problem, here is my notice, and I'm going away to deal with it."

"That's it. Be really fuzzy on all of the details. We are going to be traveling light, very light, so we have a lot to get done in the next week and a half."

Vincent DeGrazzi made a call to a friend of his. "Hey Bernie, Bernie Lanza, how youse doin'?"

"I'm doin' good, Vinnie. What's up?"

"Hey, I heard you is workin' on that golf tournament that's coming up over at Chambers Bay."

"Yeah, I just went to an all-day meeting for that job yesterday. They is goin' first class with everything over there. Russell Williams is even coming in for a couple days."

"Ain't that something? Hey, so you is workin' on security and everything, right?"

"Yeah, just the outer grounds though. I ain't doin' nuthin' with the golf course or the players. But, how can I help you anyway?"

"Well, me and a buddy was gonna come by next week and watch the ladies, but we want to bring a friend wid us, and he is kind of hot, you know what I mean? He loves to watch the ladies play golf, but he can't have no fuzz around him, not right now, capiche?"

"Nah, there shouldn't be no problems. Not until you get inside the gates anyway. My major concern is outside the course. They don't want nobody sneakin' in, and they don't want no fender benders with the cars coming and going. But there's no cops around outside nowhere."

"There ain't no cameras even in the players lot or nothin'?"

"Not from the LPGA. The only security cameras are on the front of the clubhouse, and they are the club's property. Once you get inside, the cops are only worried about the bigger players, and there will be so many people milling around, there shouldn't be no issues. Just be careful. Wear sunglasses and a hat. You know what to do. Hey how's your golf game anyway? We gotta get out some time."

"Yeah, we'll play pal. Why don't we wait until after the tournament? I'm sure you'll be plenty busy until then."

"Sure thing Vinnie, I'll come by the bar and say hello. You need a pass or anything?"

"Nah, I already got our stuff. I shouldda thought of you first though."

"Never too late pal."

"Thanks Bernie. You hang low, baby."

Vincent clicked off his burner phone. Slam dunk. I didn't think it was going to be this easy he thought and walked over to the wet bar to make a drink. Angela was in the kitchen prepping dinner. "What are you so happy about?" she asked him.

"I'm gonna make you a rich woman one of these days," he responded, snuck over and kissed her on the back of the neck.

First thing the next morning Vincent called Tommie Thurston. "Hey buddy, Vincent here."

"What's up?"

"We gotta have a meeting with the kid. Stuart, Stuart the kid. What a damn name anyway, huh?" Who would ever name a kid Stuart? Some gangster this kid is going to be. So, he called me late yesterday afternoon, Smooth Stuart the Gangstah, and he is telling me stuff over the phone. Like he is calling the shots or something."

"Whadda ya mean, calling the shots?"

"He says him and his girlfriend didn't know nothin' about havin' to be at the house, and if there was any trouble and somebody gets messed up, they are outta there."

"That little dork, if anybody gets roughed up, it's probably going to be him."

"Yeah, really. Let's sit him down this Thursday or Friday and work out the fine points. Explain a few things to him. What does he think anyway? He is going to sit at home and play with himself, and we do the work. Just like I said at the start."

"And he gets half a cut? Ha. What a dumb ass. I don't think he understands who he is dealing with."

"Yeah, let's meet wid him on Friday, and then if we need another sit down, do it on Monday or Tuesday. I am starting to get a little nervous about this guy. Do you think we should tell him about we gonna just keep his cut? All of it?"

"Nah, probably not. I think it might hurt little Stuey's feelings."

"Hahaha."

"By the way, I talked to Carlo this morning, and told him we might have some product to wash. No problem, he says. He can fly it to Sicily in his private jet, and exchange it into euros for ten percent, and some minor transportation costs. Then we wire the euros to Switzerland, and we're set for life."

"Great news. That guy Carlo is a piece of work, no?"

"He sure is. He is my man."

"I thought I was your man," Tommy joked.

"You are, but he has a private jet, and connections in Sicily," Vincent replied.

"Yeah, well we can have a private jet pretty soon, too. Right here, baby."

Stuart and Monica met with Vincent and Tommy on Friday at noon. They endured another once over with the wand, before Vincent dismissed his tough guy. There was also no extravagant Italian spread waiting for them. "Sorry about the shakedown," Vincent said. "It's just we always have to check. If we ever found anything, big trouble, eh?" Vincent said it more for Monica's benefit, as Stuart had heard his hectoring more often than he cared to recall.

"Why would we be wearing a wire Vincent? Even if we were, it would be entrapment, and inadmissible as evidence."

"So now you is a lawyer too?"

"No Vincent, I was just trying to state the obvious."

"Don't be a smartass kid, we don't like no smartasses, and we don't trust nobody. If you was any kind of smart, you wouldn't either."

You idiot, Stuart thought. I have downloaded your business files. I am sitting across the table from you with my phone in my lap. It's on video with the volume turned up, so everything you say is being recorded. I have full access to your computer, your emails, I could destroy your world with one PDF file sent out to the wrong people. Instead Stuart said, "Yes sir, I think I understand you very clearly now."

"Get with it, kid. This is no time to be thinking about it. By now, you need to know what you are doing. Capiche?"

"Yes sir," Stuart nodded solemnly, and poked Monica in the leg to stop her from smiling.

Vincent continued on. "Okay, this is maybe our final face to face meeting, but I will be talking to you every day from now on only on the burner phones."

"Yes sir."

"So, we are aiming to make the snatch on Thursday or Friday evening. Yeah?"

"Yes sir."

"Me and Tommy is going to do it ourselves, because we want to keep this operation as small as we can. Less problems to deal with. That is also why we want you and Monica in the house. I have one of my best people lined up, to work with you there. His name is Lennie. He is one my key boys here at the bar, and also does some collections for me. He has been with me for over five years, and I trust him big time. I think you and Monica need to move over to the house this weekend so people in the neighborhood get used to seeing you around a little. Me and Tommy will call you when we are on the way with the goods. You have the garage open, we will slide in, and Golfer Girl goes directly downstairs."

"Yes sir."

"So, I gave you money for supplies and everything, right Monica?"

"Yes sir."

"You gonna have to get food for everyone, plus personal stuff for the girl."

"If I need to buy food for four people for a week or two, it will take more money than you gave me."

"Okay Monica, I will give you another five bills today when we is done here. Me and my associate don't think it is a good idea for her to have no TV down there or nothing like that. She'll just sit around and watch her coverage on the news, and she may get some kinda crazy ideas. We will threaten her when we bring her in, and tell her if she shuts it and don't cause no problems, then nothin' ain't gonna happen to her. I think she will be scared enough, at first anyway, that she will behave herself. You need to keep her comfortable and happy Monica, and everything will be alright. If she starts yelling, or acting crazy or something, she is gonna get whacked, and shackled to the bed. Nobody don't want that, so you keep her calm.

Another thing, anyone who goes downstairs needs to cover up. You need to wear one of them face cover up things the rug heads wear. That will confuse the hell out of her, she will think we are terrorists. And get a couple of ski masks for the guys."

"I will get everything, but I am also going on record, that if anyone gets rough with the girl, I am out of there."

"Whatever, ain't nobody gonna get tough wid her unless she axks for it. Stuart, you and Lennie will be on twelve-hour shifts. Twelve on, and twelve off. One of you needs to be with Monica whenever she goes downstairs. Just open the door for her, and keep watch while she is down there. Monica, you feed her twice a day, a late breakfast and an early dinner, find out what she likes to eat. If she ain't gonna have no TV, get her some books and some women's or golf magazines. Whatever she wants within reason, get it for her, as long as she is behaving."

"Yes sir," in unison.

"Stuart, you and Lennie need to be alert when you is on duty. If you doze off overnight, okay, but you stay on the couch close to the basement door. Don't you let no neighbors or nosey kids start coming around the property. I will call in every morning around ten am. Youse need to tell me about anything unusual that happens. After one week, you and me can get active on negotiatin' her ransom. Find out who she banks with, who her manager is. That would be a good person to start talking with. The FBI will be all over this, but they won't have no idea where she is if we're careful. Any questions?"

"Vincent, when we start the negotiations, we will need more help. I can't be doing guard duty, and then trying to get a deal done. And you know the FBI is going to be involved. We need to be entirely focused. That is the most important part of this whole deal."

"Sure Stuart. You is right. I'll have extra help for us when we need it. Anything else?"

"I think that covers it. We gotta talk every day from now on. I will load up on burner phones from different locations, and we will move in this weekend, but still keep a low profile," Stuart said.

"Good, let's eat these burgers, and get out of here."

"Can we go for a bike ride?" Stuart said to Monica. "I need to get some fresh air, clear my head."

"Why don't we ride over to the house in Gig Harbor and check it out?"

"That's a great idea, it's such a primo day."

Stuart's Stealth Black Triumph 500 was his pride and joy, and it didn't take much coaxing for him to trot it out. Especially with Monica holding on tightly behind him. It was such a great day, Stuart was looking forward to a ride, and also thought it might be a good idea to let Monica get some more practice doing the driving. She might need that experience someday soon. I'll let her take over on the way back, he thought.

"Let's go get the bike, and if Chet is there, we can schedule a sit down with him, and get all up to date, and on the same page."

"Good call."

CHAPTER TWELVE

Steve Reed picked Chrissy up at Miami International, on Sunday evening. They embraced warmly, he helped get her clubs and two medium sized roller bags into the trunk, then they headed east to South Beach. The Jaguar's convertible top was down, and the summer breezes billowed over them while they rolled along enjoying the last of the evening's natural light.

"Nice ride, Reed," she chirped.

"Nothing's too good for my girl."

"I want to be your girl this week. All week. Maybe even longer if you can handle it."

"Don't worry about me, woman, I'm a seasoned professional."

"Well, that makes two of us. Should be some fun times."

They were staying at the Cardozo Hotel. Their roof top penthouse suite seemed quite a bit smaller than a commercial hotel would be, but the location was great, the house restaurant was spectacular, and occasionally there was even a Gloria sighting.

Check in at the elegant front desk went smoothly. An attendant served them fresh hibiscus nectar as a welcoming beverage, and Chrissy admired the sumptuous fresh flower arrangement in the middle of the lobby while Steve completed the paperwork. Arriving in their suite, Chrissy suggested they get comfortable, and their outer clothing came off quickly. Effortlessly. And they got busy immediately.

"What's for dinner?" Chrissy finally asked around ten thirty.

"Definitely some Carne Frito at the grill downstairs. We can send out for some snacks now if you are hungry."

"I'm starving. Why don't we just send down for dinner and stay in? I've had a pretty long day."

"That's fine with me. It will be nice to have a relaxing night. Let's turn the phones off and just chill." Dinner was ordered, Steve was looking forward to his Carne Frito, and they continued to chat.

"When are our tee times?"

"We have an eight thirty Wednesday morning at Doral. Eight thirty so we can beat the heat a little bit. Then on Thursday, we have another eight thirty at Coral Gables. It will be nice to take a couple days off of the golf course for me. We could drive down to the Keys for the day on Monday if you want to."

"That would be fun. We are still flying out together, right?" Steve asked.

"Yeah, we're booked for an eight o'clock on Sunday morning to Kennedy. Will has he and I set up for a round with a couple of sales reps that afternoon at Bethpage Black, then some more meetings on Monday. On Tuesday morning I'm off to Wisconsin for the Kohler tournament, then, yahoo, back to Seattle for the new Amazon hooptedoo. That is going to be so much fun. Why don't you fly out for that, you could meet the fam? We have a big house rented, so you would have a place to stay."

"Could work, but I'm getting pretty close to my report date for training camp. Would I be sleeping in your bed with your parents around?"

"Well, that depends more on your performance this week than my parents." They began kissing and fooling around again, when they were interrupted by a handsome Cuban room service waiter knocking on the door. Chrissy ran for the bathroom, and Steve quickly put on some warmup pants, and ushered dinner in. It smelled great.

"You can come out now," Steve called to her.

Chrissy returned from hiding, threw a T-shirt and some panties on, and sat up on her side of the bed propped up with a couple of oversized pillows. "It's been a while since I had dinner in bed with a man while I was nearly nekkid," Chrissy said.

"Me too. I mean while I was nearly nekkid, not while I was with a man," replied Steve. They laughed, and proceeded to ravage everything in sight.

Monday morning, the happy couple did decide to head on down to the Keys. Steve called for the Jag, they took a change of clothes and some toiletries in case they wanted to stay over, and were headed through scenic (sic) South Miami by tenish. It was another hot July day, but with the convertible's top down, they had their natural air conditioner working.

It was great staying in a celebrity hotel, because there were other all-star guests around, which helped divert the paparazzi away from them to some extent. They did pose several times before leaving the Cardozo, but no big. They were a beautiful couple, and posing now and then was a part of their lives anymore.

"Can we stop for lunch at the Barracuda Grill?" Chrissy asked. "It's in Marathon."

"Why not?" said Steve.

"One of the girls told me it was a great little seafood place. Five stars."

"By southern Florida or New York standards?"

"Southern Florida, probably. But I'll bet you the seafood is fresher here than it is in New Your City."

"You are probably right about that," Steve replied, while putting the Jimmy Buffet channel on Sirius Satellite Radio. They rolled down Highway 1 with the music blasting, Chrissy's hair flowing in the wind, and enjoyed the uniquely incredible bays and cays of the Florida Keys.

Driving the rest of the way to Land's End after lunch, they arrived in time for the sunset, and found a spot on the southern wall at the tip of the Keys. Tip of the USA actually. They enjoyed the sunset, people watched the informal carnival going on in front of them, and cruised around on foot some. A quaint little Bed and Breakfast with a big, old Banyan tree in the front yard, caught their eyes. After checking in, they went out for some lump crab and conch fritters, with a good bottle of Chardonnay at The Fisherman's Restaurant.

"You must know how good it feels to get some quality down time," Chrissy told Steve. "It's probably a lot like your bye week in the NFL. Thanks for being here with me."

Steve leaned across their little two top table and gave her a kiss. They were both starting to feel something warm and fuzzy.

The rest of the week went smoothly. As smooth as the Pure Silk body cream the ladies of the LPGA like to use. Chrissy and Steve got back to Miami and had plenty of pool time. They played golf from the black tees together, and split their two matches, so each had some bragging rights. Chrissy had a more polished swing, but Steve was very athletic and she gave him three strokes a side. He aggressively exploded through the hitting zone, and was longer than Chrissy, if more erratic. She kept her swing tuned up, and enjoyed the friendly competition.

"You are so smooth through the ball," he complimented her.

"Well, you know what the girls on tour say."

"What's that?"

"Shoulder to the chin, vagina to the pin."

"Ha-ha. I'll remember that one."

They went to the beach, held hands, dined out, did some clubbing at as many of the hot South Beach night clubs as they had time for, made lots more love, and just generally lived the dream.

Of course, Sunday morning was on them before you could blink and say Pure Silk. Against both of their wills, they were returning the Jag to Hertz, checking clubs and bags, and were sitting in the VIP Lounge near their Delta Airlines gate. It had been a spectacular week. Now they were flying to New York, where Chrissy would go on to her business commitments. Will was meeting her at the airport, and the two of them would drive the hour and a half east to Bethpage. Steve had a connecting flight, and was heading on to his hometown of Chicago where he would spend the rest of his off season with friends and family. Finally, they got ready to depart, deposited their empty latte cups in the recycling canister, and filed out into the terminal when the call came over the loudspeaker for first class boarding.

After settling in, Steve turned to Chrissy. "I will come for the last day of the tournament, and help you celebrate your win," he said.

"That works for me, baby" Chrissy replied. "Will you call me?"

"Sure, I'll call you, are you crazy?"

"Everyday?"

"Every morning and every night." They snuck in a kiss. Nothing earthshaking, as the coach passengers were filing by like cattle, and had nothing better to do than stare at the privileged business flyers. What an ordeal it is for first class travelers to endure the interminable parade of losers stumping by to the coach section. Overburdened with carryon bags, usually staring, until finally they clear the forward cabin, and allow the more entitled flyers their just due.

But Chrissy was happy. Very happy. She felt like she was falling in love. She had recharged physically and mentally, and was ready to get back to the grind. Get back and kick the grind's butt.

"You know, this was a very important week for me," she whispered to Steve. "Golf is such a mental game, it is not good if you can't get away every so often, and clear your jets of all of the clutter. It seems to me that in football you need much more of a break from the physical pounding."

"It's both," he replied. "There is the physical side, but there is always the pressure to perform at your highest mental level, often when you are partially injured, or else someone is right there to take your spot."

"No one will ever take your spot with me," she whispered back to him, and they kissed again.

"Jeez, why don't those yuppies get a room," the last shmuck heading back to coach said to no one in particular. To think, he could have had a double autograph if he had had his wits about him.

Delta flight 434 touched down smoothly two and a half hours later. As always, the profusion of humanity in New York, in all shapes, sizes and flavors, took Chrissy's breath away. "For a girl from small town America, this is such a rush for me," she told Steve. They continued to fight their way through to baggage claim, and after picking up her bags, it took them another ten minutes to say their proper goodbyes. Halfway through their last big clinch, Will showed up to help her into a waiting town car, and soon enough they were heading east for Uniondale, and the Long Island Marriott. Chrissy quietly wiped a tear from the corner of her eye, and left Steve stoically waving good bye from the curb in front of the terminal. He wished he was in that car with her, instead it was back inside the terminal to reenter security and head for his life in Chicago. A life he felt had changed inexorably in the last week.

"Where we staying, brother dear?" Chrissy asked quietly to break her mood and start some conversation.

"We're booked in Manhattan tonight, but we are going to stop at a Marriott on the way to Bethpage, pick up our rental car. Then, it's about ten minutes to the course. We'll just change in the locker rooms. A couple of Titleist reps have a game all arranged for us. One does golf balls and clubs, the other one contracts. Does your boyfriend need a new driver? Now's your chance."

"That would be cool. And yes, I want to spoil him."

"You might want to be a little careful about making out with him in front of God and everyone. The paparazzi would love to catch that on film," Will chided her.

"Well, he's a doll, Will, and a hunk. And I love him. We had an incredible week, and I invited him to come to Seattle for the Amazon Tournament."

"Hey, all the rooms at the house are spoken for."

"Oh well, I guess he'll just have to sleep with me, you dork. He's only coming for the last day anyway."

"Whew. Well, for the golfing today, those guys want to play our three best balls against you. I will tell them you want a new driver if you win, or you will buy beers. They won't let you buy anything anyway."

"No way. We'll play sixes, then I get a chance to partner with everyone for a few holes."

"Okay."

"I still want a new driver for Steve though."

"You keep wearing Titleist on your hat girl, and I don't think that is any kind of a problem."

"Are we signed up for another couple of years?"

"That's what we're here for."

Bethpage Black is considered by most experts to be the toughest public golf course in the USA. It was designed in 1932 by the premier Golf Course Architect of the era, A.W. Tillinghast, and renovated in 1997 by Rees Jones prior to the 2002 US Open. The Black course is so difficult a warning sign is posted as one approaches the grounds, suggesting only low handicap golfers should attempt to test their mettle there.

Chrissy and Will were ushered ceremoniously into the pro shop, where Chrissy signed a couple of publicity photos for the golf pro, and they were off. The foursome had elected to walk the course with caddies, as Chrissy wanted to keep her legs tuned up. Both Jensens were excited to play the venerable Bethpage links, the Titleist reps probably less so, as they were from Long Island, and had played the course numerous times. But it was still a treat to play with one of the leading professionals on the LPGA Tour, especially one as talented as Chrissy. So off they went, and the banter began.

Four hours later they trudged into the nineteenth hole, hot, and tired, but with that quiet elation that a good round of golf brings. Chrissy had done well, and her rotating teams won all three matches, which had her winning the small money. The bigger money was agreed to as well, paperwork to follow, with the stipulation that Chrissy got her new driver.

"My friend swings hard, and is strong, so he will need a stiff shaft. He's six foot one, and is a wide receiver, so his hands are larger than a normal person's. The grip will need a little building up, etc."

"Who is he?" the reps wanted to know.

"A friend who I owe a favor. He plays for the Chicago Bears."

"Tell me his name, and we will have the club personally engraved for him." The reps were always happy to have a professional athlete playing their gear.

"Steve Reed. But you just drink your beer, and don't even think about starting any dang rumors," Chrissy told them playfully.

"Got it. Where would you like to have it sent?"

"Send it out to me in Seattle, during the LPGA Amazon tournament. Will can take care of the address. Do you think that is doable? It would be way cool."

"That should work out just fine. And then, if need be, Steve can have it fine-tuned at Chambers Bay. We will have some reps there for the tournament."

"Works for me."

"We aim to please, Chrissy."

"Thanks again, that would be super." Chrissy never failed to be impressed at the perks that came with winning a few golf tournaments. Like the great champion Nancy Lopez once said, "Golf is wonderful. The more money I win, the more stuff people want to give me."

The conversation drifted back to chatter about the round, how much fun was had, and how happy Titleist was to have Chrissy under their umbrella for another couple of years. A good time was had by all.

Will and Chrissy drove the rental Jeep Cherokee over to the bag drop, picked up their golf clubs, and headed back west towards Manhattan.

"What's next, bro?"

"We have a meeting with the Rolex people tomorrow morning at ten, and then a one o'clock with a rep from Golf Digest. They are interested in you doing some tutorials for their magazine. We are staying at the Phillips Club on West 66th Street. It is a private residence hotel, and we can have our meetings there in their Library/Meeting space. It is very private. Then I made reservations for four to Carole King's musical in Times Square."

"Who are we going with?"

"Johnny Williams and his wife Geraldine. He's an old buddy of mine from college who works on Wall Street. He and his wife live in Brooklyn, but we are going to meet them at La Masseria, for a bite beforehand, and we can walk to the theatre from there. He helps us with some financial advice."

"Nice. Thanks for arranging something fun while we are in the city."

"No problem. It's not the newest play on Broadway, but I heard it was a great musical. Now all I have to do is navigate traffic into Manhattan."

"Ah, it shouldn't be too bad on a Sunday evening."

"No, probably not. Why don't we find a good pizza joint and have a couple of slices for dinner tonight?"

"Yeah, let's wait until we get into the city. There is pizza pie everywhere in that town."

"I'm gonna call my buddy, and see if he has a suggestion."

"Ah, don't bother him, we can find something easy enough."

"No, I'm going to call him. He may know someone."

"Whatever."

"For tomorrow, you won't be needing a Rolex for your new boyfriend, will you?"

"Gee, he already has his own spectacular Oyster. But, it's not a bad idea."

"Well let's lay off then, I don't want to get too greedy with these people too soon."

"Yeah, I know. Hey, you are the first person to call Steve my boyfriend, and you have done it twice now."

"Isn't that special!"

"Let's take the subway to dinner tomorrow night? I love to people watch during commuter hours."

"Sure, the A Train station is right outside the Phillips Club, and I'm not driving anywhere once we get settled in."

"The Phillips Club. The Phillips Club. Sounds like some kind of hang out for the petroleum crowd."

"Shut up, will you? It is a very sophisticated establishment."

"Johnny Williams recommends Highline Pizzeria, on West 28th right under the Highline overhead walkway. It's close to our hotel digs. Scottie is the owner, and if he is around, he will take good care of us."

Actually, Johnny called Scottie, who does a lot of catering for his firm and told him who was coming by, so Scottie made a point of being there to meet and greet them in person. He had a boisterous New York embrace for Will, a hug and a kiss on both cheeks for Chrissy, and a custom pie of his own design waiting. He even took them across the street to the rooftop of his residential building, brought out a great bottle of Santa Margarita Pinot Gris, and they sat and watched the last of the sun's rays linger over the Hudson River while they ate and sipped.

"You don't need no silverware," Scottie told them. "Just fold your slice over, and go for it." It doesn't take long to learn that trick in NYC.

"Once you eat New York pizza, you don't want to eat pizza anywhere else," Chrissy said after they had done major damage to Scottie's delicious custom pie.

"Once you eat Scottie's Highline Pizza, you don't want to eat pizza anywhere else in New York City," Will chimed in.

Ideally, that made Scottie's Highline Pizza the best in the world on this particular evening, and Scottie beamed with a New Yorker's pride at these celebrity clients, these beautiful people, who were saying the right things, and who made all the aggravations of running a restaurant in NYC worthwhile. Scottie lived to please his people, and as a confirmed Italian bachelor, the more beautiful his customer, the more he strived to please.

Will brought out a couple of eight and a half by eleven pub photos, one of which Chrissy signed for the restaurant, and the other one for Scottie personally. She autographed it with "all my love," and made a big lipstick kiss on it for him.

Of course, Scottie comped everything much to the protestations of the Jensen's. But you can fight all night over a check in NYC with a restaurateur, and you will never win. So, Will and Chrissy gave up trying, hugged Scottie warmly, and headed off to their evening's lodgings.

"What a wonderful man," Chrissy said. "Ain't New York grand?"

"Yep. Life is good, sis."

Will checked them into a double suite on the seventh floor of their Residence hotel. And Monday's meetings went well. Rolex was interested in doing business with Chrissy, and the feeling was mutual. Will would negotiate a contract. It didn't hurt that Chrissy had her own Lady Rolex draped luxuriously around her left wrist. Which certainly didn't go unnoticed by the Rolex people.

The Golf Digest deal on the other hand, Miss Chrissy wasn't so sure about. She liked the exposure, but felt like she didn't want to take on the monthly obligation of communicating some kind of swing tip or lesson back to a copy office somewhere. "No problem," one of the magazine's assistant editors told her. "We can do all of the production work; we just need your permission to byline the weekly series."

"I don't know if that would work," Chrissy told them. "If it has my name on it, I wouldn't want it to be ghostwritten." They left the sit down with the understanding that she would think about the opportunity for a week or two.

"Maybe in the off season, when I have more time," she told Will when they were back up in their suite. "For now, I am going to go in, take a bubble bath and relax for a while. What time do we leave for dinner?"

"We should leave for the subway about six," he replied.

"Okay, buddy. Six it is." Chrissy was happy to have a few hours to herself. It had been a busy couple of days, and she was off to Wisconsin first thing in the morning.

Six o'clock came in a couple of New York minutes, but Chrissy was up, dressed, and ready to go. Not too ultra-fancy, as they would be riding into midtown on the subway, the commuter train at that, but she could wear mink or burlap on just about any subway train in New York, and not raise an eyebrow. She chose a silky, black sheath cocktail dress, that would be basically covered by her slate grey cashmere wraparound shawl until they got to the restaurant. Her outfit would function just fine for this night, I mean, we aren't going to the Kennedy Center or anything super fancy, she thought to herself. Will was ready to go in designer jeans, a Sapphire blue dress shirt and a navy-blue blazer. They took off across 66th Street for the subway station, dodging traffic and fellow pedestrians as they went.

The underground was hot and buzzing with activity, which made the muggy platform even more stifling, and it held a perverse fascination for Chrissy. There were hordes of people moving like ocean waves of flesh off the trains, and then back on again. Their Number 1, Redline Route ran every ten minutes, and by the time they had gotten tickets, people were already boarding. Chrissy tore herself away from the two black dudes playing a Charlie Parker sax/trumpet duet, with their backs pressed against a grimy, white tile back wall, and followed Will into the train car.

It was standing room only, and as they jostled their way down to the forty second street exit, they unavoidably experienced the sights, sounds and humanness of big city life. The ethnic variety was extraordinary, and all of this street theatre was accompanied by the clackety-clacking rhythm of their subway train.

Chrissy thought it was kind of depressing that more than half the swaying crowd had their noses buried in a cell phone. But she loved the sensation of being right in the middle of this animated herd, then popping up from the underground, and seeing another whole world of hustle, bustle, and skyline on the busy surface streets above. A different, but contiguous mob of bobbing heads, this time walking furiously, headed elsewhere-with that benignly vapid facial expression so unique to big cities. In this case, they were all navigating through Times Square, New York City. With its' super-sized urban canyon of electronic neon billboards, blasting out commercial messages nonstop 24/7/365. It is the marketing capital of the world, and Chrissy reveled in the excitement of being a tiny spec in the middle of it all.

She and Will were a bit disoriented when they emerged from the underground. Had they been NYC natives, who struggle daily to solve the puzzle of getting from point A to point B on public transportation, they would have known that Broadway runs one way to the north, and they would have turned right, and headed the six blocks up to their restaurant reservation.

"I guess it isn't as unique and compelling if you have to deal with the crowds every day," she told Will. "But it sure is a rush once in a while, and it's a world away from Yakima, Washington, huh?"

"Yeah, Times Square is definitely one of the busiest intersections in the world." After being jostled around a couple more times, they got their bearings and headed off to dinner.

The Italian food was yum. Their menu claimed another superlative, i.e.-the title of "Best Clam Linguini in the City," and it probably was. Chrissy and Johnny Williams both had it, and neither of them were prepared to argue the point. Will and Johnny caught up on old times, and Chrissy made a new friend in Johnny's wife Geraldine. Everyone but Chrissy had a limoncello after dinner, before they dashed off for the theatre. But Chrissy was now back in training, and that meant alcohol in very limited quantities.

The Steven Sondheim Theatre is on West 43rd Street, so the group had to walk a few blocks back south, but it was refreshing to work off dinner a little bit, and it was more live theatre walking the streets of NYC.

The Sondheim is a smallish venue, intimate actually, with state-of-the-art sound and lighting. The group's loge seating box was private, and provided a bird's eye view of the stage. *Beautiful*, the musical has been running there since 2014. It is a classic bio of American musicality, and is woven around the genius of Carole

King, a child prodigy on Broadway, who evolves into a soft rock/pop cultural icon and super star of the 1970's and 80's. The musical productions are toe tapping and upbeat, and you can't help but come out of the theatre with a lot of *Love in your Heart,* to paraphrase one of Beautiful's show stopping numbers. Before the curtain rose, Will slipped back down stairs, met the Sondheim's Managing Director, and arranged a back stage visit after the show.

The theatre world is about as different from professional golf, as NASCAR auto racing is to the Metropolitan Museum of Art. But variety is what makes the world go around, and Chrissy loved the show. She was honored to be able to go back stage to meet and schmooze with the cast.

Introductions were made all around, and everyone spent another fifteen minutes chatting, before heading back to Times Square. Musicians and actresses were fascinating to Chrissy, and she was delighted to spend a little time with some bona fide professionals from another genre.

Times Square was still buzzing at midnight, but Will and Chrissy bade their goodbyes with the Williams, and this time hailed a cab, rather than brave the midnight subway scene. It was getting late, and an early morning wakeup call awaited them.

"How much fun was that?" Chrissy commented to Will on the way back to the Phillips Club. "And I loved your friends. They are very nice."

"I'm glad you had a good time. That was a killer show. And I don't even like musicals."

"Well I love 'em, and I will be loading the Best of Carole King on my iPhone tomorrow."

They got back to the Club, and prepared to retire. "We need to be on the road by six thirty tomorrow morning, can do?"

"All good to go here. I packed my stuff up before we left for dinner."

Chrissy slept fairly well, albeit with some tossing and turning. She was still a bit amped from all the excitement of Times Square, the walking about, and the live musical theatre.

By six thirty the next morning, they were loaded up, back in the Jeep Grand Cherokee, and on the road, drinking a cup of steaming coffee compliments of the front desk. Will was cursing and fighting the early morning traffic, mostly made up of obnoxious NYC cab drivers with their incessant, bleating horns, which blared away at everything and nothing. They slowly crawled away from Manhattan for the Queensboro Bridge and Kennedy Airport.

Chrissy was flying into Green Bay where she was to be picked up by Bobby, and they would make the hour or so drive down to Kohler, Wisconsin, and the Whistling Straights golf layout. Whistling Straits is a majestic development located on the western shore of Lake Michigan, and it was a quality tournament coming up. But to Chrissy, it was nothing more than a tune-up for the Amazon at Chambers Bay. She had had a nice break from the game, a busy week off, now it was time to get her head back into the world of championship women's golf. Will was flying directly out to the west coast, to start on his organizational duties in Seattle for the next two weeks.

Chrissy called Steve while she was waiting for Bobby. They had a nice chat. She told him all about New York City, how much she missed him, and how she was ready to get down to golf business. He told her he missed her more, and wished her well. It was the best thing he could have said.
Bobby showed up with another SUV rental, and off they went. It was early afternoon of a warm, muggy Wisconsin summer day.

The tournament went pretty well. Many of the women would have been happy with a top ten finish, but a tie for sixth place was somewhat ho-hum to Chrissy now. She was focused on prepping her total package for next week, and Whistling Straits was an excellent course for her purposes. It is long, narrow, near the lake, and challenging with loads of sand to deal with. She was able to work on accuracy with her driver, and control with her short game. The trick was not getting overly psyched up for next week. Off the course, she stayed to herself, avoided the social scene, talked to Steve once a night, was in bed early, and out at the practice facilities first thing every morning.

On Sunday evening she and her little brother had a flight out of Green Bay, with a brief layover in Minneapolis, for SeaTac Airport. She was excited. It was time to head for the Emerald City, and she felt as ready as she could be for her big homecoming.

CHAPTER THIRTEEN

Stuart and Monica got back to their townhouse, and Chet wasn't around, so they changed into riding gear, and headed Stuart's Triumph 500 south to the I-5 freeway and Gig Harbor. It was a gorgeous afternoon, and a ride over the Tacoma Narrows bridge seemed like just the thing to do. Half an hour was all it took to get to the rental, and everything looked copacetic when they arrived. Spectacular actually. It was quite a house. Established, but secluded. Private, but accessible. Big and roomy, modern but comfortable, and nicely appointed. So, they poked around for half an hour to get familiar with the place, and decided they would spend the rest of the afternoon riding out towards Mount Rainier on old Highway 410.

As they were going through the bedrooms, Stuart turned to his girlfriend and told her, "this scam better work out, because if it doesn't, I am going to have to rob a bank to pay for all of this stuff. The boat, the house, all of the IDs, plus I haven't worked in three weeks."

"You are turning into a regular gangster," she laughed and told him. "I want the master bedroom for us. Shouldn't we try it out?" and she grabbed Stuart's shirt, and pulled him down on top of her on the king-sized bed.

After their afternoon delight, they buttoned each other back up, then buttoned up the house. Leaving took some effort, as it wouldn't have taken much to keep them in bed all afternoon. But the happy lovers got out on the road again, and in half an hour they were back over the bridge, through the City of Tacoma, and headed out of town. The farther east you go, once city traffic has been cleared, the sight of Mount Rainier looms so close and profoundly majestic, it takes your breath away. It feels like you are in another world, a make believe, fantastical world. Especially on a motorcycle, with the wind in your face and the sun on your back. They rode southeast for an hour, stopped at an old roadhouse for a beer, after which Stuart let Monica take the wheel of the powerful machine. He had to admit that she handled herself pretty well as a biker chick.

They continued on for another hour, and were well into Mount Rainier National Park, before pulling into a vista point for a final, closeup gaze at the mountain, and a couple of selfies, before heading back. Stopping at the same crusty old roadhouse, they gassed up the Triumph, and went inside for another beer. The bar was a rustic haunt, filled with relics of its rural, mountaineering way of life: a moose head over the wide river rock fireplace, antique climbing gear stacked around the room, a couple of used up and weathered, old riding saddles, etc. They sat in a back corner, and quietly reflected on where they had just been. It was so overpoweringly beautiful, so gloriously awe inspiring it made small talk seem very small indeed. Mount Rainier captivates you so well, it makes one high without having to actually smoke any weed.

"Wow, what a ride," Monica finally commented. She could still feel the elements embracing her.

"Yeah, I'm gonna miss this place."

After a half hour of basking in the glory of the mountain, making chitchat, and enjoying their beers, Monica got back to business. "Does Chet have the boat ready to go?"

"Yeah. It is all prepped up for an extended sailing. We have been stocking up supplies, and all-weather gear. The navigation equipment is on board, Chet has the scuba gear ready. The boat is docked at one of the outer slips in the Tacoma Narrows Marina, she's a beaut. All we have to do, is pick up the cash, shoot down the narrows, load up, and sail away into the night."

"There better not be any transmitters in with the cash or you are screwed, partner."

"Well, they will know that Chrissy's life depends on them not trying anything cute, trust me. We will have hauled in the money long before Chrissy is cut loose, so I think they will get the timing on that."

"You know Vincent wants me at the house for security, so that you will be keeping the dough safe, don't you?"

"Yeah, I figured that out. What concerns me is that he might want to keep you in exchange for our half of the money. We need to create a diversion, maybe leave the basement door open for Chrissy so she can try to escape, while that is going on, you grab the Triumph and split for the airport. You already have the new set of ID's I got for you, right? I will leave the bike stored in the utility shed, and you will have to beat it the hell out of there. I'm going to set up a closed-circuit cam of the drop site and the crab pots, so Vincent and Lennie can be busy monitoring that. I'm sure Vincent is going to be at the rental when we are making the pickup. Your job is to get out of there and jam it to the airport."

"As in my life depends on it?"

"That's about it, girlfriend. It is definitely the most dangerous part of the op for you. Don't forget though, that we have plenty of goods on Vincent and all of his businesses, so we should be able to handle anything he wants to throw at us. I am going back into his computer one more time after midnight tonight, print out his latest data, and we will have him by the short hair."

"I hope this Chrissy girl doesn't start any crap. I don't want to have to deal with that right off the bat.

"Just befriend her, and she won't cause any problems. She has a lot more to lose than to gain, if she starts to make waves."

"I hope you are right."

"I mentioned to Vinny goombah, that we should maybe take the drop to another location in case it is bugged, so we don't lead the feds back to the rental. But he seems to think we should still come back with the cash to the hideout. He wants to get his hands on the money as fast as he can. That makes it even more of a timing thing, where you have to get out of there before we are supposed to be back. When we are gone too long, he is going to get suspicious. He already don't even trust his own mother. You know how he is."

"Well, I will have my pistol stashed in the house somewhere, and I'll shoot my way out of there if I have to. I don't want anything to happen to you or the girl, but Vincent, I don't give a damn about him."

"I don't think it will come to that if we have a good idea what we are doing. We will have at least a week to get a plan in place once the snatch is made, and we are both at the house together. I already don't trust this Lennie guy as far as I can spit either. You know he is going to be a snitch for Vincent. The key for us now is to clean up all of our personal loose ends, and by this time next week, we are wiped off of the map. We don't exist on paper anymore."

"Starting with the townhouse. Did you terminate the lease?"

"Yep. Terminated the lease, I'm turning my Accord back in. The rest of my stuff goes into a couple of duffle bags, or off to the Goodwill. Everything else in the townhouse is good, we certainly didn't damage any of their stuff."

"How you gonna turn your car back in?"

"I bought a hardship termination clause when I first leased it."

"Smart. My 4Runner is paid for, I have the title, and a guy at the casino wants to buy."

"All we will have left is the motorcycle, and we can just leave it in long term airport parking. It is completely registered in a false name to a PO Box anyway."

"That's too bad. You love your motorcycle."

"Well, that's life. I can always buy another one."

"So, let's go out to dinner and enjoy the rest of this dope day before everything gets completely crazy. We are going to be so busy for the next week."

"Wait a sec, there is one more thing."

"What's that."

Stuart pulled a little velvet box out of his right leather jacket pocket. Monica's eyes widened. Stuart kicked a chair from the next table aside and got down on one knee.

"Will you marry me?" he asked her softly.

Monica looked at Stuart, deep into those hazel eyes of his. Their eyes met, held, and Monica couldn't help but think what an awkward situation this was.

"I love you," she finally said. "Of course, I will marry you, but can we wait until all this is over with? We have enough on our plates here. I'm not going anywhere, and quite frankly, your timing is terrible, Stuart. Ask me again when we are safely in the Philippines, and I can have a proper wedding."

Stuart paused, thought about it and said, "I'm an idiot, a fool in love, baby. You're absolutely right." He smiled self-consciously, and touched her cheek with his fingertips. He was feeling stupid, but at least she had kindly rejected him, and half accepted his proposal.

"Of course, I am," she replied. They paid up and went outside to their ride. "I wanna drive," she said.

"Okay, but no wheelies."

Dimitri Zarkova was one of Vincent's foot soldiers. He picked up collections, worked security (was a bouncer) at the bar three nights a week, and did the computer work for Vincent's numerous enterprises. If it was a bigger company, he would have had the title of IT Director. That is, if he wasn't a thug, and in the country illegally. He had come to the US on a commercial flight from Moscow via Frankfurt, and connected through Newark on to Seattle a year and a half ago. He had a letter of introduction to Vincent DeGrazzi, and once Vincent hired him, he had just stayed on in the country illegally. Even though he now had altered identification, he was very careful driving, was paid in cash, and lived as far under the radar as he could get.

Dimitri enjoyed working for Vincent. His little studio apartment was close by in the south Seattle City of SeaTac, and in reality it was little more than a place for him to crash at night. He took his meals at Vincent's bar, enjoyed the discounted female companionship made available to him as a perk of his employment, sent his extra money back to a brother in Bulgaria, and other than that, his needs were few. He was considered a masher by the working girls, as he was rough with them, and never tipped. He was medium of height, but stocky and thickly muscled, and according to rumor, was smattered with course black body hair. The girls liked to mimic his heavy eastern European accent when he wasn't around. A few of the more senior women had actually gone to Vincent and refused to sleep with Dimitri, so the Russian made a point of "dating" the newer girls who were as yet unaware of his reputation. For all anyone knew, he was legal, but you couldn't be too careful. If anyone dropped a dime on him, that would not be good.

As it was slowing down, on this uneventful Saturday night, Vincent finished his late-night sandwich with a double shot of Stoli Vodka, and decided to go back to the office and spend a little time in QuickBooks Pro.

His admin work actually took up a couple of hours every day, as Dimitri had to do two sets of entries. One for the government, and a private set for Vincent and Ronnie. There was so much under the table cash coming through the business from so many areas, that it needed constant tracking.

A lot of the hourly and security payroll was paid under the table, and Dimitri had to enter that into the system. Then there were the bank deposits to be made, and the cash to be processed, documented and put away in the safe. But the Barber's system also kept official payroll and the related payroll taxes to a minimum, and Ronnie was very particular about how the books looked when they were handed over to him quarterly. Vincent's businesses were doing very well, and Dimitri enjoyed his part in keeping things organized and going forward smoothly.

Dimi stepped into the dark office, and turned on the overhead lights. He unlocked the lower drawer, and removed the company laptop. That crazy old bastard Vincent insisted the laptop stay locked up in the desk, which Dimitri found amusing. But he grabbed the HP computer, and booted it up.

He logged on, clicked into Microsoft QBs and did a double take. He thought he saw a cursor navigating through the end of the check register. He blinked, and stared at the screen again for a couple of seconds, watched the screen execute a slight surge, and saw the cursor disappear. Dimitri immediately went to the firewall and looked for any intrusions. He checked for internal security alerts, went to systems and scanned for any foreign apps or programs that he might have been unaware of. He found nothing. He doubled checked all of the software again to be sure, and scratched his head. He was sure he had seen something odd, but there didn't seem to be any threatening footprints or elements anywhere. It was late and he was tired, but he was positive he had seen something out of line. He would have to mention it to Vincent ASAP.

Dimi entered a day's worth of transactions, but his heart wasn't in it. If someone had compromised their computer, he didn't want to disturb the system until he could come back tomorrow, when he was fresh and clearheaded, and do a thorough technical audit. He would have to wait until Monday to talk to the boss, as Vincent refused to be disturbed on Sundays. "It's my family day," Vincent told anyone who was remotely interested.

Dimitri was unaware that Vincent had a couple of busy weeks coming up, or that he had allowed someone into the laptop when he was in Atlanta on business a month ago. But the hell with it, he said to himself, I am going to call him tomorrow after I check things out. Even if it is his Sunday down time, he needs to know about a possible computer breach of his confidential information.

CHAPTER FOURTEEN

Monday the eighth dawned to perfect July weather in Seattle. It would proceed to be a beautiful, clear Northwest day in the low eighties. A light summer breeze floated by, taking the edge off of the heat in most inland locations. It was a perfect day for golf, but probably too light of a breeze for any world class sailing on Puget Sound's placid waters.

Will had been back in Seattle for a week getting the house organized, tying off the Rolex deal, and prepping the way for Chrissy's arrival. His job depended on everything being smooth and organized so Chrissy could concentrate on her craft, and he was good at what he did. Bob and Ginny Jensen had driven in last Friday, and Ginny was getting the roomy pantry stocked and ready. They had brought along an insulated ice chest full of prime grass-fed steaks and chops with them, plus four cases of Yakima and Walla Walla wines from their personal cellar. It should be a great week, win or lose, of celebrating with friends and family.

Bob's brother Richard and his wife Emma would be staying at the house, along with Will, Bobby Jr., and their older brother Charlie. Bob and Ginny, Chrissy and Steve, Ginny's sister Elaine and her husband Calvin (up from Portland, Oregon), and Ginny and Bob's close friends Alan and Trisha Snapp. Alan being the current President of Yakima Golf and Country Club. Then there were another two dozen friends and relatives from around the state that would be dropping by as well. Monday night was an informal gathering, with beer and burgers, and people coming and going as they saw fit. Will had scouted out a catering service that supplied contract personnel by the week so there should be plenty of domestic help for the family. Tuesday was a more formal invitation only dinner affair, with the BBQ glowing, the wine flowing, and was the kick off night of the week.

Chrissy would be around later on Monday evening after her pro-am tournament. Then Tuesday was a day of practice for the girls, and an LPGA sanctioned fund raising/auction dinner for the Susan B. Komen Breast Cancer Research Foundation that night at Point Defiance Zoo and Aquarium. Pt. Defiance would be a lot of fun, but she would miss the activities at the house. Wednesday was a free practice day for the ladies, with the tournament, of course, starting on Thursday morning.

After Tuesday, the schedule on the home front quieted down, so everyone could focus on the tournament. Then things would begin to ramp back up with early gatherings on Friday and Saturday, but both would be concluded by nine pm so as to keep the peace and quiet for Chrissy's sake. Chrissy was in and out throughout the week, and no one expected too much from her until the golfing finished up on Sunday. Everyone knew well of her penchant for practice and focus on her game, and no one was about to disturb her routine this week. Hopefully, they would all be celebrating a victory on Sunday afternoon. Chrissy was certainly one of the odds-on favorites. She would be playing in her home town, on a course that was very familiar to her, and conformed to the length of her game. An appropriate analogy might be Arnold Palmer returning to Latrobe, Pennsylvania, or Jack revisiting Columbus, Ohio.

Sunday's closing party was planned as the grand finale. A large gathering with friends and family, fellowship, good times, fun and games. Will would have the bocce ball court open; the volleyball net was set up in the pool, he found a mini mariachi band in South Seattle, and the caterer was scheduled for six o'clock. In addition to the older crowd, Chrissy, Charlie, Will and Bobby all had friends from both Seattle, Yakima and college days in and around town for the festivities. They would be at the tournament, and were also invited to visit at Jensen manor.

Tommy knocked on Vincent's front door at promptly five thirty Sunday evening. "Well, come on in stranger," Angela greeted him with a smile and a hug. "Vincent is out on the back deck having a cocktail. What can I get for you?"

"Gosh, Angie, I'd love cold beer. You look great girl, here these flowers are for you."

"What a lovely bouquet. Aren't you just a sweetheart, Tommy Thurston! I'll join you all out there in a minute."

"Howdy partner, how you doin?"

"Great Tommy. Good to see you. What can I get for you?"

"Oh, Angie is bringin' me a beer."

"Well, looks like we are going to have some fantastic weather this week, eh?"

"Yeah, should be a great tournament. It will be an exciting week."

"I think we are all set. I have been over to the house, Stuie and Monica are already staying there. The town car is set up, you can pick it up on Tuesday. Monica has got the house stocked up. Carlo is going to be ready with the plane. There is one little problem though."

"Yeah, what is that?"

"Dimitri called me around noon today. He's feeling like he saw something funny going on in the laptop computer."

"What kind of funny?"

"Well, he went into the office late Saturday night, and thought there was something unusual going on in the damn thing. He went back on Sunday morning, and couldn't find nothin', but he was concerned enough to call me on a Sunday. It's a big deal for him to do that."

"Geez Vincent, you know Ronnie warned you to be careful with that kinda thing. And really, this don't have nothing to do with me. It's between you and Dimitri and the kid. If he hacked some stuff off your computer, I think that could be a big problem for you."

"Yeah, I know. I got a meeting with Ronnie tomorrow. But I think the kid has got to go when we are done here."

"Vincent, this is all your business. I told you I would drive for you, and that is it for me. I don't really even want to know about any of this other crap." In Tommy's mind, his involvement was limited to completing the snatch. Everything else was Vinnie's problem, and the V needed to know that implicitly.

"Even if I call the Contractor, and put a hit out on him?"

"Let Dimitri and the Contractor take care of it. I don't want nothin' to do with it. I'm drivin', I've got my alibi all set up, and I don't know nothin' else about nothin'." Tommy was beginning to be annoyed by what was becoming Vincent's obvious computer naivety. What they all didn't need right now, was some private information leaking out on his little syndicate. "You better be sure you speak with Ronnie tomorrow."

"Yeah, I will. We can finish talking after dinner. Hey, it might not even be anything, and if it is, there's ways to make the little shit talk if need be."

Angela came out of the sliding glass door from the den, and brought a tray of drinks with some Italian olives and cheese to nosh on. She saw the dark look on Vincent's face, and asked "all is good, fellas?"

"The coffee's on," Monica told Chet late Sunday morning. She was the first one up and about for their scheduled meeting. Stuart stumbled in a minute later. The boys grabbed a cup, Monica refilled hers, and they all sat down around the kitchen table.

"We're all good?" Monica asked. She seemed to be the partner who was most concerned about the logistics of the coming week.

"Good to go here, baby," came from Stuart. "Chet?"

"I am done working by the middle of the week. The boat is stocked and ready. It will be my new residence as soon as you two leave for the house in Gig Harbor today."

"You are packed up already?"

"Yep, my stuff is all out. I will come back on Wednesday, and clean up anything else, make an appointment with the leasing rep to inspect the place, and get our deposit back. It was a pleasure rooming with you two."

"Likewise, Chester," Stuart replied. "Should we take a full-on trial run down the Narrows this week with the scuba gear?"

"Absolutely. I know those waters a lot better than you, but we need to run through it at least one more time. I will check the tables for some similar tide movement, and we can give it a go. Everything okay with things on the other end?"

"Yeah, I think so. I downloaded the latest data from Vincent's laptop last night, terminated the access program, and deleted it out of his system. I have run off a couple of Zip files for us."

"You better be careful with that stuff man. If he ever found out, he would kill you big time."

"Sorry, but I will be long gone, and he will be in jail."

"Well, you know what? I am the captain of a thirty-eight-foot yacht. I am sailing to the south seas for an undetermined length of time, and a friend asked me if he could come along. That's all I know, and that is all I care to know." From Tommy Thurston to Chet Lincoln, everyone seemed to be quite interested now in covering their own backsides.

"Not to worry. It is my auxiliary laptop. If they ever could possibly trace anything back to it, the computer is registered fictitiously. As a matter of fact, for the record, it is Joy Inslay's computer. Get it? It is a close enough match, that they would be investigating the Governor of the State of Washington."

"You dummy," said Monica. "If Vincent even thinks anyone was poking around in their business, you would be the first person they would suspect. They would grab you, and pull it out of you one fingernail at a time."

"Monica is right on, Stuart. You be careful man."

"I will be." Their gloom and doom was getting to Stuart. Did he really think he noticed Vincent's laptop turn on Saturday night just before he erased himself out of the system?

"When are they going to try and snatch her?" Chet asked. He considered himself a minor accomplice at best in this whole escapade. As an all-county cross-country runner in high school he was in great physical shape, he loved the water, and was experienced both above and below the surface. He was twenty-seven years old, his personal program was together, he had money in the bank, was willing to shoulder his share of responsibility in this caper, while he considered Stuart and Monica to be taking the major risks and exposure. But they couldn't do it without him, and if there were any complications, he could always just sail down the coast, and away on his own. No problem.

"They want to grab her on Thursday or Friday if possible. Saturday there would probably be too many people around. Friday would be ideal if the opportunity was right. Then we hold her for a week, and start negotiating with bankers the following week."

"Okay, I'll start watching the tides for our trial run. Monica, what is your plan?" Chet asked.

"Well, I'm the nursemaid after they grab the girl, then before the money gets dropped, I have to make my break between then, and when you two are supposed to show up back at the house. I don't want to give Vincent any opportunity to pull any tricks, so I'll split on Frankie's Triumph, and head for SeaTac. My travel bag will be there in a locker, along with a ticket to Manilla. I will be a homesick working girl, going off to see her mama. Frankie and I will refine my getaway plan while we are there at the house next week."

"Don't use my real name, Please!"

"Jesus, Frank. What possible difference could it make at this point in time?" Monica was becoming annoyed with Stuart's nitpicking.

"Okay you two, calm down. Stuart, FYI, I bought a Casio transceiver set, which is a surface to under water communication device. You and I can be submerged, Vincent gives us a one-word command like -NOW- and we go for the gold. We can stall him a little, tell him there are some kind of obstructions in the water or something, to give Monica a little more time, and then we split. Be sure and tell Vincent about it, that should give him some peace of mind. Also, I got us some bigger underwater propulsion devices from a friend. These will be fantastic aides for getting through the currents, and back to the Marina."

"That's awesome, Chet. I can't wait to try them. On my end, I need you two to sign up on the Find My Friends App with me this morning. That way we can trace each other's whereabouts at all times on our iPhones. Like when Monica takes off on the bike, we will know when she makes it to the airport, and be able to track her exact location. And I have another question here for us. What if we just dropped the hammer on Vincent right after he snatches the girl? He gets her to us, and then we forward his zip file to the cops. They would be on him, and that would keep him busy enough that he wouldn't even be thinking about messing with me or anyone else. Yeah?"

"Whoa, bro, big time whoa. That is some heavy shit right there. You are talking about messing with the damn Mob? I for one, don't want any part of that. We should keep the zips on hand in case we need them. Otherwise, we don't even use them. We don't want to step into anything unless it is absolutely necessary. What do you think, Monica?"

"I agree, Chet. Very bad idea Stuart. Why stir up a hornet's nest? These are miserable people, and they can be very dangerous. We are not dealing with the boy scouts here. Plus, if the cops got the file, Vincent and his guys would surely know it came from you."

"Okay, okay it was just a thought. I will continue to work Vincent like normal. As long as he is square with us, we are okay. I like the transceiver thing though, Chet. That is a good idea for both operations and Vincent's morale. Anything that makes him feel like he is in control, is a good thing."

"Do you have a set of ID for me, Stuart?"

"Yes, I do. And I hope I don't have to tell you both to be very careful. You know that carrying false identification is now a federal offense and potential terrorist activity."

"What do those ID's cost anyway?"

"They are fifteen hundred bucks in cash each. Five bills to make them up, and a thousand bucks goes to someone in the DMV to record them, and make them legal. The passports are even more expensive."

"Well, I won't even use mine until we get into a foreign country. What about you Monica?"

"Let me think about it. I probably won't need to use anything like that unless something goes sideways. But I will have it with me just in case. My ticket to the Philippines is in my real name."

Alton Walker strolled into his temporary office cubicle at the Chambers Bay admin trailer, and slung his wind breaker over the back of a desk chair. He sat down, and logged into the LPGA website. His Pro-Am was the first scheduled activity of the week, the first official task of his career actually, and he wanted to make sure all the ducks were in a row.

Penny Brown stepped into the cubicle soon after him. "Allo boss," he said.

"Hi Alton, how is it going?"

"Chipper. I think we are ready. The tee prizes are all in and put together in their individual bags. The volunteers have been scheduled, the caterers are set, the awards are in the closet, the evening's program has been confirmed, and the tee times are all filled up and paid for. I just stopped in to make sure we didn't have last-minute emails to tend to, or any late cancellations."

"Sounds like you are ready to go. There is a change of plans for you after your event on Monday though."

"What's that?"

"Cynthia wants to relocate you to the Marriott Hotel at the airport. You will have the town car, and be responsible for transporting anyone as needed to and from Sea-Tac to the tournament, or anywhere else they may need to go. That sound okay? You will probably get a few celebrities. That would be fun, eh?"

"Whatever you and Cynthia need, I'm on it. Just give me a tinkle on the tellie."

Great. I will give you the keys to the town car tomorrow, and they have a reservation for you at the hotel. Good luck, I'm sure everything will go well. I'll be on my cell at all times, should you need me."

"Thanks, cheerio."

"You'll still come visit me in Tacoma, won't you?

"When do you want me?"

"Every night."

"I'll see what I can do."

CHAPTER FIFTEEN

Chrissy and Bobby Jr.'s flight from Minneapolis was on time, and Will was waiting for them at Sea-Tac's baggage claim.

"Howdy y'all, welcome to Seattle."

Chrissy was soo pumped to be back into her adopted home, and the city of her college alma mater. She couldn't wait to see the myriad friends and family who were in town, and then Steve would be here too. Jackpot, homerun, slam-dunk.

"Mom and dad get in okay?" Chrissy inquired.

"Oh yeah. They have been busy getting ready for everyone."

Chrissy and Bobby Jr. had had lots of time during their flight to review the coming week's schedule. She didn't need to remind him they teed off in Monday's Pro-Am at the one o'clock shotgun start, and she wanted to be at the course by ten am.

"Willy, can you run me up to Nordstrom's in Seattle on Tuesday morning before I go to the course?"

"Sure sis."

"Better yet, let mom take me and she and I can do a little damage up there together."

"Yeah, yeah, I will be happy to drive you and mom." They didn't bother to invite Bobby Jr.; he would be sleeping in as usual.

Chrissy was chomping at the bit on Monday morning. She was sitting down eating whole wheat toast and drinking coffee in the kitchen with her mom and dad when Bobby Jr. stumbled downstairs. Ginny poured him a cup of mud, they bade everyone good bye, and hustled out of the house at nine thirty. "Come on baby boy, we got some golf balls to hit."

Bobby didn't need to be at the course this early, but Chrissy was excited, and wanted to get going. He would review the layout while she was hitting balls, before the pro-am teed off. It was also a good time to catch up with his posse, and find out where the caddie action was going to be this week.

Chrissy was paired in the pro-am with Jennifer Caan, the fairly new Athletic Director from the University of Washington, and three other amateurs. It was a modified Scotch format, where the lady pros drove off the tee, and then everyone picked the best shots after that, and scrambled the rest of the way into the hole. They usually ended up playing the pro's shots, so if they had a good day, you did too, and the pros got a practice round in in the bargain.

Chrissy was up for the pairing with Jennifer, and keen to catch up on all the U Dub athletic department gossip. What was going on, and who was doing who? She was very proud of the University of Washington for hiring a woman in the male dominated Athletic Director's position, and was also proud of Jennifer's performance once she was in the job. She had helped keep the football program in the national spotlight, extended the football coaches' contract, brought in a new basketball coach who had revitalized that program, overseen the expansion of the football stadium, helped reduce some substantial athletic department debt, all while going to countless fundraising and operational events. It was going to be a lot of fun to get caught up with Jen.

"Hey, things have been pretty calm since the old football coach left. Those guys were party boy city, but the new guy is a real straight shooter. Our new basketball coach is batshit crazy. But good crazy. Everyone loves him, especially his players, and he is a great recruiter with nationwide connections. Women's softball and volleyball have been killing it, and both women's and men's crew teams finished top two or three in the nation last year. We had to dump the ladies' crew coach, but hired a new woman to take his place, and she is doing great. The golf teams are competitive, but there haven't been any top tier players like you emerge, to help us elevate that program. I am engaged to a great guy from the Provost's Office, he is an attorney. What's new with you?"

"Just right in the middle of the golf year, but it's been very good so far, especially at Pelican Hill a month ago. I am so excited to be back in Seattle, and it is really cool that they paired us up together. I just had a week off to psych up for this tournament, and spent the time in Miami with Steve Reed. Remember him? Wide receiver for the Seahawks and Bears? He was with the Seahawks for three years. We hooked up good. He is major yummy and is coming out to Seattle for Sunday's round. I hope I do well. That would be bank to win it while he was here. I am really so excited to be home; I have to try and cool my jets. You should come by our place this week. We are having a huge party after Sunday's final round." Yadda, yadda, yadda. The girl talk went on for most of the day's round.

Chrissy and Jenifer's group came in in the money. They didn't win the pro-am, but then no one really wants to win the prelims anyway. Most of the players considered it bad luck, like winning the par three tournament at the Masters, and you will never win the real tournament. Well, maybe a few of the girls wanted to win everything in sight. But the prizes were mainly gift certificates and merchandise from the pro shop, and the amateurs loved the bling, but lady pros didn't have much time to use the certificates, and certainly already had plenty of merchandise from all the sponsors in their travel bags.

The post tournament party was a standard affair. Chatter and cocktails were plentiful, the awards were presented, the buffet dinner was mostly bland and unexciting, and by the end of the evening most of the LPGA players were long gone. Tomorrow was a practice day, with the fund-raising dinner in the evening. It would be another full day of activities.

Bobby and Chrissy called home for an early ride, and Chrissy wanted nothing more than some down time with mom and dad before bed, and another busy one tomorrow.

Ronnie "the Barber" Barbieri met Vincent in the bar at three o'clock on Monday afternoon.

"Thanks for coming over, Ronnie, can I get you anything?"

"Sure Vinnie, how about a glass of red wine?"

"Great. I have a nice bottle of Martini Cabernet right here, let me open it." Vincent wasted no time in making Ronnie comfortable.

"Thank you. What's on your mind?"

"Well, I think you might have been right about the computer kid. Dimitri went into the office late on Saturday night to do some posting, and thought he saw someone poking around in the check register. Whoever was in there, went scram as soon as Dimitri entered the system, and he couldn't find no trace of anyone hacking into us. But he was almost positive he saw something that didn't seem right to him."

"That ain't good, Vinnie. I told you to be careful."

"Well, since that first time I let the kid in, no one else has been near there besides Dimi and I insist it be kept locked up 24/7."

"Yeah, but if he planted some kind of search tool in your software, he would have access to your laptop no matter where it was stored, and he would be smart enough to remove it if he had to. You say the kid was on your laptop just that one time?"

"Just the once."

"Were you watching him the entire time he was there in your office?"

"Yeah, except I might have gotten distracted a little bit with a phone call."

"Jeez Vinnie, that is all it takes. One minute, and the guy has access to all of your records and files. It happens just that quickly."

"So, what do we do now?"

"If I was you, I would assume the worst, and hope for the best. Are you still going ahead with your heist thing you was talking about?"

"Yeah. That should happen this week if everything goes right. We're all set up for it."

"With the kid?"

"Yeah, with the kid."

"And he hasn't said anything to you about anything?"

"Nope. He ain't said nothin' about nothin'. And if he did, his ass would already be toasted."

"You have to be extremely careful here, Vinnie. If he has had access to your files, he has certainly backed them up, probably in several places. If those files got into the wrong hands, you have serious problems my friend."

"What do you mean backed them up. How could he do that with me right there by him?"

"Not at that time, Vincent. Sometime later he went into your system, then made copies of your files. Most probably multiple copies, and he can do that remotely from anywhere."

"I am going to kill that little meshugenah!"

"Not until you get those files back. He likely installed some kind of remote access to your system, and downloaded your files as insurance so you didn't rip him off when the job goes down. But if you are straight with him, he will most probably be straight with you. And when everything is done with, well then you can deal with him."

"How about we get the job done, and then I keep the cash, and wring those files out of his sorry little neck?"

"I would urge you to use the utmost care when dealing with this situation, Vincent. Even if you do him bodily harm, he could arrange to have copies of those files accessible to all of the wrong people."

"Not if I have a blowtorch on his balls."

"Vincent, you are not listening to me. For example, he may have your files set up in an email. If he does not deactivate that email every forty-eight or seventy-two hours, it will be automatically sent. In this case, most probably to the Tacoma cops or the News Tribune paper. Think about it. You would not only do major damage to yourself, but you could bring a lot of other people down with you. I don't have to tell you how ugly that could get, Vincent."

"So, you are saying that I would have forty-eight or seventy-two hours to get the location of the files out of him?"

"That could be the scenario, Vincent, but maybe not. And if you didn't get the files back, it would be complete disaster for you and a lot of other people. Myself included."

"What if I was to have Dimitri going through his phone while we was workin' the guy over?"

"Jesus, Vincent, use your damn head. He could have you set up on his laptop, his girlfriend's phone or computer. His freaking mom could have a letter to mail if he disappears. Don't you get that? He could be coming at you from anywhere."

"Yeah well, his girlfriend is working for me now too. Maybe I take both of them, and start on her right in front of him. See how he likes that."

"I would strongly advise you to download your files off that machine, and then destroy it. Change all of your passwords and access information, and do this immediately. Have Dimitri go out and buy a new laptop tonight. And then, if it was me, I would keep the kid close to me. You know, the keep tight with your enemy's thing. Don't let him suspect nothin' about you knowin' what he was up to. Don't let on about anything, and in the next couple of weeks when the time is right, you finish your business with him. Remember, he has your files, but we have coded everything in, and been very careful not to use any official names or places. Also, we download everything every three months, and start a fresh file quarterly. So, there is not a ton of information to go on in there. Any reasonable prosecutor could have trouble making much of anything stick on the basis of that evidence alone. But who is reasonable anymore? The Feds could make a case out of it just to harass you, and the negative heat would be intense. It would ruin the business you have going now, and would probably ruin you financially. And that is even if they didn't get a conviction. No more restaurant, no more Escalade, BMW, Angela, good life. That's what I'm talking about here."

"You are right my friend, and thank you so much for your advice."

"Vincent, you are one of my oldest friends, and I would be very, very careful in the short term if I were you. You do not want or need to be attracting any undue attention to yourself or your operation here at the bar right now. You have a very good, safe thing going. Your life is very comfortable. Why jeopardize any of that for some hair brained idea? And if you do go ahead with your scheme, I would be most cautious. If things don't look right, or come together just the way you have planned, you walk away from it. Hear me? Whadda ya got to lose? Nuttin' pal."

"You're right as always, Ronnie. First of all, tanks for setting up the books so they is so safe like. Secondly, tanks for the advice. I think you is right on, and trust me, I will be very careful. Third, and I understand you don't want no part of this thing, but could I possibly retain youse to help prep us up to negotiate with these people for the ransom?"

"I don't have a problem with that Vincent. I will spend as much time with you and the kid as you need. My rate is five hundred bucks an hour. I think we will need a minimum amount of time to develop a strategy, work on technique, prepare you both for some of what the FBI might counter you with. I would strongly suggest you let the kid do the talking. Your accent is too distinctive. They would be all over it."

"Works for me, Ronnie. I guess step number one is grabbing the girl. If that goes well, we would have all next week to prepare."

"You two will have to come to my office. I ain't getting anywhere near that girl."

"Fine, fine. I will call you on a burner phone and make an appointment."

"Okay."

The two old friends finished their wine, and Ronnie rose to leave. "I gotta go, I got another stop to make. You be careful for Christ's sake, will you?"

"Sure, sure. Let me see you out."

Vincent showed Ronnie to the door, then returned to the back room of his bar, and poured himself another glass of wine. His mind was working overtime, and he was steaming with anger at Stuart Melman. "That little shit is going to wish he was never born when I get through wid him," he said aloud to no one but his pride. In the meantime, I should be calm, and keep him close to me like Ronnie said, and his broad too. If things ain't exactly perfect when we go to make the snatch, the heist is off, and then I will still whack the little fucker out before I am done with him.

Vincent picked up his cell phone, and dialed home. "Hi Angie, it's me. Put on something fancy will ya, I feel like going out for a nice dinner tonight."

"Sure, Vincent. How sweet. When you coming home?"

"I'll be there in half an hour. I just need to make a couple more calls. I love you."

Angela held the phone a foot away from her head, and gave it a strange look. "Love you too, baby," she replied. "See you in half an hour." What in the world has come over my husband she wondered, and shook her head in curiosity? He must want something, or else he screwed up pretty good.

Vincent hung up, and put a call in to Dimitri. "Stop on your way in, and pick up a new laptop." He relayed the rest of Ronnie's instructions, hung up, and grabbed his car keys. He felt much better having talked to Ronnie, but was still angry with Stuart for having made a chump out of him.

Ronnie Barbieri walked out to his C Series black Mercedes sedan, settled in the driver's seat, started the engine, and let the car idle smoothly for a minute. He shook his head and began to understand the need to watch Vincent more closely from now on. First off, the V was old, old school. In the second place, he was tough, but no rocket scientist. Damn good thing I run a tight ship with him and his books Ronnie thought. But I am not going to jeopardize myself or my career over some pazzo, who seems to be having a midlife crisis. I will help him out to some extent, but mainly so he don't shoot his own feet off, and take mine with him. At least he is smart enough to ask for my help with the negotiations.

That kid is lucky, Ronnie thought. In the old days, kaboom. The kid, his girl, her sister, his mother, all of them would be long gone.

CHAPTER SIXTEEN

Steve called Chrissy at eightish on Tuesday morning, and they had some pillow talk for half an hour.

"Things are winding down here, how about if I show up on Saturday morning? I can get there in time to catch Saturday's round, and we could have an extra day together. That okay?"

"Dude, you can come this morning if you want. As a matter of fact, why aren't you here already. Don't you love me anymore?"

"Love? What is love? I know lust, as in I want you right now, but what is this love thing?"

"Well, it's an aura really, where you feel so close to someone no matter where they are, you don't ever want to be away from them. And in that case, I'm pretty sure I'm in love with you. There, I said it."

"Yeah? Well, all I do is think about you, and want to be with you all of the time, so I must be in love too."

"Wow. Then it's official. We must be in love."

"Yes, I admit to the world I am in love. I love you, baby."

"That was so beautiful, I am in tears here. I love you back. And forth, and back again." It seems so much more natural after you say it a few times.

"Me too. I have an appearance at a tournament on Friday, and I will catch the first flight out on Saturday morning. I can't wait to see you again, and meet your family. I love you."

Chrissy got up at eight thirty, and was floating. This was the first I love you talk she had ever shared with a man other than maybe her family guys, and that was different. She was in love with Steve

Reed, and he felt the same way. Those are the three best words in any language in the whole world, she thought. I love you. I LOVE you. I love YOU. And he was coming on Saturday. She couldn't wait to tell her mom all about him. It was great to have three brothers and a doting dad, but what would she ever do without her mom? I love you mom, I love you Steve, I love everybody today, and she skipped off to the shower singing love songs. Pink was running through her brain, and her mind was rocking. Legato tones flowed out of her. She fantasized about launching a singing career. I would definitely want to start out on Broadway. I could sing to Steve every night.

Bob and Ginny were in the kitchen as usual when Chrissy came downstairs. "You want some eggs, hon?" Ginny asked.

"Sure Mom. Hey, guess what. My friend Steve is coming a day early. He will be here on Saturday. I can't wait for you to meet him."

Ginny Jensen could see and feel Chrissy's excitement. It was hard to miss, as she was glowing like a Roman candle. "How wonderful, honey, I will look forward to that."

"You will love him, Mom. He is such a great person, and so beauteous too."

Ginny had never seen Chrissy looking so radiant. Well, maybe after winning her first Major, the ANA Invitational, but that was another kind of glow. This was love, and it was pretty obvious.

Damn. She's high as a kite here, Bob Jensen, ever the practical dad realized, hoping this wouldn't throw her off of her game. "What did you say his name was?" Bob asked.

"It's Steve, Dad. Steve Reed. You are going to love him, too. Where is Will? We should get going, so we can be the first ones in the store. I have to be back by one at the latest." Chrissy was still hovering about a foot off the ground.

"He is up and about hon, but have some breakfast. If we get there too early, nothing will be open anyway."

"Whatever mom. If we get there early, we can just stop by the Pike Place Market, and get some Salmon for dinner or something."

Chrissy was so love struck, she just wanted to get moving. Get some action going, leap over a downtown building, do anything physical. Just somehow, make Saturday come sooner.

"Have a bite to eat, and I will go put on some lipstick. We can leave in fifteen minutes."

"Okay Mom. Will," Chrissy called out to her brother.

The drive north to downtown Seattle was the usual mix of industrial/commercial mishmash; airport congestion, casinos and cardrooms, Boeing Field, car and RV lots around the I-5 freeway, but it all looked beautiful to Chrissy today. Bob and Will sat in the front seat of the car chatting, while Chrissy and Ginny were in the back seat together. Chrissy told her mom all about her time in Miami with Steve, how she had met him in Seattle at a party, and known him for two and a half years now. What a cool guy he was, and how good they were together. Basically, how she thought he was just about perfect. Ginny was so happy for her.

It was nine thirty by the time they found parking in the north end of downtown, and they did decide to stroll down to Pike Place and hang in front of the fish vendors, waiting for someone to step up and buy a whole salmon. Then everyone could cheer when the guys performed the classic and sacred Seattle ritual of throwing the slippery, glistening body of the fresh catch back over the counter to the packers. To stimulate the crowds, and open some wallets, the fish hawkers were tossing around a surrogate salmon. A sample study. The surrogate was dented and bruised from being tossed around so much, but no one cared. They all just wanted to see flying fish.

The Jensens had been to the Market numerous times over the years, and never tired of the scene. The fresh seafood, from brilliant colored rock fish to eerie looking octopi, all artfully and exotically laid out on the shaved ice display tables, the tossing ritual, the bustling crowd cheering, and rutting around for better viewpoints. The smell of fresh brewed coffee wafting over from the original Starbucks across the street, already starting its own line of patient customers, queued around the block awaiting their custom-made lattes. It was a Seattle tradition like no other, and everyone in the Emerald City embraced the familiar conventions. Especially Chrissy this Tuesday morning. It was just what she needed to calm herself down, and distract her emotions away from the love planet and back to real life again.

After a few more minutes in the fish market, Chrissy told her mom, "Let's go up to Nordstrom's, and the guys can hang out here for a while, eh?"

"Sure, hon. That sounds good." The girls made arrangements with Bob and Will to meet at noon back at the car, made a U-turn, and headed up hilly Pike Street for the flag ship Nordstrom store.

Love, the market, Nordstrom's, gorgeous weather, shopping with mom, what a day this is going to be. Who cared about the grungy panhandlers and the druggy riffraff on lower Pike St. today? Chrissy was not letting anything bother her. I am going to let someone else worry about it this morning, she thought, and the Jensen girls hustled through the snarky street activity, and on towards another Seattle mecca: Nordstrom's Flagship Department Store.

Entering Nordstrom's for a serious shopper, who doesn't have the opportunity to visit there twice a week, is akin to being invited through Saint Peter's Heavenly Gates. It is inspiring, captivating and enthralling. Especially to someone bitten with love.

"Where do we start?" Ginny asked.

"I need some lingerie, then I've gotta find a new sheath for tonight's dinner, and finally some shoes. How about you?"

"I should get a few casual things in sportswear for the week. What about a golf outfit for you? Don't you need anything for the course?"

"Oh no, Mom. Adidas supplies all of my golf apparel. I have my own buyer, and she sends me half a dozen outfits whenever I need them. They will be there waiting for me when I get to whatever city we are playing if I call her. After the tourney, I usually donate some of them to the local high school golf programs."

"How nice, sweetie."

"Yeah, Mom. Life is pretty good right now."

"You have worked hard, and earned everything you've gotten, baby."

"I know, but I still feel so special most of the time. It's like a bonus, a gift, how you are blessed with this physical talent, and it's almost unreal, how great people treat you. Crazy, Huh? Hey, let's go find lingerie, or I can go there, and meet you in formal wear."

"Sure, sure. You get your private stuff, and I'll see you in half an hour. Call me, my phone will be on."

Chrissy hustled off. She wanted some new intimates that were sexy, ravishing, and unseen, unenjoyed as yet by Steve Reed. She was in the right place. Where's the sexy stuff now? she wondered and headed off. Let's see watcha got, Mr. Nordy.

Will and Bob strolled through the market. They both enjoyed the jostling crowds, the samples of fresh Rainier cherries, and alder smoked salmon.

"So how are you guys doing?" Bob asked.

"We are great, Dad. Chrissy is just kicking it. She is playing so well right now, and with that comes all of the endorsement opportunities. We are actually turning down deals right now, and I mean five or six figure deals. But Chrissy has such great common sense, and tends to keep the perfect balance between her day to day life, her commercial life and her golf. It can be stressful, but she just takes it all in stride."

"She isn't spreading herself too thin, is she?"

"She is rock solid, Dad. You may not be aware of how much people love her out there, so this week should be awesome. This is her homecoming, and she is like a female Freddie Carson to this city. They idolize her, and they are going to love her even more by the time this tourney is over. She has been looking forward to and prepping for this week ever since the tournament was announced."

"That's great to hear. The most important thing to all of us, especially to you and her, is to keep your feet on the ground. Be yourselves, don't let her celebrity dictate your values and life style."

"Well, we have a great family to thank for keeping us grounded, Dad. That is another thing about golf, as compared to say an acting or a major league team sports career. The outside pressures to conform don't seem to be as strong. In a golfer's world you can set your own pace, and create and maintain your own destiny, so to speak. It is an axis where earning potential and your own personal values come strongly into play. There is a reasonable work/life balance, if you play your cards right. I mean it is often a complete grind, and sometimes things get overwhelming, but you are still your own boss. Know what I mean?"

"Sure son. Hey, look. There is a little Mexican market over there with a Fresh Homemade Tamales sign in the window. Let's go try a couple." Father and son crossed the cobblestone street, and entered the little tienda. So much for the morning sermon, eh? Will thought.

Sure enough, there were still some homemade pork tamales with Hatch Green Chile sauce left. Living in an agricultural community like Yakima, and its' preponderance of Hispanic population, tamales are a cultural staple and often an integral part of any daily diet. The guys ordered two each, and crossed back over the cobblestones to go and sit on a city bench, overlooking a grassy knoll and out onto Puget Sound. The tamales were fresh out of the steamer, and melt in your mouth moist and tender. The view was spectacular.

"So, you think she has got a good shot this week?" Bob asked.

"She is going to kick it," Will replied. "She has been working her tail off for this. Taking a week in Miami to charge up her batteries didn't hurt anything, and now she is ready to go to work."

"This new boyfriend isn't going to be a distraction?"

"No way. He is a professional athlete, and understands what goes into prepping for a major event. If anything, he will help her stay focused and competitive on her golf, but give her some added incentive. If she wins, then she will want to take a break, and spend some more time with him."

"In that case, I may like this guy already."

Will and Bob sat on their bench, and watched the carnival like atmosphere continue to scroll by. While not as exotic as Venice Beach, it nevertheless makes for some capital people watching.

"Are these people punked out, or is this the way they dress all the time?" Bob asked Will while trying to digest the often-whacky looking parade of Seattle's finest passing in front of them.

"It's about par for the course, Dad. Seattle can get pretty grungy and political sometimes. Remember the WTO riots a few years ago? That was a real scene."

Finally, Will gave Chrissy a call. "It's about eleven thirty, babe, you need to start wrapping things up, no pun intended, if we are going to get you to the course around one."

"Nah, Mom and I have decided to shop all morning, then go to the spa for a couple of hours, and after that, it's dirty martinis for happy hour."

"Funny girl. We'll meet you at the car in twenty."

"Come on Dad. We've got about half an hour to kill, let's run over to Emmett Watson's and grab a dozen oysters on the half shell."

"On top of the tamales?"

"Sure. You only live once. We can get a microbrew to wash them down."

"Okay. Hey, I need to talk to someone this week about getting our peaches in this market. We could make a killing selling direct down here."

"Okay, Dad. Give Charlie a call."

The ride back to Tacoma was uneventful, just the usual traffic for Will to deal with. They picked Bobby up at the house, and headed straight for the course.

"Can I call you around five thirty after my round? I need to come home and change, and then I will need a ride to the event. Which one of you gallant gentlemen will be escorting me tonight?"

"How about Charlie?" Will asked. I am picking him up at the airport this afternoon. That would give you two some face time."

"Cool. As long as he has a jacket to wear. This is a formal affair."

"Seattle formal, or Yakima formal?"

"Yakima formal is fine with me. These women are gonna love him. Come on Bobby, I think our foursome is waiting for us."

Yakima formal it was. Charlie wore a fresh pair of Lee jeans, his favorite cowboy boots, a floral pattern snap button western shirt, with a big cowboy buckle on his belt, and he had on his favorite suede leather coat. "You look beautiful brother," Chrissy told him.

Charlie drove, and Chrissy navigated them to the Point Defiance Event Center. The party was underway when they arrived and headed for the check in table at the registration desk.

"Welcome Chrissy," the volunteer girls at the desk cooed. "We are so happy to have you with us tonight."

"It's a pleasure to be here with y'all. I'd like you to meet my brother Charlie Jensen."

The girls welcomed Charlie warmly. Who doesn't like to have a real cowboy at their party?

The reception was in full swing, about three hundred people strong, when they entered the ballroom. Charlie ordered a beer from the hospitality station, and Chrissy was drinking ginger ale.

"Hi Chrissy, hi Chrissy, hi Chrissy. What a cute outfit, etc." Chrissy was killing it in her new lavender colored ensemble from you know where. Charlie was enjoying meeting the ladies, who were like bees to honey for Chrissy and her handsome, rugged looking blond-haired brother. Every which way they turned, there was someone new to meet. Even if they preferred female company, the ladies were all warm and welcoming to Charlie. He was happy to reciprocate with them, and recognized many of the faces he had seen on television while watching Chrissy's tournament play. He was impressed with the golfing star power in the room, and was also made aware by Chrissy when they would walk by an executive from Amazon, the Mayor of Tacoma, or a professional athlete from one of the local pro teams.

Charlie was impressed. In Yakima we have sweeping blue skies, and fertile, rolling hills of agricultural crops. In Seattle and Tacoma, they have star power and Chrissy is one of the biggest and brightest, he realized succinctly.

Chas and Chrissy circulated over to the silent auction tables and began to check out the goods. There was a considerable amount of quality merchandise to be had, and well-dressed couples slowly filed by, perusing the auction items. Charlie was more interested in the backsides of the young women who were bending over to write in their bids. He thoroughly enjoyed the silky scenery before him, but he restrained his carnal self, and was happy to continue meeting so many of his sister's friends from the LPGA Tour.

Chrissy found her spa package, and bid the maximum, insuring her successful acquisition of item number 129. It was an eight-hour, three process visit for two, with your own personal attendant. She returned to Charlie's side, just before the LPGA Director of Marketing, accompanied by a very tall, red headed man walked up to them.

"Hi Chrissy, I'm Penny Brown and this is Alton Walker, we are a part of the Tour Marketing team. I just wanted to tell you what big fans we are of your game, and we want to wish you the very best this week. Aren't you from Seattle originally?"

"Hi Penny, this is my brother Charlie. Hi Alton, so nice to meet you." They shook hands all around. "I am originally from Yakima, Washington, but went to school at the University of Washington up in Montlake. It is so nice to be back in my adopted city, my home state, and with a ton of friends and family here for the tournament."

"I'm from Kansas City, and Alton is from Australia. So, he is a long way from home."

"I think I may have seen you around, Alton. How long have you been working for the tour?"

"Over a year now. I was doing some basic grassroots marketing research type stuff, so I was on the courses a lot. Now I am officially on the Marketing Staff. I ran the tournament yesterday, how did it go for yew, Chrissy?"

"It went very well. Everyone I spoke with liked the format, because it kept things moving along, and we got done in four and a half hours. Sometimes those pro-am rounds take forever if it is straight metal play. Come to think of it, I know I have seen you around. You are kind of hard to miss, especially when you make it to all of the different venues. How tall are you anyway?"

"I'm six foot two plus the hair, and it has been so much fun being around your tour. I tell anyone who will listen to me, that I think you ladies, pound for pound, are some of the best athletes in the world."

"Wow. Penny, give this man a raise. What a nice thing to say."

"Oh, we do our best to keep Alton happy, eh?" she smiled intimately up at him. "What are you doing to stay out of trouble, Charlie?"

"I manage our family ranch back over in the central valley. We process about a hundred acres of Yakima peaches, and breed and train thoroughbred horses. You should come visit sometime."

"That would be a delight." Penny took out her cell phone, and put it to work entering Charlie's information. It was the polite thing to do, but they were both pretty sure Penny Brown wouldn't be showing up in Yakima, Washington anytime soon. "I will give you a call whenever I can."

"Please do."

The chimes rang, and Chrissy looked up in surprise. She hadn't yet begun to think about where they were supposed to sit for dinner. "Come with us," Penny said. "We're all seated together up front."

Dinner was surprisingly good for a crowd of three hundred people. Dungeness Crab cakes for a starter course, then mesclun lettuce salad with arugula and pea vines, an entrée choice of grilled salmon or filet mignon, and blackberry slump for dessert. There was some piped in music and a comedienne during the dinner hour, and as the dessert plates were being cleared, the main event of the evening, the live auction, started to ramp up.

Bill Curtain, host of the local *Seattle TV Tonight* show was the emcee and auctioneer. "We have a boatload of stunning items assembled for you tonight, folks. Don't make me work too hard up here, so please bid early and often. We also have some special prizes for a select few of the LPGA ladies, please give them a hearty round applause at the appropriate times. And don't forget folks, this is all happening to support Susan B. Komen Breast Cancer Research. So please give generously from your hearts."

Bill launched the auction with a weekend golf trip for four to the Bandon Dunes Golf Resort on the Oregon coast, complete with lodging, caddies and clubhouse dining and gift packages. That was received well, and went for over eight thousand dollars. Bill possessed the classic auctioneers sing song, rapid fire delivery, and was whipping the urbane crowd into shape quickly.

After half a dozen items had gone out the door, Bill announced that the first of the special awards was to be presented. "And now ladies and gentlemen, we have an inaugural presentation for the 2018 Rookie of the Half Year Award, will Ms. Christina Tam please come up here." Christina arrived on the large center stage, and Bill shook her hand. "Christina, for your outstanding achievements so far this year, and in the true spirit of the Northwest, we would like to present you with this native Chinook Salmon." An aide came out onto the stage, holding the large, fresh salmon, and extended it out to Christina with a steady hand. Of course, Bill had a pair of latex gloves for her. Christina froze in bewilderment, and while she was putting on the protective gloves, she wondered what in the heck was going on. The look on her face was priceless, and the crowd roared in delight. Bill Curtain quickly stepped in, and helped her hold up the slippery fish, they grabbed it by the gills and the tail, and camera flashes went off like Fourth of July. Christina loosened up, realizing she was being hazed a bit, and the crowd continued to roar. Bill brought out a wash basin to rinse their hands afterward and announced that Christina's prize would be professionally packaged and held for her in the catering kitchens.

The auction went on, and at various points would be stopped for another gag gift to one of the girls. A new coffee maker, and a case of Starbucks coffee to Michelle Yee for long drive of the half year. Of course, she had to pose with her gift in a crazy grunge wig and flannel shirt. A bikini and a belly board went to Wendy Carr for best sand play for the year to date. The action droned on. Chrissy didn't buy anything, but held her numbered bidding paddle up in the credit card call for a thousand-dollar donation.

As the live auction wound down, Bill once again interrupted the program to announce, "and now ladies and gentlemen, for the final special award of the evening, a gift for the Sweetest Swing on the LPGA Tour right now, Ms. Chrissy Jensen, will you please come up here." Chrissy gasped, and blushing a bit, rose, touched the corners of her mouth with her dinner napkin, gave Penny Brown a sideways look, and walked slowly up to the stage.

"Chrissy, we have a pitching wedge here for you, and were hoping you would be willing to demonstrate that sweet swing of yours for us."

Chrissy, tomboy extraordinaire, was never shy when challenged, even if she was in a fitted cocktail frock and was standing in front of three hundred people. She kicked off her new Christian Louboutin pumps, hiked her skirt up a bit, grabbed the pitching wedge, and took a few practice swings. The crowd thundered their approval. But wait.

Bill had an aide bring out a hitting mat, and three plastic whiffle balls. "Ladies and gentlemen, Chrissy is going to hit these three balls into the crowd. Each ball contains a special gift for whoever recovers it, the kicker, is you cannot leave your seats to recover any of the balls."

Taking Chrissy by the shoulders, Bill spun her gently around three times, and led her over to the hitting mat. "Ladies and Gentlemen, the first ball contains a one-thousand-dollar gift certificate to Seattle's fabulous Canlis Restaurant. Thank you to the generous folks there on Lake Union for their support." Chrissy dropped the ball on the mat, snuggled her bare feet into the soft AstroTurf, and with a half swing, sent the ball arcing out into the seated crowd. It came down nicely on top of table number thirty-two, and was promptly snatched up. Everyone applauded.

Repeating the process, Bill informed his audience that the next giveaway was a case of Cabernet Sauvignon wine from Leonetti Vineyards in Walla Walla, Washington. Leonetti is the premier vintner in the State of Washington, making this particular item worth well over twelve hundred dollars. The crowd went nuts, and Chrissy turned in the other direction, opened the face of her golf club, and flopped a shorter shot into the second row of tables. The ball took one bounce, and was grabbed out of thin air by a gentleman with a sure hand and quick reflexes.

For her third shot Bill again twirled Chrissy around, and announced the final prize, this time it was Alaska Airline tickets for two, anywhere in the USA. The crowd quieted in anticipation, and on her final sweet swing of the evening, Chrissy blasted the ball, and sent it flying. It hit the ballroom ceiling, and bounced directly down into the lap of a Seattle matron. The crowd went to crazy town.

"We would like to thank everyone for coming tonight, especially our good-natured LPGA ladies. And for you Chrissy, we have a new cowgirl hat and a case of Washington Red Delicious Apples. Your box of apples will be waiting for you as you leave the registration desk tonight, but you would you please consider wearing your new cowgirl hat back to your seat." The crowd had one good roar left in them, as Chrissy donned her new headgear, tipped it graciously to Bill Curtin, and left the stage.

She got back to her table, winked at Charlie and sat down. Her hat stayed on, and it nicely complimented Charlie's outfit. "You two are in big trouble," she said to Penny and Alton.

Mac Tenderson mounted the stage, and gave a final salute to the crowd on behalf of the LPGA. He thanked all of the event organizers, the sponsors, the auction donors, the tour's talented players, and the attendees. On behalf of the LPGA and the Susan B. Komen Foundation, he wished all of the players good luck in the tournament, and this wrapped up the evening's official program and activities. "We invite everyone into the lounge, which is set up right outside of the ballroom for your entertainment and dancing pleasure. There are refreshments available. Thanks again for coming out, and please drive home safely."

Chrissy was ready to go. It had been a long, full day, and tomorrow the practice rounds and preparation for the tournament continued in earnest. She needed to wrap her head around some serious golf time, and they bade goodbye to Penny and the rest of their tablemates.

"Well, at least they aren't peaches," Charlie commented, as they stopped at the registration desk to pick up their goods. Chrissy put the spa certificate in her purse, and signed off on her contributions. Charlie grabbed the apples like they were a box of toothpicks, and they got ready to depart for the parking lot and home.

"Thank you so much for coming out and participating tonight," Penny told Chrissy. "I'm sorry I couldn't give you a heads up about being called on stage, but I was sworn to secrecy."

"Okay girl, but you know pay back is a bitch." Everyone laughed, and headed out. Chrissy, still wearing her cowgirl hat, had to shake a lot of hands along the way.

"Oh, Alton, you have a late request for your services tomorrow afternoon. A couple of the girls have friends flying in to SeaTac, and wanted to know if they could get a pickup. I think they hope to do some kind of an early, happy hour pub crawl. Can you help out with that?"

"Sure Penny."

"Talk to Katie Kramer tomorrow about the arrangements. She will be around all day."

"Can do."

Chrissy and Charlie made it back to the Cherokee, and loaded up. "Geez, sis. You are a rock star now."

"Did you have a good time, Charlie?"

"Heck yes. That was total fun. I, we all, are so proud of you."

"Thanks for coming with me tonight. I love you."

"Most of all?"

"Absolutely Charlie. You are my man." Charlie tweaked her nose, and they drove off.

Chrissy was in her nightshirt, and had tucked herself into bed ten minutes after they arrived home. Tomorrow was the start of showtime.

CHAPTER SEVENTEEN

Chrissy was downstairs eating breakfast with her dad and mom at quarter to eight, when brother Bobby strolled into the spacious kitchen.

"Good morning everyone," he said pleasantly and gave his mom a peck on the cheek. "You ready to go, sis?"

"Good to go, Bobby. Grab a bite, and we are off."

"No, I mean are you goooooood to goooooo, baby?" He exaggerated his words to the extent that no one in the room would have any trouble understanding what he meant: Are you ready to go out and take this course by the back of its neck?

They got to Chamber's Bay in good time, and Bobby hauled Chrissy's clubs to the practice range. I am going to go look around while you hit some balls, sis. How much time do you want?"

"We have a tee time with Paula and two other girls at nine thirty. We will want to take our time, so it will probably be around two when we are done. Then let's grab a sandwich, and go back out. Paula wants to go with us again this afternoon. If all goes well, we can be home by seven."

"Works for me, see you in an hour."

Paula Chapman was another darling of the LPGA Tour. She was a steady player and five-time winner, but she was also cute as a bug's ear, adored by the media, and a prominent spokesperson for women and children's issues. As successful as she was, she still had a good work ethic and will to win about her, which Chrissy liked. They were both competitive enough to play for a hundred bucks a hole, and bragging rights with the other LPGA ladies. Practice rounds were where the majority of the action is. Most of the ladies didn't like to be distracted with side bets and such during tournament play, but practice rounds, that was something entirely different. Chrissy and Paula would have a money game, and the other two Asian players, would be doing their own thing.

It was also the last opportunity to test the course; the speed and break of the greens, the texture of the sand in the traps, the location of the traps (they are everywhere), the subtleties in the course during different times of the day, the lighting, the wind, the sun, etc. And so it was on this beautiful mid-July Day in University Place, Washington. While it was relatively warm in the Northwest, it was a very pleasant respite from a lot of the rest of the country's often repressive heat and summer humidity.

And at their appointed hour, these four self-possessed young women, so successful and independent, headed out to do what millions of other people all over the world must pay money to enjoy. Carefree were they, yet focused on the job at hand. Setting out to practice their craft on a flawless day, all of them tied for the lead in the upcoming tournament at this point in time. They unintentionally, but symbolically represented the progress and aspirations of young women athletes all over the world.

"Tell me about these greens, Chrissy," Paula asked. "I have heard so many negatives about them."

"Well, from what I understand, the USGA insisted that the greens be seeded with fescue for the US Open. Fescue isn't natural to the northwest, so that is what caused the problems. But I hear they have been converted to poa annua, which is our native species, and things are much better now."

"I hope so. They looked absolutely brutal during the PGA Open."

"It appeared worse than it actually was. I was here, and it had been so unusually hot and dry in Seattle, the course just looked burnt out on TV. But it wasn't as bad in person. I actually played here four months ago, and it was still February, but the course was just fine and the greens were very puttable. I hope they are, because I don't want to hear any whining when I kick your fanny today."

"Ha. You still owe me a dozen Pro V's from Wisconsin, you biach."

Crissy liked the banter, but she quieted down and began to concentrate on her game. Like any professional golfer, taking the pulse of the course is essential to one's success. The roll and break of the greens necessitate challenging the hole from all angles during the tune up rounds. A crucial putt on Sunday afternoon might well depend on your preparation today.

Simply enough said, she loved this place and not just because it was her adopted home course. Not just because she thought it was an exacting test of championship golf, and it made her feel comfortable just to play here. But she couldn't think of a more spectacular layout anywhere, with the authentic links layout, and the incredible water views. She knew that being home again was not enough to assure her a victory on Sunday afternoon, but her experience, preparation, and knowledge of the tricky layout at Chambers Bay would definitely help. Not to mention the fact that she was piping the ball a mile, and putting well.

They played their morning foursome, took all the time needed to inspect the nuances of the course, and then broke for lunch. They took the shuttle back up to the clubhouse, where Chrissy made Bobby a sandwich from the players buffet, and they sat with Paula and her caddy out on the veranda and ate quietly. Chrissy and Paula had actually postponed their standing wager to the afternoon round, which would be more conducive to match play. After half an hour, they all headed back out for the first tee and their second go round. Chrissy teed off at eleven oh seven Thursday morning, so this would be the last chance she had to play the course. Tomorrow morning, she could hit all the range balls she wanted, but this was her last real test of what the course had to offer.

Three and a half hours later, they wrapped up the day. Chrissy won the match with Paula three and two, and pocketed a couple of

Benji's. "Thanks, girlfriend," Chrissy attempted to be gracious in victory, but it was a little hard not to needle her best friend on the tour a little bit.

Bobby was done in. Toting a tour sized bag for thirty-six holes in eighty some degrees weather, on Chamber's often steep, hilly links, was overtime work. Although he was tired and sweaty, he was still willing to put in whatever time and effort it took to get Chrissy prepped and ready. And she seemed like she was all good to go. This was a five hundred-thousand-dollar tournament to the winner, and if Chrissy took first place, that meant fifty grand for him. Plus, she was always very generous with his living and travel expenses, so he was fully committed when it came to practice time.

Chrissy and her little brother tromped back out to the Jeep Cherokee, stowed her clubs, and headed for home. Bobby was dying for a cold beer, but that could wait for a few more minutes. He would stay in at the family compound tonight. All Chrissy wanted to do was cool off, sit out on the porch with her mom, and chat for a spell.

They would have a light dinner, maybe play some gin rummy afterwards, and then she would give Steve a call, and go to bed early.

Alton Walker caught up with Katie Kramer, and got the information for his afternoon pickup at the airport. He was enjoying the company of all the different ladies, touring them around, and was learning the ropes of Seattle traffic. There was plenty to learn in that regard.

Leslie Mancebo and Leslie Buford, two Leslies interestingly, were his tour contacts. His clients so to speak, and he was a little puzzled that several of the ladies would want to go out drinking the night before the tournament started, but he decided it was their call, and none of his business.

"Gud dai, laydies," he greeted them cordially. "Wazzup?"

"Some friends are flying in on United. We want to pick them up and stop off at a couple of places. They have never been to

Seattle, so we want to show them around a little bit. But we don't want to stay out too late, and not get crazy at all. This is just some old friends from college connecting. You are welcome to join us, but you would probably be bored to death."

"No worries at all. I get the concept."

"Do you know any good places?"

"Sure, sure. There are a couple of brew pubs up in Georgetown, but that's a bit of a rough neighborhood. Sharp's has a great happy hour, but it is kind of airporty, if yew know what I mean?"

"How about Thirteen Coins? I heard that is really old Seattle," one of his ride offered. He thought it was Leslie Buford.

"Why don't we go there, and then we can cruise around a bit. They might be getting hungry by then, eh?"

"Good idea."

The girls were excited to see their friends and get caught up. The flight was on time, and Alton loaded up the luggage, and took off for Thirteen Coins.

"I'm just going to stay in the caaw." He announced with his nasal Aussie accent when they arrived at the restaurant. "You have fun, and I will be right here when you are ready to go."

He had a good book going, a new Jack Reacher novel, and actually was looking forward to a little down time. Ms. Penny Brown was the culprit who had been keeping him up nights of late.

The four young women were escorted to a benchmark Thirteen Coins banquette in the lounge, one of the high-backed booths made famous at legendary restaurant, and they began to chitchat nonstop. They had their privacy, but were also able to look out over the bar's main seating area and enjoy some people watching while they were talking and sipping wine.

After an hour or so, Leslie Mancebo suggested they go out and cruise around some, and look for a dinner spot. "It is still so nice out, we should take advantage of the beautiful evening."

Alton was dozing off when the ladies rejoined him, no problem, he saddled up, and off they went. Highway 99 runs north and south in the greater Seattle area, and is the main alternative to the busy Interstate 5 Freeway. Although it is no Rodeo Drive on the south end of town, they all decided it was a better shot than getting on the interstate, and dealing with all of that rush hour traffic. Maybe head north a bid and get up to Southcenter, a major destination shopping mall in south Seattle. There would be good restaurants choices there.

"Fiddle, laydies. It looks like traffic here is almost as bad as I-5, eh? I think there must be an accident up ahead or something."

The group slogged on for another half mile, and everyone seemed to be getting hungrier, and more frustrated with the traffic. "Why don't we just find someplace to eat around here, and wait it out," Leslie B asked. "It will still be light enough for a drive afterwards won't it, Alton?"

"Sure," Alton replied. He turned around and began heading back down south towards the airport.

"Hey there is an Italian restaurant right over there. It looks okay." he said.

"Vincenzo's. Let's go." The other young ladies responded.

Alton announced he would like to come in and get a bite to eat, but the girls should do their own thing, and he would sit at the bar. They hit the little foyer, took a right turn, and found themselves in a darkish room with high windows, tall plants in all of the bar's corners, and a large glassed in wine storage unit on their right. There were European flags and World Cup banners all over the walls. The room was three quarters full, felt darkly intimate, and somehow a little dangerous in an anything could happen in here kind of way.

There was a mixed crowd in the bar, some young, construction worker types drinking beer, a few more tables of blue-collar men sitting around, several small klatches of golfer type guys, drinking after a round maybe. It was a mostly male clientele, then there were half a dozen single women sitting at the bar sipping something in bucket glasses. There were two bartenders and a cocktail waitress working the room. One of the bartenders was an attractive woman with a floral tattoo running up her left arm. She appeared to be in her early thirties. The other bartender was a buff Italian looking dude. The sign at the door said for them to seat themselves, and as they paused to let their eyes adjust to the dimness of the room, an older gentleman emerged from the back of the bar, walked behind the service area to say something to the female bartender. Alton suddenly became very agitated.

"Vincent, Vincent," he called out impulsively. The LPGA ladies were taken aback, and a little embarrassed at the attention he was attracting. As all heads turned to the entryway of the bar, Alton took half a dozen long strides, and was standing at the middle of the horseshoe shaped bar. The young Italian barkeep flexed defensively, as if there was going to be a confrontation, but Alton extended his right hand toward the older gentleman, and said "Vincent how are you doing? It's me, Alton Walker from Pelican Hill, remember?" Not that anyone could forget a six foot five, flaming redheaded Australian drinking partner and self-proclaimed LPGA golf groupie.

"Hey, how are youse? Whataya doin' up in Seattle anyway?" Vincent asked, and looked over at the four attractive young women who were still standing in the doorway staring at Alton and Vincent.

"I am up here for the tournament at Chambers Bay, mate."

"Looks like you is doin' okay for yourself."

"Doing okay? Heck Vincent, pot is legal up here, and everything else is on my expense account. I work for the LPGA now."

"That's great, man. Why don't we get a seat for your friends," and Vincent nodded his head to one of the bartenders in a nonverbal suggestion to get the girls situated. "Get the ladies a drink on me, will ya please?" Vincent said to his other bartender.

"Thanks a lot, Vincent. Dang me, I completely forgot you even owned a bar up here."

"Yeah, well, this is it. Make yourself at home. Are those ladies' players?"

"Two of them are, and two are friends just into town. You should come over and say hi."

"I can just say hello, I was going out the door when I seen youse." Jesus, Mary, Joseph, Vincent thought to himself. He is about the last guy on earth I want to see right now. He will be hanging all over that tournament like a gold chain around one of those rapper's necks. And me and Tommy if he sees us.

Vincent exited the back bar, and walked over to the now seated quartet of women. Alton was already at the table, and introduced them.

"Welcome to Vincenzo's," he said with his best Italian accent. "Good luck this week, I hear the course is in great shape."

"Thank you," Leslie B responded. "Yes, it's a beast, but it's in beautiful shape."

"Well, enjoy yourselves ladies. I recommend the Italian sausage pizza, it's wunnerful, and the antipasti is also a good way to start off. I am going to take care of everything for you tonight, so when you win this thing, you tell everyone you eat at Vincenzo's, eh? Then come back over here, and we gonna throw a big party."

That brought a chuckle and a thank you from the ladies, and the young Italian barman was now standing behind Vincent, waiting to take an order. "I gotta go now, youse have a good time." He turned to Alton, "Good to see you again," he said, spun around on his heel and was gone.

"I'll be right over there at the bar if you need me, laydies," and Alton was also gone, leaving the women with the handsome barman. He flirted with them a bit while taking drink orders, and left them some bar food menus.

"I feel like I am back in Sicily somewhere," Leslie Mancebo offered. The young ladies had too much to talk about though to pay too much attention to the ambience in Vincenzo's.

"Yeah, it's dark, but it sure smells good in here," one of the girls chirped.

Alton sat on the left side of the horseshoe bar. There was a single lady sitting two stools over on one side of him, and another single woman three stools over the other way. No wonder they are single, he thought to himself, they are pretty tough looking. As Alton was probably the friendliest person in Seattle, he nodded at the women buddy-buddy like, and ordered a beer. Not surprisingly, Vincent's bar offered some good Northwest microbeers and a few Italian choices, but definitely no Victoria Bitter. The working girls nodded back, not too interested in a guy who had come in with four pretty, young women. He must be some kind of a limo driver they thought. He is pretty cute though, in a striking kind of way.

One of the construction guys came over to the woman on Alton's left, and they chatted for a few minutes in low voices. Alton could only pick up a smattering of their conversation, but he was wise enough to understand there was a transaction being conducted. The woman was too young to look as hard as she did, but she got up and led the guy out of the bar. He had his hand on her ass as they walked away. Oh shit, Alton thought. I have brought the LPGA to a hooker bar. The dark side. Vincent, that damn dog, I should have known.

Now he had a quandary on his hands. How to get his charges out of there, without causing a scene. Realistically, Alton was too new in town to know that the south end of Seattle on old Highway 99 was no stranger to bars and hookers. But also, in reality, Alton himself was no stranger to shady bars. The Italian bartender had witnessed the situation, and was watching Alton to see what he was going to do.

He had a sip of beer, got up and went out to the town car to collect his thoughts. He came back in, went over and knocked his beer back, and motioned to the bartender for the check. The bartender sauntered over and told him he was Vincent's guest. So, he dropped a twenty-dollar bill on the bar top for a tip, and crossed the room to his girls. "It is really beautiful out there, laydies. We should finish our drinks and go for that drive."

All four women looked at him in surprise. They were chatting busily, were totally into it, and wanted to order some food. But he turned his back to the bar, and gave them a distressed grimace of a look on his face and a tip of his head, meaning let's get the hell out of here. So, they grabbed their phones and sunglasses, had a last sip of wine, and followed him out to the car.

"What's going on?" they all asked as they reached the town car in the parking lot.

"It's a house of ill repute," Alton replied. "All of those single women sitting at the bar were prostitutes. I would get in big trouble for bringing you in there."

"Turn around," the women chorused. "We want to go back and look at the girls."

"No way," Alton replied. "I'll tell you a story instead."

"Bullpucky," Les B said. And the four young women turned around and stomped back into the bar before anyone had had time to clear their drinks away.

"Damnit," Alton said to himself. "I am herding cats here. How in God's name am I supposed to know where to take people, when I have never been in this city before?"

The LPGA ladies were quietly fascinated by the underbelly of Seattle night life. And it was just getting started. But they ate antipasto and focaccia bread with olive oil and balsamic vinegar, and watched as the crowd expanded and contracted. As liaisons were formulated around the bar, they voted their approval/disapproval on the hookups with a thumb up or down signal. It was usually disapproval, and after an hour or so, they realized it was more degrading than glamorous, and decided that enough was enough. Their intrinsic curiosity at seeing some real live working girls, no matter how cheap it now seemed, and as long it was someone else being cheapened, had been satisfied. They all thought Vincenzo's had been better than a reality TV show.

Back on the road, Alton looked for the I-5 south on ramp, and along the drive launched into the tale of how he had met Vincent and his friend Tommy in Newport Beach, and they had gone drinking. He managed to omit most of the details of the transsexual. More about them hanging out together and doing some partying. He finally summarized the evening for his ladies: "Vincenzo's Restaurante would be highly frowned upon by my bosses. It's not even close to the LPGA image, and I can't take you there again. I could get fired. Please don't even tell anyone we were in there."

Alton missed his access ramp, but kept on driving, trying to wind his way back to the freeway. Somehow, they ended up in a south end town, that was not too far from SeaTac airport.

"Look," one of the newbie girls squealed while the car was stopped for a signal, and pointed up at an official roadside traffic sign. The Municipal Posting said --*Do not pick up hitchhikers. This is a prostitution abatement area.*

"No way," said Les M. "Where are you taking us, Alton?"

"Look over there," the other visiting twenty something said, and pointed across busy Highway 99. "It's a cannabis store. Come on Alton, we've got to go check it out."

"No way. You Sheila's are trying to get me in big trouble."

"Oh, come on, Alton. It won't hurt anything to just look."

"Please," the young women cried in unison. One of them said, "this place is Sin City."

"Come on Alton, be a sport," Les B implored. "They don't have anything like this in Ames, Iowa. Trust me. Just let 'em have a look. That won't hurt anything."

"All right. Ten minutes, go have a look."

Once across the street, and into the parking lot, the four young women tumbled out of the town car, and pushed their way into the marijuana store. The two more experienced LPGA players followed at an appropriate distance. Alton stayed back in the car, and tried to watch and see if anyone recognized the players. After their ID's were checked, the young women strolled about looking at a real life weed shop. "Look at this, look at that." Ten minutes went by in a blink, and soon enough Alton stuck his head in the door, and said it was time to go.

"Thank you, for stopping Alton," the girls crooned. They would not forget their first pot store visit. It seemed more like a whacky pharmacy with all its now legalized products displayed so officiously. Fortunately, there were no photographers around. A front-page pic of the ladies in the pot shop would be a complete disaster, and Alton couldn't wait to get out of there.

"Look what I got," Alton heard one of the girls say, as she held up a gram of Obama Kush weed in a vial marked "from Bondi Farms." "It only cost nineteen dollars."

"Check this out for five bucks," the other visitor held up a small glass pipe, and a Bic lighter.

Alton was busy driving, and the next thing he knew, he sniffed the sweet, saccharine smell of marijuana smoke.

"Goddamnit," Alton griped at the back seat. "I have to take Mac Tenderson to the airport in the morning, and this car is going to smell like a rock concert. Open up the rippin' windows, will ya please."

The women just giggled happily. "Seattle is a lot of fun," one of them said. Leslie Mancebo declined to smoke, but Les Buford who hadn't been playing that well lately, thought a couple of hits might be just what her golf game needed. So, they rolled on, swaying pleasantly to oldies music from the eighties, body rushing to Prince, and gazing out at the hard edges of South Seattle.

The girls were still floating, but it was time to begin heading back, so they continued to enjoy the sights while visiting sporadically, and Alton navigated his way south. Commuter traffic had largely dissipated, and the driving was much more relaxed.

"Let's go back to Vincenzo's," one of the girls funningly implored. "I want to take that bartender home with me."

"You women are so hot, if we go back there, they will probably kill me, then they would kidnap all of you, and turn you into Vincenzo sex slaves."

"That bartender could slave over me for a few days," the girl replied.

"Which one?" Leslie Mancebo asked her, and got an elbow in the ribs for her trouble.

"Hey, watch it," she shot back. "I've got some golf to play tomorrow morning."

CHAPTER EIGHTEEN

Vincent got home, and kissed Angela warmly. "You ready for a cocktail?" she asked him.

"Sure. Make me a double martini would you please? I gotta go change and make a quick call."

Vincent went into his home office, and dialed Tommy up. "You ain't gonna believe who I just saw in the bar," he told his partner in crime.

"Who?"

"That fucking moron from Newport Beach."

"Which fucking moron? It wasn't that bartender from the hospitality tent wanting a job in your restaurant was it?"

"No way. I would kill that dope if he ever set foot in my place. It was the tall, red headed Aussie that saved your reputation, remember him?"

"Oh yeah, that guy. What was he doin' in the bar? He must follow these women all over the country, huh?"

"Yeah dat guy. He said he was up here for the tournament. Told me he was workin' for the LPGA now."

"Well, his prayers musta been answered."

"He's gotta be doin' okay though, there was four good lookin' broads wit him in my place. Two of them was players, he introduced me," Vincent told the T.

"No lie. Well, I hate to say it, but I hope we don't see him no more this week. You know what I mean?"

"My thoughts exactly. Hey, let's meet one more time tomorrow morning before the tournament starts, can we?"

"Sure. At the bar?"

"Yeah. Ten o'clock. I will call the kid, and have him be there."

"Nah, you have him come after me. I don't need to see that little dirtbag no more."

"Okay."

Vincent went into the master bedroom, changed into casual clothes, walked back outside, and sat down in a padded lounge chair on his knotty cedar deck across the patio table from Angela.

"Thanks for the drink, baby."

"Sure, Vinnie. How was your day?"

"It was pretty quiet. I got a fair amount of stuff going on for the next coupla weeks, so I am just checking on things, making sure everything is good to go."

"You gonna be around? You promised to take me to Vegas don't forget."

"Sure. I ain't forgot. But it is too hot to go down there now. Wait until I get done wid my business, and we can go down in September."

"You promised me."

"Geez, why you wanna leave right now for? It is so nice here, and Vegas is like a hundred and ten degrees. Give me a break. Why don't I make a call, and we can invite Ronnie and Julia to a show at the Emerald Queen. We can stay over in the Casino penthouse, and have a good time right here. I'll get us front row seats."

"Yeah, well who's playin' over there?"

"I dunno. I'll check tomorrow. By the way, if anyone should ever axk you, for the next couple of nights, I am sitting home with youse right here in the house, having a quiet dinner, and watching the ball ballgame, capiche?"

"What's going on Vinnie?"

"Nothin'. Just a little business is all."

Tommy strolled into Vincenzo's at a quarter to ten on Thursday morning, and found Vinnie sitting in his usual spot drinking coffee. "Hey, bud. Whatcha wanna talk about?"

"Let's go in the back room."

Safely tucked in his meeting room, Vincent said, "Ah, I just wanted to check one last time. We all ready to go?"

"Yeah sure, Vinnie. The car is squared away, I got my phony beard and chauffeur's cap. I been spending a lotta time over at Chambers, and know that place like the back of my hand now."

"Okay, here are the parking/access passes. Why don't you pick me up around three this afternoon, and we can drive down there, and check it out. Work on our timing, that kind of thing. Then we go over earlier tomorrow. Not be seen together, but hang around, and watch her finish, and be ready if she goes over to hit balls. Have the car parked nearby."

"Yeah, I was there early yesterday morning checking it out. Chrissy come drivin' up in a black Jeep Cherokee SUV. It looks like her caddy is driving her around. I think he's her brother. What time you wanna leave here?"

"Around two. The crowds are lighter during the week, so I don't wanna get too cozy over there. More of an in and out thing, eh?"

"Sure. It will take us at least a half an hour or so to get to the course. I know the car, so we can check that out. We need to watch out for that redheaded guy. He shouldn't see us over there at the course at all."

"No kidding, see you at two. You have your piece in the car?"

"Yeah, just in case."

Stuart and Monica were also right on time. "Hey, Vincent, how are you?"

"I'm good kid. Let's go in the back room."

"We weren't going to wear any clothes today, then you wouldn't have to wand us. But we thought we better not."

"Well, Monica I am okay with. You not so much."

"Just kidding, Vincent.'

"I know, you little schmuck."

Ivan wasn't working this morning, and Vincent didn't want to wave the wand himself, so he just asked them, "you two wearing a wire?"

"Not today, boss. Not any day, boss."

"Good. So, I just want to go over every last detail. Youse ready to do this?"

"We're ready."

"There is no backing out once this thing gets rolling. You got that, right?"

"As long as she don't get hurt, Vincent."

"Yeah, whatever. We are trying to go for tomorrow evening. We will be out there today to scout it out, a kind of trial run. I guess if the situation was perfect, we would go today, but we would both rather wait until tomorrow."

"Okay. Just keep us hooked up with one of your burner phones," Stuart said.

"Right. Now, if things don't look like they should when we is over there, no matter when it is, we ain't gonna go. The whole deal is off. But if and when we do go on it, I will call when we are on the way, and let youse know when we should be there. You have the garage door open, and in we go. Then we transfer her down to the basement. If she gets hysterical, then we will have to calm her down. I will have a blanket over her head, so she can't see nothing. Once she is in the basement, you need to take care of her, Monica. I got some sedatives from a friend of mine, if she was to get noisy or hysterical, you gonna have to put them in her food or just make her drink them down."

"Got it. Feed her twice a day, and get her what she wants, as long as she behaves herself."

"Yeah, and don't spend too much time with her, okay? Just take her food down, and make sure she is alright. Tell her she should be sitting on the bed, eyes down, when you come in the room. If she won't do that, then tell her we gonna tie her ass up. I will be in and out for the first couple of days, to make sure everything is okay. You got that rug head face thing I told you about, right?"

"Yeah. It's called a niqab, and I've got one."

"You make sure you wear it whenever you are in the room. She may try to get a good look at you, but as long as we got something on our faces, she won't be able to make any of us."

"Look Vincent, I will take care of her, and I will cook for me and Stuart. The other guy is on his own."

"That's ain't no problem. I will tell him. Just have some food in the house, in case he wants a sandwich or breakfast or something."

"Okay."

"Stuart, once we get her in there, you and Lennie are on for alternate twelve-hour shifts. Then during the day, you and me are gonna meet with a friend of mine. So, it looks like you gonna have to work the night shift. I got a buddy who is a very smart, and he's gonna coach us up on negotiating with these guys. They is very good at that stuff, and we is new at it. So, he is going to get us prepped and ready. He said for youse to get a voice distortion device."

"Good idea, Vincent. I need to tell you also that we got a transceiver set which will let you communicate with us while we are under water. I was going to set up a closed-circuit camera on the crab pots for you at the house, and you can tell us when they make the drop. We will be over there and on it fast."

"You don't need to do that. I have a place to watch the drop from the bluffs on this side, and I can signal you when they are done dropping. Then I will leave for the house, and meet you there. How long you gonna take to get back with the cash?"

"If we get to the cash in five to ten minutes, secure it, then it will take us a least fifteen or twenty minutes to get back across the channel, up the bay, and in under the boat house. Don't forget, we will be towing a couple hundred pounds with us."

"The pots are still gonna be off Point Defiance, right?"

"They are going to be on the east side of the Point. And we will be down the shoreline in Salmon Beach. When you signal us, we start up the channel to get to the pots, then we come back across the Narrows, and over to Gig Harbor. Like I said, that should take at least fifteen to twenty minutes depending on the currents."

"Do you love this woman?"

"Sure Vincent, we are engaged to be married."

"Well, she is your security deposit, Stuart. Anything happens to that money, and she is going to descend into hell one limb at a time. You understand me?"

"What are you talking about? What could possibly happen to the money? We come back here, and we split it up, and we go away. Then you cut Chrissy loose, and we are all done. Isn't that our deal?"

"Well, it better be, Sonny. So, once we get golfer girl in the house, and call her golfer girl. I don't want to be usin' her real name, then you and I start meeting with my friend next week. He thinks you should do the talking, but I will be with you all of the time."

"Okay."

"Also, I rented you a car for while you is at the house. Nothing fancy. Just a little sedan to run around town in. It is rented in a phony name, so you be careful not to get any prints on the car. Always wear gloves when you are in it, and drive carefully. Anything else you need from me?"

"A couple of things. I will be doing an underwater trial this afternoon, which will help us have everything down to a science. After that, I will be available twenty-four seven. And then, shouldn't we have code names for ourselves or something?"

"Yeah, we probably should. I will be called Jack." He nodded to Monica, "we can call her Florence, like in Florence Nightingale." Vincent laughed at his own attempt at humor. "Lennie is Leroy, and what about you?"

"Call me Sugar."

"Sugar? What kind of a damn name is Sugar? We gonna call you Sammy. Who are you doing the diving thing with?"

"My friend and roommate. He isn't sure of what is going on, but I just told him he would be making a good chunk of money to help me."

"Can you please do your trial run tomorrow? Now that you and Monica are moved in and settled good, then you can have all day to do your thing tomorrow. Make sure you have your timing down right, because this is gonna be tricky, and we got one chance to pull it off. On the big night, you guys have to be very careful, because the heat is gonna be all over the place. They will be watching for anything and everything. Come to think of it, we is gonna have to talk more about this next week."

"Whatever you say Vincent. My buddy won't cause any trouble."

"Good, because he is dead meat if he even thinks about it. And in the meantime, Monica will be at the house with me and Lennie, waiting for you to return with the dough."

"Got it, Vincent."

Stuart was a little worried about Monica. He was sure Vincent had spooked her with all of his talk about tearing her limb from limb.

"You okay?" he asked when they got back to her 4Runner.

"Am I okay? That shrimpy little bastard had better watch his mouth. My dad was an Airborne Ranger. We moved every year of my life until I left home at eighteen. You think he didn't teach me some stuff that I didn't need to use every time we arrived at a new base? Plus, I will have my Glock with me. That guy had better watch his own self. I might just tear him a new one."

Stuart was impressed. He was convinced she was going to do just fine.

Vincent made a call to Lennie. "I got your first job at the new place for you."

"Yeah, what is it?"

"You just gonna sit out on the dock at the house tomorrow, and wait for Sammy to swim into the boat house."

"That's it?"

"That's it."

Vincent made his second call to Dimitri. "I got a job for you tomorrow."

"What is it boss?"

"I need you to follow my little buddy around tomorrow."

"Stuart?"

"Yeah. He is going to do a diving project for me. I want you to pick him up at his townhouse, then tail him all day. Watch where he goes at all times."

"No problem, boss."

CHAPTER NINETEEN

The Jensen Compound was up early, and it was all hands-on deck. The non-immediate family members had arrived at various times the night before, and everyone wanted to wish Chrissy well this Thursday morning.

She was starting to stir when her cell rang. "Good morning, baby," Steve murmured in her ear. "You ready to go?"

"Morning my love," Chrissy cooed back. It was only seven o'clock, but Steve knew she would be awake.

"I will be watching for you on the golf channel today. What time do you tee it up?"

"Twelve oh seven. We are going to be leaving here in an hour or so. I like to get there early, and go through my routine. I was just getting ready to do some stretching when you called."

"Well, I won't keep you. I just wanted to say I love you, and to hit 'em good today."

"Thanks, baby. I am going to win this one for you, because I love you, and I am going to see you on Saturday."

"Please don't let me be any kind of a distraction. You stay focused on your job, and we can celebrate afterwards, win or lose."

"You are right, and you are a dream. I love you, and I havta go now."

"Love you too, bye."

Chrissy finished loosening up, and started getting ready. She felt relaxed and confident as she headed down stairs to start the day.

"Good morning everyone," she greeted the fam. "It smells so good down here."

"Good morning Chrissy," they chorused back.

"It's great to see y'all, thanks so much for coming."

Ginny had knocked out a chafing dish of scrambled eggs, bacon, sausage, toast, etc. for everyone, and aunts, uncles and cousins were scattered throughout the kitchen and dining room. But she turned the gas burner back on, and made Chrissy's scrambled eggs fresh from scratch.

"There is some cut up fruit and yogurt in the refrigerator, sweetie."

"Thanks Mom." It felt pretty special to have so much family around. It definitely pumped her up when they were all here at the house, and then out cheering for her on the course.

Chrissy had her coffee, ate breakfast, visited and she, Bobby and Will left for Chambers Bay in the Jeep Cherokee at a quarter to nine.

"The Golf Digest people haven't given up yet," Will told her during their drive. "They came back with an offer of twenty-five grand for a six-page spread on you and your swing, and then hope you will do some continuation pieces for them at five grand per for the next six months."

"That is going to have to wait until the season is over, Will. It would be really hard to slow down and fit something like that in right now. You know how much time it would take. They would want to start by going back to the ranch and talking about all that old stuff, and then they would pester me to death for the next six months."

"Heck, Chrissy, why don't they do the spread on me?" Bobby chimed in. "I do all of the heavy lifting around here anyway, and I can probably tell them more about your swing than anyone. Plus, I need the twenty-five grand more than you."

"That is a great idea, Bobby. It could be the launch of your professional coaching career. Except in your case it would be more like five hundred bucks."

"Ha. Thanks a lot, sis."

"Just kidding Bobby. You are worth way more than twenty-five grand. Will, can you make this happen?"

"Chrissy, I am not a miracle worker."

The sibling banter continued, until they pulled into the player's parking lot some ten minutes later.

Chrissy got out of the car, and stretched her legs. She looked up at the sky, and couldn't see a cloud anywhere. "Can't blame it on the weather if we go south today," she said.

"We are going north, sis," Bobby replied. "I don't care what the weather is doing. How you feelin'?"

"I'm a tiny little bit tired from all the walking yesterday," Chrissy replied. "But hopefully, that will keep me from swinging too hard today."

"I've got some people to see," Will interrupted Bobby and Chrissy's conversation. "Knock 'em dead today you guys."

"We gonna try like hell, big bro."

Chrissy was too busy fussing with her golf bag to listen to her brothers.

Her warmup went well, and Chrissy felt loose and relaxed on this gorgeous July morning. She was standing at the first tee chatting pleasantly with Bobby, and waved at her family who were poised behind the tee, waiting to start their eighteen-hole trek down the first fairway. She was paired with a couple of the Asian ladies, so there wouldn't be too much chit-chat during the round, which was fine with Chrissy. She was focused and ready.

Twelve oh seven rolled around, and the starter sent the threesome off without incident. Chrissy pounded her drive down the middle of the first fairway, the Jensen clan applauded supportively, and off everyone went.

The front nine ended two and a half hours later, and Chrissy was not in a good mood. The younger of her two Asian opponents was painfully and tediously methodical, to the point of a slow play warning to their group from the rules official, and Chrissy's rhythm was struggling as a consequence. She was hitting the ball well, but when they got to the greens, the interminable waiting was aggravating her. It was almost as if the other player was deliberately attempting to affect her game, and then to make matters worse, the player causing the slow play couldn't miss a putt, and Chrissy couldn't make one. By the end of the front nine, Chrissy was one over par, and steaming.

"Calm down, sis," Bobby told her.

"You calm down, damn it," Chrissy replied, miffed that Bobby wasn't being more supportive. "She should be on the clock, not the whole threesome. What's the matter with the officials today?"

"It is what it is, sis. You need to slow your pace, and not let her bother you."

"Slow my pace? We are on the damn clock here. How can I slow my pace?" Chrissy said as she glared at her brother. It wasn't the first time they had had words on the course, but what Chrissy perceived as sass from her caddy, was not very well received on this highly anticipated day. It was pretty close to heresy in her mind. Very often, the players get wired with tension over the game, hay wired actually, and of course, it is always the caddie's fault.

"Geez Chrissy, calm down will you. Getting upset won't help anything. I'm on your side here, I'm just trying to be helpful." Is it the full moon? Is her period starting? Did this guy Steve's coming have her amped up? Bobby was doing his best to interpret the mood of his golfer. At this rate, he was pretty sure things weren't going to get any better by the end of the round if she continued to lose her composure.

"Just shut up and carry the bag, will you please. We can talk about this later." Chrissy was obviously frustrated. And she was even more aggravated because this was the damn Chambers Tournament, and things were not supposed to be like this.

"Yeah well, just make a few putts, will you?" Bobby snapped back, turned, shouldered Chrissy's bag, and trudged off to the tenth tee box.

Unfortunately, the second nine didn't go much better. Chrissy did make one birdie, and got back to even par for the day. But by the time she was off of the course, and into to the locker room, she was exasperated, cranky, and near tears. Bobby knew enough to keep his distance, and leave her well enough alone.

"Will you please leave my clubs at the putting green?" She asked/commanded her little brother.

"Sure thing. See you tomorrow." With that, he left to join his caddy brethren, glad to be away from his bitchy sister. There was a party tonight, there always seemed to be a party somewhere, and it would be a pleasant change of scenery for him.

Vincent and Tommy watched Chrissy come off of the course and head to the scorer's tent. They saw Bobby tote her clubs to the practice green, and figured she would want to work on something after an even par round. She still had her game face on, so not too many people could tell she was upset, but it was pretty apparent to her parents who had followed her for eighteen holes. Her mom wanted to talk her back down, but unfortunately, after the scorer's tent, Chrissy had to go to the bathroom, and then there was always the throng of adoring fans to stop and sign autographs for. Being alone and hitting balls or working on her putting stroke was all she wanted to do right now. She didn't want to talk to anyone.

So, Ginny Jensen waited patiently until her daughter had fulfilled her obligations, and they were able to chat for a few minutes over the fence that separates the public from the practice putting green.

"You okay, Hon?"

"Yeah, Mom. I kinda lost it out there today. I just need to be alone for a while, and work on my putting."

"You want to talk about anything?"

"Nope. I'm okay. I need a little time here by myself is all."

"Well then, we will wait for you over there by the bleachers, and we can ride home together. Will and dad are going to meet us at the house, and I don't know where Bobby went."

"We?"

"So, Elaine and Trisha are looking around in the pro shop, and they are going to hang out with me, if that's okay with you."

"Whatever Mom. I just want to be alone right now."

"Sure baby. Take all the time you need."

An hour and a half later, Ginny wasn't sure she had made the right call, but Chrissy was wrapping things up, and the four women finally headed for the player's parking lot and the black Cherokee.

Vincent and Tommy were sitting patiently in their Town Car when the threesome of women and Chrissy showed up.

"Oh man," Tommy blurted. "Good thing we weren't going to do any snatching today, eh?"

"Yeah. If this is the case every day, we can just fuhgeddaboudit."

"Well, we'll see what happens tomorrow."

CHAPTER TWENTY

Chrissy and the ladies made it home in due time. The caterers were getting ready to set out dinner, and the rest of the family was gathered and enjoying a subdued cocktail hour. Chrissy helped herself to a glass of Chardonnay, and sat down with everyone for some conversation. The chit chat and the glass of wine would surely help to get her mind off of her frustrations, and after that, she would have some dinner, probably go for a walk, talk to Steve and retire early.

"Where's Bobby?" Aunt Elaine asked. "We are almost ready to eat."

"I dunno, let me text him," Will replied.

A minute later Bobby returned Will's text, and announced that he would be out for the evening. That annoyed Chrissy even more. The little roofer can't even be home for dinner when our whole family is here from all over the place, she thought.

Dinner was good. It wasn't Ginny's home cooking good, but was edible none the less. Tomorrow was the semi big party anyway, what with Bob grilling up steaks and getting the good wine out. After dinner, the ladies went for a walk around the neighborhood, and that picked up Chrissy spirits quite a bit.

How annoying was that stupid girl today, was the general consensus? And don't get us started on the officiating either. "It wasn't a great start, but I am only five strokes off of the lead. There are still three days of golf to be played. A lot can happen." As all of the walking women were amateur club golfers, they easily identified with her situation, and began to share stories of some of the annoying players they had gotten stuck with over the years.

"You'll come back strong tomorrow, Chrissy," they agreed. "Five strokes really aren't insurmountable. Look at Pelican Hill, you killed it there."

"Yeah, but that doesn't happen all of the time. You guys know that."

"So, tell us about your friend who is coming on Saturday."

And then Chrissy was able to yak about something much more pleasant than her bothersome golf round. The ladies walked for an hour, enjoyed another Maxfield Parrish evening, and were excited to hear about Steve Reed. They were all so happy and proud to be sharing this special family moment together.

The Infinity Lounge was rocking. It is a landmark south Puget Sound nightclub up in Southcenter, and Thursday nights they host the big weekly Lip Sync contest. This is where young people gather in costume to mime their favorite musicians, get tipsy, let off some steam, maybe win a prize, possibly get laid, and be able to go to work on Friday with a pretty good hangover and a few stories to tell. This Thursday was no different, if anything, it was made more rowdy by the group of about twenty caddies from the big golf tournament in town. They say golf tournaments are a great stimulus to the local economies, and twenty thirsty caddies certainly were stimulating beverage sales in the Infinity Lounge.

Bobby borrowed a cowboy hat from a young woman nearby, went up on stage and sang along with Hank Williams Jr. *on There's a tear in my Beer.* He finished his number to a rousing ovation, came down from the stage and rejoined his new lady friend. They danced and laughed and made a night of it. Actually, they literally did make a night of it, but not before Bobby made her promise to drive him to Chambers Bay Golf Course first thing in the morning.

Of course, the young, first time lovers overslept, and Bobby had to text Will that he was running a little late, but on his way to the course. When Chrissy got this update, she was furious, and was even madder when he finally met her two hours later on the putting green, blamed his absence on traffic, smelled like a distillery, and was wearing the same rumpled clothes under his caddy bib as yesterday. Fortunately, her clubs had been in the Cherokee, and Will had brought them to the range for her. She was about ready to ask him to carry her bag for the day, but he was off somewhere talking business with someone. Chrissy glared at Bobby, and continued putting.

Sensitive young man that he was, Bobby knew how annoyed she was, and tried to apologize. To no avail. He was on thin ice, and Chrissy, who was a structured, routine oriented professional was again, through no fault of her own, off on the wrong foot. Fortunately, the always resourceful Ginny Jensen had brought along a change of clothes for Bobby. But by the time he got back into the caddie's locker room, cleaned up, and changed clothes, he didn't have time to do his usual prep work, and this made Chrissy spitting mad. That little nitwit is done, she fumed. This is it. I will not tolerate this kind of behavior, brother or no brother. I bend over backwards to take care of him, he knows how big this tournament is to me, and he pulls this kind of a stunt. How dare he?

As they were five strokes back, their tee time was earlier today, and at eleven ten Chrissy prepared to tee off. At least she was happy to be playing with her good friend Paula. She was greeted warmly by the legend of Seattle golf, Mr. Freddie Carson, and at her introduction, the crowd gave Chrissy a boisterous welcome. The extended Jensen clan cheered wildly, and Bobby stood glumly with his eyes focused downward, intently studying the grain of the tee box turf.

Chrissy again striped her ball down the center of the fairway, and they were all off. She intentionally walked faster than usual, just to make Bobby work harder than he normally would have. But she realized she had to let her frustration go, and get her head into the game.

A lot of times, that is easier said than done on the golf course, and again Chrissy and Bobby struggled on the front side. She was one under, and was putting better. Unfortunately, since Bobby hadn't studied the pin sheet that morning, neither of them were quite certain of the exact flag placements, and therefore Chrissy wasn't sticking the ball as closely as she could have to score well. Not that she was inclined to take any of his suggestions anyway. This created more frustration and friction on the team, which caused her to swing harder. Well, this will always affect one's natural rhythm, and so more vexation arose. She was near tears at the end of the first nine, when Bobby sidled up to her.

"Listen Sis, I know I screwed up. But you are hitting the ball really well, and Paula's caddy is going to help me out with the pins, so we can get through this. Let's just concentrate here, and if you want Will to finish up the tournament on the loop for you, I understand. But if you give me another chance, I won't ever mess up again, I promise."

"The whole family is here Bobby. How could you do something like this?"

"I know this is a special week for you, Chrissy, and I can't change anything now so let's just go play golf. For your sake, let's don't make it any worse than it already is." Right then, a pretty girl in a cowgirl hat wiggled her way up to the ropes, and called out a friendly hello to Bobby Jensen.

Chrissy sighed, shook her head in annoyance, and rolled her eyes. She looked past the cowgirl hat, and up at the crowd surrounding the tenth tee box, where she saw her older brother Will. He seemed to be escorting one of the female Golf Channel commentators around, and was obviously amused and enchanted by her company. He was laughing merrily, while hovering over this attractive young woman, and seemed completely absorbed. With everything but my game, Chrissy thought. What a team I've got behind me. The hell with it, Bobby's gone right after today's round, and none of these negative thoughts are conducive to making birdies. So, let it go.

The back nine was better. Chrissy started scoring again, and made four birdies. That made her five under par for the tournament. But she was still six strokes back as the leaders were now at eleven under. But I know I can catch them, she thought.

"Bobby, will you please take my clubs to the driving range for me?"

"Sure, Sis. Anything else you need?"

"I just want to be left alone to hit some balls. Can you please find Will and get the Jeep keys and bring them to the range? Also tell mom and dad, I will be home later on, and please don't wait dinner for me. Will can probably get a ride back to the house from his new friend. And when I get home, you and me need to have a serious chat."

"Okay."

Chrissy submitted her score, went into the women's locker room to freshen up, and went back outside to wade through her fans. She signed autographs for forty minutes and then headed for the driving range. "Well, I guess the day wasn't a total loss," she thought. "We were four under on the back nine, which is a heck of a lot better than yesterday. Maybe I am being too hard on Bobby. He is just a damn kid, after all."

When Chrissy finally got back to the driving range, the crowds had thinned somewhat. The car keys were sitting on top of her golf bag with a Hershey's chocolate kiss Bobby had gotten from somewhere. Probably from his new girlfriend. That boy can't resist something pretty in a short skirt and cowgirl boots, but he is still in the damn doghouse. She tucked the keys into one of the zippered compartments of her golf bag, threw the chocolate kiss in the trash, put her cell phone in the compartment on the other side of the big bag, took out a five iron, and started hitting some balls. This is where she was at her best. Her mind would clear, and hitting balls was certainly relaxing, but it also served to ease a lot of her frustrations. Whack, she hit her first practice ball. Bobby would be at his loving best tomorrow after his screw up today, and they would close some ground. Everyone else was taken care of. Bob and Ginny were back at the house, preparing to entertain friends and family. Will was occupied, Bobby would have Ubered home by now and would be sleeping it off. Whack, another one. And Steve was coming in tomorrow. She would stay on the range for another hour, then head home, slip in and sneak upstairs. She didn't feel like being part of the crowd tonight. Maybe she would stream up *The Greatest Game Ever Played* and watch it again, alone in her room. In the meantime, whack, whack, whack.

Chrissy's threesome had finished their round at three thirty. By the time she was done with her obligations and got to the driving range, it was almost five. She would hit balls for another hour or so, and call it a day. The leaders were well in and off of the course by now, and there was only a fraction of the day's crowds left as this LPGA Friday wound down to dinner time.

The hour turned into an hour and a half, as Chrissy was deep in thought as to what she needed to do tomorrow in order to get herself back into contention. She hit a wide variety of clubs. Simulating each hole, and mentally scoring herself. Her efforts seemed to please her, and she decided to hit a dozen more balls with her driver before calling it a day. She wanted to wrap things up with a completely positive feeling as she departed the course for home.

Finishing her practice routine, she tucked the oversized head cover over her favorite club, put her sticks all back in the bag, pulled out the car keys, hoisted her bag, and headed for home. She was tired, not so much from her normal activities, but from all of the drama and emotional baggage of the day.   No more of this crap, she thought to herself. If I can catch up, and win the Tournament, Bobby will survive. But if we are too far behind, and I don't pull it out, then he is gone.

CHAPTER TWENTY-ONE

Chrissy caught the shuttle from the driving range back up to the main clubhouse, her mind still deep in thought, and began her walk out to the players parking lot. She crossed around the back-terrace veranda of the clubhouse that faced the setting sun and the golf course, and couldn't help but observe how much the small crowd of remaining revelers were enjoying themselves. How nice it must be to just be able to drop in, and have a cold, refreshing beverage whenever you wanted she thought. Of course, there was no way that was going to happen for her today. So, she smiled to herself, and kept on going. She would get home, have an early dinner, have a serious sit down with Bobby, and be ready for tomorrow.

"Here she comes," Tommy said. He had the best viewpoint from the driver's side of the of the town car. Vincent was sitting directly behind Tommy, and was wearing an oversized hoodie, dark sunglasses, and a New York Yankees baseball cap pulled low. The parking lot was virtually empty, and the attendant and admin personnel were all long gone. The players assistance golf cart was locked up for the night, and the boys couldn't have hoped for a better set up.

"Be sure and pull past her car, so I have room to open my door once we are by the rear end of her Jeep. You have your door open and you are outside too. Just in case."

"I know man, we have gone over this a thousand times." Tommy was annoyed by Vincent's incessant redundancy. It was obvious that he was the ops guy, and Vincent wasn't.

But for all of the T's experience, both of their adrenaline pumps were pounding like four-barrel carburetors. Vincent was happy to be onto something big. Sex, crime, danger, whatever. Although he was a little nervous, it had been a long time since there had been this much excitement in his middle-aged life, and he was loving it.

Chrissy, more so than usual when she came off of the course after a round, was in her own oblivious world. She was trying to finish mentally digesting this frustrating day, when she saw her black SUV, and clicked the unlock button on the vehicle's key fob. She walked around to the back of the car, and laid her clubs gently on the ground. She was glad the lot was almost empty, and no one was there to pester her for an autograph or want to make some idle, inane blather. She opened the back-hatch door, and tossed the keys on the cargo deck, and as she retrieved her clubs to stow them away, she noticed another vehicle in her peripheral vision.

Now, she became quite aware of the other automobile as she set her clubs in the back-storage compartment of the SUV, and a black town car edged in right behind her. It was angled so that Chrissy was blocked in behind her Cherokee on the left, and when the doors of the black car opened, she would be boxed in on her right. It pulled by until they were adjacent to her, when it stopped rather abruptly, and both doors opened simultaneously.

Chrissy half turned to see who was there, wondering why her space was being invaded like this. She thought it might be Will and his commentator friend, when a shortish man with a hoodie pulled down around his head, wearing large, ugly sun glasses, jumped out of the back seat and pointed a gun at her stomach. She blinked with surprise. Back in Yakima or anywhere else she knew of you didn't just go around pointing guns at people.

"Get in the car," the little man said to her. She didn't even notice that there was a bigger guy standing behind her.

Chrissy blinked, and stared numbly at the guy. WTF, she thought, they have me mistaken for someone else.

"Get in the goddamn car, sister," the unpleasant man snapped at her again.

Chrissy's mind couldn't process what was happening, she was still half in and half out of her own world. They have me confused with someone else she thought again. Then she heard her voice say "Hey, I'm Chrissy Jensen, I'm playing in the tournament here tomorrow." She continued to stare vacantly at the guy in the hoodie. He was becoming agitated.

"No, you ain't, and don't make me use this," he said, and jabbed her in the rib cage with the barrel of his pistol. "Get in the damn car, now."

"Ow, that hurt. I'm not getting in your car, you asshole. Get the hell away from me." Chrissy was now fully focused, getting very angry, and took a step backwards. While the pistol pointed at her was an eminent threat, she remained convinced that this was all a terrible mistake. She was at least as tall as the man with the hoodie, and somehow, she didn't feel physically threatened by him. She stood her ground, and repeated "I am playing in this tournament tomorrow, will you please leave me alone." Why don't they get it? she wondered, and started to reach for her keys. She knew she needed to get out of there.

"Sorry, honey" she heard a voice say, when Tommy Thurston stepped up close behind her, grabbed her ponytail in his left hand, jerked her head back and placed what felt like a razor-sharp knife to her throat. "Get your fucking ass in the car now, or I will kill you. I will cut your throat." Chrissy knew instantly that this was real, very real, and she was in trouble. Big trouble. She felt herself being pushed forward and into the back of the town car. Now it was surreal to her. Like it was definitely happening, but to someone else. Here she was however, being thrown around like a rag doll by a couple of complete strangers.

"Get your ass onna floor, and keep your mouth shut," the mean sounding voice said to her.

The first guy jumped into the car after her, and awkwardly finished pushing her down between the two car seats. A blanket was thrown over her, and she heard the back hatch of the Cherokee close. Are my golf clubs safe? she instinctively thought.

Once Chrissy was in the car, it was a done deal, and it had all happened just that quickly. No one could possibly see anything because of the heavily tinted windows. She felt hoodie man's feet.

One on the small of her back, and the other one on the back of her lower thighs, and felt the pistol again. This time it felt very real, and very threatening. She was furious and terrified, but wise enough to remain calm. The gun was pointed firmly at the base of her skull, and when the car started to move out, the barrel of the gun smacked into the back of her head.

"Don't move, and shut it, and youse won't get hurt," Vincent told her.

She could feel and hear the car start to drive away, and listened while the man in the back seat said to someone that they were on their way. Vincent made his call while Tommy scanned the parking lot and their immediate surroundings carefully as they began to proceed.

"Coast looks all clear."

"Good, let's get the hell outta of here."

It takes about half an hour to drive from the Chambers Bay Golf Complex in Olympic Place to Gig Harbor during peak traffic hours, and it took Chrissy about fifteen minutes of that travel time to get her breathing and emotions back under control. Rather than be overwhelmed with fear, she remained angry. How dare these bastards? And, because of her enmity, her collegiate behavioral science background kicked into gear. Her first reaction was mindfulness.

Instinctively, she knew she needed to absorb anything and everything possibly to help herself as much as she could. Start by recalling and filing the most detailed physical descriptions of her assailants, and put them in the memory vault, she told herself. The little guy with the hoodie and the ugly, cheap aviators, the Yankee ballcap, the black town car, the time of day, how long this ride was going to last. She was already analyzing and assessing.

They are not robbing me she knew, because they had left her golf clubs behind, and not demanded any other physical property or money. It wasn't a case of mistaken identity, because she had made pretty damn clear to the two men who she was. There hadn't been any sexual advances at her so far, and the two men didn't seem like terrorists, therefore, she assumed that she was being kidnapped for ransom. She prayed for that to be her situation. If she was being abducted for ransom, she would probably be okay for the short term, as it is pretty hard to ransom a dead person, and so she must find a way to resist. And she must stay strong.

She told herself to assume the persona of a helpless female, let them think she was scared and vulnerable. Weak. Pretend to be clueless and overwhelmed, and in the meantime, use her brains and her physical strength to reverse the field, so to speak, and attack her attackers. She felt like she was in superior condition physically to overpower either of her captors if they were weaponless, especially the smaller of the two men. He had seemed hesitant and unsure of how to get her into the car, even as he held a gun to her stomach. The driver, she wasn't sure about. She could feel he was bigger, stronger, meaner, and more decisive than his partner. More dangerous. Only time would tell, but she needed to be ready should any opportunity present itself.

The T made his way east from Carr Inlet to Bridgeport Way, turned left and headed north toward the Tacoma Narrows Bridge and Highway Sixteen. He encountered no problems other than the normal city traffic congestion, and their passenger was cooperating nicely. She sounded like she was crying under her blanket, and Tommy mentally condemned her for being just another fragile female.

Reaching the highway access, Tommy turned left and continued north towards the westbound Narrows Bridge. The town car was headed for the older of the two twin suspension bridges that span the waterways between mainland Tacoma, and the Olympic Peninsula. One supporting traffic that ran to the west, and the newer edition's traffic which runs to the east. The older of the two bridges had replaced what was known as Galloping Gertie, the original bridge over the Narrows passage.

Galloping Gertie had been aptly nicknamed by locals, and was opened to the public on July 1st, 1940. It was designed by an internationally respected bridge architect, one Leon Moisseiff, who hailed from New York City. He had been involved in the construction of other significant bridge projects such as the Manhattan Bridge over the East River, the Benjamin Franklin Bridge across the Delaware River, and San Francisco's Golden Gate Bridge. But this particular bridge, unfortunately, was built on the cheap, was woefully under supported, and quickly gained her quirky nickname, as it would oscillate by two or three feet in the mildest of winds. Pictures of Gertie flailing wildly on the day of the severe windstorm that created her demise, are still circulated in engineering classes, and are a textbook case of aerodynamic-aeroelastic design failure.

On the ill-fated morning of November 7, 1940, a mere four months and one week after her public service debut, strong winds howled throughout the region, and Gertie began to convulse spastically. Prudent travelers opted to wait the storm out rather than attempt a crossing, and later in the day the bridge could not withstand the aggressive gusts, and collapsed into South Puget Sound. Fortunately, there was no loss of human life, the only casualty being a mixed breed, three-legged dog named Tubby.

Seven years later in 1947 a new bridge commission was convened, resulting in the construction of the bridge that Tommy and Vincent were now planning to cross. The west bound bridge suited their needs perfectly, as the newer east bound span was a toll bridge, and had cameras mounted across all five lanes of traffic. The older west bound unit charged no tolls, welcomed all comers, was clean of any photo or video cams, and the boys sailed across Puget Sound actually admiring the setting sun, and the placid waterways as they transported their human cargo to the safehouse.

Tommy exited Highway 16 at Wollochet Drive, continued driving slowly north through the picturesque little, waterfront town of Gig Harbor, around the far end of the bay and on toward their destination. They rolled onto the eastside (of the harbor) property, where Sammy and Leroy, as instructed, had the lights out and the garage door open. Tommy eased the town car into the first space on the left, and Sammy pushed close on the double door remote control.

When it was down, Vincent took the blanket and draped it over Chrissy's head. "Sit up," he growled.

Chrissy turned over, and sat up as best she could in the constrained space. She was stiff, could only see downward with the blanket covering her head and upper body, and felt a rough hand grab her left arm and drag her up onto the back seat. They are right-handed she thought, as she continued to be pulled out of the car, and led through what must be a garage, and up a short staircase and into a house. She felt Vincent's pistol pressed against her back as she was led into the house. She could see the flooring as she looked under the blanket, and noted that it was of a good quality, custom wood installation. Therefore, the house must be fairly new and somewhat substantial. She began to whimper for the sake of effect, and Vincent told her to shut up. Isn't he a real tough guy? she thought.

The hand on her arm continued to lead her into the house, and she finally was pushed through a doorway, and told to descend a flight of stairs. There were fourteen steps. Once down the stairs, she was led across the room. The hand turned her around, and pushed her down onto what seemed like a low bed, and into a sitting position.

"This is your new home," Vincent told her. "You will be staying here wid us for a while. If youse cooperate, and don't cause no trouble, nothin' is gonna happen to youse. If you try anything, we will chain you to dis bed, and your life won't be so good. You unnerstand me?"

Chrissy whimpered, and shook her head yes. He sounds very Italian she thought.

"Florence here is gonna take care of you, she will feed you twice a day, at ten in the morning, and five or six at night. When you hear a knock on the door, you come ova here to dis bed and sit down, with your head and eyes lookin' at the floor. You get me?"

Chrissy shook her head yes again. "Where am I?" she tearfully asked.

"Shut up," was her answer.

"We will bring you down some food tonight. You got any more questions?"

Crissy shook her head no. "Stand up then, so we can frisk you."

Monica reached up under the blanket and patted Chrissy down thoroughly. "No phone boss, no car keys. Just some golf tees," she heard a woman say.

"Take 'em," she heard the little man say, and just like that, they were all gone. She thought there were four of them in all.

It was getting on to eight o'clock, and Vincent was ready to depart. Tommy was long gone. Actually, he hadn't even entered the safe house. He still had on his fake mustache and his chauffer's cap hat, and as soon as Chrissy was out of the town car, he trudged across the driveway to where he had parked his own car earlier and took off. He decided that rather than returning to the mainland via the Tacoma Narrows Bridge with all of her cameras, he would drive the twenty minutes north to Southworth, and take the Washington State Ferry back over to Fauntleroy in West Seattle. It was only another twenty-minute drive from there to his place down in Normandy Park. He would return as arranged to pick up the town car in three or four days when the proverbial waters had calmed down.

Tommy felt like everything had gone reasonably well, other than Vincent struggling to get golfer girl into the town car, and he knew it had been a veteran move to bring his blade along. That had certainly gotten her attention. As he pulled out of the Gig Harbor driveway and headed for Highway 16, he was about as sure as one could ever be under these circumstances that things had gone well. Now he needed to get back to Normandy Park and his awaiting girlfriend. He tuned into Sirius Satellite Radio, where the channel 60 Outlaw Country station automatically came on, and headed north.

"Youse need anything else?" Vincent inquired in his pidgin Italian accent. He had grown up on the west coast, and was an American citizen through and through, but he still enjoyed lapsing into gangster talk whenever it seemed fitting, or necessary to impress.

Back upstairs, Stuart said, "I think we got it here, Jack. I am taking the night shift like you said, and Florence already has her food ready. If anything comes up, I will call you. How did everything go anyway?"

Leroy simply grunted.

"It went just fine, kid. Tommy drove, I made the snatch, and here we are. You call me if you need anything, eh? I gotta go."

Vinnie checked to make sure the garage was locked up tight, and walked over next to where Tommy had parked and also took off. Like Tommy, he was convinced that things had gone well. It wasn't his fault that the stupid girl had frozen up on him. He wasn't sure why Tommy had got himself all nervous and stepped in like that, just when he was going to use stronger measures.

He pulled out onto East Shoreline Drive and headed his Cadillac Escalade back for the bridge. While he was driving to the highway, he tuned his car radio in to 710 AM, and the Seattle Mariners baseball game.

Chrissy waited a couple of minutes to be sure everyone was gone, pulled the blanket off of her, and looked around. The basement room she had been transported to was sparsely furnished, but it was not totally unpleasant. It was carpeted with the kind of indoor/outdoor floor covering you would find in a rec room. There was a beanbag on the floor in the middle of her new quarters, and the single bed she was sitting on. Three or four magazines and a couple of paperback books were scattered around by the beanbag, and there were two overhead light fixtures appropriately spaced in the middle of the ceiling, making the room a little dim around the corners. The walls were all wood paneled. It appeared as if there was a bathroom cattycorner from where she was sitting.

She got up and went over to take a look, and had just washed and dried her face, when she heard a knock on the door. She splashed some water back into her eyes for effect, returned to the bed, and sat down, with her head and eyes averted to the floor.

Chrissy heard someone fumbling with the door locks. It was the Florence person, who opened the door, and stepped onto the landing of the staircase with a tray of food. She descended the stairs, while Stuart stayed at the top of the staircase observing the room. She looks about the same as high school, he thought to himself. If anything, a ten-year level of added maturity/worldliness, and a lot more buff looking. Monica crossed over to the bed, and set the food tray down next to Chrissy.

"I am Florence, as in Florence Nightingale, and I will be your caretaker. As long as you don't cause any trouble, we are going to get along fine. If you behave yourself, I will get you whatever you need within reason. There are toiletries, towels, and changes of clothing for you in the bathroom." Chrissy inadvertently looked up and saw the olive-skinned young woman in her niqab.

"Don't look at me, keep your eyes on the floor at all times, or I will blindfold you," the woman told her. She didn't sound Arabic, and Chrissy thought it a strange combination to have an Italian Mafioso older guy, and a young Arabic type woman working together. It made her shuddered to think they might be terrorists, and wanted to blow up Seattle or something even crazier. She had been able to catch a glimpse of Stuart standing on the stairs with a ski mask over his face before she returned her gaze downward.

Florence turned away and walked back across the room. "You need anything else?"

"No," and Chrissy again began to whimper for dramatic effect.

Florence took the stairs two at a time, exited the room, relocked the door, and left Chrissy alone in her new digs. She looked at her tray of food, and saw a big bowl of Mac and Cheese, a green salad, a bottle of water, and several Cliff bars. There was a plastic fork on the tray, and a couple of napkins. The food looked processed, and barely edible. She had been starving to death when she left the course, and now her appetite was completely gone.

She got up, went up the stairway, and quietly inspected the door. It was solid oak, opened in, had a regular lock, and a keyed deadbolt both of which were locked up tight. Trying to turn the door handle proved useless and testing the solidity of the door got her nowhere. She wasn't exactly sure how many people were in the house, but thought she would find out soon enough. It was very quiet in the basement, and she could hear nothing other than some TV noise coming in under the door at medium volume from the house's interior.

Returning to the bed, Chrissy tried to pick at some of the mac and cheese, gave that up, and took a bite of one of the energy bars. That did nothing but make her nauseous. She was in shock, and a lot of her early bravado was beginning to wear off. A real tear slipped from her right eye, and she laid back on the single bed, and cursed her fate. Her eyes eventually got heavy, and she drifted off into a restless, fitful sleep.

CHAPTER TWENTY-TWO

Will's new friend gave him a ride back to the Jensen compound, and he invited her in for a glass of wine. When they made their entry, the party was rolling along.

"Hey, Willie boy," Uncle Calvin greeted him. "What can I get for you?"

"Just a beer for me, unk, what would you like Tina?"

"Glass of chardonnay would be great, thank you."

"You are in luck, girl. We've got some Abeja in the house tonight."

"He loves Abeja," Will whispered in Tina's ear. "Thinks it's the best white wine in Washington."

"Well, let's have a taste." Tina was from San Francisco, and knew her chardonnays.

Will and Tina grabbed their drinks, and eased on into the house which faced to the west. They continued on, and joined the majority of the family who were out on the front deck in the evening sunlight. Will wanted to stop by the kitchen and say hi to his mom, then go see how papa Bob was doing at manning the grill. You could smell the delicious aroma of the sizzling steaks all over the neighborhood.

"Come on, I will introduce you to my parents on our first date," Will said kiddingly.

"You must really want to marry me," Tina joked back at him.

They sipped their beverages, courtesy of Uncle Cal, and began to mingle. Ginny Jensen was out on the front deck near Bob, chatting and cocktailing when they found her.

"Hi Mom, this my friend Tina. How you doin'?"

"Good honey. Hi Tina, so nice to meet you. Welcome to the party. Are you from Seattle?"

"Thank you, no I'm actually from San Francisco, but I work for the Golf Channel, so I travel all over the country."

"How interesting. That would have been my dream job when I was your age. Except, there wasn't any golf channel then."

"Yeah, it's a great job, I love it. So, you must play then."

"Oh yes. Chrissy and I have been playing together since she was about eight. We live in Yakima, and are members at Yakima Valley Country Club."

"Wonderful. I hope we can tee it up sometime. And good luck to Chrissy by the way. She looked like she was starting to make a run on the back nine today."

"Yes, she struggled some yesterday, got a little frustrated at the pace of play, but today was better. Speak of the devil, where is your sister, Will? Have you seen her?"

"No, mom. Not yet. Bobby came and got the car keys from me, and said she wanted to stay and hit some balls and be alone. That usually takes a couple of hours, so she should be here pretty soon."

Will and Tina continued to mingle. Will whispered in Tina's ear, off the record of course, that Chrissy was miffed at her little brother/caddie today. He related how Bobby had stayed out all night partying Thursday night, and was late to the course on Friday morning.

"When she gets annoyed, all she wants to do is hit golf balls."

"Those darn caddies," Tina replied. "Her secret is safe with me." But she still filed this tidbit in the back of her mind, in the tour gossip file. It might come in handy when/if Chrissy decided to change her looper.

"Hi Dad. I'd like you to meet Tina Borenson."

"Hello Tina, nice to meet you. Haven't I seen you from time to time on the Golf Channel?"

"So nice to meet you, Mr. Jensen. Yep, that's me, I am a backup commentator, and do all of the stat work for our producers, announcers and color people. Looks like you are doing a bang-up job on the grill there."

"Yeah, I'm almost done. Hope you can join us for dinner. These are prime, grass fed steaks from my buddy's Yakima ranch. He raises certified Angus beef, and they are melt in your mouth tender and delicious."

"Sounds too good to pass up, Mr. Jensen."

"Good, you stay then. And please call me Bob."

"Dad, you are too modest. I heard it is actually the grill master that makes the steaks melt in your mouth."

"Well, if you must know, it is probably a combination of the two. Just don't let Tim Traynor hear you say that." He winked at Tina, and took a sip of his red wine. Other people were crowding up to the BBQ, as of course, everyone wants to sniff around the grill, and if you are lucky, you might get a tidbit to taste. So, Will and Tina walked over to the edge of the large deck, and gazed out at the high bank view to the west.

"It's a beautiful evening, isn't it?" Will observed. "Chrissy actually went to the University of Washington, so she was very excited to be back in Seattle in July for this Tournament."

"It really is. The whole area just glows when it is nice. This is definitely one of the best places in the country this time of the year. Besides, I know exactly where your sister went to school, I am the stat lady, remember? Hey, I even know you went to Washington State University on a basketball scholarship, studied Computer Sciences and Business Management, and are Chrissy's Agent/Manager."

Before Will could reply, Trish and Alan Snapp stopped by to say hi, and then one of the caterers was ringing the chimes to announce that the dinner buffet was now open for business.

Ginny Jensen approached Will and Tina. "Honey, will you please call Chrissy, and see where she is. I hope she can join us, even for a little bit."

"Sure Mom." Will autodialed Chrissy, and got no answer. "Why don't people leave their dang phones on?" he asked Tina.

"Just text her. No one answers their phone anymore."

Bobby, refreshed from his two-hour snooze, joined the crowd, cracked a Pepsi, and rolled into the back of the buffet line.

"Have you heard from Chrissy?" his mom asked.

"No mom, I left her at the golf course three hours ago, she wanted to hit balls, and she had the keys to the Cherokee. And thanks for the change of clothes today. You saved my backside."

Ginny frowned at her youngest son, and shook her head, "We can talk about it later, and don't do something like that again." Bobby knew she was not happy with him either, it didn't take a psychic to figure that out. Damnit, I'm gonna be in the doghouse for a while, he thought.

The dinner party droned on. Bob's steaks were as tender and savory as advertised, and everyone was enjoying the excitement of the next two days of the tournament, as well as the ambience of the meal, and the excellent Washington wines shared with family and friends. There were almost forty of Yakima's finest at the gathering.

Ginny Jensen didn't expect Chrissy to hang with them throughout the evening, but it would certainly be nice if she could at least show her face, and say hello. By now it was well after eight, and Ginny slipped away, and trudged up the stairs to check Chrissy's room and see if she had somehow gotten up there without anyone seeing her. That was highly improbable, but it was worth trying.

Chrissy's room was empty, untouched since her morning departure. "Something is not right here," Ginny thought, and went back down to find Will and have him track Chrissy down.

"Will, I am a little worried about Chrissy. She's not home yet. Isn't it unusual for her to be out this late on a tournament night, especially with so many friends and family around?"

"I called and texted her mom, I don't know what else I can do."

"Well, it's going on nine, and I am getting concerned."

"It is a little unusual. I don't know why she wouldn't be home by now. I think she might have been a little upset today when she came off of the course."

"I know she was, and with good reason."

"If she isn't home by ten, I will think something is wrong," Ginny said.

"We can take my car and go back over to the course if you want to Will. It's only ten minutes away," Tina offered.

"Would you mind, honey?" Ginny asked.

Bob Jensen, sensing some discord, edged over to his wife and son. "Where is Chrissy anyway?" he wondered aloud.

"That's what we were just talking about," Ginny replied. "I am worried about her, and Will and Tina are going to run back over to Chambers Bay and see if she is still around."

"Good idea. Do you want me to come with you?"

"No, we can handle it Dad, you stay here with your guests. I will call from the course if we find out anything, Mom."

Will and Tina pulled away from the compound in Tina's rental sedan.

"This is not at all like Chrissy," Will said.

Arriving at the course, they found it largely deserted in the lingering twilight. Tina drove by the clubhouse, and the lights were all off. Even the bar had been shut down.

"Try the players parking lot," Will suggested.

Tina took a right and drove two hundred yards over to the lot. The first thing Will saw was their car sitting exactly where he had parked it that morning.

"What the heck," he said. "Pull over there, will you?" and pointed. No need, it was the only vehicle left in the lot.

Will got out, and approached the Cherokee. He walked around the vehicle, and looked in the driver's seat area. It was undisturbed. Next, he checked the storage compartment behind the rear seat, and noticed Chrissy's clubs. He tested the hatch handle, and surprisingly, it opened. He looked at Chrissy's bag, and saw her cell phone tucked into the outer mesh side pocket. He took it out, looked at it, and turned the phone on. He saw his incoming call and text of an hour ago still on the home screen. Tina got out of her driver's seat and came up behind him.

"Something is wrong here. She would never leave her clubs in an unlocked car, and she would never leave her phone behind. Now I am concerned too."

"Look, the keys for the car are right there. What do you want to do?"

"I think we better go back to the house, and start a phone chain. See if anyone has seen her."

"Let's go."

Will reached in and retrieved Chrissy's cell phone, looked around to see if anything else was disturbed, and lowered the hatch back down.

"Better leave everything alone," Tina advised. "Just in case we have to call the cops."

Tina's comment stunned Will. Calling the cops on Chrissy's behalf was about the last thing he thought he might be doing that night.

CHAPTER TWENTY-THREE

Vincent arrived home in forty minutes, parked in his garage, walked into the kitchen and gave Angela a kiss.

"You're late. I was just about to start dinner without you."

"Sorry, hon. Things ran a little long today. What's for dinner?"

"I threw some leftovers together. They came out pretty good."

"You wanna drink?" Vincent asked.

"No thanks, I already had a glass of wine. Maybe with dinner. How was your day?"

"Quiet. Nothing much going on. Then the one day I can come home early, the delivery guy is late."

"What delivery guy?"

"Just a messenger bringing some paperwork that Ronnie needs for the taxes."

"Someone else couldn't be there? You are spending way too much time at the bar anymore, you know that?"

"Nah, this was certified, coming up from Phoenix, and I had to do the signing."

"Where you want to eat?"

"I just wanna relax and watch the ball game for a bit. Can we eat in the den?" Vincent replied, while he busied himself with the martini shaker. His adrenaline was starting to calm down.

"Whatever you want. I have about a hundred pages to read tonight to be ready for my book club meeting tomorrow afternoon. So, you do your own thing."

Will and Tina hurried back to the compound, and Will grabbed Bobby and hustled him and Tina into the office/computer room of the house.

"Bobby, meet Tina. She is a friend of mine, and works for the Golf Channel. Dude, I think something has happened to Chrissy. Our Jeep Cherokee is right where I parked it this morning, and Chrissy's clubs, cell phone and the car keys were in the back, but the car was unlocked. Her phone was in her golf bag, but she is nowhere to be found. The Clubhouse was all shut down. Do you know anything, or where Chrissy might be?"

"No, man. I took her clubs over to the driving range for her this afternoon when she came off of the course, and she asked me to go get the car keys from you. I took them back, and left them on top of the bag for her and took off. She isn't home yet?"

"No. All is not right here. We need to get on the phone to anyone who might know where she is. I will call Paula, and any of the golfers I can on her cell. You call some of your caddy buddies, see if anyone saw anything. Tina could you possibly call tournament security, or anyone else that might have been around, and see if we can find out anything? Maybe the club manager is still there, and see if he knows something. I am going to tell Mom and Dad that we are on the phones, so they can get rid of everybody out there in case there is a problem. But I don't want Mom to start freaking out."

"Uh, has anyone checked her room? She may just be up there sleeping."

"I'll check, but I think Mom was already up there." Will left the office, and Bobby and Tina got on their phones.

It took Bob and Ginny an hour to get the house cleared out, and by this time it was eleven o'clock. All three of the phone team had called everyone they could think of, with negative results, when Bob, Ginny and Charlie all filed into the office.

"Any luck?" Bob asked. Worried strain was already showing on Ginny's face, and her boys could tell she was on the verge of tears.

Tina went over and put an arm around her shoulders. "Everything is going to be okay, Mrs. Jensen," she said. "Chrissy probably just ran into an old friend or something, and lost track of time."

"Steve Reed couldn't have come into town early, could he?" Bob asked.

"Damn it," Will said, "I'll call him right now." *Why didn't I think of that* he thought?

"Isn't he in Chicago? It's one o'clock in the morning there."

"Doesn't matter, dad."

Will dialed the number, and roused an obviously sleeping Steve Reed.

"Hi Steve, it's Will Jensen, Chrissy's brother. Sorry to call so late, but we were wondering if you had heard anything from Chrissy this afternoon or evening?"

Steve tried to shake the grogginess out of his head, and replied, "No man, I haven't. Is something wrong?"

"We're not sure, but it about eleven o'clock here, and she hasn't come home from the golf course yet. That is just not like her. Plus, we found her phone and golf clubs in our unlocked car back at the course, but no Chrissy anywhere."

"No, that is not like her at all," Steve agreed. "I don't know what to tell you, except if I hear anything, I will call you immediately."

"Thanks. What time are you getting here tomorrow?" Will asked.

"Around noon. Will you be at the course? I was going to go straight there."

"I don't know, depends on what's going on around here."

"I will call you as soon as I get into town. This is weird." *Really weird*, Steve thought.

"I know. I hope she shows up soon."

Will looked at his family. They looked back at him. "I don't know what to say," was his response. Ginny was crying softly, and Tina was holding her left hand, while Bob was on her right side with his arm around her shoulders. My baby girl, my baby girl, kept racing through Ginny's mind.

"Should we call the police?" Charlie asked.

"I don't know," answered Bob.

"Tina, what do you think?" Will asked.

"Gosh Will, I am not a family member, and I can definitely see the concern in this room. So, all I can say is if, or as soon as you call the police, all hell is going to break loose. If you do contact them, I would suggest going down to the station personally, because if you call it in, someone, very possibly the press, will pick it up on a scanner, and then the word will be out. Besides, I think the police will just tell you that she hasn't been missing for at least twenty-four hours, so they can't do anything yet. I am going to go back to my hotel, and let your family have some privacy here. I hope and pray this situation resolves itself quickly."

"Thanks for all of the help, let me walk you out to your car."

"Will," Tina said as they got out to the front of the house, "if it was me, I would wait until first thing in the morning before I called. I didn't want to say that in front of your Mom, but Chrissy is a big girl. I feel sure she'll get back to you as soon as she is able."

"This is just so out of character for her. She was ready to kill her little brother just yesterday for doing this very same thing. This is not the way she rolls."

"Bobby?"

"Yeah, he is her caddy." I know that you big lunk, I'm the damn statistician, she thought.

Tina gave Steve a hug, and told him to "call me first thing in the morning. If she hasn't shown up yet, we can contact the police, and I will deal with all of the LPGA and media stuff. We should call Cynthia Summers and Carmen Ayala. Carmen is local, well connected, and she will certainly know who to contact as far as the cops go. We should probably go for the top people on this thing. No doubt about that."

"Thanks, you are a star." Tina got in, and started her car. She wished she could have stayed.

Will went back into the house office. "You guys want to call in the police now, or wait until morning?"

"Why don't I call Alan Snapp, and ask his advice," Bob suggested. "He's an attorney, and I'm sure he would have some good thoughts. Will, do you or does the LPGA, know anyone in law enforcement who might be of any help?"

"We are working on that dad, but call Alan and see what he has to say. Tina suggested we call the Ops Director and Sponsor's Rep first thing in the morning, if Chrissy isn't home by then. They will put us in contact with the right people. I don't personally know any local cops, but the LPGA office will surely have some contacts. Tina said she would be on top of that first thing, if we need her help."

"I am scared to death," Ginny composed herself enough to tearfully admit. "This is absolutely not like Chrissy. She would no more go out alone until all hours of the night like this, without letting one of us know than she would fly off to the moon. I am convinced something bad has happened, and I think the sooner we get in touch with the authorities the better."

The male Jensen's in the room couldn't totally disagree with Ginny, but when to make their move was the question. All poor Bobby could do was hang his head.

"I think we should wait until the morning," Will finally said. "If we call in about a missing person now, some desk sergeant may or may not file a report. The most he would probably do was call out an APB, and what good would that do with the Cherokee still sitting at Chambers Bay? If she is not home by morning, we can make the right calls, and get the big boys working on it right away. Which reminds me, Bobby, can you go back over to the course, and at least get her clubs out of the car."

"No, no, don't do that Will. As much as I hate to say it, that may be evidence," Charlie interjected.

"Sorry, you are right Charlie."

"I will take another car, and go sleep in it next to the Cherokee," Bobby volunteered. He was thrilled to be getting out of the house.

"Good idea, Bobby. Dad, you better brief the other family members who are here, and then go call Alan Snapp. If Chrissy doesn't show up, we are going to need some help on this thing big time. I am going to try and sleep for a couple of hours, and if she isn't here by dawn, I will get the ball rolling."

"I am going to stay up in Chrissy's room," Ginny told everyone. "Trust me, you will know if she comes home tonight."

"I will sit up with you Ginny," Bob said. Already the aged, grass fed beef and fine red wine in his belly had started to sour.

CHAPTER TWENTY-FOUR

Ginny didn't sleep a wink, and by six in the morning was an exhausted, nervous wreck. She nudged Bob who had dozed off, and went to look for Will. He was sleeping in his room, and Ginny woke him.

"Chrissy didn't come home. Come on, we've got to do something."

"Okay, Mom. Let me get up, and call Tina. Put on some coffee."

Ginny also woke Charlie while she was still upstairs, then went down to brew a pot.

Will called Tina, rousing her from a sound sleep.

"Something is definitely wrong. Chrissy didn't come home all night. This is absolutely not like her."

"Oh, I am so sorry. Let me get up, and I will call Cynthia." Her adrenalin had kicked in as soon as she heard the urgency in Will's voice.

"No, if you could give me her number, I feel like I should make that call. Can you call the other lady, the one from Amazon?"

"Sure Will, it's ....."

Will dialed Cynthia's cell phone, and awoke his second professional woman of the day.

"Good morning Ms. Summers. This is Will Jensen, Chrissy's brother and business manager, I'm so sorry to disturb you." He proceeded to blurt out to her the events of the previous evening. "And she is still not home. We are very worried, and are asking for your help in knowing what would be the proper authorities to contact."

"Oh gosh, Will. This is terrible news."

"Yes, it is. We have a gathering here for the tournament, it's just not like anything Chrissy would do, especially with her mom and dad, all of her extended family, and closest friends here staying with us."

"When was she last seen?"

"She went to the driving range yesterday afternoon after her round, and that's the last any of us have seen or heard from her. Our SUV is still in the parking lot where we left it yesterday morning, and her clubs and car keys are in the back of the car. But no sign of Chrissy."

"Let me call Mac Tenderson and Carmen Ayala, and see what they suggest. I assure you, Will, the full support and resources of the LPGA are at your disposal. Can I call you back at this number?"

"Certainly, Cynthia. We have not contacted the authorities yet, we wanted to talk to you first."

"Yes, I appreciate that Will. I can tell you the Mayor of Tacoma was out here yesterday, and he will certainly know what would be the best path going forward. Carmen will have his number. Let me call you right back."

The wheels had begun to grind. Tina was in touch with Carmen Ayala. Cynthia called Mac. Carmen had contact numbers for the Mayor and Police Chief of Tacoma.

Twelve minutes later, Cynthia called back.

"Hello Will, Cynthia here. I just spoke to Carmen, and she immediately called the Tacoma Chief of Police. He and his Chief of Criminal Investigations would like to meet with us at your SUV in forty-five minutes. I assume it is in the player's parking lot at the course?"

"Yes, it's a black Jeep Cherokee, and it is parked around the middle of the lot. Our younger brother is there securing the vehicle. It was unlocked, so we didn't want to disturb anything inside the car, or have anyone steal something from the vehicle. I haven't spoken to my brother this morning, but I know he is still with the vehicle until he is notified otherwise. I will call him as soon as I get off with you."

"That sounds good. On behalf of the LPGA, I will be there at the meeting with the authorities this morning, as will Carmen Ayala, and Tina Borenson, from the Golf Channel. I believe you know both of those women. So far, the media has not been notified, but as you well know, this will become public knowledge pretty quickly, and then it will become big news. We would like to manage the flow of information as well as possible, but I need to ask, and this is a difficult question. Will, can you give me your complete and 100% solid assurance that you and your family feel Chrissy is missing, and has not been detoured somehow, someway, somewhere in a non-threatening manner? We will pull out all of the stops here, and should Chrissy show up for her tee time today as if nothing had happened, it would create an embarrassing situation for all of us. God help us that the press would get ahold of anything like that."

"Cynthia, I can assure you this is so out of character for Chrissy, we her family, are 100%, no 1000%, fearful of her health and wellbeing. Nothing remotely like this has ever happened with her before. Ever. We are worried sick about it, and it is so unlike her, it could not be a situation created by her own volition."

"Thank you for your reassurances, Will. I know Chrissy personally, and know she is one of the most well respected, hardworking, and grounded members of our tour. We will do our utmost to help get her home, and playing golf again as soon as possible."

"Thanks Cynthia. See you soon. Should the immediate family come along?"

"How many of you are there?"

"Mom and dad, myself, and her brothers, Bobby and Charlie."

"I think that is manageable, but let's keep it as small and low key as we can."

"I agree. My dad might bring our family attorney along, but that would be it."

"Okay, see you in forty-five minutes."

Will hung up, and called Bobby.

"Hey, you awake?"

"Yeah, nothing much going on here. People are starting to dribble in, but no one was around all night."

"We are coming over there in half an hour. I will bring you a cup of coffee. Cynthia Summers from the LPGA will be there, along with the Chief of Police from Tacoma, his Chief Investigator, and a couple of other LPGA admin people."

"Awesome. See you soon, bro."

Chrissy rolled over and stirred. She was still tired and felt groggy. Suddenly she realized where she was, and sat up with a start. Her room had no windows, so she had no idea what time it was. She had no cell phone to help her out. Why hadn't she worn her Lady Rolex yesterday she fumed at herself in hindsight. But then realized it would probably have been stolen or confiscated from her.

She got up, crossed to the bathroom, freshened up, and changed into the warmup suit Florence had left her. Under the circumstances, she felt pretty ridiculous in her cute little Lululemon designer golf outfit.

Her stomach was starting to growl, so she went back and sat down on her bed and ate the other Cliff Bar. That made her feel better. She shook herself, to get rid of the lingering shock of what was happening, and began an attempt at mentally evaluating her situation. She was certain she had been kidnapped for ransom. But, how long will they keep me here, I wonder? How many of them are there? Where is this house? I think I am relatively safe for the time being, but what can I do to protect myself? She looked around her room. There was nothing she could see that might come in handy as a weapon. Chrissy was physically strong, and she had had some martial arts training in Yakima, as her dad had insisted on it before she went off to college in the big city. But without a weapon of some kind, she would have to be extremely careful. Approach any opportunity with great caution. "But I might get a shot, and I will be ready," she said aloud, reinforcing it to herself.

She decided the two priorities she must incorporate, would be to try anything and everything to develop a rapport of any kind with Florence, and to work out as much as possible. The first option might get Florence to lower her guard at some point, and open a door for her, no pun intended. The physical training would help pass the time, and also prep her up for any potential hand to hand confrontations that might arise. She felt, and rightfully so, that her captors wouldn't anticipate her physical strength. But she needed to lay low for a day or two, and let things fall into some kind of pattern. A routine.

After her team meeting with herself, she dropped down on the floor, and began stretching, followed by some pushups. Her mind was still churning, as she worked out, and finally, as her tenth set of twenty pushups was halfway over, she heard the morning knock on her door. Workout in the mornings, yoga in the afternoons, was her final thought as she quickly got up, and sat down of the side of the bed. Her eyes averted to the floor.

Florence walked down the stairs wearing her niqab, and balancing a breakfast tray, while a new guy stood inside the doorway with a ski mask on. Chrissy was already becoming an expert at looking upward with her head pointed downward. This new guy was bigger, much burlier than the last guy.

"Here you go," Flo said as she crossed the room. "Scrambled eggs, ham, toast, and an apple."

"Thank you," Chrissy replied softly. "How long am I going to be down here?" she asked in a fretful voice.

"A couple of years probably, won't that be fun?"

What a smartass, Chrissy thought, as she kept her eyes down, and said nothing. But Monica's comment made her steaming mad. This was supposed to be such a special day: the tournament of her dreams, Steve coming to town, all her family around, back home again in Seattle. Enjoy yourself while you can, little Flojo, you will be spending a lot more than a couple of years in some hell hole jail by the time this thing is all over. And Chrissy began to steel her mind for the challenges that lay ahead.

Tacoma Chief of Police Lawrence Mills rolled into the players parking lot with his Chief Investigator Danny Chong sitting shotgun in his unmarked cruiser. He could have had his aide drive for them, but preferred to project a hands-on persona in a case of this magnitude.

There was already a small group of people gathered when they drove up. Not enough to make the first of the players who were arriving stop and gawk yet, but they were definitely turning some heads. The early golfers continued to file in, and some of them recognized the faces of the LPGA executives who were standing around and wondered what was going on.

"Good morning," Chief Mills offered, and introductions were made all around.

Danny Chong prepared to start taking the crime scene report. He had his tape recorder out, and Will launched into the details of what was now Chrissy's obvious disappearance.

"Has the vehicle been disturbed in any way?" Danny asked. Will responded to the question, and Danny asked his Chief to call for a Forensics Team while he was busy launching his report.

"Has this type of behavior been a previous pattern of the alleged victim?"

"Absolutely not. She is a very successful LPGA golfer, and takes her profession most seriously. She is not a party girl, and she doesn't go out and carouse around. As a matter of fact, her whole family and her close circle of friends are in town for this tournament. She would never, ever disappear like this. We are all very, very concerned," Will related.

"Mr. Jensen, we will release a missing person's report and create a hot line. Perhaps that will produce some input from the public. I need a picture of Chrissy. Our department will launch the investigation, and we will also be in contact with our local FBI team. They have a satellite office here in Tacoma, with the divisional office up in Seattle, but we will maintain jurisdiction in the case. After our initial dossier is completed, we will notify them of our findings, and confer as to any assistance they might be able to provide."

"Thank you, Mr. Chong. We don't care who has jurisdiction in the case, as long as we get my sister back. And of course, you realize, that time is of the essence here. The quicker we can get the ball rolling with your investigation, the better chance we have of bringing her back home."

"Yes sir, we are well aware of that, Mr. Jensen," Chief Mills interjected. "We will do everything in our power to bring your sister back to you safely. I can confirm for you, that as of now, we have very little to go on, pending the forensic inspection of your vehicle. May I ask you Mr. Jensen if it was a habit of hers to stay late and practice like she was apparently doing yesterday?"

"Yes sir, it was. She is somewhat of a workaholic about her golf game as a matter of fact, to the degree that none of us really pay much attention to her comings and goings any more. Both her brother," he pointed over to Bobby, "who is her caddy, and myself were here at the course yesterday. As was her immediate family, who left after Chrissy's round to prepare for a family reunion at our compound later on last night. Just another reason why she would never have stayed out all night, as well as leaving her golf clubs, keys and cell phone in an unlocked car."

"No one has reported seeing her cell phone in the car, Mr. Jensen."

"Oh, that's right. I took her phone home with me last night when we came down here from the house to look for her."

"Who is we, Mr. Jensen?"

"Tina Berenson from the Golf Channel and myself."

"Where was the phone, where is it now, and for what reason did you remove it from the vehicle, Mr. Jensen?"

"When we got here around ten thirty, we found the car where I had parked it yesterday morning. Chrissy's golf clubs, and car keys were in the back-trunk area. Her phone was in one of the side pockets of her golf bag. As we were not one hundred percent sure she was missing at that time, I took her phone with me, so we could use her contact list to check with some of her close friends, and see if anyone might know of her whereabouts. It is back at the house."

"Thank you, Mr. Jensen we are going to secure the crime scene and this vehicle now, and the Forensics Team is on their way. I need everyone to step out of the immediate area, and you need to return the phone to me down at the station. If you and your brother Bobby, could drop by the precinct at your earliest convenience this morning, that will greatly assist in getting our investigation started. I am also going to need a photograph of Ms. Jensen. Please bring one with you when you come in."

"We can come down right after our meeting here is finished, sir. I will need to drop by the house to pick up a publicity photo of Chrissy, and I can also retrieve her phone, and bring it along." This guy is kind of a dick, but he seems to be all business, Will thought. Good cop/bad cop maybe.

"Thank you, everyone," Chief Mills spoke to the assembled crowd. "Here are Inspector Chong's and my business cards with both of our personal cell phone numbers. I will have a staff Information Officer assigned to help us manage our efforts, and be a liaison with the press. If any pertinent information should emerge, don't hesitate to call either of us, at any hour of the day or night. This is an extremely visible case, and I am putting it on our Department's highest priority status. We will interview all of our uniformed personnel who were deployed to these premises yesterday, and I will be in touch with you Ms. Summers so that we may contact your appropriate personnel. In the meantime, I am respectfully asking for all of your patience while we initiate our investigation. These cases can take time, sometimes a consider-able amount of time, and your support and cooperation are greatly appreciated. Any questions? No?" and Chief Mills concluded his closing comments.

With that, the official gathering was over. The Jensen family was now confronted with the reality that their beloved Chrissy had in all probability been abducted, or at the very least was the victim of foul play, and there was very little if anything they could do about it. The LPGA and other related tournament personnel were also critically aware that they had a serious situation on their hands.

Cynthia Summers spoke up. "May I please ask everyone to convene in the clubhouse meeting room for a few minutes, we have a significant amount of issues to discuss and anticipate here."

Will turned to his family, "I can deal with this, if you all just want to go back and get some rest."

"No way in hell I am leaving," Ginny responded, and that seemed to be the popular opinion of all the Jensen family as they trouped across the parking lot towards the Clubhouse.

Once in the Meeting Room, they were joined by Carmen Ayala of Amazon; Ralph Dexter, Director of Security; Bernie Lanza, with Puget Sound Event Management; Penny Brown, LPGA Marketing Director and her assistant Alton Walker; Alexander Heron, Chamber's Bay General Manager; and Anthony Palmer, Tournament Director. Cynthia's assistant had been busy this morning notifying the right people, and Alexander Heron had coffee service set up for everyone. It looked like they would all need it to help power them through the day.

"Ladies and Gentlemen, we have a serious situation on our hands," Cynthia said, and proceeded to brief everyone in the room who had missed the gathering with the Tacoma Police Officials. She continued on for a few minutes, and in closing related: "I am happy to announce at this time, that I apprised Mr. Mac Tenderson, Assistant to the Commissioner of the LPGA, of our situation this morning, and he authorized a $100,000. reward for any information that would lead to an arrest and conviction in this matter."

"The Jensen Family will double that amount," Bob Jensen immediately said.

"I am sure Amazon will participate in any reward funding," Carmen Ayala spoke up. "I will have to speak to my home office this morning as to the specific amount."

"That is wonderful," Cynthia murmured. "Now then, we need all Department Heads and Task Leaders to please check in with their respective people, and see if anyone saw anything unusual. I will send out a memo to ALL staff this morning informing them of Chrissy's nonappearance, and the proffered reward. Penny and Tina, we need to create a press release. Carmen if you could check in with your people and we could get a final number from them, we could include the total reward figure in the press release. The sooner we get the word out the better. Will, I trust you will be the spokesperson for the Jensen Family. Penny, as Marketing and information Director, I am putting you in charge as the contact person for the LPGA. I will expect you to be in very close communication with me at all times. Tina, I'm sure you will handle things with the Golf Channel? I am opening the floor now to any more discussion and/or suggestions."

The room began to buzz with conversation. Soon, Ralph Dexter and Bernie Lanza excused themselves, so they could go and begin talking to their staffs. Alexander Heron left to go interact with the greens and clubhouse staffs. The crowd was dwindling when Carmen Ayala returned, and announced that Amazon was also going to guarantee 100K to the reward fund. Tina Borenson left immediately after that to get to her production people with her scoop of the year. She put her left hand to her ear, gave Will the thumb and little finger up signal to call her as she left.

"I think this was a very productive time we have spent together," Cynthia declared. "I am not sure what else we can accomplish right now, other than to be vigilant and stay patient," and called her meeting to a close. Everyone stood up and began milling toward the exit doors.

"I think Cynthia is right, there's not much else we can do. Why don't you all go home and get some rest, and Bobby and I will make a trip downtown to see Investigator Chong?" Will said.

The family trouped off to their cars, and by now the player's lot was over half full. People were rubbernecking. The Police were still very much combing the Jeep Cherokee for any clues, prints or fragments. Will approached, and asked Danny Chong if he could please secure Chrissy's golf clubs when the investigation was completed, and he would come down and retrieve them at the station.

"I think you can take them now," the Detective responded. "They were the first thing the team inspected when they got here.

"What about the car, when can we get the car back?"

"The car has to go downtown to the lab. It usually takes at least a day. I can call you when they are finished with it. I am just leaving for the station, when can I expect you?"

"We are on our way right now, Inspector."

Paula Chapman had just arrived at the course, and headed straight for the Cherokee and Bobby Jensen.

"What's going on?" she whispered.

"Chrissy is still missing; she didn't come home at all last night."

"Oh my God, that is so not like her. This is terrible."

"I know. You call me if you hear anything."

"Will do."

CHAPTER TWENTY-FIVE

Monica and Stuart were happy with the onset of the caper. They were as close to positive as they could get that Chrissy Jensen's abduction had gone flawlessly. Heck, Bonnie and Clyde couldn't have conceived or executed a plan any better. And as they sat and watched KIRO news on Channel 4, they were intrigued by the details of their crime. Kind of like a golfer watching a replay of their last round, except there weren't any bad shots to regret.

"Wow," Monica observed. "They sure got three hundred grand reward money raised up pretty quick, eh?"

"Yeah, I told you golfer girl was worth some dough."

"The important thing is that they don't seem to know anything. If they did, they wouldn't be hyping such a hefty reward so quickly. I'll bet you there will be more money added to that, too."

"Yeah. If they don't have anything on us now, they ain't gonna get anything either."

"This is so awesome, Monica. I think we just nailed Phase One here."

"Golfer girl and me is gonna get along just fine. She is meek as a little lamb down there. I think Vincent scared the crap out of her."

"Good. Just keep her happy and quiet."

Leroy didn't appear to want to help much. He showed up for the ten o'clock feeding, but went back in his room and appeared to be sleeping, although he had inquired of Monica when his lunch and dinner would be fixed. He was already starting to get on her nerves, and he was apparently quite a night owl.

Vincent was in his office bright and early, and gave Tommy a call about 10 am.

"Hey buddy, youse seen da news this morning?"

"Who is this?"

"It's your damn partner, who you think it is?"

"You're on a burner phone I hope."

"Of course, I'm on a burner phone."

"Well yeah, I did see the news this morning, and don't call me anymore until you got your thing wrapped up over there." Tommy hung up.

"Jeez, what a jerk," Vincent muttered.

He was happy as a fat little clam with the way things had gone, and thought Tommy would be too. Vincent had gotten in so smoothly last night, even Angela didn't suspect anything. She is probably getting ready for her book club luncheon as we speak. Forget Tommy, I will call Ronnie.

"Hey Ronnie, how youse doin'?"

"Fine, just fine. Sounds like your package came in okay last night."

"Oh yeah, there was no problems, dat's for sure. No problems at all."

"You are on a burner phone, right?"

"Sure, sure. That's the only way to go from now on."

"Right."

"Hey, I was callin' youse about Monday. When we gonna sit down and chat?"

"We will have to do it over a burner, buddy. I can't be in any kind of personal contact with anybody right now."

"Okay. What time youse want me to call you?"

"Around two. I will go on a late lunch break, and take the call outside in my car."

"I can only talk for thirty minutes or so."

"Gee, I thought youse was gonna talk us through this thing."

"I will get you started, and I can talk to you again if there are any questions, but I gotta lot going on right now."

"Yeah, whatever. I will call youse at two on Monday."

"Here is the burner number I will be on."

What a bunch of chicken shits, Vincent thought. Oh, they'll be happy enough to show their crummy faces when the dough comes rolling in.

"How the receipts look for this weekend," Vincent asked his bookkeeper.

"It was the usual good weekend for you, boss" she replied.

"Alright then. I'm leaving early today. Take messages for me will ya?"

"Sure Vincent."

Will and Bobby GPSed the Tacoma main Police Precinct Station and arrived forty-five minutes after the meeting with the brass at Chambers Bay had ended. They parked in one of the spots designated for visitors, and proceeded in to find what turned out to be a surly duty sergeant seated behind the counter in the anteroom.

"We are here to see Inspector Chong," Will said.

"Do you have an appointment?"

"He is expecting us."

The sergeant picked up his phone, and made a call. "Sit down over there," he told the guys, and pointed in the direction of an old wooden bench sitting against the wall across the room.

After waiting for twenty-five minutes, Will walked back up to the sergeant's desk. "We need to see Inspector Chong now. We are here at his request, and if he isn't available, we will have to come back at a later date."

"Let me make another call."

"You do that."

Two minutes later, a couple of uniformed policemen emerged from the secured area, and approached the Jensen brothers. "Sorry for the delay, gentlemen. Won't you please come with us?" one of the officers said with a smirk on his face.

All four of them proceeded back through ominous looking double doors, which slammed shut behind them, and on down a long, scruffy hallway that was ill lit by bare lightbulbs, which had metal cages around all of their ceiling outlets. They finally took a right turn at the end of the corridor, and another officer met them.

"Please step inside," the first officer said, opening a heavy white door with a small, wire mesh window built into in it at eye level. Will and Bobby started to file into the small, rectangular room, when the second officer blocked Bobby's pathway, and told him: "You need to follow me."

That startled Bobby, but Will was already in the first room, and by the time he turned around, Bobby was gone, and the door was closing.

"Where is my brother going?" Will asked.

"No worries, he is going to be close by. If you could please have a seat, the inspector will be right along in a few minutes."

The officer turned and left Will to his leisure, and the door banged shut behind him. Will looked around the battered, scuzzy room, and sat down on one of the two chairs. The one that faced the door. There was a scarred, beat up table between the two chairs with a metal ashtray on it. Otherwise, the room, was empty except for another glaring light fixture with the metal cage surrounding it. I am in a damn interrogation room, Will came to realize.

He waited another twenty minutes, and was livid with frustration. Getting up he went to exit the room, so he could find Bobby and they could get out of there. Reaching the heavy door, he turned the handle, and found that it was locked from the outside. He was being held against his will in an interrogation room for common criminals? Now his blood pressure was really climbing.

Another ten minutes went by, and finally a smiling Danny Chong rapped lightly on the door, made his way in, and sat down opposite Will.

"Is this your idea of a fucking joke, Mr. Chong? I demand to be released out of here immediately."

"I apologize for the delay, Mr. Jensen. It has been a very busy morning, as you might imagine."

"What do you want with me? I am out of here."

"Mr. Jensen, I want to assure you that this is no more than a routine component of our investigation. By law, I am directed to speak with anyone who was closely involved with the case, and we always begin by talking with family members first. Do you have any objection to my recording our meeting this morning?"

"Of course not. Are you insinuating that I had anything to do with Chrissy's disappearance? Am I a suspect here? I think I will leave now." And Will again began to rise from his folding chair.

"Mr. Jensen, the door is locked, and if you would just calm yourself for a few minutes, we can get this over with."

"I am very calm, and you had better make this quick." Will sat back down, and eyed Danny Chong with a death glare.

"Please tell me everything you know about Chrissy, and why she didn't come home last night."

"I already told you everything I know about the case when we were at Chambers Bay this morning."

"Mr. Jensen, why did you remove the alleged victim's cell phone from the scene last night?"

"I already told you that."

"Did you bring the phone back with you?"

"Here it is," Will said as he reached down into his attaché case.

"And a picture?"

Will again fumbled in his case and produced one of Chrissy's publicity photos for Inspector Chong.

"Your sister is a beautiful young woman, Will. Do you know of anyone who might have reason to benefit from her disappearance, or wish to do her harm?"

"Absolutely not."

"Did you have anything to do with your sister's disappearance, Will?"

By now Will was on the verge of erupting, but realized going ballistic wasn't going to do him any good. How can this be standard operating procedure he wondered?

"No inspector, I had absolutely nothing to do with my sister's disappearance," Will enunciated slowly, as if speaking to a child with special needs.

"You have people who can vouch for your whereabouts at all times last evening?"

"Of course."

"And you would be willing to take a lie detector test to confirm your statements, if necessary?"

"Of course."

"To the best of your knowledge, did anyone else in your family have anything to do with your sister's disappearance?"

"No fucking way."

"Does Chrissy have any life insurance policies?

"Yes, of course she does."

"And who are the beneficiaries of those policies?"

"Her family."

"In what amount are the policies?"

"Two million dollars."

"Are you one of the beneficiaries?"

"Myself, her other two brothers, and her parents would share equally in any benefits."

"I have no further questions Mr. Jensen, and I would like to apologize to you for this intrusion into both your time and your sensibilities. I know my questioning has been unpleasant, but it is a necessary evil in any kidnapping case. You have my card, and my cell number. I might suggest we communicate several times a day from now on. If this is a kidnapping case, at some point in time, you will be contacted and we should know about that as soon as it happens. For your family's sake, I truly hope it is not another scenario, where someone out there wishes physical harm for your sister. I would also like to assure you that we will do everything possible to secure Chrissy's return and safekeeping." With that, Danny Chong extended his hand to Will for a conciliatory hand shake.

Will ignored Inspector Chong's courtesy, and rose to leave. "May I go now?" he asked.

"Yes sir. Your brother is waiting for you out in the reception area."

"When will I get Chrissy's phone back?"

"I can have it for you by tomorrow afternoon."

Will and Bobby got out of the police station as quickly as possible.

"Did they put you through the same bullshit as me?" Will asked.

"Well, they wanted to know if I had anything to do with it, that's for sure."

"What an f'ing jerk. Was it Danny Chong who spoke with you?"

"Yeah, him and another guy were both in the room."

"He must have talked to you before he came to see me. I should have punched the guy out."

"Yeah, I was ready to."

"Then he wanted to be all buddy buddy again, said he was just doing his job."

"Good cop, bad cop. Let's get back to the house, mom and dad are going to need us to be around."

"What are you doing home so early?" Angela asked.

"I came home to spend some time with you, baby cakes."

"Well, I have my luncheon at one thirty. Hey, did you talk to Ronnie? When are we going to the Emerald Queen?"

Jesus, Mary, Joseph, Vincent thought. "Yeah, I spoke with him this morning, he's pretty busy right now. Says he don't know when he can get away."

"See Vincent, damn it. I knew you would try and blow me off."

"Hey, it's not like that at all. I'll take youse to lunch right now. Wherever you want. Anywhere. Let's go up to the damn Space Needle. C'mon let's go."

"I've got my ladies luncheon, Vincent. You know that."

"Well, I told you a coupla days ago that I would be pretty busy for the next two weeks or so, too."

Vincent stalked into his office, and turned on the TV. Christ, everyone is a ton of fun today, he groused to himself.

Tina met with her production people, and was set up for a live feed into the Morning Drive Show on the Golf Channel. That morphed into social media releases/feeds, and soon the ladies of the LPGA were buzzing. Everyone was stunned that one of their own had apparently fallen victim to some kind of foul play, and all of the ladies were hoping and praying for Chrissy's safety. While she wasn't the warmest, fuzziest gal within the circle of LPGA players; as far as bonding and socializing, as far as tweeting incessantly, she was nonetheless a huge star on tour, and if not Miss Personality, then she was still highly respected. But now that she had gone missing, there was sure an awful lot of unconditional love for her going around.

Next, ESPN picked up the feed, then the local sports radio stations, and finally the local TV stations sent crews out to the course. The regular news teams were just as interested in this developing local story as the sports reporters, and Penny Brown was busy as a beaver trying to keep up with all of the activity. She had Alton Walker with her of course. He was manning the phones, while Penny handled the electronic side of the local interactions. They had a press conference scheduled for noon. Tina Borenson was working with the National Sports Media, and even had spots going out on this evening's national news networks. Penny and Tina were pushing all of the right buttons, and couldn't have gotten any more comprehensive, professional style coverage going. Including continuous reports of the reward monies.

After their morning interaction with the police brass, and the subsequent organizational meeting in the Chambers Bay conference room, the Jensens returned home, where they still had family and house guests staying. Everyone tried to be brave and put on a courageous veneer, but they were all in shock. The reality of what horrors could befall someone in these often sick and depraved times, was too overwhelming to think about. All of the family felt personally violated and sickeningly helpless. Especially the women.

Ginny Jensen had been a rock throughout the night, but now she was deeply disturbed, faced exhaustion, and extreme emotional distress. She was experiencing every loving parent's nightmare, and felt as if she had been run over by a truck. She thought she knew what it was like to be a piece of roadkill, maybe worse if it is possible. Ginny's sister contacted her primary care physician in Portland, and had him call in a prescription for some sedatives. She dispatched Calvin to the drug store.

The men gathered in the den and it was like a morgue in there too. No one had much of anything to say, and the most frustrating element of their situation, was the interminable waiting around. It was just starting, and was going to get worse. A lot worse. Chief Mills himself had forewarned them about that. Unfortunately, men are not very good at patience and forbearance most of the time, but now they had absolutely no choice.

In addition to the denial stage of the grief they were all suffering, there was an unspoken aura of guilt being felt by a lot of the guys. They were vaulting over the anger phase and beginning to bargain with their personal emotions. If there was anger present, it was directed inwardly for each of their lack of support for Chrissy. Bobby especially was badly stricken. There were so many things he could have done to help prevent this catastrophe. In the first place, he should have been home two nights ago, and not upset Chrissy and his family like he did. Then, he should have stayed with her at the range.

Will felt the same way. He could have insisted on giving her a ride home, and not been distracted by spending time with casual, new acquaintances. Bob Jensen was pounding himself for not being with Chrissy at the range. He felt guilty for being at home getting ready to party it up. Indulging himself, and using Chrissy's fame for his own ends. Those feelings were particularly hard for him to swallow, and he felt, whether justifiable or not, that he had abandoned his daughter.

Will and Bobby were unable to do much of anything to alter the general mood of the house when they returned. They did keep the personal anger and frustration which had evolved from their experiences at the police station to themselves. Both brothers agreed on their way home that on top of everything else, it would do little good to get everyone else as perturbed as they were.

Steve Reed arrived around two o'clock, and he was also somber and serious. Will introduced him around, and he could do nothing more than sit and commiserate with the rest of the men once the small talk about his flight had subsided. Steve was in the same state of shock, tension and disbelief as everyone else in the room.

Back at the course, all of the LPGA women were experiencing a lower level of trauma than the family, but were still clearly affected, especially Chrissy's closer friends and playing partners. Will thought about these issues, and from back at Jensen compound around three in the afternoon, he sent out a tweet to the LPGA members, asking them to stay the course, and play their best. "Do it for Chrissy," he encouraged, "that's what she would want you to do." It was a classy move, and did not go unnoticed or unappreciated.

Late in the afternoon several small groups of the players began to drift by the compound to pay respects, commiserate, and show their support. The visits meant so much to the family, and it served to galvanize the household as well as providing some much-needed distraction. The Jensens began to stir a little from their shock and depression, and the visitors served as catalysts to stimulate them from being comatose to at least partially functioning. Even if it was something so mundane as accommodating their guests with coffee or tea, it changed the family's collective mood, and kept them functioning at a very basic level.

Will's tweet was also an inspiration to everyone. Between that and the visiting lady golfers, the family continued to rally. About five o'clock Bob announced that he was going to try and get an adult beverage down, and the male members of the family gathered to support him. They were happy not to let Bob drink alone, but in truth no one was in much of a mood for libations.

They all knew it was just a feeble attempt to try and pass some more time. To act normal.

The six o'clock news, both local and national, released the details of Chrissy's abduction, and trumpeted the substantial reward being offered. In closing, they panned to a support site already set up for Chrissy in front of Chambers Bay Clubhouse. It had been started by concerned fans, and was inundated with flower bouquets and hand lettered signs encouraging the family, and calling for any information that could help lead to Chrissy's speedy return. The overwhelming and instantaneous support of the media and Chrissy's fans continued to lift the family's spirits significantly.

CHAPTER TWENTY-SIX

Saturday evening crawled by slowly and uneventfully for everyone. The Jensen compound out of habit, had watched the Amazon Tournament on TV. But it was now more subdued than ever. There were numerous updates of Chrissy's abduction, lengthy conjecture and postulation by the local television commentators, but nothing had emerged from the morning police investigation. Will called Chief Lawrence Mills to verify possible details or progress and was told that there was nothing new to report, and he was directed to make all future calls to Inspector Chong. His Sunday morning chat with Danny Chong revealed lots of frustration on behalf of the TPD but no progress of any kind.

Chrissy's evening was much the same. Some kind of a frozen meatloaf and sticky, lumpy potato dinner, then solitude and boredom for the rest of the night. She picked up a couple of the magazines Florence had left for her and did what she could do to distract herself and pass the time. For an outdoors person like Chrissy, being locked away from family and friends in a stuffy, barren basement was akin to solitary confinement. She felt like most common criminals were having a better night than she was. At least they probably had TV, and someone to talk to.

In the morning Chrissy was up early, and had gotten most of her heavy workout in when she heard the knock on her door. Room service, she thought, and fanaticized that Steve Reed was bringing in her breakfast tray with a red rose on it. She would have run to him in a New York minute right now, even if he was in his dirty, sweaty football practice uniform.

Monica/Florence brought the tray in with Chrissy's scrambled eggs and sausage. She set them down on the bed, and was preparing to leave the room, when Chrissy spoke to her in a subdued tone.

"The old guy said I could have anything I wanted within reason, if I didn't cause any problems, right?"

"Well, whattaya want then?"

"I want you to talk to me while I eat my breakfast. I am down here by myself, with no outside light, no fresh air, and I am going crazy. I need to talk to someone."

Monica looked at her inquisitively. What does she want, she thought? I guess she has a point, and what do I have to do but sit around upstairs with that jerk Leroy anyway? So, she sat down on the edge of the bed, and said "Whazzup? Whatta ya want to chat about?"

"Nothing, anything, I don't care. How is the weather. Who is leading the golf tournament? Can I have a television? What's for dinner? Thanks for cooking for me by the way. Who does your hair? I don't care, what we talk about, just sit down with me for a few minutes. I'm going crazy down here."

"The weather is great out there. No, you can't have a TV."

"Why not?"

"Because Jack said he don't want you having no TV down here." She got a totally American accent, Chrissy thought.

"How about a radio then?"

"I don't know, I will ask him."

"Thank you."

"What you want for dinner?"

"How about some broiled salmon, with asparagus hollandaise, and mashed potatoes."

"Ha-ha. How about a grilled cheese sandwich and a bowl of chicken noodle soup?"

"You need to leave now," the big, burly guy said from the top of the stairs in his heavy Eastern European brogue.

"Whatever," Monica replied to him, and under her breath quietly turned and said "see you tonight" to Chrissy.

Well, that's a start, I broke the ice Chrissy thought. She just may be approachable. Then she heard some screaming and yelling from inside the house, and rushed up the stairs to better hear what was going on.

"Don't you ever tell me what to do, asshole," Chrissy could hear Florence screaming at burly boy. "You are not the boss of me."

"Yeah, vell Jack said he don't vant nobody sittin' around talking to da broad."

"He also said if she was cooperating, she could get whatever she wanted."

"Jack said…."

"You stuff it, I will call Jack myself. I need to ask him about something else for her anyway."

"You need to watch your mouth, woman. Or I will clock your ass."

"Try it, big man."

"Hey, hey, what's going on in here?" Stuart came rushing into the kitchen from outside the house. "The front door is wide open; I can hear you guys all the way out on the deck."

"Tell this moron to mind his own business, will you, Sammy?"

"Everybody please calm down. Florence, just call Jack, and see what he says. We don't have to argue all day here."

"I will call Jack, and you can tell Leroy here, to clean up the damn kitchen. Look at the mess he left from making his breakfast. I'm not the maid around here." Chrissy was taking it all in.

Leroy gave her a scathing look, and went over and laid out on the couch.

"Hi Jack, this is Florence. I have a couple of questions for you."
"Yeah, what is it?"
"Well, our guest has been very cooperative, and when we went in this morning, she asked me if it was okay for her to have a TV, and I said no. Then she says, well what about a little radio. And when I took her breakfast over to her, I think she just wanted some human contact, and she asked me to sit down and talk to her for a couple of minutes. I didn't think it would do any harm. She was

getting ready to freak, and I thought it would help to keep her calm if we talked for a minute. She just asked me about the radio, and we talked about what was for dinner. She has been doing everything we asked of her, Jack."

"Yeah well, she better. I don't care if you get her a little portable radio, but you keep the chitchat wid her down to a minimum. Next thing you know, youse will be talking, and somebody's name will slip out or something like that, and then we got trouble."

"Okay Jack, you are the boss. By the way, I need another five hundred bucks, this guy Leroy is not only a jerk, but he is eating us out of house and home."

"Why you call him a jerk?"

"Jeez, he makes a huge mess all over the kitchen, then starts telling me what to do. I don't need that, Jack."

"Let me talk to him."

"I'll tell him to call you," Monica said and hung up.

That annoyed Vincent. He hated being cut off on the phone.

"Jack wants to talk to you," she called over to Leroy. Then "Sammy, I need the keys to the car. I'm goin' out."

Monica drove into Gig Harbor and up Borgen Ave, to first the Target store where she bought an am/fm clock radio. Then over to Albertson's, where she picked up a side of salmon from the seafood counter, and some potatoes and asparagus in the produce section. This will give me something to do this afternoon she thought, and will annoy Leroy boy even more, when he doesn't get any.

Leroy called his boss, and Jack lit into him. "You calm down, man. The last thing I need is to have yawl fighting amongst yourselves like a bunch of three-year old kids. Just lay low, and do your job, and don't start no trouble. You hear me?"

This made Vincent really cranky. Do I have to go over there and babysit the bunch of them he wondered?

Having returned from her errands, Monica cleaned up the kitchen, and began to do some prep work for dinner. Peeling potatoes, trimming and blanching the asparagus, etc. Stuart relaxed on the front deck, and Leroy was asleep on the couch. He was snoring pretty good, so Monica dropped a couple of pans to make sure she would wake him up. Leroy got up and stumbled off to his bedroom.

The third round of the Amazon tournament at Chamber's Bay had proceeded almost as normal. The girls sucked it up and tried to put Chrissy out of their minds. Play was consistent, if not spectacular. The first thing most of them did when coming in from their individual rounds, was to inquire about any updates. Her failure to show up on Saturday had certainly confirmed the rumors that she was missing. Everyone was still afraid to mouth the word kidnap. If anything, some of the girls who didn't know Chrissy all that well, and therefore weren't as close to her or concerned in general, picked up some ground on the field.

Will was beginning to establish a modest routine with Detective Chong, had taken a call from him around two on Saturday afternoon, and now the detective had was calling again first thing Sunday morning.

"Will, I received a message from the FBI satellite office here in Tacoma. They want to sit down with us by Monday afternoon if nothing has transpired over the weekend. If this is a kidnapping for ransom, we should anticipate some contact from the perps any time now. We have calls in to the local stations to encourage them to continue broadcasting the reward information. Hopefully, something will shake out this weekend. The statewide crime prevention show comes on tonight night at nine, and they can often help produce good leads and end results."

"I will have my phone on, trust me."

"The FBI agrees this is either going to be a kidnapping for ransom, or not. We are all hoping it is a ransom case, and then it is a matter of negotiating for money. The majority of these type cases are resolved successfully. I'm sure I don't have to tell you what we don't want, is some psycho who has other ideas. You should also know Will, that I have received calls from law enforcement personnel from Seattle to Portland, all over the west coast actually, who are offering whatever support they might be able to give us. Your sister is a much-loved young woman, and you can tell your family that we are doing everything humanly possible to find her."

Local news was on in the den of the compound. Without much enthusiasm, Will relayed most of Inspector Chong's comments to everyone, everything but the psycho stuff, but there was still nothing breaking on the case. Ginny had ordered pizza, but Will and Tina were going out to meet with Penny Brown, and do some strategizing. There was a large jigsaw puzzle going in the dining room, and four of the guys were playing cribbage, but everyone was basically just laying low, hoping the phone would ring with some positive news.

Ginny couldn't help but wonder/worry herself about what Chrissy might be eating for lunch, if she was out of danger, if she was safe from harm. These thoughts overwhelmed her, and she couldn't get them out of her mind. She alternately cried, prayed, waited and cried some more.

At six o'clock on Saturday evening Chrissy could hear the lock on the basement door jiggling, and she went and sat on the edge of the bed. Monica/Florence began her descent down the stairs. Burly boy came in behind her and stood on the landing. Chrissy could feel him glaring down on her, and felt the enmity seething from him. She had analyzed Florence as best she could, and projected her to be a somewhat extraverted personality type, independent, with doer and maybe some nurturing tendencies. She had thought about it all afternoon, and felt like Florence was going to be approachable, and was certainly more empathetic than anyone else around the place.

Flo was carrying her dinner tray, but it was balanced on top of a cardboard box. Chrissy could almost feel her smiling behind the niqab. She walked over to the bed, and set her package down. Chrissy was excited to see it was an AM/FM radio. She was more than excited, she was elated. So much so, that she didn't notice what was on her dinner tray, until Florence said, "Your dinner, madam."

Chrissy did a double take when she saw a fat filet of roasted salmon coupled with mashed potatoes and asparagus on the plate. She whispered, "thank you so much," and knew instantly they had connected in a personal way. She had gotten the nurturing part at least partly right, and she would now do anything possible to deepen the relationship. She should also do her utmost to continuing fostering the hostility between Flo and burly boy.

"You are welcome, we can talk more in the morning," Florence whispered back. She turned on her heel, crossed the room and ascended the stairs. The door locked behind her.

Chrissy was beyond elated. She had launched some, if minimal, dialogue, had gotten her radio, and was going to have a great dinner. She told me we would talk more in the morning; I feel like the door is opening. I should ask her if I can talk to Jack, and get a message out to my family that I am okay for the time being. Now that would be a real breakthrough!

Chrissy dug into her dinner. All of her working out was helping her appetite return. I should have asked for a glass of chardonnay she thought, and wished she was out at a nice waterfront restaurant with Steve.

Will and Tina met Penny in the Chambers Bay Grille Room midmorning on Sunday for a quick breakfast and organizational meeting. During the drive over from the compound, Tina told Will she had a surprise for him, and she would share it at the restaurant. Penny was five minutes early, and upped their reservation to five. They sat by a big screen TV, so they could watch the pre-tournament talking heads while they were strategizing. Alton Walker, Penny's Marketing Assistant was there and also Cynthia Summers. Everyone exchanged greetings, and sat down to peruse the menu. The aromas emanating from the open kitchen had peeked Will's appetite. He wanted something light but tasty, and then some positive conversation. Anything to alter the depressing reality of the last miserable day and a half.

The group opted for coffee, and after it had arrived, Tina tapped her mug with a spoon to get everyone's attention.

"I have some important news, and am thrilled to announce that the Golf Channel has agreed to contribute another one hundred thousand dollars to the reward fund," she glanced over at Will and smiled.

Will was moved, he almost couldn't speak he was so appreciative of all the support Chrissy was receiving. Not only financially, but his phone, twitter and Instagram accounts had basically exploded since Saturday morning, and everyone wanted to help. He thought about it for a moment, and replied to Tina and the table, "I believe Chrissy would want me to commit another hundred thousand from her personal assets. It would bring the reward to 500K. That's a significant number. It's gotta turn some heads, don't y'all think?"

Everyone agreed, and their coffee mugs were raised, and came together in a toast.

Being the senior executive at the table, Cynthia took over the conversation, and launched her pitch. "As this tournament is winding down, and in addition to all of the incredible publicity we have received, I think we should make a major push on Chrissy's behalf. I am talking local TV stations, the Golf Channel-- not only during our own tournament broadcasts-- but throughout the next couple of days. I will call the PGA and have them express their support. We need to have the local sports radio stations do an on-air marathon. I will talk to our own broadcast teams this morning; we need The Seattle Times and Tacoma Tribune to run feature stories. Penny can you get a social media package going: hit Facebook, have all of the LPGA players shout out on Twitter and Instagram? We need to create a firestorm of activity. I would love to see all of our contacts not just make a report, but start a concerted movement to get Chrissy back now. Buy into a rescue, get'er done, make this a regional movement. As soon as we are finished here, I am going to get on the phone and get to work. I hope you all will join me. We have got to utilize this last critical window of time available to us. Especially as the reward has gone up another 200 grand."

They ordered and began to delegate responsibilities. Tina: national network media. Penny: local electronic and print media. Alton: social media. Cynthia: the LPGA Staff, PGA, and ESPN.

"I will call Chris Leavitt, the Groz, and Brock Huard at the sports radio stations; those guys know everybody in greater Seattle. Heck, I will tract down John Clayton, and hopefully get him to give us some air time," Will said.

"John Clayton, the football guy?" Tina asked.

"Yeah. He is a football guy, but people love him up here. He is a Seattleite, and would kill it for us," Will interjected.

"Call anyone and everyone you can think of. I'm talking about Good Morning America, The View, The Football Guy, whoever," Cynthia continued.

"Just email me," Penny advised, "and let me know who you are contacting. "I am going to start a spreadsheet so we can track what we are doing, and make sure we don't duplicate our calls."

Breakfast came and was woofed down. Everyone had become charged up by Cynthia's motivational speech and couldn't wait to get back to work.

"The communications center is open to anyone, if you need working space," Penny volunteered as the table separated.

Alton lingered with Penny for a minute, until the rest of the guests had departed.

"Pen, you need to ask Cynthia if we can stay on for another week. Tell her the LPGA will need a presence here to monitor the progress of the case, and I will be your aide. I am going to get into this thing. For half a million bucks, I am going to get to the bottom of all this."

"I like your idea, Alton. But how are you going to help find Chrissy Jensen?"

"I need to start sniffing around. Go old school. Get over to the tournament, and just start walking around, and talking to people like I did all last year. Keep my ears open. There's got to be something people are missing."

"I think Cynthia would go for us staying on. I will talk to her this afternoon if I can get through to her."

CHAPTER TWENTY-SEVEN

Mount Rainier emerged from the ashes of dawn much like Poseidon might have erupted from the sea to meet Aphrodite. There were streaks of crimson in the wispy clouds, as sunrise lingered temporarily, then the sun overpowered the horizon, and illuminated another flawless landscape well worth enjoying for anybody who cared to be up at this early hour.

Chrissy didn't need to set the alarm on her new clock radio to wake. She had grown up as a farm girl, and on a farm, most people get up early and go to work. She cursed her fate as she had a depressing thought about her Sunday tee time, and the fact that she wasn't waking up next to Steve. That was a cruel joke on her, and she realized she had partially reconciled herself to the fact she was shutting down a bit. There was work of another kind to do today, now she was supremely pissed off, and she told herself to stay aggressive.

She sat up on the side of the bed in her warmup suit, having decided she would sleep in her clothes, should any emergency situations arise. As a big yawn escaped her mouth, she got up and stretched, and went into her little bathroom to shower. She locked the door behind herself, stripped down, and let the hot water stream over her. It was soothing. She changed into fresh everything, thinking it was considerate of Florence to anticipate her needs, and the fresh clothes were more than necessary with all of the working out she was doing. She hand washed her panties, hung them to dry in the shower, and finished up her morning business.

Florence would be coming down at ten AM, and she wanted to continue working on her. I've got to get a message of some kind to my family that I am okay, and I need to get my hands on a weapon of some kind. Florence probably won't bring me a set of brass knuckles, but I need to think of something innocuous I can use to my advantage.

She returned to her chamber and began doing stretching exercises.

At nine thirty, Chrissy heard the door locks jangle. "Hmm, they're early today," she thought, and then realized that by moving up the schedule, she might be avoiding burly boy. Chrissy went and sat at the head of her bed.

Florence came down the stairs, and indeed it was the other guy. Florence and this guy seemed to have some kind of rapport. They were just more comfortable around each other, there was less friction in the air. She crossed the room, set Chrissy's breakfast down, and parked herself on the foot of the bed.

"Sorry about Leroy yesterday. He's a butthead."

"Thank you so much for the salmon last night, and for just sitting with me a little bit. Dinner was delicious." Everyone knows the cook loves compliments.

"No problem. I did it as much to spite Leroy as anything."

"Can I ask you for just a couple more little things?"

"What?"

"Do you think the head guy would allow me to send a message to my family, just to let them know I'm alright?"

"Oh, I don't think Jack would ever go for that."

"Well, what if I promised you fifty thousand bucks to bring me a cell phone?"

"You know Jack would kill me, if he ever found out what you just said? Don't even talk about anything like that, or I will have to leave."

"Sorry, sorry. I just want to let my family know I am okay, that's all. I don't want anyone to get in trouble. Especially not you."

"Just be patient," and Florence dropped her voice to a whisper. "I think they are going to start negotiating to get you out of here sometime next week."

Chrissy was disappointed, but in reality, had thought the possibility of getting any communication open with her family was going to be a long shot. "Do you think I could talk to this guy Jack? If he will just let my family know I am okay, I will do anything I can do to help him get whatever he wants."

"I will pass it along. Don't get your hopes up."

"I won't," and in a moment of inspiration, Chrissy said, "I do need something else."

"What?"

"It's kind of personal."

"What is it?"

"I want a vibrator," she said, blushed, and took a bite of scrambled eggs to diffuse her discomfort.

"Ha, ha," Florence giggled. She scooted over a little, and touched Chrissy's leg with her left hand. "Are you getting a little lonely down here?"

"Nothing fancy, just a regular old vibrator." Chrissy said, moved her leg away slightly, and focused on eating breakfast with her head down.

"Whatever. Jack said to get you what you wanted, as long as you were being cool."

"Please don't say anything to the guys, especially the Russian dude. Please."

"Our little secret, honey."

Florence patted her leg, got up and crossed back over to the stairs. "Enjoy your breakfast."

"Thank you."

"I am going to go get on the phone, Alton."

"Righto Penny, I will get started on Facebook and Twitter, then I want to go over to the Tournament and sniff around a bit. I want to hang out like I used to before you came along and rescued me."

"That five-hundred-thousand-dollar reward has piqued your interest, hasn't it?" Penny said with a smile.

"Maybe. I'm going to get going, and then go over to the course. I want to circulate around over there today."

"Hope it does some good."

"Yep, and don't forget to talk to Cynthia about us staying on."

"I will call her later. Meet you back at the hotel around five? I will take an Uber."

"Make it six."

"Okay."

Penny contacted half a dozen News Directors from the local network TV and the major radio stations. After three hours of nonstop dialing and talking, she took a break and rang Cynthia's cell phone number. Surprisingly, Cynthia picked up on the third ring.

"Hi Cyn, how's it going?"

"Good. I'm talking with a lot of people and getting nothing but enthusiastic support."

"That's awesome. I have different question for you."

"What is it, Penny?"

"I was wondering if it wouldn't be feasible for me to stay on here for another week or so, until there is some headway in Chrissy's case. I could be a presence for the LPGA, and also communicate to you what is going on. I would need Alton to stay and help cover the bases. Don't you think next week is going to be a critical time? Either Will or the cops should get a ransom demand, or something else will happen. If a demand doesn't come in pretty soon, it is going to make a lot of people pretty nervous. We should be here to monitor the situation, and help out. If nothing else, I can be your eyes and ears."

"I was thinking along the same lines Penny, except there is one problem."

"What's that?"

"I haven't had a chance to chat with you privately in the last couple of days, but the problem is Alton."

"Alton?"

"Yeah, I got a call from Mac Tenderson on Thursday afternoon, and he was annoyed with Alton. Seems like when your boy drove him to the airport on Thursday morning, he said the town car smelled like a frat house. He wants Alton to get drug tested, and said a haircut wouldn't hurt either."

"Oh no. You want me to talk to him, and see what was going on in the town car? I know he was driving some players and their guests around on Wednesday evening."

"You talk to him, and find out what happened. Ask him who was doing what. If he swears to God he wasn't smoking pot, I can stall Mac off until you guys get back to Daytona, and we can schedule him for a test. But, if we cover for him, and he goes back there and tests positive, I will have no alternative other than terminating him."

"Let me talk to him, Cynthia. And what about staying on for another week?" Penny said.

"I will have to check with Mac. I'm okay, but he'll have to sign off on it," Cynthia responded.

Penny thought for a moment before replying to her boss. "I will get back to you later on, as soon as I can track him down, and find out what happened." I wonder why Mac doesn't want to talk to the players Alton was driving around, Penny wondered.

"How is it going with your local contacts?" Cynthia asked.

"Everyone has been super supportive," Penny said.

Alton flashed his staff credentials to the player's parking lot monitor, and she ushered his vehicle in. There was still some room available towards the back of the lot, he parked, and got out of the LPGA town car in casual clothes. He wanted to just circulate around this afternoon, and see if anything might come to him. He walked over to the middle of the lot, as near to where Chrissy's SUV had been parked as he could get and started milling about.

He was deep in thought. If her golf clubs were in the car, and her cell phone was in her golf bag, she must have just put her things in the automobile before she was confronted. Tired from a long day, focused on getting home to her family, she would certainly not have been particularly mindful of her surroundings. Heck, he had personally seen her leave the course before, and knew that she usually stayed later than any of the other players. That would put the time of her disappearance around seven. With the long, lingering Pacific Northwest summer evenings, she could easily have lost track of time, and assumed it was earlier. At seven o'clock or so, the lot should have been largely vacant, making it easy for someone to approach and threaten her. Alton's assumptions, while right on, didn't even include the distracting personal issues Chrissy had had with her caddie that Friday.

What type of person or persons would attempt something like this? Alton thought. Surely, it wouldn't have been amateurs, or some spur of the moment thing. Anyone who knew anything, couldn't help but be aware of the firestorm that abducting someone of Chrissy's profile would bring. So, there must have been some premeditation and also weapons of some sort in play. And there was surely more than one abductor. The Tacoma PD Forensics Team had found no evidence in Chrissy's SUV, so maybe these were professional criminals.

He was heading over to the parking attendant, when his cell rang. He checked the phone's screen. It was Penny. "What's up?"

"I just talked to Cynthia, and she and Mac Tenderson are upset with you. Mac said the town car smelled like dope on Thursday morning when you took him to the airport, and now he wants to have you drug tested. What was going on anyway?"

"I was driving the girls around, and the Leslies' friends saw a pot shop, and wanted to stop. I guess they don't have anything like that where they are from. I didn't want to, but they insisted, and I gave them ten minutes to go in and look around. They came back out, and we drove away. The next thing I knew they were in the back of the town car, and were smoking weed."

"Did you smoke it with them, Alton?"

"No way. I was driving, and as a matter of fact, I told them to knock it off."

"Alton, please tell me the truth. If you swear to God you weren't smoking, Cynthia will cover for you, and stall off a drug test. But when the time comes, if you test positive, she will have to fire you."

"No worries, pet. Just don't test me for alcohol."

"You swear to God?"

"No worries, I already told you."

"Okay, baby. I think we are good for another week then."

"Great. I am working on things here, I gotta go." And Alton ambled over towards the parking attendant. He groaned mentally, and said, damn sheilas, to himself. I knew they were going to be trouble.

"Allo, I am Alton Walker, with the LPGA," Alton introduced himself. "And your name is?"

"Hi, I'm Jenny. I'm a volunteer."

"We are trying to gather up any possible information concerning Chrissy Jensen's disappearance. Do you remember anything at all unusual about last Friday evening?"

"No sir, isn't it terrible? She was so nice to me all week, always came in with one of her brothers, and would wave. The police have already been here several times. I left at five o'clock on Friday evening, which is my regular time, and everything seemed pretty quiet to me."

"Did you observe anyone lingering or seeming to loiter about?"

"No sir."

"Is this gate secured when you leave? I mean, do you stretch a chain across the entrance or anything like that?"

"No sir. That would be difficult to do, because there are still cars in the lot at five when I leave."

"There are no security cameras around, is that correct?"

"Yes sir, no cameras."

"And all of the transportation people were already gone?"

"Yes sir. They get here early to accommodate any needs the ladies might have. But by the time the last players are on the course, their work is pretty much done. I think most of them go on over, and watch the tournament."

Alton and the attendant were interrupted by a black SUV approaching. There were two middle aged gentlemen sitting in the front seat of the car as it neared the gate, and as they passed, Alton lost sight of the men because of the heavy tinting of the vehicle's windows.

Turning back to the lot attendant, Alton couldn't think of anything else to ask. So he thanked her and ambled slowly back over to the middle area of the parking lot. As he retraced his steps, the two guys who had just entered the lot in the SUV, crossed his path on their way to the entrance gates. One of them was a bit on the rotund side. He had on Bermuda shorts, and a polo shirt. But his skin was the clammy white of a Northwesterner. The other fellow was a little shorter, with a darker complexion. He looked like he might be Italian or Middle Eastern. He was also dressed casually. There was something vaguely familiar about them, but Alton couldn't put his finger on it. Whatever, he thought.

He turned his mind back to Chrissy's situation. Had to be a minimum of two guys, had to be some type of imminent threat involved. He closed his eyes and tried to envision Chrissy toting her clubs out to the car, stowing them and turning about, only to have someone in her face.

The snatch would had to have happened quickly and quietly, or it would have attracted attention. Someone probably pulled their car up alongside her, or maybe behind her, and then threateningly forced her into their vehicle, and sped away. It had to have been someone with the proper credentials to get into the lot in the first place, and it had to have been a vehicle that fit into the general landscape. Nothing that would give Chrissy or anyone else any cause for concern.

This felt like a professional job to Alton. He had a hard time convincing himself that a couple of amateurs would have the nerve to just drive in, and kidnap a world-famous athlete and get away without a hitch. And if it was a pro job, then it would surely be a kidnapping for ransom, and he was surprised no one had heard of any demands yet.

For whatever reason, that that stage hadn't yet been reached. Hell, he had just had breakfast with Will Jensen, and nothing was said. If it wasn't a snatch for pay, it had to be some kind of pervert, God forbid. But why would some perv, unless he was a stalker, go to the trouble of snatching a celebrity, when anyone would probably fit his sickening needs? If it is a ransom job, when will the kidnappers contact them he wanted to know?

He thought the LPGA kept a record of all the vehicles with access to this parking lot. Surely, they must, because those parking passes had to have been purchased, and then it became a revenue tracking matter for accounting, so he would check on that. The thought occurred to him that the office would probably have the names of the package buyers, but not a record of the vehicle types. I also need to review the closed-circuit film from the front of the clubhouse, and also any other film footage, from any other locations that might be available. He would want to speak to Bennie Lanza, the outside security contractor if possible. It was going to be a busy afternoon, but he felt like he was making a little bit of progress. If nothing else, he was certainly more familiar with the possibilities of last Friday evening than he had been before. Somehow, he felt like there was still something to be gleaned out here in the lot. Some kernel of wisdom or knowledge he was missing, but he felt confident it would come to him in time.

Back at the Jensen compound, things were plodding along. The men decided amongst themselves to go back over to the course and watch the tournament. There wasn't much they could do at the house. Chrissy certainly wasn't here; she was out there somewhere. Maybe by some miracle, someone might overhear something or pick up a random clue over there. The women decided to stay in the nest, so to speak, and watch the tournament on television. They wanted to be close to home should anything materialize.

Steve Reed was hanging with the guys. Chrissy's family had been very warm and welcoming to him. As a matter of fact, he had slept at the compound last night. It felt weird being in his lover's bedroom, her actual bed, without her, and he knew what a huge decision it had been for Ginny Jensen on where Steve should spend the night. He knew she preferred to keep Chrissy's room just the way Chrissy had left it and volunteered to go stay in a hotel. But Ginny wouldn't hear of Steve staying in some hotel, and she was sure in her heart Chrissy would want him to stay in her room.

In Gig Harbor, Leroy got up at ten, and went out into the kitchen in his boxer shorts. "Let's go feed the bitch," he said to Monica.
"We fed her already."
"Whatta mean you fed her already? Feeding time is ten o'clock."
"I didn't want to wait around, and so Sammy and I already went in and took her breakfast down. Why don't you go put some clothes on anyway? You look like hell."
Leroy was badly hungover. An ice hockey brawl was raging inside his head causing a splitting headache, and now he had gotten up for nothing. Plus, he felt like Monica had gone early without him, just so she could sit down there and chat it up with golfer girl, despite what Jack had told them."
Nor was Monica happy after having had to clean up Leroy's kitchen mess following his dinner making and late-night snacking the previous night. She would not work in a pig sty of a kitchen, and her job was to feed Chrissy, so what was she supposed to do? Leaving Leroy a clean kitchen was hopeless, and besides, what was worse, her chatting with Chrissy for a few minutes, or Leroy getting bombed out of his gourd every night here at the house. What a miserable loser this big shmutz is, she thought.
Leroy pushed her aside as he headed for the coffee pot. Monica turned, gave him a hard two-handed shove in the middle of his back, after he had passed her, and hissed at him, "Don't ever touch me, you pig."

Monica's shove landed Leroy face first into the corner of the back counter and the edge of the kitchen cabinets. His left hand hit the coffee pot, which burned him, and he turned back toward her with his fists clenched in fury. But Monica snatched up the ten-inch French knife from the cutting board on the sink, and invited Leroy to come any closer. She was smiling as she flashed the knife at him.

"You want some of this?" Monica asked.

"Fuck you," he mouthed at her, belched, and left the kitchen.

Monica turned and walked out to the deck where Stuart was again lounging around sunning himself. "I am going to kill that Russian mobster friend of yours," she told him.

"Now what? And he ain't no friend of mine."

"Now what? Well the son of a bitch just put his hands on me in the kitchen. I let him know I would stab him if he ever touched me."

"Jesus, Mon. Can we just stay out of each other's way a little bit?"

"I want you to call Jack. I want to talk to him right now."

"Mon, you know it is Sunday. Let's just calm down, and I will call him in the morning. If we call him now, he will just get peeved at being bothered on the weekend, and side with the Russian. Why don't you come outside and sit with me and enjoy the nice weather? I will cook dinner, and cleanup tonight, okay?"

Monica was still fuming, but she didn't want to make things worse than they were, and she knew they couldn't be calling Jack ten time a day. "Okay, but you go talk to that shithead."

Stuart got up and went into the house. Leroy was nowhere to be seen, so Stuart went and knocked on his bedroom door, and found him stretched out on top of his bed with a pillow over his head.

"Hey, can we all just calm down a little bit?"

"Fuck you, wussy," Leroy returned in his heavy brogue.

"Look buddy, we are both going to make some money here if we just chill out. I will call Jack first thing in the morning. We can't go around here at each other's throats all day."

Leroy considered Monica's threatening him with a knife about the equivalent of a flea bite. "I am KGB, you tell that little bitch of yours to stay away from me. Or I make schnitzel with her."

"Okay, big boy, I will tell her while she is outside on the deck loading her Glock. So why don't we just have a full-on shootout and bring the cops around. Jack will really like that, and we can all end up in jail."

"Get out of here, wussy boy."

"Up yours," Stuart replied, turned and slammed the door.

"Just stay away from him. I told him you were packing."

"We are calling Jack in the morning."

"Alright, alright."

Alton dialed Bernie Lanza and asked if they could meet in the Pro Shop and talk for a few minutes. It was Sunday of the Tournament, so Bernie couldn't be away from his roving post for too long. He hadn't seen anything suspicious anyway.

Next, stop was the admin offices of the Chambers Bay Golf Club. He was able to get access to the club's security tapes from Monday to Friday evening, and that took him an hour to scroll through with no results.

He chatted with Alexander Herron, CBays General Manager who had conducted interviews with all of the operating departments of the club, and found nothing.

The parking permit records were with the club's accounting offices, and not a part of the LPGA's records at all he discovered. Thumbing through 300 some permit applications took some time, but he didn't see any names that looked familiar. All of those individuals would have to be contacted personally, and a lot of them were from out of town. Over half of them were players, friends of players, friends of friends of someone. The other half were just people who would rather pay five hundred bucks for a permit, as opposed to riding in on public transportation with the masses. Profiling a list of 300 people could take hours, and might be another dead end. He finally decided to just go out to the course, walk around some, and try to collect his thoughts. Somehow, he needed to find that needle in the haystack.

By now, the leaders were well into the back nine of the Tournament. It looked like a dogfight that might come down to the last hole or two between a couple of the Asian girls, one of Spain's premier players and the reigning Canadian Champion. He felt sure Chrissy Jensen would have been in there, had she been able, slugging it out for the title as he continued to mingle about in the crowd. Alton had enjoyed his time on the courses working as a grass roots marketing rep for the tour. He basically just did a walk about and chatted people up at every opportunity, trying to ascertain and continue to define hot spots the tour could capitalize on.

He began to stroll back towards the eighteenth hole and the hospitality tents, when he saw the two blokes who had driven into the player's parking lot while he was talking with the attendant. They were ambling along, drinking beers and stopped to look at the leader board. They started off again towards the eighteenth fairway, and for some reason, Alton was drawn to the two men. He couldn't take his eyes off of them.

And suddenly, it hit him like a crisp Muhammed Ali jab to the jaw. He was looking basically at two older white guys. They had arrived in a black SUV, they were kind of dorky looking, trying to be cool in their own way. That's basically Vincent and Tommy he realized. We are back on the Pelican Hill Golf Course. He looked around at the crowd, and wondered where Vincent and Tommy were anyway?

Two guys who were so interested in the LPGA they had come all the way down to Southern California, then made a point of returning to the course to sit in a nearly empty grandstand to watch Chrissy Jensen hit golf ball after practice golf ball, and waited so long, there were only a few cars left the parking lot when she departed. He bolted for the executive hospitality tents. If they are so infatuated with the LPGA and Chrissy he wondered, where are they today or where have they been all week? Today, on this beautiful day, in practically their own back yard, and they are nowhere to be seen.

Alton raced through the hospitality areas, he went back out to the eighteenth green, and checked the bleachers. He went into the clubhouse, the pro shop, the restaurant and the bar. All of the locations were crammed full of people. It was pretty obvious that Seattleites had flocked out in numbers to support this ground-breaking tournament. But he sure didn't see Vincent and Tommy around anywhere.

"My work here is done," he thought. "I need to go and pay Mr. Vincenzo a visit first thing in the morning."

CHAPTER TWENTY-EIGHT

Monica took off Sunday afternoon to run some errands, but mainly to get out of the house, and away from Leroy. She did some food shopping and also stopped at Lover's Erotic Boutique in the Tacoma Mall and picked out a basic seven-inch, ivory colored vibrator with batteries for Chrissy.

"Good for her," Monica thought to herself. "She might as well have some fun while she is sitting around doing nothing down there 24/7."

That night Monica wrapped the vibrator up in a cloth napkin, and took it down with her on Chrissy's dinner tray. Leroy failed to notice anything unusual.

"You didn't get this from me," Monica whispered to her. "If anybody discovers it, you found it under the bed or something."

The rest of the evening was uneventful. Stuart had made dinner for everyone, and included Leroy as a good will gesture. It was nothing fancy, just ground beef tacos and a Caesar Salad, with fresh Rainier Cherries for dessert. But Leroy seemed pleased by Stuart's courtesy, and willing to bury the hatchet.

Chrissy scarfed her dinner down, and picked up the vibrator. She balanced it in her right hand, and closed her fist around it. Not brass knuckles, she thought, but it's solid, and it will have to do.

She walked up the stairs and onto the upper landing. It was about four feet from the door to the stairs, and six feet wide. The door opened in, but it had been framed out on the interior of the deck landing, almost as if it was added as an afterthought. A railing skirted around the outer edge of the landing and extended from the back wall to the front of the little deck. It then took a ninety-degree left turn and when it met the stairs, it turned right, and proceeded downward.

As the sheetrock had never been completed, there was a space about fifteen inches wide between the door framing and the back-right deck railing. Because the door had been inset, there was some available space set back in from the front of the doorway by about six inches due to the expanded framing codes of the Pacific Northwest. It was just wide enough for her to squeeze into, and if she compressed herself back against the wall, she felt like she would be fairly well concealed in the dim light at the top of the stairs.

Maybe everyone would be half asleep on a Monday morning, and she could sneak up on them. Especially if she rolled the bean bag up in her bed like she was still sleeping. It was worth a try.

Chrissy descended the stairs, retrieved her vibrator, clenched it firmly in her right hand, and began to spar. She could see her shadow from the overhead light against the far wall's paneling, and she stood on the balls of her feet, and began throwing punches for the next half an hour. Right, left, right, left, right. One, two, one, two.

The alarm on her clock radio went off at seven am on Monday morning, and Chrissy got up to began her preparations. She took a hot shower, and put on the navy-blue workout suit, which was the darker of the two outfits Florence had left her. She said a silent prayer it would help conceal her in the dim lighting, then she rolled and flattened the beanbag out as best she could. It was old, and pliable. She laid it on the bed in as close to a sleeping posture as she could get it and covered it with her blankets and pillow. Then she did some stretches and waited.

She hated violating Florence's trust, but if she could do anything to get herself out of here, she would go for it. Turning on KJR Sports Radio 950 am, she listened to the morning talk show hosts, one of them was a young woman, and she was talking about Chrissy's disappearance.

Wow, I'm worth half a million bucks on the street, Chrissy thought. It made her feel super good that she remained on people's minds, and everyone was still looking for her.

Time crawled by. Chrissy wondered if Florence would come early like she had yesterday. She was upstairs and ready by nine fifteen, but by nine forty realized she was back on the regular schedule. Make it ten then she thought.

At nine o'clock Stuart called Jack. "What time do you want me today for our training session?"

"Be at the bar by two."

"The usual place?"

"Yeah."

"When are you coming for the other one, the black one?" Stuart asked, referring to the town car that was still sitting in the garage.

"Tommy is coming with me this morning. We will be there around ten. I am driving us, and then Tommy will do his own thing."

"Okay see you later on."

"Everything else going okay?"

"Pretty much. We had a little dust up yesterday between Florence and Leroy, but I think we patched it up. It got pretty hot for a while. Probably be a good idea if you sat down with us for a few minutes, and just told everybody to start getting along."

"I can do that. See you in an hour," Vincent replied in an annoyed voice.

Leroy stumbled out of his bedroom at ten. He wasn't as hung over as Sunday morning, but he was still groggy, and he headed straight for the coffee pot. At least he has on sweat pants today, Monica observed, but he was still shirtless. He thinks he is a stud, but doesn't he realize how bad his body odor is?

Crazy times call for crazy measures, I guess, Chrissy thought, but the irony of the situation brought a smile to her face, and reminded her of the Psychology Department, History of Sexuality class she had taken in her junior year at the U. It was one of those courses no one really forgets. From Chaucer's *Canterbury Tales* to the Victorian Era, where Chaucer's early volumes (written in the fourteenth century) had been the first major work of any note to proclaim that women were more powerful than men in governing sexual contact and control in a relationship. Continuing on, the curriculum taught how Western Women were still treated largely as chattel throughout the middle ages, and culminated in the Victorian Era. Where, during these sexually repressive times of the nineteenth century--little more than one hundred years ago, and the author is not taking any poetic or literary license here--women were still often treated either at home or in a medical facility for hysteria and "ladies" type afflictions by professional physicians. Hysteria had been considered a malady of women since the Roman physician Galen in 300 BC, and when the female patient was diagnosed as suffering from anxiety, depression, nervousness, etc. by the (usually male) doctor, they were scheduled for an office visit, and were given a pelvic massage and stimulated to vaginal orgasm by the attending physician. Called a "Hysterical Paroxysm" by the medical professionals of the day, the treatment wasn't considered sexual in nature, rather it was therapeutic and clinical, and the successful climax that was achieved, would temporarily alleviate the maladies and vaginal blockage of the long-suffering patient.

The treatment was so widely practiced, physicians of those times, found it to be tiresome and physically taxing, and often delegated it to young assistants.

Around the turn of the twentieth century, the development of what was called a vibrating appliance was invented and formulated. At first, these devices were very cumbersome and expensive, but by the nineteen twenties had evolved into sizes more conducive to personal use.

Still, there were stigmas to obtaining one of the new appliances by any "respectable" woman, and they were still costly. This did not apply to the privileged classes, of course. Then came the Great Depression and World War II, and diverted the nation's attention to the more pressing issues of the cratering economy and the nation's defense.

As our country steadily returned to postwar normalcy, the nineteen sixties rolled around, and the advent of Gloria Steinem and the modern Women's Liberation Movement gained considerable prominence, visibility and momentum. Into these euphoric times, the personal vibrator began to reinsert itself. No pun intended. By the nineteen eighties, studies have indicated that over half of the female population in the United States of America, either owned or had experimented with a personal vibrator. And in response to the dramatic spike in demand, countless number of products entered the marketplace that promoted convenience, sensuality, options in materials, size, color, variety or function, and anticipated results. A person could even get a discretely packaged, affordable sex toy delivered to their home from a mail order house or catalogue now. Often couples began to shop together for products which would help in satisfying their mutual needs. "You've come a long way baby" was a popular slogan of the times.

And now, Chrissy thought, here I am concealed, and ready to assault a man with the very phallic substitute that had partially replaced the need for his services in the first place. Not assault him sexually, but in a much broader sense of the term. Her humble vibrator had evolved into more than a sex toy. It was going to multifunction for her as a weapon of self-defense.

At ten o'clock or a couple minutes after, Chrissy felt footsteps approaching the basement door. She took several deep breaths to quiet her nerves, and heard the door locks turn. She sucked in her stomach, which wasn't hard to do, and leaned back into the wall as tightly as she could. She had left the closest of the overhead lights off, which was unusual for her, but it made the lighting much darker than normal. Monica advanced onto the landing, but hesitated when she noticed things appeared to be so much dimmer. She began descending the stairway carefully, partially assisted by the light coming in from the open door above and behind her.

"Chrissy," she called out. When she got to the bottom of the stairs, she found the light switch on her left, and flipped it on. She could now see Chrissy's body form in the bed. Maybe she's not feeling well or this whole ordeal is just starting to get to her, she thought.

Leroy walked halfway onto the landing, and bent at the waist to see what was going on down the stairs.

"Now," Chrissy said to herself. She stepped forward, clenched her right fist tightly around her modified brass knuckles, and uncorked a solid roundhouse at a still bent over Leroy's head. She swung with all of her might, turning her body nicely into the punch, and got her full weight and momentum behind her arm and shoulder. She caught Leroy between his right ear and temple, and knocked him forward. Then she gave him a vicious kick to the rear area of his right ankle and Achilles Tendon. He was dazed, wounded, and pitched headfirst toward the steps stretching out in front of him. He couldn't catch himself on the railing, fell forward, and began to thump face first down the stairs. Chrissy felt no remorse for him.

"What the hell," Florence shouted, and ran to the bed. She whipped the top cover back, saw the bean bag, and dropped the breakfast tray on the floor. She realized what Chrissy had done, and turned around, she saw Leroy crumpled at the bottom of the steps. She heard the basement door slam shut, and realized they had left the key in the deadbolt as always, awaiting their departure. She hurried over to the bottom of the stairs and shoved Leroy with her foot to see if he was still alive. He was breathing, so she brought her foot back, and kicked him in the head to make sure he would stay out for a while. She thoroughly enjoyed that, then she vaulted up the stairs, and began to scream Sammy's name out.

Stuart was half asleep up in the master bedroom, and heard some commotion going on. At first he thought it might be Monica and Leroy going at it again, but it sounded more like muffled screams coming from Monica. He jumped out of bed, stumbled into some pants, pulled his ski mask on, and bolted for the basement.

Chrissy had already pulled the heavy, solid oak door closed behind her, and turned the deadbolt with the key Leroy and Florence had so thoughtfully left behind. She turned and squinted her eyes into the brightness of the first full sunlight she had seen in three days. Thinking there was some movement coming from somewhere, she sprinted through the mud room, into the open kitchen, and saw the front entryway across the large, open room to her left. She made a dash for the front door. It was her passage to freedom, and it was just steps away.

Vincent picked Tommy up at the auto body shop where they were to drop the town car upon its retrieval. Tommy wasn't too happy to be returning to the rental/stash house in Gig Harbor, and proceeded to carp at Vinnie most of the way over the Tacoma Narrows bridge.

"Why couldn't the damn kid bring the car back?" was the crux of his complaint.

"Jeez T, we are getting a half a share. The least you could do is help take care of the stupid town car for me. I'm doing everything else here."

"Whatever. Let's just get this over with." The two mobsters rolled down into the Gig Harbor house driveway, and parked in the secluded turnabout. Tommy already had a fake beard on, and just to be safe, he pulled on his chauffeur's cap, and Oakley sunglasses.

"Let's go into the garage through the house," Vincent said. He was out of the Escalade and walking nonchalantly ahead of Tommy. Adjusting his aviator sunglasses in the glare, he hopped up onto the front porch. Vincent was six or seven steps from the massive front entryway, when he heard the door handle rattle.

Chrissy on the other side of the door, turned around one last time to see if she was in any danger, or if anyone was pursuing her. She heard Sammy's movement, which seemed to be coming closer, and she flung the door open, squinted into the bright sunlight, put her head down, and started running out of the house at full speed.

Vincent who thought Stuart or Monica was opening the door for him, looked up and saw Chrissy come barreling out of the house, and right at him. He was so shocked at seeing her, he stood gaping, rooted to the porch, and in an instant, one of those slo/mo moments where you know what is coming, but are powerless to do anything, Chrissy ran right into and over him. The crown of her head caught Vincent on the side of his nose, and the left cheekbone/eye socket area. She broke his sunglasses, as she slammed into him. It was as if she was an NFL linebacker and had speared him with her helmet. Vincent went down like a sack of cement.

Tommy who had a little more time to react, bent at the waist, and let Chrissy's momentum bring her right to him. He braced himself for their collision, and he grabbed her legs behind the knees, and straightened up. This threw Chrissy over his right shoulder, and he bolted for the front door. He shoved the door open with Chrissy's protruding buttocks, and kicked it shut with his left foot. All this while Chrissy was slamming him on the back with something hard and pointy in one of her fists, and was screaming "Help me, help me," like bloody murder.

Tommy back hurt from Chrissy's blows, and he ran with her in to the great room. To quiet her down, Tommy threw her off of his back, and down onto the hardwood floor. That knocked the wind out of her, and gave Tommy time to reach down with both hands, and in spite of Chrissy trying to kick him in the groin, he flipped her over onto her stomach. He was sitting astride her lower back, with her pony tail in one hand, and was getting ready to smash her face into the floor to shut her up, when Stuart ran up.

"Don't hurt her, don't hurt her, she's under control now."

He heard Monica yelling at him from behind the basement door, and told Tommy he would be right back. He hustled over to the door, and unlocked it. Monica emerged shaking, and saw Chrissy on the floor. "Thank God," she said.

"Where's Leroy?" Stuart asked.

"He fell down the stairs. He's out cold," Monica told him.

"Let's get her back downstairs," Stuart said. He wanted to get Chrissy away from Tommy as quickly as possible. They forewarned Chrissy to keep her mouth shut, before grabbing her legs and dragging her to the basement door. She was still struggling, but the two men had overpowered her, and once in the basement she was manhandled downstairs and thrown onto her bed.

"Lay down on your belly, face to the wall, and shut the fuck up," she was told.

Tommy told Monica to go back and take care of Vincent. She rushed toward the front door, and was able to grab Vincent's arms, and drag him back into the house. Everyone was glad they had an obscured driveway.

Going into the kitchen after some cold water, Monica saw Chrissy's vibrator lying on the floor, half under the back of the wraparound couch. She wasn't sure if Stuart or Tommy had seen it, but she scooped it up and took it into the kitchen and stashed it in the dish towel drawer for the time being.

Bringing some water back with her, she was strong enough to horse Vincent up onto the couch, and got a cold compress on his head. He began to slowly revive. Stuart and Tommy were doing the same thing with Leroy in the basement. Vincent began to shake his head and regain consciousness. Monica tried to help him as best she could. He was still laid out on the couch, and she refreshed his cold compress with another one, and cleaned away the blood on his face from where his sunglasses had shattered and lacerated him.

Suddenly there was a knocking on the front door. Monica scooted over to the basement door, and told Tommy and Stuart to keep quiet, she closed that door and went out to see who was on the front porch.

"Hello honey," an older woman said. "I live two doors down, and I thought I heard some commotion over here."

"You know ma'am, I thought I heard something too. Maybe it came from some kids playing out on the water."

"Hmm, well, I just wanted to make sure everything was okay with you."

"Oh yes, thank you so much. We are here vacationing from Portland, and I'll keep my ears open for anything. What did you say your name was?"

"It's Wilkinson, honey. Margie Wilkinson."

Margie looked like she wanted to come in and visit for a spell, but Monica told her she had something on the stove, and needed to get back in the kitchen. "I'll bring you over some fresh made blackberry jam," Monica threw out as a peace offering.

"How sweet of you honey, that's very thoughtful," Margie said.

"Think nothing of it. I'll come by tomorrow if I can, and we can visit for a spell." Monica smiled, and closed the door gently.

Margie headed back home, but left wondering why a girl wearing a niqab would be making homemade jam, and then, how the niqab got so messed up and crooked looking anyway. Strange people, those Portlanders, she concluded.

Monica's timing was exquisite. The door had no sooner closed, when Vincent groaned loudly, and almost fell off of the couch. He was trying to sit up, and he was not happy.

"Who in the hell was that?" he asked gruffly.

"Some old lady from down the street. She wanted to make sure everything was okay."

"What in the devil just happened here? You people are supposed to be keeping that broad locked up, and she almost killed me."

"It seemed like she was tame as a little lap dog, then she ambushed us this morning when we went in to feed her. She had one of the lights out, and after I went down the stairs with her breakfast, she was hiding up on the landing, and she attacked Leroy. He took a tumble downstairs, and I don't know if he is hurt bad or not."

"Amateurs, miserable amateurs. All you had to do was keep her quiet and locked up. Hells bells, she probably got your stupid radio, and starting listening to all of the news reports about her ransom, and got some crazy ideas. Go and see how they are doing with Leroy down there will you." It was a direct order, not a request.

Monica went downstairs, and saw Chrissy lying face down on the bed. The guys were trying to arouse Leroy, and had actually gotten him into a sitting position, but he was pretty dazed. His forehead had a large lump on it, the left side of his face was all scratched up, and he had the glassy-eyed look of someone who was suffering a grade 2 or 3 concussion.

"Let me get you some ice, maybe that will help."

Hurrying back up upstairs, Monica found Vincent on his feet and stirring about. She got a mixing bowl, filled it with ice cubes, grabbed a couple of dish towels, and headed for the basement.

"You people are lucky me and Tommy was here. The cops would be on your asses already. You would be in the back of a patrol car right now," Vincent growled as she passed by him.

The ice seemed to help Leroy out. "WTF," he mumbled, and Stuart and Tommy helped him to his feet, and guided him up the stairs and to his room. Monica wasn't sure if Chrissy needed any ice, or if they had just thrown her on the bed and told her not to move. Whatever.

Monica followed the guys up the stairs to where Vincent was standing in the kitchen, and he told her to go back down and get the flipping radio. Vincent was about ready to grab the radio and beat someone's head in with it.

What a pain in the butt this thing is turning into, she thought. Maybe I should just bail now, and head for Manilla. I've already got my airline ticket.

Leroy made it to his bed, but his head was spinning, and a severe headache wracked his thick Slavic skull. Tommy returned to the great room, and saw Vincent was back on his feet.

"Great job partner, you slowed her down for me. I am out of here."

"No kidding I slowed her down. That stupid little tonta almost killed me."

"Get over it. I'm gone." Tommy walked into the garage, and hit the door opener with his knuckle. He would drive the town car back to the south end, and then be rid of these incompetent boobs. Forever, he hoped.

"Damn it, Sammy. What the hell is going on around here? I leave you to watch the broad, and if me and Tommy don't come over this morning, youse is in jail now. Probably squawking like a pregnant canary too."

"Hey, don't blame me. It happened on Leroy's shift, not mine. He's your guy."

"Whatever."

"Listen, why don't you just take off, go look after your eye. We are back on top of it now. We don't really need Leroy around here anyway. Why don't you take him with you?"

"No. Let him stay here and sleep it off. I have some Oxycodone at my office, you can pick it up when you come see me at two o'clock. I'm going to go back and ice up my eye. How does it look?"

"You gonna have a shiner pretty quick, but I think you'll be alright."

"See you at two. Don't be late. You want me to have Dimitri come over here later on?"

"No, we will be okay."

"Don't anyone go in that basement alone with her. We should just go down and tie her to the damn bed right now."

"Then how is she supposed to go to the bathroom?" Monica asked.

"Give her a damn bedpan." Vincent replied.

"And who is supposed to empty that thing?" Monica said.

"Ah, the hell with it. Don't have no more screw ups around here, got it? I just want to get her out of here. We gonna call them tomorrow. You start gettin' ready for that."

Vincent was fuming. His head ached, his eye and cheek were sore and swelling. Now he was going to have a black eye, a migraine, and have to manufacture up an excuse for everyone, especially Angela. He wobbled out to his car, started it, and slowly backed up. Thank God for small favors me and T was here, he thought.

"What happened to you, boss?" Vincent's bartender asked when he walked in the side door of his restaurant.

"You should see the other guy. Get me some ice in a plastic bag, will ya?"

Vincent walked to his booth in the rear corner of the room and sat down heavily. The barkeep came over with his ice, and he asked her for a cup of coffee, and a double shot of scotch. It was five minutes to twelve, and his regulars and some stragglers were drifting in for lunch.

"You want something to eat?"

"Nah."

She walked away to get Vincent's coffee and liquor. He laid his cell phone on the table, and reached into his back, left pants pocket for his burner phone. He changed his mind about eating, and leaned his head out around the edge of his bench-backed booth seat, to ask for a bowl of soup with his drinks, and found himself looking directly down the hallway at Alton Walker. Alton was standing at the end of the bar checking things out, and now he had found what he was looking for.

He walked down the aisleway to Vincent's booth, got there, said hello, and slid into the bench seat directly across from Vincent.

Ah shit, Vincent thought. What else could possibly go wrong today?

The bartender caught up with Alton in two seconds flat. "You need an appointment to come back here, buddy," she snapped at him.

"Oh, I won't be but a couple of minutes," Alton said."

"You want me to get Dimitri, Vincent?"

Why make it any worse than it is? Vinnie thought. "He's okay, Betty. Let him stay for a couple of minutes. How you doin', kid. Where is your broads?"

"The tournament is over Vincent. Everyone's gone down to San Francisco for the next one."

"Sure. How come you is still here then?"

"Well, Chrissy Jensen is still missing, and they wanted me to stay around and help look for her. I figured with your contacts, we could chase her down, and collect that half million-dollar reward money."

"What in the hell is you talking about? My contacts. I ain't got no contacts."

"Gee, Vincent, I did some checking around this morning, and you seem to be a pretty well-known guy. I googled you, and found out you were in the joint a few years back. You must know some kinda guys who could pull off something like a big-time kidnapping, eh?"

"You being some kind of a wise ass, kid? I don't know nothin' about no damn kidnapping."

Alton wondered why an old guy like Vincent would need a burner phone to go along with his cell. Looked like he was just about to use it too, it was sitting on the table right in front of him. Alton felt like grabbing both of the cell phones, and getting his fanny out of there before he had to deal with Dimitri. But he didn't want to totally alienate Vincent. "Hey sorry, I didn't mean to offend you, my man. Did you go to the tournament at all? I didn't see you out there?"

"No, I been busy with family in town all weekend. I been playin' tour guide for the last four days. It almost drove me crazy. How did it go over there, except for the girl got snatched, I mean?"

"It went okay. I guess. It was kind of a downer though, because everyone was upset about Chrissy. It was all about Chrissy, Chrissy, Chrissy all weekend."

"Yeah, she seems to be a fucking handful, don't she?" Vincent, still semi-foggy from his collision with Chrissy's head offered up an interesting description to Alton.

"A handful? What's that supposed to mean?"

"I mean maneater. She's a bit of a pain in the ass, I heard. A real bitch." Well, there is another strange comment Alton thought. Chrissy, a bitch? Not hardly, buddy.

"What happened to your eye, man? Looks like you got popped pretty good. You get out of line with your mother-in-law just now?"

"None of your damn business what happened to my eye. So, what else can I do for you?"

"I told you, Vincent, I'm after that reward."

"Well there ain't no rewards around here. And if you don't mind, I need to get some work done. I've got a couple of meetings this afternoon. Maybe you could come back another time, eh? We could go out and drive around and look for golfer girl, make us a half million bucks."

"Yeah, okay. I better leave anyway you so you can take care of that eye. It's starting to swell up pretty good. Can I ask you one more question man?"

"Whatever."

"If someone were to snatch the girl, why wouldn't they have called in a ransom demand by now?"

"Why you keep asking me about Chrissy Jensen? I don't know nothin' about her. Why would I know anything about that broad?"

"I just thought you might know something, is all."

"Get the hell outta here will ya? I got work to do.

"Sorry to be a bother, but, good to see you again. I'll call before I come by next time. Hey, by the way, where did you get that burner phone? I need one."

"How should I know, Dimitri gets 'em."

"How is the reception? What kind of phone is it, anyway?" Alton reached down and quickly picked up the phone. He turned it over and saw the ALC@TEL brand logo on the back of the phone case before Vincent snatched it out of his hand.

"Don't touch my damn stuff, man."

"Sorry, I was just wondering what kind of phone it was. How did you say the reception was?"

"The reception is fine. I don't use it all that much." Just when you want to call in a ransom demand Alton thought.

"See you around Vincent."

"Later, Kid. Hope you find da broad."

Alton went out and sat down on the far side of the bar. Lunch was halfway over, and as things were slowing down, Alton thought he might as well have a beer.

Betty glared at him from down the backbar. "Whadda ya want?" she asked.

"Sorry to bust in on you earlier, doll. I ain't seen Vincent in so long I got excited and forgot to call ahead."

"Don't ever do that. He don't like no drop-ins."

"Well, sorry again. He is just such an old friend to me, like a father really."

"Ha, ha, that's a good one. Vincent a daddy again. You could be his red headed stepchild."

"How many children does he have?"

"He's got kids, but he ain't got no family close by is all. That's why he sits around this bar of his all the time."

"Anyone visit him this weekend? I mean like from his family?"

"You need to start minding your own business, buddy."

"Sorry, sorry. I would just like to meet them is all." Hmmm, Alton thought.

Betty moved on down the bar to tend to her customers.

Alton's early beer went down smoothly, and he decided to move along. He doubted if Betty would serve him again anyway, even if he wanted another one. He left a twenty-dollar bill for Betty, and headed out of the darkened bar for his car.

Betty walked back to Vincent's booth as soon as Alton was gone. "Who the hell is that guy?" she asked.

"Some goofball I met at a golf tournament a while back."

"He come back in the bar, ordered a beer, and was asking questions about you."

"You're kidding me. What did he axk you?"

"Wanted to know about your family."

"What did you tell him?"

"I didn't say anything specific, and then he wanted to know if any of them had visited you this weekend. He was asking all innocent like."

"You didn't say nothing about nothing did you?"

"Hell no. I told him to buzz off. I just thought you should know he was askin' is all."

"Thanks, Betty."

His bartender's comments gave Vincent pause for concern. What was this damn redheaded hoser up to, and why did he come barging in here today? In his younger days, Vincent would have already been on the phone, arranging a meeting for Alton with Dimitri and a couple of his buddies.

CHAPTER TWENTY-NINE

Stuart made it to Vincent's bar at one thirty on Monday afternoon and was ready to get on with phase two of their operation. Chrissy's near escape had rattled both he and Monica. Stuart was beyond aggravated at how devious she had been, at how close her escape attempt had come to succeeding, and Monica hadn't even told him about the vibrator. They would have been in deep shit had golfer girl made it out of the house, and from now on, she was on a very short leash.

Monica was especially flummoxed at being played by Chrissy. But it wouldn't, damn well wouldn't, happen again. Now when she went into the basement, she would go with her pistol in hand, set the food tray on the stair landing, while Chrissy was instructed to lie face down on the bed, and then she would leave straightaway. No more clean linen, no more broiled salmon, no more chit-chat, no more jack for you honey!

Stuart and Vincent went into the back room, "How's your eye?" Stuart asked while Vincent called Ronnie on the burner phone at two o'clock sharp. "It's fine," Vincent mouthed while the phone was ringing. It sure looks like hell, Stuart thought.

"Good afternoon Bill," Vincent opened the conversation.

"Good afternoon."

"Bill, we are at your disposal on how to best handle these negotiations. Please share your ideas with us." He put the phone on its' speaker setting.

"In the first place, gentlemen, this is not a negotiation. The last thing you want is a negotiation. These people are expert negotiators. You will not get into that arena with them. This is more of a paradigm for you to follow." Neither Vincent or Stuart knew what paradigm meant, but they continued to listen intently. "You are to deliver your instructions to a significant person of interest, and deal with that person exclusively. You will not talk to or deal with any law enforcement personnel of any kind. Especially not anyone from the FBI. Also, Vincent, your accent is too strong, the kid should do the talking."

How does Bill know who I am? Stuart wondered.

"Have you decided who you will be dealing with yet?" Bill asked.

"We believe it is her older brother," Stuart replied.

"You find out who is her significant money person, her manager, her agent, her father, her brother whoever, and you deal only with that one person. But you need to practice a few things first. Make sure you speak confidently. You are strong and sure of yourself. You give them your demands, and you keep your communication short and sweet. And I mean short. You start with a phone call on a new burner. You buy a distortion device to camouflage your voice. Give them your instructions, give them your expected delivery date, and hang up. You maintain control of the calls at all times. Then you will get back to 'um the next day to make sure they understand what is expected of them, and make sure they are busy raising money. You do not stay on the phone. The FBI has extensive tracking equipment, and they will be pulling out every stop on a high-profile case such as this. You will have no more than eighty seconds to make your call. Capiche?"

He is another Italian, Stuart thought. Mob connections? That ran through his head too.

"Yes sir."

"By the third day, you continue to inquire about the money. Is it all collected? Are they ready to perform? Hopefully, they are. If they want to ask questions, or debate with you, hang up on them. By Thursday, they should be almost ready to go. You make sure they have gathered most of the money, and are conforming to your demands. They will be given the general drop information, for example, they gonna need a boat, they gonna package the dough a certain way. This stuff is of course, non-negotiable. You tell them that if they don't perform, she will lose a finger for every day they delay. You can Fed-Ex them a finger if you like, just to show them you are serious."

"Yes sir." Where are we supposed to find a freaking finger laying around Stuart wondered?

"You call them on Friday morning, and set the pickup time for Friday evening, am I correct?"

"Yes sir."

"Again, you are dealing with the same person all week, and they are not any kind of law enforcement personnel. If the fuzz ever gets on the phone, you will hang up. You give them the specific details of the drop late in the afternoon on Friday. In the meantime, they need to have their boat, they need to have the money, the money is packaged properly. You will give them no window of time for the cops or anybody else to set up any kind of trap, or have a chance to surveil any of your activities. You must make it extremely clear to them that if they fuck with you in any way, and I mean in any way, their girl is in eminent danger of losing her life. Are we clear on that one?"

"Yes sir."

"I certainly hope you have planned your exchange thoroughly. I can't help you with that. I am just here to help with your prep, and assist in setting up your deal.   Any questions."

"What if the cops take over any of the conversations, and turn it into a negotiation?"

"Don't you listen? You will never, ever talk to the cops. Period. If they attempt to interfere or interject themselves into the conversation, you hang up, and send them a fucking finger. You make it clear to whoever you talk to in the first place, that under no circumstances do they ever put a cop on that phone. The pigs will have everything recorded anyway. They will hear every word you are saying. They will be doing traces on you, they will be doing voice modulations, they will be monitoring your diction, analyzing your conversations. You get on that phone and you be short and sweet. You give them your demands, and you hang up. And you do it with a fresh burner every day. Preferably a different brand of burner, and you use a voice distortion device."

"What if they want some kind of proof she's okay?"

"I have considered that, and decided it would be okay to let her talk to her guy for maybe ten seconds on the first day. You have a gun to her head, and she can say to them, that she is okay, and if they play ball and follow your orders to a tee, she will continue to be okay, but to please, please help get me out of there. That's it. And I'm serious, you have a gun to her head. If she gets any ideas, you better deal with her pronto."

"Got it. But she don't know who none of us is. She don't even have no idea where she is or anything. She couldn't do too much damage, even if she did get ideas, which she won't." Vincent continued, "We will explain to her that the end is in sight. Behave and you will be out of here in one piece. It ain't a good idea for her to mess up. She will know that."

"That's about it, gentlemen. Good luck," and with that, Ronnie the Barber terminated his end of their phone call.

That guy sure sounded a lot like the asshole who ripped into me at lunch that first day, Stuart thought.

"You got everything?" Vincent asked.

"I'm good," Stuart replied.

"Hi Cynthia."

"Hello, Penny. What's going on?"

"I just wanted to let you know I have spoken with Alton, and he has sworn to me that he wasn't smoking pot in the town car. He said he was driving the girls around, and Buford and Mancebo's friends saw a pot shop, and wanted to stop. I guess they had never seen one before. They pretty much demanded he stop for them, which he did. Unbeknownst to him, they ended up buying some weed, and fired up in the back seat of the car while he was driving. He is in an awkward position, because he is just the driver, and they are the tour players. He was pretty mad at them actually."

"You swear to God?"

"Absolutely. And I told him what would happen if he went back to Headquarters, and failed a test."

"Okay. You stay for the rest of this week then. And there is some more good news. I spoke to Lannie Yang the International Players Rep this morning, and twenty of the international ladies stepped up and donated five thousand bucks apiece right after the tournament yesterday. Isn't that awesome? That will bring the reward money up to six hundred thousand."

"That is so awesome, I can't believe it, Cyn. Have you talked to anyone about it yet?" Penny said.

"I have a call in to Tina right now. Yeah, the ladies gathered in the locker room, and had an impromptu meeting after the tournament. They wanted to do something to help, so twenty of them chipped in. Tina is going to contact the Golf Channel and ESPN. If you could contact the local stations and print media, we should have the word out by this afternoon. Anything else going on?"

"Not that I have heard. Alton worked on social media all morning and was over at the course scouting around this afternoon. Other than that, everything is still same, same."

"Okay, I'll let you go. Get on the phone and social media, and let people know about the additional reward money."

"Will do."

Penny sighed and began dialing. She was starting to hit the wall.

After their teleconference, Vincent was worn out and ready to hang it up for the day. But he still had a few things to review with Stuart, who apologized profusely over the morning's snafu, and promised nothin such would ever happen again.

"How did your test run go on Saturday?"

"It went well," Stuart replied. "We got there in just over ten minutes, and were across the Narrows in another twenty. About a half an hour in all, door to door."

You lying little shit Vincent thought. "You get up under the dock okay? It's not too shallow out there is it?"

"Nope, it's about eight feet deep at the end of the dock. Should give us plenty of coverage."

"Yeah, I think your buddy is going to have to come into the house with you. There will be too much danger in him trying to swim his way back out of there."

"Whatever you say, Vincent."

"You go back to the house and practice your little speech with Monica. You're gonna need to get a distortion device."

"No, problem, Vincent. I already bought one on line."

"Okay then. I will be over there about nine thirty tomorrow morning. We go down and talk to her, find out who she wants us to call, and we get it going," Vincent said.

"I can talk to her tonight, and get an idea who she wants us to deal with. I think that might help me prepare a little better," Stuart replied.

"If you can do that without her kicking your ass and running off down the street, do it."

"Not to worry, boss. Anytime we go in there again, Monica has her Glock drawn."

"Monica has a weapon?"

"Yeah. She brought it along for safety sake," Stuart said. "I think it might come in handy."

Vincent stared at Stuart as if he was thinking about what needed to be done. When in reality, he was recalling Dimitri's report on Stuart and Chet's diving run. How they had never in fact returned to the dock at the house, where Leroy was waiting for them. How they had started out at the Tacoma Narrows Marina and then finished the trial run back there, rather than at the house in Gig Harbor. How Dimitri had learned of the nice new sailing yacht they had stashed in the Marina, and had actually gone aboard and done some snooping after the boys left.

"That oughta do it, eh? Now I havta go home and explain to my wife how I got this black eye." Which by now, was swollen shut.

"So sorry about that, Vincent. See you in the morning, boss."

"Yeah, see you." You incompetent, lying little shithead, Vincent thought.

"KIRO News Desk, how may I help you?"

"May I please speak to the News Director?"

"To whom I am speaking please, and in what regard you are calling?"

"Certainly, this is Penny Brown, I am the Marketing and Information Officer for the LPGA here in Tacoma, and I have an update on the Chrissy Jensen case for you."

"So nice of you to call Ms. Brown, let me get Mr. Rollins for you."

"Penny Brown, how nice to hear from you again. This is Marcus Rollins speaking. How can I help?"

"Mr. Rollins, I am calling to let you and your viewers know that some of the actual players, the international women of the LPGA tour themselves, called an ad hoc meeting with their peers after the tournament ended yesterday afternoon, and pledged an additional one hundred thousand dollars to the reward fund for the rescue of their friend and fellow professional, Chrissy Jensen. Any person or persons who can furnish information that would lead to the arrest of the kidnappers or lead to her physical recovery would be eligible to collect the six hundred-thousand-dollar reward."

"I think the incremental increases in the reward have caused your story to remain in the spotlight, Penny, and hopefully some resolve will be coming soon. We at KIRO News, will continue to lead off our nightly broadcasts with your updates, and six hundred thousand dollars is certainly an impressive sum. It's is bound to produce some results very soon."

"Thank you so much, Mr. Rollins, we certainly hope so."

"Please call me Marcus."

"Thanks Marcus, bye."

Penny made the same call another half a dozen times that afternoon to both local radio and TV outlets, people she had spoken to once already that day, but her latest update was still equally well received wherever she dialed.

She got back to their Embassy Suites room that night about five minutes after Alton had rolled in. He was drinking a beer in the kitchenette, and came over to give her a hug. She undid her belt, and let her business skirt drop to the floor. She unbuttoned his shirt and pushed him backward onto the couch. She took off her silk tee shirt, straddled him on her knees and sat forward in his lap. She put her arms around his waist, snuggled into his chest, and began to sob quietly. Alton held her on his lap for a long time.

"I just can't get the image of Chrissy's and her brother, from the fund raiser, out of my head. I had to deal with all of the local media again today, and I am just so scared that something bad has happened to her."

Alton caressed her beautiful strawberry blond, shoulder length hair. "Well, no news is good news, baby, something is sure to turn up soon." Alton hadn't said anything of his activities or suspicions to Penny. He knew as soon as he did, she would want to run to the police, and he wasn't sure that was 100% the right thing to do just yet. As conflicted as it made him feel, he decided to let things ride for another day, and kept his arms clasped tightly around Penny's warm body, while he rationalized his next move.

Tacoma Chief of Police Larry Mills and Inspector Danny Chong were sitting in the Chief's office, when the aide on the Jensen case came in and announced the new increase in the reward money. Both of them just groaned at the amount of additional calls from the general public this was going to generate. The main precinct's switch board had been lit up like a Christmas tree with helpful citizens calling in their suspicions. Most of them, as bogus as a knife at a gunfight, but nonetheless, all of the calls had to be entered, evaluated and properly catalogued. Which was even more frustrating for a department who had uncovered next to nothing substantial about the case to date. Chrissy was still missing, there was nothing new to report, and about all Chief Mills and Inspector Chong could do, was to sit around and commiserate with each other over their lack of success in probably the most high-profile case of either of their careers.

"Honey, I'm home," the words ran off of Vincent's lips like water bubbling down a mountain brook. Angela turned to greet her husband, and almost dropped the pizza dough she was kneading.

"What happened, baby?" she gasped, and went over to him and touched his wounded face with the back of a flour smudged hand.

"Oh, I was screwing around with Dimitri in the kitchen, and slipped right when he was throwing a fake punch. He caught my eye, and then I tripped and scraped my face on some burlap potato sacks."

Potato sacks my ass, Angela thought. "What are youse doing horsing around with those guys? They're half your age, and they play rough."

"Ah, we was just foolin' around. It was nothin'. I could take all dos guys in a minute."

"Baloney." Now Angela was really getting agitated. "Sit down at the counter, and I am going to get some ice for your eye. Your face is cut, you got a huge bump on your head, and your eye is swollen shut. What am I going to do with you? You wanna damn drink?"

"Christ, I thought you would never axk, baby." It was a day Vincent would just as soon forget. He was getting extremely tired of herding cats to get this job done, his head was aching like crazy, and he was sick to death of working with amateurs and risking life and limb for what? His little "partners" were trying to bend him over, and were screwing around with the cash drop not to mention his computer. It don't matter none, he thought, I could be a made guy when this is all over and the bunch of youse is dead if you ever think of messin' wit me.

The Jensen compound was maybe a notch above a morgue. It was Monday night, the tournament was over, most of the houseguests were gone. Steve Reed had extended his stay for another day or two, but the rest of the family, except for Ginny's older sister Elaine, were departed back to their individual lives and routines. Tina and Will had consummated their relationship, and she was staying over at the compound now. Ginny found great joy in having another bright, mature, young, together woman around the house, and was growing accustomed to leaning on Tina for emotional support during this painful time. Tina seemed to have become a surrogate daughter to her.

Bob, Will, Charlie, Steve and Bobby were hanging, hoping and praying something was going to break soon.

"Hey, come look at this," Bob trumpeted from the den. He was watching SportsCenter on ESPN, and was the first to see the generous gesture from Chrissy's peers on the tour, when a news flash interrupted his show. "Some of the girls are pitching in another hundred grand in reward money."

One hundred thousand dollars is not a trifling amount or a small gesture, and it is amazing how a generous token like this can spike emotions and aspirations. "This is going to put us over the top. I know it will. I can feel it," a jubilant Bob Jensen spoke out. The immediate family crowded into the den, including Will and Tina, who of course, already knew of the players largesse. But for Ginny and Bob it was like a life line.

"Something is happening," Ginny said. "I can feel it. You mark my words, tomorrow we are going to have a breakthrough in this sickening thing."

Bobby gave his mother a hug. "I'm feelin' it, mom, I'm feelin' it, too."

CHAPTER THIRTY

Vincenzo Joseph DeGrazzi's parents were born in a boot, a Sicilian Boot, and migrated to the US in 1943 as one of the last group of immigrants to ever pass through venerable Ellis Island. They were newlyweds, still in their late teens, had in-laws in the so-called Garlic Gulch region of Seattle, Washington, to which location, they continued their migration. Federico DeGrazzi was an automobile mechanic, and his wife Martina an artist in the genre of Italian cuisine. After ten years of hard work and pinching pennies, they bought a five-acre dirt farm in the south end, down towards Rainier Valley. RV was dubbed Garlic Gulch because of the predominance of Italian settlers and immigrants in the area. It was an ethnic farming community that stretched along the south eastern corridor of the brawling Pacific Northwest city of Seattle.

While Seattle proper had outfitted the miners and sourdoughs who set off for Alaska to claim their fortunes in early gold stampedes, while fishing, timber, and burgeoning airline manufacturing industries thrived in the early 1960's, Garlic Gulch offered more of a pastoral lifestyle in the shadow of Mount Rainier. To most of the emigres from the often hot, dry, bony peninsula of Sicily, it was lush, green, and heaven on earth.

Vincenzo was born in 1969. He was a gift that came late to the DeGrazzis, and understandably, his parents and three older sisters cherished the chubby little boy. When Vincenzo arrived, the small family farm was flourishing, and Vinnie as the family called him, grew up in relatively thriving times in the Pacific Northwest. The DeGrazzis enjoyed these modern times, but they also lived a traditional Italian life style they had brought to America with them from the old world.

Family meals were celebrated festively. Their family land supported several dozen laying hens, kept a couple of milk cows and goats, maintained a large green garden, and Martina commanded her kitchen with skill and finesse. Vinnie grew up eating four-star Italian cuisine, all made with love and fresh milk, eggs and butter by his mother in the farmhouse kitchen. Her summer salads, vegetable dishes and baked goods couldn't be touched by any of the other neighborhood ladies. In addition to selling some of her fresh produce up at Pike's Place Market, Martina even started importing olive oil from the old country, and made another small business providing it to her friends and neighbors. When he had time, Federico took Vinnie fishing to supplement their table. Desserts like Cannoli and Tiramisu were packed into his school lunchbox every day. His mother and older sisters doted on him.

Vinnie could have gotten himself a pony had he asked for one, but the cars, trucks, and engines his father worked on were much more interesting to him. Federico taught the boy well, and by fourteen, Vinnie was running various errands for his mom and dad in the trusty, old family pickup truck.

High school for Vinnie was more of a place to meet girls, and compete with the guys. He would grow to be five foot ten inches in stature, but was built like a fireplug, loved athletics and was tough as an uncracked walnut. He played halfback and defensive back on his high school football team, and was a star shortstop on the varsity baseball team from his freshman year on. Academically no one was quite sure of Vincent's capabilities as he was not one to apply himself much in the classroom, but he was polite to his teachers and did average work, so no one complained much. There were rumored to be several colleges interested in his baseball talents.

As soon as he turned sixteen, Vinnie took a job driving for Mr. Santini, who was like the Mayor of Garlic Gulch. He owned several businesses, and ran the Sons of Italy at the Catholic Church.

Everyone knew Mr. Santini, and most of the community had at one time or another come and knocked on his door for a small loan, some business advice, some personal council or a little help smoothing over a scrape with the law. He also ran the numbers syndicate from the Gulch to Boeing Field, down to SeaTac Airport and over to Kent, a smallish sister city southeast of Seattle. Driving for Mr. Santini was a great honor, and Vinnie's parents were justifiably proud of their son.

And drive he did. He had a knack for beating traffic on the semi urban roads. If Mr. Santini wanted or needed to get something somewhere in a hurry, Vincent was his (young) man. And he made the most of the opportunities that came to him. By his senior year in high school he carried around a modest wad of bills given him by Mr. Santini, and Vincent's employment and his father's vocation had also enabled him to purchase a 1957 Chevrolet coupe, with a bored out 283 cubic inch engine and a British racing green paint job. He was the toast of his high school.

Graduation simply allowed more time for Vinnie to work for Mr. Santini. He wasn't interested in any formal education, and by the time his twenty first birthday rolled around, he was one of Mayor Santini's regular bag men. If there was a collection problem, Mr. Santini might send a couple of the older guys out. But Vinnie was already capable of handling most any issues that should come his way, and as far as driving the highways and byways of South Seattle, no one was better at it than Vinnie DeGrazzi.

One Friday night in the summer of 1988 Vincent met a girl at a dance in Rainier Beach. She was verging on voluptuous, but was better described as amply endowed. An hourglass perfect figure of a beautiful, young Italian woman that reminded Vincent of Sophia Loren in her early prime. She was a looker, and a graceful dancer. Her five-foot eight frame seemed to float in Vinnie's strong arms, and matched his height appropriately. Dark brown, wavy hair complimented her olive skin and mahogany eyes. She was a catch, and knew it, therefore her personality was bright and playful. Her name was Angela, and her features were actually, in Vinnie's youthful but somewhat experienced eyes, angelic. They began dating, and soon enough were talking about the future. Vincent pulled out all of the stops, and invited Angela up to Vancouver, Canada with him one weekend. This was a bit of a hazardous adventure, as Angela's father kept a close eye on her.   But a trip across the International border was always a special occasion, and right there in Stanley Park on the magnificent shores of English Bay, Vincent dropped to one knee, and popped the question. Angela accepted, shed a brief tear, they embraced, and when they returned to Seattle, Vincent went and asked for her father's blessing.

The young couple were married in a beautiful June ceremony at Angela's home Parrish of Saint Anthony's Catholic Church in Renton, Washington. Following a week long honeymoon to Hawaii, they settled into a nice two-bedroom apartment near the south sound city of Burien. Vincent was now a sergeant in Mr. Santini's enterprises, and took his budding career very seriously. Angela didn't seem to mind Vincent's irregular hours, or his night work. She was a contented young woman, happy to enjoy her newly married life, putter around their apartment, spend time with her own mom and sisters, and continued to take classes part time at the Seattle Design Institute.

As time passed, and Mr. Santini approached retirement age. Vincent was already a trusted soldier for the aging capo, and he had also launched a sideline career as a restaurateur. Operating out of a small leased storefront in the picturesque little neighboring town of Pacifica, he collected his mother's recipes, hired a daughter of one of his mom's friends to do the cooking, and was up and running. Angela decorated the space for them, and helped with the bookkeeping. Vincent did the purchasing and tasted lots of Italian wine. Mr. Santini loved to eat there, and cherished the old world feel and food of the cozy restaurant. Vinnie's Trattoria, was small, but was a big hit with more people than Mr. Santini, and had lines out the door on weekends. I mean, where could you get good, authentic Italian anymore?

The Norwegian man Vincent had leased his space from, saw what success his new tenant was enjoying, and after five years, refused to renew the lease. He had visions of doing as well on his own, so what did he need Vincent for? Apparently more than he realized, as no sooner had he evicted Vinnie, and set up his own operation, than an aggressive fire destroyed his wood frame building. The cause of the fire was never determined.

One of Mr. Santini's final acts of largess was helping Vincent buy his own piece of dirt on Highway 99 for a new restaurant. It would be called Vincenzo's, and was in a better, much more active location. It would feature a full bar, and ample parking. Mr. Santini also sold his number's syndicate to Vincent, and helped him run it for the first year. Now, Vincent spent more time counting money, and less time out on the road. He kind of missed it.

Vincent actually fell into the "entertainment" business by accident. As more and more single, working women seemed to be utilizing his new bar for their own personal gain, Vincent and a couple of his right-hand men convinced them they should all work together for the common good. Vincent would provide them a safe contact area for a 35% percent cut of their action. He purchased a couple of run-down motels nearby for them to ply their trade by the hour. He protected them from local law enforcement, and it only took the threat of a couple of broken legs to convince the ladies how beneficial their new arrangement would be for everyone.

Having enjoyed this illustrious background, Vincent finished his morning coffee and breakfast Stromboli with Angela, readied himself to meet Stuart at the house, and get the ransom demands called in. Between Monica squabbling with Leroy, hostages head butting him, and Tommy acting like a jerk, he was ready to move on. "Have a good day, sweetheart," Angela told him. "Don't come home with any broken bones."

Ha, ha, Vincent thought as he went out to his three-car garage, and decided to take the BMW 330Ci today. It was another beautiful July day in Seattle, and he enjoyed cruising in the fuel injected, convertible roadster during such fine climes.

Letting the car warm up for a couple of minutes, he backed out of his garage, and wheeled around to head out of the drive. He instinctively checked the street both ways for approaching vehicles before he pulled out onto the asphalt. Not only for safety's sake, but also from his old driving days, when he had to be sure he was not being followed. Either by plainclothes cops or any other criminal elements.

Angela had insisted on buying this home in the Renton Highlands. He could have taken or left it, but that was neither here nor there this morning. He noted a beige colored sedan pull out from the curb about a block in back of him. Paying it little mind, he proceeded down the hill to the 405 freeway and then on towards the southbound I-5 freeway. Traffic was light, and his progress was better than steady. It was eight thirty in the morning.

He slowed at the on ramp to the 405, and soon he was shushing through the 405 s-curves. He loved the way the BMW handled given a bit of a challenge like the curves, thrived on the throaty purr of the powerful engine, and kicked the accelerator up a bit. Glancing in the rear-view mirror, he noticed the same beige sedan following a half a dozen cars back, and thought to himself that another morning commuter was heading out to begin their day in South Seattle.

Nearing the merger with the I-5 freeway, he caught the tail end of the early traffic commuters. He had a good forty minutes to the Tacoma Narrows bridge, and he hoped the morning highway activity was clear, and free or any accidents. He glanced up because the congestion had compacted, and the beige sedan was still back there. Now he began to monitor it a little more closely.

Hitting I-5 just north of SeaTac Airport, Vincent opened the Beemer up, and goosed it to a solid eighty-five MPH for five miles. The sedan was still with him, so Vincent crossed to the right lane, and slowed considerably. With any luck, he might get a look at the driver through the tinted windows, but the sedan slowed, and also pulled off into the right-hand lane.

What is this idiot trying to prove, he wondered, and was annoyed that he had to deal with such a distraction on this important morning. Vincent took a sharp right hand turn off of the freeway, and onto 320th Street South in Federal Way. He spun in and out of traffic to 214th, hung a left, and took 356th Street down to the 509 Freeway. That curled around to Ruston Way in Tacoma, and quickly he navigated himself to Pearl Street which leads down to Highway 16 and over the Narrows bridge. He pulled to the curb in industrial south Tacoma before he got to the bridge and waited for a good ten minutes to make sure he had lost his traveling buddy. He had.

That has got to be Aussie boy, he mused. Who else would it be?

The mood at the Jensen Compound was somber as the family headed into the new calendar week, but their collective strength would not allow them to be dispirited any longer by Chrissy's disappearance. Ginny's sister Elaine had stayed behind with her, and Tina had settled in at the house with Will. Penny Brown dropped by daily, so did Carmen Ayala as often as she could. The girls job today, and every day, was to keep Ginny busy. The plan was basically living the oldest sports cliché of all time, i.e.--we're taking this one day at a time. Whether it was the giant jig saw puzzle on the dining room table, an afternoon matinee at a local movie theatre, one of those ubiquitous sale catalogues from Macys in the mail-which would necessitate a trip to the mall, they were going to distract Ginny and fill up her days. Every morning's chant from the household from now on would be, "today is the day."

The boys were also finding ways to keep busy. Charlie was running the family ranch from the Olympic Place house. Will headed up communications with the police (Danny Chong), and the outside business world. He had already been contacted by a couple of publishers with serious book deals. Bob Jensen, who loved to cook, had taken over the domestic duties, and planned the day's meals. He did the grocery shopping, cooked breakfast, lunch and dinner, and was looking forward to bartending for everyone at five p.m.'s cocktail hour. Bobby spearheaded the cleanup after meals, and spent the rest of the time on his laptop responding to Social Media activity. As well as replying to the avalanche of well-wishers, he was always watching, scanning, surfing the web, and looking for a break in the case.

Chrissy's emotions had basically turned upside down along with her immediate environment after the aborted escape attempt. She was overcome with remorse at how closely she had come to springing herself, and was proud of how hard she had fought with her kidnappers, only to be foiled by a last-minute twist of fate. But now she was struggling with apprehension that her captors might inflict physical harm as a means of retribution for her rebellion, and for the assault on burly boy. She felt a small pang of guilt for manipulating Florence, and was also concerned with some push back there. Her overriding emotion was one of anger. She was getting more and more vexed and frustrated, at being held against her will, and being unable to do anything about it. She was furious at being unable to play in the rest of the golf tournament, at not seeing Steve, at missing any interaction with her family, her fellow golf pros, her fans, and was sick to death at being stuck in this hot, airless basement. She was often reduced to tears thinking about one of the most spectacular weeks of her life turning instead to complete dirt. Still, she was very thankful she was alive, relatively unharmed and hopefully out of here someday soon.

Now that her radio had been removed, she was existing in a vacuum of monotony and excruciating boredom. She had only a rough idea of what time it was. Her meals had devolved into some kind of crappy fast food, essentially thrown down the steps at her. She was afraid to eat most of it, and inspected very carefully, anything she thought about putting in her mouth. Florence, with a revolver in her hand, and in a profanity laced diatribe, had instructed her to lie face down on the bed whenever she heard someone approaching the room, which she found singularly humiliating and offensive. She was getting annoyed and rebellious to the point of thinking about hatching another escape plan. If she could somehow overpower Florence, and get hold of her revolver, she might be back in business.

No one had laid a hand on her physically, for which she was greatly relieved, but what were they waiting for? Make the call dudes! Are they trying to increase the pressure on her family to perform once they finally make their demands, Chrissy wondered? She was filled with angst whenever she thought of her mom, and what all the family must be going through at the compound. And they are still at the Nike compound, she thought. There is no way they would ever leave town with me still being gone. She knew they could never do that, and would instead be doing everything humanly possible to pinpoint her whereabouts. As her emotions raged, Chrissy felt like she was on an out of control rollercoaster ride.

She also had ample time to think about her life. Of her week in Miami with Steve, her recent trip to NYC with Will, her golf career, of her past life in general. She delved deep into her personal history. If she had brought this ordeal down upon herself, she wanted to know why. Her mind flitted to the Carol King musical, she and Will had attended together. "You've got to get up every morning, put a smile on your face, and show the world all the love in your heart," took on a twisted meaning in her present circumstances. But the bouncy, uplifting melodies and the catchy lyrics, were stuck in her head and competed with Donna Summer's 1980's classic women's anthem, *I Will Survive*, to give her hope and inner resolve. Otherwise, she spent the time replaying past rounds of golf in her head. Cementing the nuances of her favorite courses in her memory bank, constantly analyzing how she could master each challenging track. It was amazing how well she could transport herself to other, friendlier places through the powers of sublimation.

She also traveled in her mind back through more pleasant times. Her childhood, the university days, and wondered why it was she, one out of one hundred twenty fellow golf pros, who had been targeted. Did she offend someone, or somehow foment, in some unintentional way, her own abduction? Had she been too independent and trusting of people, when she should have been more cautious, more circumspect considering her financial status, her physical attractiveness, and all of the inordinate success she had achieved in her twenty-seven years? Had her work ethic made her vulnerable? And why was it almost always women who were abducted? She had never heard of a PGA pro disappearing overnight.

She did her best to etch into her mind the facial and bodily characteristics of her captors. Although they always disguised or secreted their identities, she was keeping track of their number, their routines, and then during her escape attempt, she had gotten a fairly decent look at the older guy. She was fairly certain he was one and the same person who had initially abducted her. Although it was bright out, and she was squinting severely into the late morning sunlight, it was as good a look as she had gotten at any of them. She worked hard to imprint his image and facial characteristics in her mind's eye.

To stay calm, and lift her spirits, she began to do some stretching exercises, and would then move on into more aerobic and/or strengthening work.

Chrissy had no sooner started her workout, when the lock on the basement door begin to clatter. Just to be perverse, and show her disrespect to whoever was coming into the room, she stretched out on her crummy, little single bed, and stared at the ceiling in defiance. The hell with them, she thought.

More than one set of footsteps descended the stairs, and she glanced over to see who was coming into her world. Florence, wearing the tan niqab, came down stairs first, and approached Chrissy's side of the room, with a drawn revolver. She stopped about twelve feet away, and commanded Chrissy to sit up on the edge of the bed, and keep her eyes on the floor. Looking down, and straining her eyes up as best she could, Chrissy could see two additional forms in ski masks behind Florence. They were males, one shorter, one about six foot one.

As they got closer, she was able to ascertain that it was the other guard, not burly boy, and the old guy. The younger guy spoke, and told her she was going to be allowed to talk to her family, and let them know she was all right. Chrissy was immediately ecstatic. Her heart jumped, and she remained outwardly calm, but her emotions were racing.

"Tell us who your money person is, and we are going to be dealing with that person alone as far as your ransom is concerned. We will give you ten seconds to say you are okay, and to please help you get back home. If they don't help, you will not make it back, you will die. Florence has a revolver pointed at you. You say one word out of line, or try anything to cause trouble, and Florence will shoot you in the stomach, and we will leave you locked up down here to bleed out and die. Do you understand me?"

"Yes."

"Who are we calling, and what is their cell number?"

"My brother's name is Will, he is my business manager, and his number is….." Stuart wrote the number down on his hand. It would be a waste of time to enter it in the burner phone, because the burners were only being used once from now on.

"Do you want to rehearse what you are going to say?"

"I've got it." You idiots!

"Here goes then," Stuart said.

It was ten thirty-seven on Tuesday morning, and the cell phone rang three times before someone answered it.

"Will Jensen here."

Stuart spoke into the hand held, voice distortion device that was plugged into his burner phone. "Someone wants to talk to you, Will." He unplugged the distorter, and held the phone to Chrissy's mouth.

"Will, this is Chrissy. I am okay, I'm all right. Please help me Will, I want to come home so bad. Do whatever they say, or they're going to kill me, I love you all, please, please help me. Do whatever they tell you to do." And as soon as Stuart pulled the phone away, he plugged the distorter back in, and Florence motioned Chrissy towards the little bathroom with her pistol pointed at her head.

"Get in there, and keep your mouth shut."

"Chrissy? Chrissy? Are you there?"

"Shut up and listen to me. You have until three o'clock on Friday afternoon to collect ten million dollars, which we will exchange for your sister's life. We want the money in used one hundred-dollar bills. No sequenced series of bills. No new money. Do not tamper with or attempt to track the money in any way. If you do, we will kill your sister. We will deal only with you. Do not call the authorities, we will not talk with anyone else but you. If anyone attempts to intrude on our communication with you, we will take garden shears, and cut off a finger from each one of your sister's hands, and mail them to you. We will give you instructions on delivering the money this week. We will call you daily on this line only. Do you understand me?"

"How can I be sure Chrissy is okay."

"Shut up, and get the money," and Stuart hung up the phone.

Vincent high fived Stuart. "Good job."

"Thanks Vincent. I am excited to get the ball rolling here."

"You ain't the only one, brother," Vinnie agreed emphatically.

Pandemonium erupted at the Jensen Compound. "That was Chrissy," Will screamed, his whole body was shaking. "She's okay, that was her on the phone, they let her talk to me."

The den was immediately flooded with everyone who was in the house. What did she say? Where is she? When is she coming home? How did she sound? Etc., etc., etc.

Bob Jensen was the first one in the room, crossing over from the kitchen, and gave his son a mighty hug. "Thank God," he said. "What do they want?"

"Ten million bucks."

Ginny Jensen heard the commotion from upstairs, and almost broke her neck racing down the stairs. Next came Tina, then Elaine, Bobby, Charlie and Steve. Everyone was yammering at once, until Will got them quieted down. He relayed all of what Chrissy had told him, and most of what the distorted voice had said.

"The important thing right now," Bob said, "is Chrissy is okay. Whatever they want, we've got to get it, and get Chrissy back."

Ginny Jensen had broken down, and was crying hysterically. She was being comforted by Tina and Elaine, but had five days of absolute anguish to flood out of her system, and it was going to take a while. At least she was crying tears of joy. Chrissy wasn't home yet, but she was alive, and that was a start. Even Steve Reed, one of the toughest over the middle receivers in the National Football League, wiped his eyes, and said a silent prayer of thanks.

As the family began to calm down, and their hysteria devolved into excited chatter, Will called Penny Brown and broke the news to her. She was as hysterical as his family had been, and when she regained control of herself, he asked "Can you please call Cynthia and Carmen Ayala and see if we can all meet in the Chambers Bay Conference Room in an hour. I will call Chief Mills and Danny Chong, and Alexander Heron. Tina will meet us there, and if you talk to anyone else, please ask for their confidentiality until we meet with the Chief and his people."

"Sure, Will. Consider it done, unless I call you back."

"Thanks Penny."

She hung up, and called Cynthia Summers immediately. "Cynthia, It's Penny. Will Jensen just got a call from Chrissy. She seems to be alright, and apparently a ransom demand has been made. But she is okay for now. Isn't that great news?"

"It really is, Penny. What's the demand? How much money do they want? Do you know?"

"I don't know yet. I'm am going into a meeting with everyone in an hour. I will be able to let you know then, and I'll call as soon as I find out anything."

"Why don't you just call from the meeting, and patch me in on speaker phone? I would really love to have a presence there," Cynthia asked.

"Whatever you say, I think everyone's going to be elated to have you on board. Will Jensen has asked that we keep the news confidential until we can meet with the police, and see what they want to do."

"Can do."

As soon as she hung up with Penny, Cynthia called Mac T. Mac T. hung up, and called Commissioner Wilson. Word was spreading quickly.

The Chambers Bay Conference Room was buzzing as the executive group gathered to process the new information and make a plan. Will opened the meeting by relating the phone call he had received that morning at ten thirty-seven am. Chief Mills requested immediate possession of Will's phone, which Will was happy to relinquish, on the condition he have it back by the end of the day in order to keep the lines of communication open. The Chief reiterated his request for confidentiality and said it would certainly help his offices operate if they didn't have the media crawling all over them all afternoon. The Chief had an aide take Will's phone downtown to the communications lab for analysis, promising they would break it down, and return it in a couple of hours.

Cynthia spoke up, and greeted everyone from her FaceTime app. "I have spoken to executive management at LPGA headquarters, and they are all thrilled at the news, Will. We are so happy for you and the family."

"Thank you."

The conversation turned to the ransom demand, and that proved to be a thorny subject. Ten million dollars is a lot of money. Carmen Ayala came in about halfway through the discussion, as she had had to drive down to University Place from the Amazon campus on Lake Union in Seattle proper.

"There has been some discussion with my Executive VP, who is in communication with our President and our Board of Directors, and they want the Jensen's to know you are not in this thing alone, Will. We are all part of a larger community here, and Amazon will do whatever it can to help us resolve this ugly chapter in American sports history," Carmen offered dramatically.

Will drew a deep breath, and responded, "Thank you, Carmen. That is much appreciated. We, as a family have access to a certain amount of assets and funds, but ten million would certainly stretch our resources. Then there might be various commercial loan opportunities we could investigate."

"Has anyone considered a Go Fund Me campaign?" Penny asked. "With the exposure this case has generated, and with the spectacular support and genuine love people across the country have for Chrissy, it seems like that would be a natural opportunity."

"I think you are right, Penny," Cynthia said. "How about you take the rest of the afternoon to do some preliminary work, and then we launch a GFM effort tomorrow morning?"

Since they had little else to go on besides analyzing the phone, and setting up an electronic surveillance post at the Jensen compound to intercept future calls from the kidnappers, Inspector Chong couldn't help but agree with Cynthia and Penny's proposal. It was confirmed by everyone, that time was of the essence. Penny felt certain there would be a leak to the press, and therefore the confidentiality thing was dead in the water anyway.

The meeting wound down, and everyone had something meaningful to do. If not actual work, certainly planning for the GFM campaign tomorrow.

Will and Tina went back to the compound and got on the phones. Will borrowed Bob's cell, since his was not due back until later. He spoke with Chrissy's commercial bankers at Chase and Wells Fargo banks. He conferred with his father about equity in the family ranch, did a projection of Chrissy's future earnings, as to the amount of collateral he would be able to demonstrate to the banks. He reconnected with the publishers about potential advances and earning streams. He was busy updating Chrissy's stock portfolio, when Tina walked into the den.

"I wouldn't worry too much about it," she said. "If all goes well, all Chrissy has to do is write a book, then go out and win a couple more golf tournaments. That should take care of the ten mil pretty easy. By the way, Carmen Ayala is trying to contact you. Here let me call her back for you."

"Hi Carmen, Will Jensen here, what's up?"

"Hello, Will, thanks so much for calling. I have extremely good news for you. Our Board of Directors in an emergency conference call this afternoon, has authorized an interest free loan to you and your family to insure the safe return of your sister. We will help with fundraising throughout this process, and guarantee that everything moves forward smoothly."

"Carmen, how can we thank you enough? We are going to get Chrissy back, and then we are going to do some major celebrating with the key players here in Seattle. Can you please express our family's deepest appreciation to the Board for their help and support?"

"I will do that," Carmen said, "and we will talk again tomorrow, eh?"

"Of course."

Carmen called Penny, Penny called Cynthia, they both called Tina, Tina dealt with the national media, Penny was back on the phone with the local media and the GFM people. They would be ready to launch first thing in the morning.

CHAPTER THIRTY-ONE

"I'm bogged," Alton thought aloud. "That old man gave me the slip. He is a lot better than I gave him credit for." How did he even know I was behind him? He continued to drive idly around Tacoma in the hopes he might be able to able to somehow stumble into Vincent again, but gave up after an hour, and headed back up to South Seattle. Well, if I lost him, he thought, guess I will have to go back to the bar and find him again.

Alton cruised through the parking lot at Vincenzo's, and when he didn't see any BMW's, he backed into a space in the rear of the lot, and prepared to wait. It was edging into early afternoon. His cell phone was backlogged with texts and calls from Penny, to whom he didn't want to talk, until he resolved his informational dilemma with Vincent. He waited patiently, actually dozing off in the process, when his phone finally vibrated for the thousandth time, and out of annoyance he answered it.

"Where in the world are you?" asked Penny irritably.

"I'm up here in Seattle trying to track some things down," Alton replied.

"Why are you acting so crazy, Alton? You know you're supposed to be in contact with me at all times. We had a big meeting today. Cynthia dialed in via FaceTime, everyone else on the project was there. Cyn was asking about you. You should have been here."

"What's going on?"

"Will Jensen got a call from Chrissy today. The kidnappers put her on their cell around ten thirty this morning, and let her talk to him for a few seconds before they made their ransom demands. She is okay, Will talked to her personally, isn't that wonderful news? Everyone is so totally relieved, and the energy level almost jumped out of the conference room today. We are going to get her back Alton, and we all think Amazon is going to help. After they let Chrissy talk, then the kidnappers started the process. They want ten million bucks by this Friday to ransom her."

"Holy smokes, love. That is a lot of money."

"No kidding. Seriously, I need you back here now. We have got a lot of work to do. I am working on the launch of a Go Fund Me campaign tomorrow, and you have to help me."

"I will head back right away. Give me an hour, in case I hit traffic."

"Just hurry up, mate."

"Yes mum."

Alton was treading in shark filled waters, and he now felt more than remiss by withholding information from Penny. On one hand, he knew he should be talking to the police about Vincent, his suspicions, and what he had seen in California. If nothing else, they would interrogate Vincent, and maybe find out something. On the other hand, Chrissy seems to be alive and if not free and clear, at least okay for the time being, and the big issue is to get her back. He rationalized that it might actually do more damage if he went directly to the cops, and they came charging in, spooked Vincent, and caused him to do something harmful. Or, I might be totally wrong about the whole enchilada, and make a bloody fool of myself, causing Vincent a lot of trouble for nothing.

Then, there is the reward money. Six hundred grand seemed like the Washington Lottery to Alton, and he had a shot at it. Therefore, with a measure of greed, an allowance of self-justification, and a pinch of denial, he decided to continue like the Jensen's were, and take things one day at a time. His overriding motivation was Chrissy's safety, and if she was alive, well then, he wanted to stay under the radar, and keep digging until he found her, and claimed at least a share of the reward.

It was getting time for Alton to go, when he saw Vincent's BMW pull into the lot, and park by the side door of the bar in his reserved spot. "Finally," he thought.

Alton waited a few minutes to let the dust settle. He thought Vincent would check in with Betty at the bar, take a leak, order a glass of wine or cup of coffee, and should be sitting in his booth reading the sports page, when I come in. Ten minutes later, Alton eased through the side door, waited until Betty crossed over into the liquor storage room, and beat it over to Vincent's booth.

"Allo, Vincent, how are you today?"

"I'm good, bozo, I thought you might show up. Whattaya want?"

"Still lookin' for that reward, Vincent."

"Why don't I give you a tour of my place here, and you can see that there ain't nobody stashed up in the attic anywhere."

"Hey, I got some news for you."

"What is it?"

Alton watched Vincent very closely, to see what his reaction might be. "Chrissy is alive, she's okay. Her family got word today, and the kidnappers want ten million bucks in ransom money."

Vincent, ever the high stakes poker player, didn't flinch a muscle. "That's great news. She seems like a nice kid. I'm glad she is okay. When did they call? I ain't heard nothin' about it on the news all day. Maybe you should go out and kidnap yourself a golfer, kid. Sounds like they is worth more than any six hundred grand reward money."

As Alton leaned across the table and lowered his voice to talk to Vincent in confidence, Betty came storming out from behind the bar. "Goddamn it, you again? I thought I told you not to come back here without an appointment."

"It's okay, Betty, he's harmless. I find him amusing actually."

Betty muttered something, and backed away, glaring intensely at our boy. Alton ignored her, leaned forward into his side of the table, and looked at Vincent. With the new information about Chrissy emerging, he felt like the game was starting to change, and Alton thought he needed to pick up the pace. Try and put a little pressure on Vincent. "Can I be completely honest with you Mr. DeGrazzi?"

"Say what's on your mind, kid."

"I want you to know I haven't said a word to the cops or anything, but I think you know a lot more about this Chrissy Jensen thing than you are letting on."

"Whoa now, why in the hell would you say something like that to me?"

"Well, there are a lot of things. You act kind of suspicious sometimes, I mean with the burner phones and the black eye and all, for example. And then I seen you and Tommy checking Chrissy out down at Pelican Hill. She was practicing late the day you dropped me off when we come back from drinking at Blackie's. I was watching you guys, and you were following Chrissy around big time. You were all over her all afternoon. Then she comes up here, and just disappears. It don't figure is all, and I think you know something."

"Them is strong words, kid. And for one thing, if you went to the police right now, you would be just another crackpot trying to get some reward money, because I am totally clean. But also, if someone went around making false accusations about the wrong people to the police, that might also land that person in the hospital. Me, I try to keep my nose clean, and the last thing I need is any trouble with the law. I don't even want to talk to those people, unless I have an envelope for them or something like that I hafta do. But I will tell you what I'm gonna do for you kid, because I like you, and because you seem to be in the know. I will axk around, and see if there is anything I can find out to help you get your hands on that reward money. How does that sound?"

"That sounds good, Vincent."

"Now, what can you do for me, while I am doing you this huge favor?"

"I don't know, what?"

"Well, as we discussed, the first thing you can do, is stay away from any cops. Secondly, you kicking me back a few bucks from the reward money, if you can get it, wouldn't hurt none. Third, and this is big, you can also keep your ears open, and let me know what you is hearing from the LPGA people and the Jensens. If they is going to raise the ransom money, I need to know, because that might run us out of time to find the girl and get you any reward money, capiche? So, I need to talk to you a couple times a day for the rest of the week. You let me know what is going on, and I will do the same for you. Is that a deal kid? Can we shake on that?"

"Yeah, I can do that. You gonna come through for me?" How does Vincent know something is supposed to happen this week, Alton wondered?

"I will make some calls okay. That's all I can do right now. So, let's exchange cell numbers, then I will walk you out, huh?"

The numbers thing done, Vincent got up, and led the way out the side door of the bar. Alton was hesitant, to follow, but what choice did he have? Follow Vincent, or suffer the wrath of Betty. Out in the pleasant afternoon sunshine, Vincent looked around his mostly empty parking lot, and saw Alton's beige Ford Taurus rental sitting there.

"By, the way kid, don't ever try to follow me again will ya? You ain't up to that task, and Dimitri would break your head in if he knew what you was doin' this morning."

"Sorry, man," Alton said. "I don't bloody well know what I was thinking."

Properly chastised, Alton drove away, and headed back south to Tacoma. He texted Penny that there was an accident on the freeway, but he was on the way, hoping she wouldn't be too annoyed with him. Leaving when he did, got him off and running just ahead of early commuter traffic. Penny texted back that he should come directly to the Jensen's compound.

The compound was in high spirits when he got there, and the den was full of talking heads busy working their phones. Tina was on the line with the Fox Sports people, Penny was again in conference with the Go Fund Me folks, it sounded like Will was talking either to an attorney, or the County Prosecutor. Penny gave him a list of calls to start on. It was going to be another media blitz that evening, only this time there was actually something substantial to report. As word started getting out, some members of the local TV stations began setting up camp outside of the compound, hoping there would be a breakthrough, and they would be the first on the scene to get a scoop.

"Go Fund Me wants to start the campaign tonight," Penny announced. "They said we will never get as much positive publicity as should come in tonight. All of the local stations have the pertinent information, and Tina has been in communication with the national boys and girls in New York and LA."

Bob Jensen came into the den, and reported there were now about thirty members of the media gathered outside, so Will called Danny Chong to see about setting up a security perimeter manned by a couple of patrolmen outside of their main entry gate. The whole house was buzzing.

Bob was prepping dinner up for everyone, and proceeded to go back into the kitchen and finish mixing up a large pitcher of margaritas. By the time everyone got off of the phones, it would be almost five o'clock, and time for a celebratory cocktail. For the first time in almost a week, people would actually be inclined to enjoy a drink together.

Finally, five o'clock rolled around, and the cell phones went away. Bob set up his makeshift cantina, and in addition to having drinks, a hug fest broke out. Will hugged Tina, who had been like an angel for he and his family, emerging at just the right time, both professionally and personally, to offer comfort, guidance and support. Alton and Penny were hugging everyone and jumping around, Bobby and his mom were dancing a jig, Elaine had her arms around Charlie, and Bob was holding his perspiring margarita glass in his right hand, and smiling like an emcee at a beauty pageant.

Will finally got the crowd's attention, and raised his glass for a toast. "Here's to Chrissy, may she be back with us soon."

Dilly, dilly. Here, here, and everyone took a healthy drink.

"Please allow me to remind all of us, that as great as our news is today, we still need to stay focused until Chrissy is safe, and back with us. We've had a breakthrough, no doubt, but a lot of work to remains to be done," Will admonished everyone.

Here, here again, and the group began to filter back into the den to start watching the evening's newscasts. That was an easy job, as the update of some initial contact with Chrissy was the headliner on local news and also got some quality coverage on the national stations. The sports stations were running hard with it, and GFM was getting some major exposure through all of the outlets. Without naming a specific ransom amount, other than its' being very substantial, the news was broken and now out there in force. Thankfully, the Tacoma Police had arrived and set up their barrier, because a significant number of media and now some paparazzi were milling around outside.

The American public was now aware that they could help Chrissy's cause greatly by simply texting a ten or twenty-dollar contribution on their cell phones. Free Chrissy signs went up in various major cities, the media blitz was off to a successful start, and GFM offices were starting to buzz.

At LPGA Headquarters, as somber as the timbre had been in the offices for the last week, staff and management were jubilant at the latest news about Chrissy. In a secondary reaction, the tour honchos were also delighted the LPGA was able to generate this kind of publicity to help recover and support one of their own.

At the safe house in Gig Harbor, Stuart and Monica were overwhelmed by the local and national response to Chrissy's update. There was hardly a channel on TV that wasn't talking about Chrissy Jensen, and Stuart and Monica were stunned and humbled, as the audacious path they had set themselves on began to fully sink into their brains. They could do no more than sit quietly on the couch, watch the news shows, and hold on tightly to each other. It seemed like the lonely two of them against the rest of the world.

After an evening of channel surfing at the compound, and as it was nearing time for the eleven o'clock news, Penny who was the official contact with the Go Fund Me site directors, and was monitoring the progress of the incoming donations, was able to report that a staggering five point five million dollars had been collected so far on Chrissy's behalf. While GFM didn't hesitate to inform their clients that donations usually peaked in the first seventy-two hours of a funding drive, the clan and friends at the compound were stunned at the response. Thinking they were going to have to mortgage all of their futures to raise Chrissy's ransom money was overwhelming, but here was a legion of friends and complete strangers coming together to help out in the most touching and munificent manner. Not to even mention Amazon's amazing offer, and other generous corporate inquiries Will was fielding. Can you say: Nike, Titleist, Callaway?

The family was worried that Ginny, who was moved beyond tears by the evening's generous outpouring, was going to have a coronary. She would be one of the few people in recorded history to succumb after suffering a coronary of happiness and relief. But they didn't need to worry too much about Ginny. She was tough as a strip of weathered rawhide, and if anyone thought for a second that she wouldn't be there to welcome her Chrissy back home- well think again buckwheat!

Around ten, Will and Tina went out to the families' front yard to say thanks to the crowd gathered outside the house. From their communication, the reporters would file their final updates back to their respective stations for the eleven o'clock local broadcasts.

"Good evening, I am Will Jensen, Chrissy's brother, and on behalf of all the Jensen's, I would like to thank you for coming out tonight. We continue to appreciate your support of our missing daughter and sister, and want you to know how much you are contributing to the effort to bring Chrissy home. The only new information we have for you at this time, is to report that over five million dollars was raised tonight to help meet the ransom demands for Chrissy."

"What is the actual ransom demand?" one of the reporters shouted out.

"The Police Team has asked us to keep those figures confidential, however, I can communicate to you, that we are nowhere near raising enough funds to purchase Chrissy's release from her kidnappers. Thank you, we will be back with you first thing in the morning, unless something should break unexpectedly during the night."

Tina turned and followed Will back into the compound. A few of the newsies were still clamoring for information, shouting out their questions, but the rest of the crews had begun to shut down. It was the general consensus both inside and outside the compound that it was time to wrap things up for the day.

The family was still gathered in the den watching the late news broadcasts before retiring, but Will and Tina wanted to see Alton and Penny off before they checked out.

"Thank you so much, Penny," Will said, and gave her a firm hug. "You got the ball rolling today, and all of us Jensen's appreciate it greatly."

"Happy to help, Will. I will check in with you first thing in the morning. Right now, it looks like the only problem we may have is shutting the fund down before it produces a surplus."

"That is a nice problem to have, but if it does go over the top, we would want to donate any extra money to some type of homeless organization."

"Absolutely. I just think we will all sleep a little better tonight. I know last night I felt like jumping off of a bridge, and now, things are so much improved." Penny's relief was very evident.

"Thanks in large part to you."

"Just part of the team here, Will."

"Goodnight Penny, sleep well."

"Gnight to you too, mate." Penny was starting to unconsciously adopt Alton's vernacular.

Tina and Will went back in the house, and directly up to bed. They had spent the last, long weekend together as a couple, their maiden voyage so to speak, but this would be the first night they slept together without the weight of the world on their shoulders. They were both aware of these circumstances, and fell into bed and each other's arms spontaneously. Both of them euphoric with the day's turn of events.

As well as the family would sleep that night, no one was feeling any better than Chrissy herself. She had actually spoken with Will, there was no way she could hear what was being said as Florence had hustled her out of the room and into the bathroom, but they were talking to Will and making their demands known. That is all that mattered, and this horrible nightmare would be over soon enough, so she could be home again. It had become very clear to Chrissy in the last twenty-four hours, that home for her was: her family, Steve Reed and a golf course. Any course.

She did an extra one hundred ab crunches and pushups before trying to sleep, but she was still too jacked up, and spent another fitful night isolated in the basement.

CHAPTER THIRTY-TWO

Vincent put in a call to Tommy on a burner phone Wednesday morning. "Can I meet you some place for lunch, we need to talk?"

"What about?"

"What do you freaking think? We had a pretty damn good day over here yesterday, and I just want to make sure all of our ducks are in a row. There's been a few changes we should go over is all. I can come up there to Normandy Park if you like."

"Why don't we meet at South Center. There's a Fantastic Wings joint there that's pretty good."

"How about noon?"

"Fine."

Vincent got to South Center first, again enjoying the balmy weather for the twenty-minute drive in his BMW convertible. He chose a back-corner table in the bar for the impromptu meeting. With loud rock music blaring, the garishly bright lighting, and all of the service noise bouncing off of the hard surfaces in the millenniumish bar/restaurant, he thought this would suit their purpose perfectly. Tommy, rolled in, and they sat on their stools, and stared at each other for a moment.

"Well," Vincent said, "if I was one of the kids, I would say yesterday was dope."

"How so?"

"You know, we let golfer girl talk to her brother for ten seconds, which seems to have released a lot of tension. The kid done a good job giving him our money demands, and I seen on TV last night, that she has already raised a bunch of money on something called Go Send Me Money, so she shouldn't have no trouble gettin' the ten mil up."

"It's called Go Fund Me."

"Whatever."

Their waitress came over, gave her head a shake which sent her blue hair flipping around, and took two orders of your basic wings. Both partners in crime ordered a beer to go with, and sat back.

"This is some shit, ain't it?" Vincent mused. "You can develop a whole restaurant concept around chicken wings now, hire kids with blue hair to sell 'em, and then go nationwide and get an IPO going. My mother is rolling over in her grave right now. I got a couple of other things for you though."

"Whaddya got?"

"This is hysterical, you gonna love this one. Your buddy from Pelican Hill, the tall redheaded kid has been coming around. He actually told me yesterday he thinks I know more than I am letting on with Chrissy."

"What did you say to that? We may have to take that guy out."

"No, get this. He is obsessed with the reward money. You know the six hundred grand. Wants me to help him get the money."

"That guy is going to be trouble, Vincent. You mark my words."

"I don't think so. I made a deal with him yesterday. One: absolutely no cops. Two: I'll make a few calls, see what I can find out. While I am helping you out, you need to let me know all about what is going on with the LPGA and Jensen people. Three: if I can find out anything, I might be able to help you cash in on the reward. We are going to be getting all of the inside info from those people on a daily basis. Ain't that some crazy shit?"

"You better be careful dealing with this clown. He is a civilian, and you don't know what those people will to do."

"Hey, he ain't got nothing on nobody, you and me are both rock solid. All he can do is help us, and he can't really hurt us in any way. I made a deal to help him if I could, that's all."

"Don't get me involved with any of these people."

"You ain't partner. That's the beauty of the whole thing."

"What else you got?"

Well, the other kid, computer boy, went on a test dive the other day. I had Leroy out on the dock at the house, waiting for him. And I had Dimitri follow him and his buddy around some. Turns out they have a pretty nice sailboat stashed in the Tacoma Narrows Marina. When they did their trial run, they didn't come back to the house according to the plan. They went straight over to their slip at the Marina. I think they got some ideas, and I had a feeling we should talk about it."

"Who in the world is Leroy?"

"That's Lennie's code name."

"Where is the boat in the marina?"

"It's in one of the covered slips at the outer edge. All they have to do, is swim in to their berth, load up the dough, and sail away. A sunset cruise, for all anyone knows."

"You talk to them about any of this?"

"Nope. But if one of us ain't there waiting, when they come out the water, they may want to take off with all the dough."

"Ain't the kid's girl still around?"

"Yeah."

"Well, she is your collateral ain't she?"

"Yes and no. If they blow her off, then they got the dough, and we got the dame."

"I would rather have the dough."

"Me too."

The wings came and Vincent snorted at Tommy after the blue haired waitress had gone. "Twelve bucks for some rubber tasting crap. This place is strictly freezer to table food."

"Will you quit bitching about the stupid wings. We are here to talk business, damnit, not start a stupid food blog."

"I'm just saying."

"So, we take the girl with us, and wait for them in the slip. Then, we off all three of them, and keep the money?"

"That's a big order, man. Whatta we gonna do with the bodies? How do we get the money out of the slip and up to a car? Remember what the kid said, the money is bulky, and weighs like two hundred twenty-five pounds. Plus, there is sure to be cameras all over the damn place. And they still might have something they stole off my computer, and they could email or text it or something that could incriminate us."

"Us?"

"Well, me."

"Okay then, we change the method of transferring the dough."

"To what? How?"

"I don't know."

"I think it is too late to change things now."

"What if we just let the kid's girl, Monica is her name, go free. Then we meet the boys at their slip, split up the money fifty fifty, and take off. That way you and me get our fair share, and everyone is happy. Think about it, this deal has had a few problems, I know, but we walk with 2.5 each in cold cash this Friday night? That ain't bad is it?"

"No, not too bad."

"I'm willing to settle for that, and walk with no more grief."

"Let me think about it. Eat some wings, they're good."

"They taste like fucking plastic."

"Whatever. I like the topping," Tommy said.

"That ain't no topping. That's Tabasco Sauce heated up is all it is."

Vincent was happy with his meeting, glad he and Tommy were close to being on the same page, and he headed back to his beloved bar. That serves real damn food, he thought to himself. Once there, he went into the back room, locked himself in, and called Stuart.

"What's up, boss man?"

"We gotta call them again this afternoon, yeah?"

"Oh yeah, did you watch any TV last night? Golfer girl was on every channel known to man. The money should be rolling in. What do you want me to tell them?"

"Come on up here. And we can go somewhere. I want to be around when you call, but I don't wanna have to drive back down there. And there's no way we gonna make the call from my restaurant."

"Where do you want to meet?"

"I'll meet you in the parking lot of the Lenny's Restaurant on International."

"I can be there in an hour."

"I wonder how the money is doin'? Vincent asked. "We gotta touch base with them every day, keep the hammer on um, get things set up right. It's going to take a while to get that much used money together."

"Plus, they need to get a boat. See you in an hour."

"Don't forget your voice thing."

Vincent rang off, and called Alton.

Will and Bob Jensen, Tina, Penny, Alton, Inspector Chong and Carmen Ayala had a ten o'clock meeting at the compound, and everyone was bursting with excitement at the universal response to Chrissy's case. Interestingly, support wasn't coming in just from the USA. The Go Fund Me team was able to report to Penny that additional money was pledged from Europe, South Korea, Japan, Australia, Thailand, even China. It was a testament to the international organization the LPGA had evolved into, as well as the greater family and fraternity of golfers. They wanted to wait until after today's close of business at five o'clock west coast time, but felt they would in all probability be able to project that collections would be approaching the ten-million-dollar goal by the end of tomorrow's calendar day. This is one of the largest, most successful private campaigns we have ever administered, they told Penny. Disaster relief, a hurricane or an earthquake, maybe a large fire will raise similar money, but this response has been nothing but spectacular.

"I can give everyone an update after I talk to them today, in the meantime, let's keep working it," Penny reported.

"We look forward to hearing the update," said Carmen. "With Amazon's guarantee of the funds, and the way GFM is responding, all we have to do is exchange the money for Chrissy, and we are hopefully done. I think we can all relax now. Maybe take it a little easier." Carmen was aware of the long hours everyone had been working, and the stress level around the compound.

"With all due respect, Carmen, I think Tina, Will, Alton and I need to keep plugging away on the phones," Penny said. "We can continue to update the media, and keep the project rolling on their agendas. They are like animals in a way, and need to be fed as often as possible. Don't ever quote me on that."

"What is the role of the police going forward?" Alton asked.

"We are observing and compiling as much information as we can at this time," replied Danny Chong. "The department is very happy the funding campaign is going as well as it is, and we will do everything in our power to help see to Chrissy's safe return. But please don't forget that there have been multiple felonies committed, and we will also do everything we can to bring the perpetrators to justice. And Will, I am asking for a half hour of your time right after this meeting to prep together for the next phone call."

"I am pretty stretched for time, Inspector, but I can probably spare a few minutes for you." Will was still highly annoyed with his treatment at Tacoma Police headquarters, and also at the TPD's lack of any real progress in solving Chrissy's disappearance. "The family certainly respects your position in law enforcement, but things seem to be going so well, we want to emphasize to you and your people where our priorities lie. We don't want you to do anything, I reiterate anything, that might jeopardize Chrissy's wellbeing, or interfere with her safe return. We feel very positive in the direction this thing is heading, and we are all completely satisfied to proceed at our own discretion."

"I understand your sentiments Will, but you need to remember the nature of the individuals we are dealing with here. Potentially, these are some very dangerous criminals, and it is of the utmost importance for us to be involved in any and all communications with them going forward." Danny Chong could readily sense Will Jensen's apparent animus. Will was starting to border on being hostile.

"Sure inspector, we can chat after this meeting."

"Thank you, Carmen," Will continued. As much as he resented Danny Chong, he appreciated Carman Ayala. Where would the Jensen's be without her and Amazon?

"You just keep us posted Will. Let me know if any of the demands change. We are getting the money together, and can collect a check from the GFM people later. I will keep all my people up to date, as I am sure you will too with the LPGA people, Penny."

"Yes, thank you, Carmen, and thank you Penny and Alton. Thanks to everyone. Let's all hang tight today, and I will send out a group email as soon as the next call comes in, or if I hear anything else. Be careful when you leave, the press is already gathering outside of the house."

"Talk to them," Penny advised. "Keep them updated. Send out cookies and coffee. They are our friends; they are here to give us continuing coverage. Chrissy has become a rock star in their eyes, and the press can't get enough of her right now. I can do it for you on my way out if you like."

"You're right Penny. I'll be happy to do the honors, but why don't you and Tina join me. Dad, can you work on some coffee, and snacks for them?"

Alton had seen Vincent's call come in, but he certainly couldn't take it in front of Penny. The two of them stopped at a Panera Bread cafe for a sandwich on the way back to their hotel suite, and Penny was still jacked with excitement and a sense of purpose.

"I mean, we could have Chrissy back in two freakin' days," she said between bites of her avocado and brie cheese sandwich. "Aren't you stoked about that?"

"Of course, I'm blimey stoked about that, why else would I be sitting here working my tail off on this thing with you?"

"You seem kind of quiet is all."

Chrissy was awake at what she thought was an early hour. Since she had very little concept of time anymore, it was hard to tell. But breakfast hadn't come down yet, so it had to be earlier than ten. She rolled out of bed, relieved herself and brushed her teeth, then began stretching. Her spirits and morale had been so uplifted by one simple phone call, and she could almost taste that first cup of fresh roasted coffee, while sitting around the kitchen table with her mom and dad. She could smell the aroma of bacon wafting off of the stove, as she descended the stairs that first spectacular morning. Steve was still at the compound, and they had just made love, were coming down to breakfast. They were holding hands, back together, and were absolutely loving being in love.

Her mind was totally given to fantasizing now. As she stretched, she packed her virtual bags, and moved into a make-believe world, where she was once again out and about and free to come and go. Much like spending time in a third world country will help one to appreciate the quality of life so many of us enjoy in the USA, being locked away in an airless basement for a week will give one a much better perspective on personal freedom and self-determination. Not surprisingly, it was the little things Chrissy missed. Her personal brand of toothpaste, and body lotion, being able to leisurely bathe and shave her legs. An afternoon spent outdoors in the sunshine. Meals with the family, waking up with Steve next to her. Not to mention playing some tournament golf with her fellow pros. And above all, the safety and security of being back home, and not having this gnawing feeling of danger, threat and uncertainty hanging over her head.

As she loosened up, she resolved to put the negative feelings of her captivity behind her as much as possible, lay low and prepare to get the heck out of here. She started her strengthening exercises with vigor, and knew she had used her time in captivity to make herself physically and mentally stronger. She was elated to feel like she was on the downside of her ordeal. Communicating with Florence was now out of the question, so all she could do was wait, and pray this thing would be wrapped up soon. She had not seen burly boy around since her escape attempt, so hopefully, he was gone. He was the one person who made her feel especially uneasy, and she was morbidly concerned she might ever be isolated or alone with him. He would certainly want his pound of flesh back.

She worked out as best she could with no weights or exercise equipment, focusing on her quads and abdominal wall, as well as her upper body. It was her only way of biding time, and keeping her body in the best shape possible gave her a sense of wellbeing. She had no idea what a tsunami of support she was receiving out in the real world.

Alton broke away from Penny long enough to return Vincent's call when they got back to their Embassy Suites hotel room.

"Sorry, I was in meetings all morning."

"No problem. How is everything going over there?"

"Everything is first rate, mate. The money is basically taken care of. They just need to bring it all together now, and have them tell 'em what to do with it."

"How did they do that so fast?"

"They are making a killing on the Go Fund Me site, and then Amazon guaranteed them an interest free loan for the full amount anyway. So, they are already over the top."

"Amazon guaranteed the full amount?"

"Amazon gave Chrissy Jensen an interest free loan for ten million bucks, and she and her family and whoever can pay it back over time if they need to. Anyway, it looks like the Go Fund Me campaign is going to cover it all. They are already over eight million dollars contributed, and it's only been going for a day. So, the Jensen's won't even need Amazon's money. What have you got for me?"

"Well, I've got a couple of calls coming back this afternoon. I will call you. If you can't talk, just take the call and hang back up. Then call my burner when you can."

"Got it."

Inspector Chong and his negotiating team sat down in the den with Will, right after his meeting in the driveway with the assembled press. "Now whatta want?" Will asked.

In addition to Danny Chong, the communications team consisted of two trained conflict negotiators from the TPD, and a communications expert who was on loan from the FBI as an advisor/consultant.

"Will," the FBI negotiator began, "we want to make crystal clear to you how important these phone calls are to our investigation. They are the portal to the body of this case. The longer you can keep the kidnapper on the line, the more information we can gather for analysis. It appears they are using disposable burner phones to call, and while we would like to back trace their location from the calls, that appears to be secondary to just engaging them as long as possible. We are hoping they will make a blunder of some kind, an error in judgement, a slip of the tongue, anything that will assist our investigation."

"Is there something specific you want me to say to them?"

"Yes, there is. The last time they called, they assumed control, made their demands, and rang off in an efficient time frame. We want you to be more abrasive today. Confront them, demand to talk to Chrissy for example, and if they refuse, which they will, demand proof she is still safe and unharmed. Confront them about the money transfer, or any of the other logistical issues that might arise."

"And why do you want me to be confrontational?"

"We feel we might be able to catch them off guard with this kind of approach, and they might commit an error in judgement or drop a tell, if you will. Anything we can use to remove them from their comfort zone is advantageous to us all, Will."

"I can tell you right now, that I will not do anything to jeopardize the health and safety of my sister," Will spat at the Officers.

"We are aware of that Will, and we wouldn't ask that of you. As professional negotiators, you need to understand that we have been put in similar positions as this one. We are trained to react to these situations, this is what we do. Please trust us. It is helpful if you think from the perspective of the kidnappers. They are obsessed with the ransom money. We want your sister back. Our feeling is that we are dealing with at least some degree of professional crime here. They kidnapped Chrissy almost a week ago. They have held her for this amount of time, largely to increase our sense of anxiety, and desire to complete the ransom exchange. They allowed her to speak with you yesterday, which is proof she is still alive. We believe your being somewhat confrontational with them today, will not change any parameters in the negotiations. We are only hoping, again, it might produce something to our advantage."

"I will be willing to confront them as to speaking with my sister, and concerning her safety. If this causes any threats, negativity, or violent responses, I will back off, and attempt to remain on civil terms with them."

"Fair enough, Will. Again, we can only encourage you to trust our judgement, and let us lead you through your conversation." Whatever, ran through Will's mind. Why don't you just stay out of this, he thought.

Vincent and Stuart met in the parking lot of the Lenny's Restaurant on International Boulevard, which is a stone's throw from SeaTac Airport. Lenny's is an iconic dive that has been a part of the SeaTac culinary world for as long as most people can remember. As hard as they try to achieve the respectability of say an IHOP, this particular Lenny's is mired in the morass of mediocrity one finds in low end restaurants near most transportation hubs. Vincent was parked on the back edge of the fairly large parking lot, when Stuart rolled up in the rental sedan Vincent had provided for their use at the Gig Harbor house.

He spotted Vincent, and was able to back into a space on Vincent's right, so he could maneuver easily over into the shotgun seat of Vincent's black Escalade. The two men exchanged greetings, and began to prep for their phone call.

"Keep it short and sweet, just like yesterday. They gotta be so happy to have heard from golfer girl, they will airmail the money to us," Vincent said.

"Right on."

"I got word, their Go Fund Me money is almost over the top already, and if that ain't enough, Amazon guaranteed the whole ten mil in an interest free loan, just to get the princess back."

"You are kidding me." Stuart was shocked at that bit of news. "I guess all we have to do is, close out the deal, and we are home free?"

"That's the idea, kid."

"Okay, let's make the call," and Stuart plugged his distortion device into his phone, and adjusted the volume.

"That gonna work okay in the car?"

"Yeah, it's just an adaption on my phone."

"Tell 'em they gonna need a speed boat, and we want the money packaged into four duffel type sports carry bags. We can tell them tomorrow about the waterproof construction bags. What time are we going to set up the drop for anyway?"

"The tides are going to be perfect around six o'clock," Stuart said.

"We still on the same time schedule to get back to the dock?" Vincent asked innocently.

Stuart hesitated for a pregnant moment, before replying. "Actually Vincent, my diving partner and I think it would be more efficient if we returned to another location. It is better and safer for everyone. We won't have to fight the tide crossing back across the channel, we won't draw anyone back to the house, and we can execute the plan in half the time."

"What the hell, you were going to tell me about this, right?"

"I just did."

"Yeah, after I axked you about it. You cannot change things around like this without consulting wit me first."

Stuart informed Vincent, "my partner, who is actually the better diver by far, just suggested it. He is getting suspicious about what is going on, with all of the coverage on TV, and is getting a little paranoid. He keeps his boat at another location, and he wants to bring the money back there."

"And how am I supposed to get my money?"

"I was going to talk to you about that today."

Vincent was both angry, but also relieved. Upset about the unannounced change in plans, but satisfied with Stuart's honesty with him. "Let's talk about it after the phone call. I want to get this over with."

"Roll the window down, will you? It's hot as hell in here," Stuart complained.

It was seven minutes after four in the afternoon, and the phone rang three times before Will answered it. Three rings were just enough for the police to get their monitors and frequencies dialed in and ready.

"This is Will Jensen."

"This is Mick Jagger again, Will. We want the ten million bucks in four separate oversized sports tote bags, 2.5 million in each. Used one hundred-dollar bills. Make sure the bags are sturdy. Be ready by Thursday afternoon, and we will call to check on your progress." Stuart's voice sounded like he had had a stroke, and was talking through a water-logged time warp.

"Thursday, that's tomorrow. That is hardly any time. Why are you pushing us so hard?"

"I said tomorrow afternoon."

"That is still hardly enough time."

"You just have the money ready by tomorrow."

"I want to speak with my sister right now."

"You what?"

"I want to speak to my sister right now. How do I know she is okay?"

"You spoke to her yesterday, that's enough."

"Can you please speak up; I can barely hear you," Will said.

"Hey, get your head out of your ass, and you will probably hear a lot better."

"Yeah, well Chrissy had better be okay."

"Are you threatening me?" Stuart asked in surprise.

"My sister just better be alright, that's all."

"Or what?"

"What kind of tote bags do you want me to get?" Will said, backpedaling.

"Get some damn Nike tote bags. Call Amazon Prime for all I care."

"We may need more time."

"Not from what I hear. Get the fucking money ready, and quit whining. Good bye."

"That was awesome Will. You did a spot-on job."

"Thanks. Those calls make me extremely nervous."

"You did just what we needed you to do. I think we pulled some great data to analyze. Let us get to work, and hopefully, we can have something for you by tomorrow."

"Whew. Why was he being such a punk today? Asking so many questions, and like that," Stuart said to Vincent.

"Probably just trying to be a tough guy, and take up for his sister."

"Like he can do anything."

"Ah, you did good, Stuart. A couple more calls, and we are done."

"We going to have to figure something out. I don't want to call from here again tomorrow. I could hardly hear him when that plane flew over. It's too noisy here, and it's hot in the car."

"Yeah, I agree," Vincent said. "Why don't I just come back over to Gig Harbor tomorrow early afternoon? We'll call from there, and go over all of the last-minute details before D-Day. How is Leroy doing?"

"I took him home. He wasn't doing well at all, and couldn't help with anything, so I just took him back to his place, and told him to call you."

"What are we going to do about the money drop?" Vincent asked.

"Whatever you want boss man."

"Let me think about it."

CHAPTER THIRTY-THREE

Thursday dawned at four forty am, and was a carbon copy of the natural beauty and pleasant livability of the Pacific Northwest in July. The temperature would rise to a moderate eighty-two degrees. Humidity might hit fifty percent in the afternoon. Oysters in all varieties, fresh from the brisk, pristine waters of Puget Sound, are a regional staple. If one extended that concept to the climate in general, they could say the world is my oyster today, and not be far from the truth.

Vincent in particular felt quite expansive after he had risen, dressed for the day, and had gotten his first cup of coffee down.

"Good morning, my sweetness," he said, pulling Angela onto his lap, and kissed her on the mouth. As Vincent was not given to frequent displays of morning affection, Angela was a little concerned with his behavior.

She gently touched his cheek which was still black and blue, but less swollen, and asked "are we going back in the bedroom?"

"If I had more time, we would spend all day inna bedroom."

"Someone is in a good mood today. Did your Viagra prescription auto renew or something?"

"You are my Viagra baby. Wanna go to Vegas with me?"

"Sure, Vinnie. And when is that going to happen?"

"This weekend if I can still get us show tickets."

"Let's go."

Vincent got to his office, checked in, then kept going into his back-room sanctum and called Tommy on a new burner.

"Hey, you got a few minutes?"

"What's up?"

"I wanted to talk about D-Day with you."

"Shoot."

This was going to be a little prickly, but Vincent thought it was doable if Tommy was in a reasonable mood. It made all the sense in the world to him personally. "I am going to have everything set up for tomorrow, but I feel like we need your services for one last leg of the operation."

"And what leg would that be?"

"There are some concerns about my visibility, as I was the only one golfer girl got a decent look at when she came bustin' out of the house and almost escaped. I'm sure the cops are going to want an exit interview wid her, and I think I should have an iron clad alibi for tomorrow."

"What do you want from me?"

"I think it would be a good idea if you met the kid and his buddy tomorrow evening when they come back to their boat slip with the money. You take our share and beat it. I will get my half from youse later."

"Did you talk to him about changing locations on his own?"

"Yeah, I did. He come clean, said he was going to talk with me about it, but it all happened in the last few days. Him and his partner feel a lot safer doing it the other way is all."

"And where you gonna be?"

"I want to get completely away from this place. Go to Victoria or Vegas for the weekend. Take Angela wit me. Don't you think that would be good for the both of us? How could they ever pin anything on me if I was outta here. And, if they could never get at me, that would be good for you too. Take the heat off both of us."

"You worried about something?"

"Nope. Just trying to be careful is all. Carrot head said everything is going smooth over there with them. The money's all in, and they told the cops to back off of the whole deal. We just have to tell 'em how to drop it. The kid picks it up, and they scuba down to the Marina. You is waitin' for them in the berth. I have an electronic scanner for you, if everything checks out clean, then you put the money in a garbage can, and wheel it out of there. You are gone, I will have a drop set up for golfer girl and it's all over and done with."

"What Marina are you talking about again?"

"Tacoma Narrows Marina." How many times I gotta tell you Vincent thought? "It's ten minutes from I-5. You could be home in half an hour."

"What would I need?"

"Just a trash can, with a cover and a hand truck. I would wear your fake beard, and a hoodie or something too, if it was me."

"You will have everything else set up?"

"Yep."

"Okay. I'll do this one last thing for you."

"For us, partner, and thanks. This makes me feel a lot safer. I just want to check with Carrot Top one more time, and if he says the coast is clear, then we are good. I think we will be iron clad." The changes made Vincent much more comfortable with their whole end game.

Tommy wanted nothing more than keeping his contact with V's people to a bare minimum, but he also thought being on the front end of the money exchange and securing his two and a half mil as soon as possible was probably a smart idea. No telling what these dildos would screw up next, or hey, maybe they get smart with me, and I just off all three of them, stuff them in the cabin of the boat, and keep all the dough.

The daily ten o'clock meeting at the Jensen Compound was under way, with nothing earthshaking to discuss. The money was in, and accounted for. Carmen and her people were compiling the funds as they had been instructed. As a matter of fact, Go Fund Me had had to terminate the campaign when it reached 10.7 million dollars. 10.6 would ensure complete funding of the project, cover the GFM people, and eliminate any clerical or computer errors in processing. Plus leave sufficient money to cover any contingencies.

As contact with the press had ramped down a bit for the last twenty-four hours, the media reps were sensing something was in the air, and were more aggressive than usual, whenever they could get close enough to shout out a questions or inquiries.

"How did your analysis of yesterday's phone call go, Inspector?" Will asked Inspector Chong.

"It is a bit difficult to get total clarity, with the distortion device they are using, but we have our techs working overtime on it. If anything of substance emerges, I will call you immediately."

"Are we even close to identifying anything about the kidnappers?" Will's frustration was again more than evident in his voice. After all of the crap about him being more aggressive with the kidnappers, and still the cops or the FBI had absolutely nothing to show for his efforts.

"We are continuing to pour our resources into every facet of this case, Will."

"My question was, do you have any solid leads, anything of the slightest substance, that would help us get Chrissy back?"

"I assure you, that this case is our number one priority, Will."

"Thank you, Danny. Under the circumstances, I am going to suggest that we comply with the demands of the kidnappers, and get Chrissy back. While that is happening, Inspector, if you would shut your people completely down, and back off, at least Chrissy will be safely home with us. Until then, the lower your profile the better in our opinion. Does anyone have any other ideas or suggestions?"

"Speaking for Amazon and myself," Carmen Ayala said, "we want to see Chrissy's abduction remedied as quickly as possible. We feel this is also the will of the public, which is evidenced by their generous and timely support and contributions. To have anything negative happen to Chrissy at this juncture, to not take advantage of this opportunity to ransom her, and bring her back safely to her family, is critically important to all of us. If somehow, by some miracle, the kidnappers were ever apprehended, that would just be a bonus. Right now, we agree with the Jensen's, and our priority is 110% with Chrissy's safe return. Please be very careful with your activities, Officer Chong. As a matter of fact, why don't you just shut it down for a few days?"

"Thank you, Carmen. That summarizes our feelings perfectly," Will reiterated.

Danny Chong twitched perceptively at the priorities emerging from the assembled group. His goal was to return Chrissy safely, as well as capture and prosecute the offenders, but he remained stoic, and sat impassively as virtually everyone in the room ignored his warnings of vigilance, and lobbied for a rapid and smooth recovery of America's new sweetheart.

"In closing," Will asked of Tina and Penny, "what are we going to tell the media?"

"This a difficult time to deal with, Will." Penny replied. "I would stay as closed mouth as possible for another day, and we must make completely sure no one has illegally tapped your phone. Paparazzi are notorious for doing that. Whether the mainstream media would go to that extent, I would certainly hope not, but we must be extra careful. I would communicate that there is nothing new to report, and as soon as there is, we will release it to our local news teams immediately. You agree Tina?"

"Absolutely, Penny. Today we are at critical mass here. Let's get through with our obligations successfully, and we will most hopefully have Chrissy back with us. We must maintain our confidentiality at all costs, and not let any of the ransom tasks or details become public knowledge. That would jeopardize everything we are trying so hard to accomplish here." Turning to Danny Chong, she reiterated Will and Carmen sentiments: "I also feel very strongly that your people should virtually disappear for a couple of days, Inspector. We have too much at stake, to blow up this rescue by your people causing anything adverse to happen."

"Tina, can you and Penny join me outside for a mini press conference? I am going to tell them we are hoping for some resolve by the end of this week, and in the meantime, if they could please respect our privacy and security, we would greatly appreciate it." Will also nodded at Tina to say thanks for your support.

Alton got a text. "Call me" was all it said.

Chrissy was up early, and finished with her morning workout by the time Florence brought her breakfast in. She was dying to ask what was going on, but knew that bridge had been burned. Yeah, she thought, that bridge is scorched beyond recognition, and laying out flat on the ground, like a tornado hit it.

Brunch today was a bowl of instant oatmeal, with a couple of individual sized containers of Dannon yogurt and a couple of Cliff Bars. Yum. For some reason, maybe sustenance deprivation, she began to recreate her family's Thanksgiving dinner traditions back home at the ranch in Yakima. The crisp bite of the late November air outside; inside, the roar of the fireplace in the great room, the fragrance of an organic bird roasting in the oven. Ginny's virtual mashed potatoes and turkey gravy, with wild mushroom stuffing was making her mouth water. And then candied yams, fresh asparagus, sourdough biscuits and homemade butter with cranberry jelly, and a glass or two of Champagne with everyone sitting around the table together. Oh sure, how about a couple bottles of Leonetti Cabernet with dinner. Then, freshly made peach, apple, and pumpkin pies. With homemade vanilla ice cream.

She laid back down on the single bed, and closed her eyes. She found more and more often now she was transporting herself to a fantasy destination of her choosing, and in this particular reverie, the sensation of being home with her loved ones was so real, she floated off into a dreamy seance like state of reality that had her drowsing off, and smiling in contentment. She was in her personal comfort zone for a couple of hours, and awoke feeling sated and consummately gratified. She continued to lie on her bed, and enjoy, embrace the warmth surrounding her and reinforced to herself that her whole ordeal would be ending soon. I am almost out of here she sang aloud to herself and the four walls.

Alton found a moment of privacy on the back deck while Penny was outside with Will and Tina talking to the Media, and quickly dialed Vincent's burner phone. "What's up?"

"How was your meeting this morning?"

"It was fine. Everyone is very anxious to get Chrissy back. They are willing to do whatever is necessary to pay the dough tomorrow, and be done with it."

"What are the cops saying?"

"They don't have a clue as to what is happening. As a matter of fact, both the family, the Amazon rep and the Golf Channel lady told them to back off, stand down, stay out of the way and completely evaporate until the exchange has been made. Getting Chrissy back is everyone's top priority. What have you got for me?"

"I think I will have something for you tomorrow."

"Something good?"

"If everything works out, I think you will be very happy. You call me tomorrow morning right after your morning meeting."

"Okay mate, I'll call you by ten thirty or so."

Vincent was going to be busy for the rest of the afternoon. He had a lot of planning to do if he was going to be leaving town tomorrow. First off, he called one of his buddies who was a pit boss at the MGM Grand. That would take care of show tickets. Next, he called the MGM concierge and asked her to book him into a suite and get two tickets confirmed on Alaska Air. Early afternoon, please. Next he called Angela, and told her they would be leaving for Vegas tomorrow afternoon.

Now, he was off to Gig Harbor to meet with Stuart and Monica. For all of Ronnie and Tommy's bitching about them being civilians and greenhorns, etc., Vincent felt like they had, except for the computer incident, basically done okay by him. And now he was going to let them wrap things up. Today he was driving his Escalade, having left the BMW in the garage. It was too flamboyant, and he understandably wanted to keep his profile lower.

"I'm on my way, be there in half an hour."

"Okay."

Vincent rolled in to find Stuart and Monica waiting for him on the living room sofa.

"You want anything?"

"Thanks, I'm good."

"I want to talk to youse about tomorrow, before we call him."

"Okay."

"I ain't going to be here tomorrow. Something came up for me. So, you two will be running the show."

"Wow," Stuart said in surprise.

"Don't worry, you can handle it. You need to wipe this house down, make sure there ain't no prints left around. Even though nobody knows where she is, we still don't want to take no chances. Tomorrow, Monica, you will get her ready to go. I want you to put her in the trunk of the Taurus rental car by six p.m. Then you park it out front of the house in the guest parking slot, and leave the keys in the ignition. I will have someone come and pick the car up, and drive it to a drop spot after the money is in safely. She should look good, why don't you go buy her some new clothes today."

"Should I restrain her tomorrow?"

"I would tie her hands behind her back with zip ties, at least until you get her in the car, and you tell her to be quiet. If she's quiet, she don't get hurt. If she makes a racket, or any kinda noise, we will be nearby, and we will have to knock her ass out. You tell her as soon as she hears someone tap on the trunk a couple of times, then she can go ballistic. Not until then. And be sure and wipe the basement down after you put her in the trunk."

"Okay. If you want her to have new clothes, I need some more money."

"No problem. Here is another coupla bills. You got everything?"

"Wipe the house down, and clean it up. And we are both out of here tomorrow?"

"Yeah, leave the house just like youse was movin' out. Leave it nice, nobody gets suspicious. Once you do all that, you are free to go. It's been nice workin' wid youse."

"Likewise, Vincent."

"What else do you want me to do?" Stuart asked.

"Tomorrow when da house is squared away, have your buddy pick you up here, and get ready for your dive. I assume you is taking care of him out of your share, we don't want no push back from him later on. This afternoon, we got to tell them what to do tomorrow. I talked to somebody today, and they said the Jensen's will do anything to get her back. They raised the whole ten large on that internet thing, and don't even want the cops around, nowhere, nohow. They just want to pay the money, and get golfer girl back, no questions axked."

"That's good."

"So, here is what we do," Vincent continued on. "We tell them again to have the dough in four tote bags, two and a half million bucks per bag. Then they need to put the tote bags in separate large construction style black trash bags. The cash bags should even be doubled up, and cinched extra tight. They gonna be in a speedboat at the mouth of Gig Harbor at six o'clock. At exactly six you and your buddy are ready to dive. Just before you go inna water, you call Willy boy one more time. Tell him where the crab pots are, and how to make the drop. As soon as you finish that call, you dive, and dump the phone and voice distorter in the water. You should be at the crab pots just a little after they get there. You grab the dough, and run for the marina. I will have someone waiting there to pick up our half. He is gonna have a trash can and a hand cart and load up and truck it on out of there, as soon as y'all check out the goods."

"Hope it goes as smoothly under the water as you say it will."

"It better. Today, we tell Will to get himself a boat, and get all the money packed up. We let him know we will be watching his every move, so we don't want no cops around nowhere, and don't even think about trying nothin'. Anything I missed?"

"I need to tell you where our sailboat is."

Vincent winked at Stuart. "No need, we got it."

"How do you know that?"

Vincent smirked and said, "A little bird told me."

"Wow," Stuart was impressed. "Okay, Let's make the call."

Stuart plugged the distorter into his phone, and dialed Will's number.

The usual three rings, then "Will Jensen speaking."

"Will, this is Mick again. Are you ready to get your sister back?"

"Yes."

"Okay, listen carefully to me. You know how we want the money packaged, right?"

"Yep."

"It is 2.5 million bucks in four athletic tote bags, right?"

"Yep." So, there are four of them Will thought.

You want to have yourself a good boat. You need to have eight heavy duty, large trash bags. You double up the bags, and put a tote bags in each double package. You cinch the inside bag, then the outside bag up as tight as you can with zip ties. You understand me?"

"Yep."

"You need to be at the mouth of Gig Harbor at six o'clock sharp tomorrow evening. No cops around. We will be watching you. You can have one of your brothers in the boat with you. But no cops. Any cops, and Chrissy don't make it home, you got that?"

"Yeah."

"Any questions?"

"Where do I go in the boat?"

"We will call you at six o'clock tomorrow and tell you where to go. Until then, don't be so damn nosey."

"So, when and how are we getting Chrissy back?"

"She will be returned to you after we check out your packages, and make sure they are all good to go with no tracking devices. If the money is tampered with in any way, your sister is dead. She is presently safe and unharmed, and will be returned to you in that condition if you do everything you are told to do. Her safety is in your hands. Don't screw this up. Do you understand me?"

"Yes sir."

"Do you fucking completely get the concept?"

"Yes sir."

And Stuart clicked off.

Vinnie stood up to go. The three amigos shook hands, and Stuart and Monica walked him out to his SUV. "I will call you in the morning just to touch base."

"Okay."

"Anyway, pretty good job you two, for stinking, greenhorn assbite rookies."

"Thanks boss, good luck."

"That is awesome Monica. You will be free to go tomorrow. No need to bust out of here, and make a mad dash to the airport. I was worried about that."

"That's really good. A lot less stress for me. I think he is finally starting to trust us. You still want me to leave the Triumph at the airport?"

"Don't know what else we can do with it."

"Maybe I'll keep the key, and mail it back to someone."

"Might as well."

Stuart took Monica in his arms, and gave her a squeeze. "We are almost outta here baby."

Vincent drove back to his bar. On the way he called his friend at the MGM, and was assured he would have a set of high roller tickets to see Ed Sheeran. He knew that would make a happy woman out of Angela. I better stop off at the drug store and get a renewal on my Viagra after all he thought.

Back at Vincenzo's, he slipped in the side door, and when he caught Betty's eye, he motioned her over.

"You wanna make some good pocket cash for a little piece of side work?"

"Sure honey. Whattaya need?"

"Sit down, let's talk."

Betty couldn't sit her thirty-five-year-old, still pretty firm, backside down quick enough. She loved doing side jobs for Vincent. He always took such good care of her.

"I need you to pick up a car for me and move it into town."

"What town?"

"Gig Harbor."

"Okay. When?"

"Tomorrow," the V told her. "You take off early, from the bar here. Leave about four. Then you gonna drive down to Gig Harbor, and park your car at the Seven Seas Brewery. It's on Udderberg Street, right near the waterfront. After youse do that, you call a cab and take it to the address in Gig Harbor I'm gonna give you. There will be a beige sedan there parked in the driveway. The keys will be in the ignition. You drive it back to the Seven Seas, and leave it in the first row of the parking lot. Right in front of the brewery. You should have the car there by seven. Make sure it is parked right in front of the brewery, got it? Then you get in your car, and head back home. You need to wear gloves in the sedan, soze you don't leave no prints around. We all clear here?"

"Yeah, I got it. It don't sound like too much trouble, Vincent."

"Twenty-five grand for your trouble is okay? There may be even more."

"Vincent, that is too much."

"Don't worry about it, Betty. I take care of youse, and youse take care of me. Capiche?"

"Hell yes, boss."

Betty got up to go. "Anything else, boss?"

"This is confidential shit. Just between you and me."

"Got that." Betty leaned over and kissed Vincent on the cheek.

"Don't get no damn lipstick on me. I'll give you the address on my way out."

CHAPTER THIRTY-FOUR

Everyone was gathered at the Jensen Compound for the last morning meeting, and Will was leading the group through their final tasks.

"Carmen, the money is all together?"

"Yes, Will. There are two-armed security guards coming down from Seattle this morning. They will stay with the money here at the compound, until you and Charlie have them load it onto your boat. The FBI has checked in with me, and they want to inspect the packages prior to loading. They need to be familiar with them from a surveillance standpoint. So they know big they are, what shape, color, heft, etc."

"I think that's okay. And thanks, Carmen, for all of your help and support."

"Will, we have a Harbor Patrol boat we will be happy to provide, if you would like," Danny Chong offered.

"Thank you, Officer Dong, I mean Chong, but that's exactly what we don't want." How dumb is this f'ing cop Will wanted to ask? And he proceeded to intentionally fracture the pronunciation of the officer's name. "On behalf of our entire family, I am reminding you to please keep your personnel completely away from every aspect of today's activities. We want your assurance that there will be no police presence anywhere near the boat, the exchange-- where ever that is going to be-- or the harbor. We do not want any patrol boats, cigarette boats, blimps, recon planes, submarines, aircraft carriers, sonar, none of it. Please take the day off, and do whatever you would like, as long as it has nothing to do with my sister or the Jensen family. Am I making myself perfectly clear, Inspector?"

"Yes, Will, you are," Danny Chong replied, thinking that Will was getting pretty damn cocky, and knowing he could arrest him right now for obstruction if he wanted to. "However, for your own protection, I will have a SWAT team ready and on high alert, just in case there are any problems. All you need to do is call my personal cell number, and we will deploy instantly. Also, Will, and this is standard procedure, it is urgent that we meet with Chrissy as soon as she is physically able to sit with us for an exit interview. If she has been physically harmed in any way, or if she appears to be disoriented or damaged mentally or emotionally, I would strongly suggest she be admitted to Tacoma General Hospital overnight for observation. If she is in satisfactory condition, she will at the very minimum require a police escort back to your compound, and then we will need to meet with her tomorrow to do an in-depth review of all aspects of her abduction. We strongly advise you to have her examined by a physician when she is recovered. If she is returned to your compound this evening, we will have armed officers stationed on your premises twenty-four seven until we meet with your family."

"Thanks, Officer, for the response team. I hope their deployment will not be necessary. As far as your other obligations, as long as that all happens after her safe recovery, the Jensen's will co-operate with you." Bob Jensen nodded his head in agreement. "As far as an ideal scenario, we deliver the ransom, Chrissy is recovered, and if she is found to be in acceptable health, I am one hundred percent certain she will want to be safely returned to her family here at the Compound."

"That's acceptable to us, Will. But the family must embrace the fact that she has been through an extremely traumatic ordeal. She may have suffered physical, emotional or psychological trauma that is best dealt with by professionals. She may be a completely different person when she gets home to you. If she is not evaluated immediately, permanent damage could occur."

"Yes sir, we are aware of that. But, again, we are a very close-knit family, and we will know in a very reasonable amount of time how she is doing. If she has in any way been abused, or is emotionally distressed, we will call and seek assistance."

"Not to change the subject, but you do have your boat lined up, right Will?" Carmen asked.

"Yeah, some friends of my uncle in Gig Harbor are providing us the use of their speed boat. Charlie and I are going over this afternoon for a test drive. Carmen, after we do the test run, I think your guys can load up the packages around five. Please have them dressed in civilian clothes, not some kind of security guard uniforms. They can be armed, but please no unnies. Then we will be ready to cast off around five thirty."

"When and how is Chrissy going to released?" Penny asked.

"They said she is safe, and will be returned to us as soon as they verify the money is all there, and has not been tampered with. They are in charge here, and all we can do is trust them to do what they say they are going to do."

"Anything else?"

"Go with God, Will," Bob Jensen said in closing.

Danny Chong wanted to continue the conversation with Bob and Will, but that door closed when everyone departed the room. He shook his head, and thought what a bunch of independent son-of-a-guns these Jensen's are. I hope they are right, he told himself as he walked out the back door of the compound, and around the perimeter of the property to avoid the lurking press. He made it to his dark green Crown Victoria police cruiser without incident.

While Will, Penny and Tina went outside to communicate to the press that they were hoping for some resolve soon, Alton slipped out onto the back deck of the compound and made a call to Vincent's burner.

"Coast looks all clear here. They have the money set to go, and will be at the mouth of Gig Harbor at five thirty. They were very clear they wanted absolutely no cops, in any way shape or form around anywhere."

"Okay, Red. Here is what you do, and you listen very carefully to me. Are you seeing anyone right now?"

"Yes."

"Is she here in Tacoma?"

"Yeah, she also works for the LPGA."

"Good. Pay attention now! Take your girlfriend out to the Tides Tavern tonight around five thirty for dinner and a few beers. It's a classic joint on the water front over in old town, Gig Harbor. Been there forever. When you are finished eating, tell your girl you want to walk up the street to the Seven Seas Brewery for a nightcap. The road bends up a little hill to the left as you leave the Tides parking lot. On your right up the street and around the corner, in a little strip mall, is the Seven Seas. There may be a beige sedan parked in front of the brewery after seven o'clock, and the first three letters of the license plate may be ARC. If you see that car, you should act as if you hear something or notice something unusual when you walk by it, and you need to stop and check it out. You may want to bang on the trunk a couple of times to see if anyone is in there. If you hear anything, go get the keys from the car's ignition, and open the trunk. There may be something very valuable to you in there."

"I got it, mate."

"I can't stress enough to you that you have never had this conversation. My name should never, not ever come up under any circumstances. If anybody was to ever hear my name mentioned, both the girl and myself could be in extreme danger. Even after this whole thing comes down, if my name is ever throwed around, they would come back after all three of us. You, me and her. You get me, Red? Have I made myself perfectly clear?"

"Yes sir, you have. I will scrub my phone history this afternoon, and we have never, ever so much as spoken to each other," Alton replied.

"You do that, Red. I gotta go." Vincent was comfortable that with Alton scrubbing his phone, and him using a burner, they would be leaving no electronic traces of their conversations.

Alton was elated, and couldn't have been happier with himself, and the situation. Chrissy was coming home safely, and by finding her, he would be able to claim the reward. All $600,000.00 of it. I knew Vincent was somehow involved in this thing, he thought. But it was also essential to remain cool at all costs. The last thing in the world he needed now, was for Penny to sense any excitement on him. This could totally blow his cover, and ruin his credibility should he find Chrissy in the trunk of that car. No, even though his heart was racing at 500 RPM's, he needed to remain quiet and concerned, pensive and hopeful like the rest of the team. He could do it.

Penny was ready to leave after dealing with the press. She wanted to give the Jensen's some privacy, and also take a break. She, along with Tina and Will had been nonstop working the phones long and hard for the last week. There wasn't much of anything else they could do now. Just wait it out. First up though, she needed to give Cynthia a call.
"Hi Cyn."
"Hi Penny. What's going on up there?"
"We just had our final team meeting. Everything is all set up to deliver the ransom money late this afternoon. Ten million bucks worth."
"Wow, that is a lotta money. We can all be very thankful that Chrissy is so well liked and respected to raise that kind of money so quickly. She is going to be returned okay?"
"They are saying yes. The kidnappers don't want the cops anywhere near anything, nor do the Jensen's. Will was very adamant at the meeting. No cops, no cops. That's what he kept saying to everyone, especially the head detective guy who is assigned to the case."

"Well, I will communicate your update to the execs, and we will all have our fingers crossed down here. If there is a good side to this story, Chrissy comes home safely, and it is completely wonderful to know that the LPGA has so much support out there. You have done well, Penny. Keep up the good work, and let me know as soon as Chrissy surfaces."

"Will do. How is everything going in San Francisco?" Penny appreciated Cynthia's positive comment concerning her performance, and was equally impressed with the world of good will coming their way.

"Going well. Everyone is still very concerned about Chrissy, and I have had to grab a couple of interns down here just to help me deal with the media in your absence. But we are doing okay. I will tell you for a fact, that Mac and the rest of the brass have got security cranked up to the max. There is staff everywhere, all over the grounds, the players, the perimeters, the parking lots, the locker room. You almost can't go to the bathroom now, without a cop or a security guard holding your hand."

"That has got to be a good thing. Being here, and seeing what the Jensen family is going through, is enough to make anyone paranoid."

"I haveta run. Exactly when is all this supposed to happen?"

"Will is going to receive the instructions at six pm this evening, about dropping the money. And then we don't know when or how Chrissy is going to be returned. But Cynthia, please keep this information to yourself. You are the only person outside of the immediate team, who knows what's going on. We have been very circumspect with the press here, as has Tina with the national media, and we are concerned that should anything get out, it could jeopardize Chrissy's safety. Once Chrissy is back with us, then we can all go for it. In the meantime, please keep a lid on anything I have told you.

"Will do, Penny. Take care, and keep me posted. As soon as anything happens, and I mean anything, I want to know about it."

Cynthia clicked off of her phone, and immediately called Mac Tenderson, to give him an update. He suggested she call a few of their key media resources, i.e. the New York Times, the San Francisco Chronicle, the LA Times, and update them. Let them know we are expecting some resolve soon."

"We have to be very careful here, Mac. We can't do anything that might create a problem. It could have a negative impact on Chrissy's safety, and the Jensen's and everyone else in the world would be furious."

"I'm aware of that, Cynthia. And we shouldn't release any specifics, but don't you think it would be a good idea to give our national press partners a leg up? Couldn't it be a boon to our ongoing press relations?"

"In a way, I think it could. But if I called them now, they may infer that the whole case is about to come to a head, and start some rumors, which would just increase the pressure on everyone there at Chambers Bay. We certainly don't need anything like that happening. They are stressed out enough up there."

"Yeah, you're right. We better wait it out. But call me as soon as anything happens."

"Can do, Mac."

Ginny and her sister Elaine were tired to the bone of waiting, waiting, waiting. Ginny especially. They all felt helpless, like they had somehow been rendered immobile, like paralysis had set in. But while Bob and Will and Tina and most of the others had some kind function to pass the time, Ginny and Elaine did their best just to try to keep busy and stay positive.

Bob Jensen recognized this, and knew that today would be an especially grueling wait. As soon as Will was finished dealing with the press, Bob asked him and Tina to sit with then for a few minutes.

"We want to spend the day preparing for Chrissy safe return," he opened the conversation. "What do you think would be the best approach to welcoming her home?"

"I think it would be wise to take Inspector Chong's advice seriously," Tina began. By all means, I would have your family physician here at the compound. No one is quite sure what to expect when Chrissy returns. And while we are hoping she will be all good, my thoughts would be to keep things very low key. You in the immediate family welcome her home, maybe have some of her favorite snacks, beverages or sandwiches available. She may want a glass of wine or milk, or maybe nothing. Let her have complete privacy. In my opinion, it would be best, not to pressure her in any way. Let her talk. Let her doctor check her vital signs. She will certainly have a lot of emotions to release. Let her know about the outpouring of support she has received. If she is appearing stressed, she may need a sedative to calm down. If any of you have some concerns, she should probably have a more serious examination first thing tomorrow morning. I mean, there could be a whole range of reactions from A to Z when she gets here. On the other hand, she may be healthy and so happy to be back with you guys, she can't contain herself. She may want stay up and dance all night."

Ginny spoke up. "I think Tina is absolutely right. We take it easy, welcome her back. Let Doctor Tomberg examine her. Let her talk it out. We should be able to ascertain if she is herself pretty quickly. I think we can make it through the night, if we do that. Should she need additional professional help, we will deal with that tomorrow. And Tina, on behalf of the family, I can't thank you enough for everything you have done here this week."

"Here, here," everyone said.

"Elaine and I will have things ready for her homecoming as best we can, and you all keep doing your jobs. I pray to God Chrissy comes back to us this evening safe and sound. Everyone rest up as much as possible, this is going to be a big night."

Bob went over and gave Ginny a hug, which evolved into a group embrace. The big house was charged with excitement and anticipation, and barring any extreme treatment during her confinement, everyone felt reasonably sure Chrissy would assimilate successfully. She was tough as nails both mentally and physically, so save any overt abuse, they all hoped she would be in reasonable shape come the end of this long day.

Tina was staying at the compound, so Penny and Alton took off for their hotel.

"I am wiped out Alton, let's go out to the pool and relax this afternoon. It has been a busy week, and I want to enjoy some of this warm weather."

"I like that. Want to go for some dinner tonight? One of the bobbies was telling me about a great old place up in Gig Harbor. It's about fifteen minutes from here, and it's right on the water. We could go eat and get back to the compound and wait for news on Chrissy."

"That sounds like fun, as long as we aren't gone too long. I am ready to take a break, do something different, enjoy life a little bit."

"Let's leave here around five. We can be back by seven or so."

CHAPTER THIRTY-FIVE

Around five thirty Will and Charlie cast off from Uncle Richard's friend's dock, and motored out to the mouth of Gig Harbor. They were carrying the goods and were anxious to get their instructions on where to make the drop.

Both brothers were calm and while not relaxed, were confident things were going to go well. Will Jensen had Tina call him to double check his phone's reception out on the water.

"Ready to go, bro?" Will asked Charlie.

He was just making idle chatter to pass the time, and Charlie knew it. But had nothing to say in return. At least there were a variety of pleasure boats to watch who were coming back into the harbor from Puget Sound proper. The day boaters seemed happy and good natured on their way in to port, and Will and Charlie received numerous jolly waves from many of the passing boats. They dutifully waved back.

Mount Rainier was perched in her magnificence to the southeast. There were seabirds of all descriptions soaring through the sky. Most of them were looking for dinner, and when their aerial reconnaissance of Will and Charlie's inboard saw nothing editable, they floated on their separate ways. It was a nice place to spend half an hour before such a strategic mission.

"We've got to stay alert," Charlie finally said. "Let's just get the damn job done and get back and get ready for Chrissy to surface."

"I know," Will replied. "This waiting is just making me all the angrier. I wish I could get my hands around one of these sucker's necks for just one minute."

"Well, that's probably not going to happen, so let's just do what they tell us, and keep rolling."

Stuart and Monica also spent a quiet afternoon at the Gig Harbor rental. They got everything straightened up, and wiped down. Monica had purchased a new Adidas workout suit for Chrissy, took it down to her, and told her they would be moving her out later that afternoon, and to get herself ready to go. In her wisdom, Chrissy left as many fingerprints discreetly placed around the bathroom as she could. Just in case they might ever be needed.

Monica and Stuart were both aware of what lie ahead, and were saddened to be separated for what looked like at least a month. They spent a passionate hour together in their master bedroom suite before Stuart had to leave with Chet. He was very glad Monica had free reign to depart as soon as Chrissy was processed. That was a huge load off his mind. Monica was equally relived, but was bummed at their upcoming separation. The thought that she wouldn't see her guy again in a long time, was compounded by the fact they had only an hour left to say a proper goodbye. It just didn't seem right. She felt like he was going off to fight in some distant war, and she could do little if anything about it.

"Don't fret, baby. I will see you in Manilla in no time. We are sailing out tonight, and you've got your burner. I'll call you as soon as I can get reception somewhere. We will be in the Philippines, and we will be living like rock stars before you know it."

"You be careful. I still don't trust that shmuck Vincent 100%. This whole thing with me might be some kind of a set up. Just get the damn money, and get out of there. And please, please for me, watch out."

"I think we are solid. Vincent assures me the Jensen's don't want any trouble; they just want golfer girl back. So, there shouldn't be much in the way of cop hassles. Vincent seems to be playing it straight with us, and don't forget that we still have the goods on him. We will be hooked up again in no time, babe. And don't worry about me at all." They showered, lingered as long as possible, and finally got dressed.

"I love you," Stuart murmured.

"Too much I love you," Monica replied, and they kissed goodbye. A long and somewhat melancholy, but loving kiss. Then Chet arrived, and it was time to go.

Stuart and Chet motored across the Sound to Salmon Beach in one of Chet's old skiffs. The ten-horse outboard motor was barely sufficient to get them across the waterway, but as they were leaving the boat and motor behind, it would have to do. They pulled into the funky, eclectic, little waterfront enclave of Salmon Beach, and tied up at a friend of Chet's dock. It was five o'clock when they arrived, and they began to pull their wet suits on over their dry gear.

To the naked eye, they appeared to be two amateur divers out for a late afternoon dip. Once they were suited up, the plan was to make the call to Will, then submerge. Their personal gear was all set, plus the mechanical stuff: sea scooters, air tanks and air suppression apparatus, the harnesses for hauling the two sacks of money, etc. were loaded and ready to go. Everything was also prepped and set to cast off back at the Narrows Marina slip. All they had to do was stow the cash, slip out of their diving gear, and sail off into the balmy evening.

At exactly six o'clock, Stuart called Will, and gave him his instructions. "Pull up the two crab pots you will find exactly east of you. They are sixty yards off of the Point Defiance shoreline. You need to navigate towards the logged-out area on the hillside. It's above the shoreline you'll see directly ahead of you. The crab buoys are white, and are plainly lettered in black marker pen with the name Will J on them. When you pull the pots, there are ropes attached to the top of the traps. Tie the trash bags securely to the ropes, then drop them back in the water and let them sink. You are free to go as soon as you make the drop. We will pull the sacks back up after it gets dark. If we see or detect any presence of any kind attempting to apprehend or surveil us, you will dearly regret it, and we will have the drop sight under observation from several vantage points.   But, if you follow your instructions to the letter, your sister will be released this evening."

"Do you have any questions?"

"Where can we pick her up?"

"She will be safe, and you will find her. Anything else?"

"No."

"Then go do it."

Stuart hung up, and he and Chet dropped into the chilly water, engaged their sea scoters, and headed to the north for the drop spot.

Will hit the electronic starter button, and the Mercury inboard engine roared to life. The two brothers bumped fists, and set off to the west for Point Defiance. It took them fifteen minutes to cross the channel, and locate the crab pots. In another ten minutes the pots were on board, and the money sacks had been tied securely, very securely, to the five-foot lines. Back over the side of the sleek speedboat the crab pots went, and the weight of the trash bags did its' work. Gravity escorted the $10,000,000. cache to the bottom of the channel, where it nestled comfortably onto the sandy bottom. A couple of Dungeness crabs skittered over and sniffed around in their top heavy, confrontational way of strutting about, but all else was quiet in the early evening depths.

"Good to go?" Will said to Charlie.

"I think so."

Will had left the boat idling while they completed their delivery tasks, so he checked one more time to make sure the crab pots were bobbing correctly, that is, none of the lines were fouled, and they were maintaining their original locations. Then, he shifted into gear, and accelerated the speed boat back towards Gig Harbor.

"We got'er done, bro," he told Charlie.

"Yeah, we're about halfway home," Charlie replied.

Once underwater and offshore about fifty meters, Stuart dumped the burner phone and distortion device and began to glide through the translucent native waters, cruising smoothly behind his diving partner. The guys stayed about forty meters down and let their head lamps lead the way. Chet was able to locate Will J's construction sacks full of hundred-dollar bills in about fifteen minutes. Then it was just a matter of getting settled on the bottom, snipping the tie lines, loading the large, awkwardly heavy sacks into the strap on shoulder harnesses he had designed for them, and setting off back down the eastern side of the Narrows passage. The incoming flow of the tide was increasing, and the channel was much more navigable closer to the shore. With their head lamps turned on, the guys stayed near the bottom, and allowed themselves to be pulled along by the tide and the propulsion scooters.

This area is one of the premier diving spots in the Puget Sound region. It is enhanced by the immense submerged foundational stanchions of both Narrows bridges and the quantity as well as quality of the sea life for which they provide habitat. The variety of the aquatic culture is staggering and spectacular, from microscopic organisms to sea shrimp, mollusks, starfish, manta rays, anemones, crayfish, sea urchins, blowfish, aquarium like tropical fish of all makes and models, trigger fish, angel fish, squid, sea otters, dolphins, predators and prey. There is an underwater utopia down there that would inspire Walt Disney. Seals blast through these waters like missiles looking for nourishment. Not only is there organic life, there is vegetation, and enough color to invent a new rainbow.

The submerged flora present ranges from phytoplankton and underwater sedge, to long willowy sea grass that wafts irresolutely in the currents like a troupe of graceful ballerinas. There is enough variety around to make a Japanese master chef's mouth water shamelessly.

As if that is not enough, there are also the ruins of the old Galloping Gertie bridge, and somewhere in all of this wealth of timeless, ageless, Darwinian plethora of activity, is rumored to be a giant octopus of Loch Ness dimensions. They call her the *Ghost of Galloping Gertie* after the failed old bridge, and if people haven't seen her in her entirety, sightings have been routinely documented of her giant tentacles slicing up through the often-turbulent waters.

But this was not a recreational dive the boys were on, so they were unable to stop and enjoy the fantastic sights, and as they glided down the channel. Chet led them expertly under the bridges and on south toward their covert moorage. The head lamps were invaluable. The underwater lighting allowing Stuart to keep pace in the more experienced Chet's wake, and the sea scooters were riding the incoming tide like aforesaid seals rambling through the surging currents.

Once though the Narrows, which is obviously the constricted point in the channel, or they wouldn't have built the damn bridge there, the guys were basically underwater surfing down to the marina. If not on powerful waves, certainly on their equal, current wise, and as their underwater adventure began coming to its' climax, Stuart's thoughts turned to who and what awaited them in the Marina at their sailboat. It was not often someone pulled into the waterfront with ten million dollars in unmarked, large bills on their backs. And in the spirit of such audacity, and in the adamant words of his lover and protector, he could hear Monica's reproving voice in his head: "You watch your ass, baby!"

Back at the Gig Harbor rental, Monica was getting antsy to go. Her mind was churning, and she wanted to start moving. She went into the garage and opened the trunk of the rental sedan. Next, she went back and unlocked the door to the cellar, and commanded Chrissy to go get on the bed. With her 9mm Glock 17 handgun at the ready, she peered down into the basement to make sure of Chrissy's whereabouts, and descended the stairs.

"Lie on your stomach, and put your hands behind your back."

Chrissy complied, and Monica went over to the bed, and put her left knee on the middle of Chrissy's thighs. She put the pistol to the back of Chrissy's head to show her who was the boss, before setting it down on the bed, and securing the zip ties around Chrissy's wrists.

"Get up, and come with me," she commanded Chrissy when she was done with her task.

Chrissy rolled over and got up as gracefully as she could off the low bed. It was not an easy task to comply with, while she was restrained. Monica tied a blindfold over Chrissy's eyes and led her toward the stairs with a hand on the nape of her neck, and they ascended into the upper level of the house. Monica walked them through the outer rooms and into the three-car garage. The trunk of the beige sedan was sitting open, and Monica helped Chrissy to sit down of the left edge of the vehicle's rear frame, then pushed her down into the trunk space. Chrissy landed with a thud that hurt her left shoulder, and felt Monica folding her legs in behind her. Monica was wearing her usual niqab, but her shirt sleeves had seemed a bit shorter to Chrissy before her blind fold went on, and she could see the base of what looked like some extensive tats starting to run up her arms. She filed that information in her mental computer

"You listen to me good," Monica, who was still peeved at Chrissy for her aborted escape attempt, told her curtly. "Your brother is dropping off the money in a little while. When the money is safe with us, someone will eventually find you. While you are here in this trunk, you keep your mouth shut. They will be either in the car or close by it, and if you make a racket, they will hear you, and come hurt you. They will break your arms, or kill you if they have to. So, you just be a good girl, and lie still until someone knocks on the trunk. I am going to cut the zip ties off of your wrists now, and there are a couple of Cliff bars and a bottle of water by your head. You keep quiet and be patient, and you will be okay."

The trunk lid slammed down, and Chrissy could hear the car start up, heard the garage door open, felt it back out, drive a short distance, and stop. She vaguely heard the garage door close a minute later, then things went quiet. Chrissy was glad she wasn't claustrophobic and tried to get as comfortable as possible. The sedan was not some roomy old Cadillac with enough trunk space for a couple of bodies, so she was very restricted in how she could move. But she was out of the damn basement and was very glad about that. She took the blindfold off and opened it so she could lay her head on something relatively clean. The thought occurred to her to conserve her oxygen intake as best she could, so she began to slow her metabolism down.

Monica returned to the house through the garage, went downstairs and wiped Chrissy's room clean, then went up to the master bedroom. Removing her face gear, she shoved it in the side pocket of her bag, and was now packed and ready to go. Walking back through the house, she did a last-minute inspection, put the garage door opener on the kitchen counter by the house keys, took the remaining bag of trash and Chrissy's personal items, and exited the house through the back door of the garage. Stuart had wheeled the Triumph 500 onto the brick, side walkway for her, so she strapped her travel bag, and the sack of trash on the rear seat, straddled the bike, put on her helmet, adjusted her sunglasses, kick started the motorcycle, let the engine idle for a minute, then took off around the big house, and down the driveway. She hit the street, and was never so glad to get away from somewhere in her life. Including all of the military dumps she had ever lived in. Oops, she thought, I forgot Margie's blackberry jam. Oh well.

The weather was still perfect for a motorcycle ride, and she wasted no time in getting to Highway 16 and heading for SeaTac airport. Except, there was going to be a little change of plans. She had made an executive decision.

Monica arrived in short term parking, dumped her bag of trash and Chrissy's personal stuff in a convenient waste can, and headed for the terminals. Once at the Philippine Airlines counter, she inquired if her flight was full, and was there a wait list? When told there actually was, she offered her seat up, and requested and received a full refund in cash. It didn't hurt that she was an attractive Philippina, as was the counter attendant and fellow country woman, who was only too happy to help her out.

Monica retrieved the bag she had stashed in the airport locker, and headed back to the parking garage. She loaded up the Triumph, and called a friend to ask for a favor. "I need a ride to Tacoma, and you won't regret it."

"Meet me at my house. Where we headed?"

"I'm going to the Boathouse 19 Restaurant in the Tacoma Narrows Marina. Let's take your car, and I am going to leave my motorcycle here for you."

"What?"

"I'm going on a sailing trip, and you can keep the bike as long as I'm gone."

"Really?"

"Really. It's all yours. The paperwork and registration are in the compartment under the seat."

"How long you going to be gone?"

"I don't know."

"Cool, Monica."

"No problem, let's get going."

They were at the Marina in half an hour. Monica thanked her friend and fellow bartender, kissed him on the cheek, and took off with her satchel bags for the inside of the busy restaurant. She proceeded out the side door to the expansive deck as her friend drove away, and headed for the little marina grocery and supplies store. After buying a couple large grocery bags of staples, she told the clerk she would be right back for her purchases. It would take her two trips to load up, and the clerk offered to send the delivery boy along to help her. Not necessary she was told, and Monica started down the steel ramp to the boat mooring floats.

Tommy was already waiting in the covered slip when she rolled in, and gave her the once over. He recognized her immediately, or she would have been floating face down, and coldly nodded at her. He sat back down on his overturned plastic bucket, and stared out at the bobbing boats around them. "I've got a few more things to get," Monica told him, and went back up to the store for her supply bags. When she returned, Monica climbed up into the stern deck of the boat, and looked around. She set her bags down and began to familiarize herself. She was going sailing with her man.

Betty was all over her job. It is a solid given that very few people in their mid-thirties with a daytime bartender job, would mess up a $25,000. cash delivery job that would take three or four hours out of their mundane lives.

She got to Gig Harbor as instructed, picked up the beige sedan as directed, and dropped it in front of the Seven Seas Brewery as instructed and without incident. If nothing else, she was very programable, and being a native of Purdy, Washington, which is just up the highway from Gig Harbor, and is the home of the infamous Washington Women's Correctional Facility, she was close to home. WWCF is a fancy name for the Women's State penitentiary. Betty knew the area well. She decided to go back to the Harbor, and stop by the Tides Tavern for a stiff drink and a bite to eat.

It was amazing she didn't end up sitting with Penny and Alton who walked into the Tides right behind her, but the odds of that would have been a bit like President Trump joining Bill and Hilary for a casual luncheon. Instead, she went directly over to the sit-down bar and ordered a pint of Stella with a shot of Don Julio Blanco tequila.

Penny and Alton managed to snag a table on the busy, outside deck of the old tavern, overlooking the tidy little northern harbor. Their table was basking in the early evening sunshine, and the recreational marine activity was bustling about right in front of them.

"I'm glad we came here," Penny said. "I was afraid it was a little too far away, but this place is really cool."

"It sure is, m'love."

Ironically, Will and Charlie were sitting in a boat in the mouth of Gig Harbor, not a thousand or so yards from The Tides. Or if Penny and Alton knew what they were looking at, they might have let their eyes wander across to the east side of the harbor, and catch a partial view of the home of Chrissy's temporary residence for the last week. Maybe Betty could have joined them, and let Alton know exactly where the beige sedan was parked. Better yet, instead of passing them on her way out of town, Monica could have turned her Triumph around, joined the table, and regaled all of them on the story of Chrissy's near escape four days ago. But as it often is in a small town, life can be precariously juxtaposed in close proximity to both the deliberate and the coincidental.

CHAPTER THIRTY-SIX

While the views of the inner harbor are extraordinary, the atmosphere at the Tides is funky/woodsy/ casual, and the cuisine, as one might expect, is definitely of the pub food variety. Penny ordered a seafood salad, and Alton opted for a couple of oyster shooters, followed by a Reuben sandwich. All of which were, edible, affordable, and served in plentiful portions.

"Let's stay 'ere all night and get a bit pissed, m'love." Alton was suggesting to Penny that they stay at the Tides and continue drinking.

"That would be fun, Altie, but we've got to be getting along." Penny motioned to their young waitress for the check. As a tenured Department Head with the LPGA, Penny made considerably more money than a first-year staff member of Alton's status. Her expense account was also much larger than his, so she was usually the person calling for checks when they went out and about.

As Penny settled up the tab, they both looked around and admired the scenery one last time. Much like anyone does who is in a newly discovered hot spot, and won't be returning any time soon.

A & P had had casual chitchat throughout dinner. Penny wondered what Alton thought about Will and Tina hooking up. "Isn't it exciting? Maybe something good can come out of this fiasco."

Alton thought they were tickety boo (okay). But since he wasn't a woman, he couldn't get as excited about it as Penny.

"I hope Steve Reed can stay around for a couple of days after Chrissy gets back," Penny said hopefully.

Again, Alton seemed disinterested on the subject.

Men, thought Penny. They have no emotions; they are either numb or dumb. She was ready to head back to Tacoma.

Alton's mind was whirling with his impending task.

"By Crickey, I wish we could stay a bit longer."

"We should really be getting back, Alton."

"Say, a bloke told me about a rippin' brewery right around the corner from here, luv. Let's stop for one more quick one on the way out of town. It is right around the corner, we could walk over, and come back for the caa."

"I really thing we should go, Alton."

"Oh, come on pet, just a little quickie."

Penny checked her phone, and didn't see any messages from Will or Tina. "All right. One quick one, then we go. But I'm driving back."

Alton and Penny proceeded left out of the Tides Tavern parking lot, and they jogged to the right as they walked uphill to the Seven Seas. They came adjacent to the entrance to the parking lot, and strolled hand in hand toward the hip new brewery. Alton's heart was pounding, and his hands were a bit clammy.

They walked up the driving lane dodging several exiting automobiles, and as they were almost ready to weave through the first row of parked vehicles in front of the brew pub, Alton stopped, and peered at a beige, four door sedan which was parked in front of them.

"Did you hear anything?" he asked Penny.

"No."

Alton walked over to the rear of the car, and tapped a couple of times on the trunk lid. This caused the Toyota Corolla to bounce on its' rear suspension, and he leaned down and cocked his ear.

Chrissy was nearly faint from the airless, July heat of the trunk space. Her legs and back were cramped from her contorted position, the ten-ounce bottle of water was long gone. Her tongue felt like the inside of a hot pizza oven, she had to go to the bathroom, and dehydration was beginning to set in. Was she even hearing real voices, or was she hallucinating? Was her mind finally succumbing to fear and defeat? Or had her angel somehow, someway sent someone to extricate her? She knew she was at the point of no return, and if she didn't cry out for help, she would soon lapse into unconsciousness. If they were nearby, and wanted to do her harm, what the hell did it matter now?

"Help me, someone please, help me," she half croaked, half screamed out as loudly as she could.

Alton jerked up, and looked at Penny. "Did you hear that? Someone is in the trunk of this caa."

"What?" Penny said, and stepped closer to the back end of the Taurus.

"Allo, is someone in there?" Alton said, as he again rapped on the trunk.

"Yes, help me please!" Chrissy said a weak voice.

"Holy smokes, Penny, someone is there in the boot."

"Yes, I heard something."

"Let me look in at the tiller, and see if there are keys inside. You call the bobbies."

While Alton ran to the driver's door, Penny dialed 911. Alton looked in at the dashboard, and there in the ignition a set keys dangled. He grabbed them, and returned to the rear of the vehicle. By now, there were several people standing around staring.

With a shaking hand Alton stuck a key into the lock. It turned in its' barrel, and he jerked the trunk open. Penny who was standing right behind him released a blood curdling scream at the top of her lungs. The outside deck at the Seven Seas was full of people on a busy summer Friday evening. Eighty-five degrees is a pretty warm day in the Pacific Northwest, and people were cooling their jets as well as their micro beer palates after a long week, when Penny's primal scream brought them abruptly to their feet. They were craning their necks at Alton and Penny, and some of the brewery's patrons actually jumped under the beer garden's perimeter rope barrier and were approaching the beige sedan.

Alton seemed to be as dumbstruck as Penny was shocked at the actual sight of Chrissy in the flesh, but managed to regain his composure, and told Penny to calm down as he reached into the trunk to help Chrissy out of her cramped little prison and back to safety.

Chrissy recognized Alton, and a flood of relief enveloped every cell of her being. She inhaled a huge breath of fresh air, motioned to Alton for some water to drink, and began to cry. Alton was the perfect person to be at Chrissy's side. He was big enough, and his presence was commanding enough, that when he told people to step back, they moved. He asked for someone to bring a bottle of water, and reached into the trunk to extricate Chrissy. He gently hoisted her legs over the outside wall of the trunk, and had her put her arms around his neck so he could lift her the rest of the way out. She was as limp as a golf towel in his arms.

Penny was there with them hugging Chrissy, and both women were crying hysterically. Chrissy was trying to regain the feeling in her legs, so she could stand on her own, and by now there was general chaos going off around them. The pub had emptied, and people were crowding around. Some of the patrons of the bar recognized Chrissy, and more women began screaming, which took the pandemonium up to Seahawks stadium level. "It's Chrissy Jensen, it's Chrissy Jensen," people were shouting, and cell phone cameras were shooting away. Alton was basically immobile as he held Chrissy up, and he shouted to several of the men standing around to help keep the crowd back. Suddenly a couple of what looked like plain clothed cops appeared on the scene, began flashing their badges, and took control of the area.

Someone passed a bottle of water up to Alton. Penny opened it, and Chrissy took a drink. This strengthened her, helped her cool down a smidge, and she reached up and pulled Alton's head down to hers. "I really, really need to pee," she told him.

"You stay here and wait for the cops," Alton told Penny. "She has to go to the bathroom."

He lifted Chrissy up in his arms, and began to weave his way over to the crowded pub. Cell phone cameras were flashing around them. As he finally broke through the crowd and into the great room of the brewery, a young woman emerged and identified herself as the manager. How can I help you?"

"She has to go to the bathroom."

"Follow me."

"The pub's manager led them back to the restrooms, stuck her head in the women's room and announced to Alton that it was empty. They walked into the room, and Alton gingerly set Chrissy down on her feet. "Can you walk?" he asked her.

"Get me into the stall, and I will be alright."

Alton trundled her into a stall, and with the manager's help Chrissy got situated, and then went for what seemed like an hour. She limped back out into the main area of the restroom, with one arm around the helpful young manager's shoulders. Alton reached down and swooped her up into his arms again, and they headed back out for the parking lot.

"Why don't you stay here in the brewery?" the manager asked. "I will lock the doors, and she can sit down and cool off."

Chrissy shook her head no. "Thanks, but I want to go home," she said.

"I agree, and it would cause a lot of trouble for your business. But thank yew so much anyway," Alton said.

He turned and continued back to the parking lot with Chrissy in his arms, and by the time they got to the car, the local Gig Harbor police were there in force, and had continued to secure the area.

Alton looked at Penny, gave her an "everything's okay" nod, and Alton asked a policeman if he could put Chrissy in the back of one of their patrol cars. "This way, sir," the officer said, and Alton and Penny followed him back to an empty cruiser. Penny stayed in the police car with Chrissy, and told Alton she had already talked to Will. They would call again so Chrissy could talk to her mon and dad. She was still cooling down and was already on her second bottle of water. Alton went back over to the Corolla and was confronted by the Police.

"What happened?" a police officer began asking Alton a series of questions.

"How did you find her?"

"What were you doing here?"

"How long have you been here?"

"Whose car is this?"

"Can we see some identification?"

The questions were flying at him. "Gentlemen, if you don't mind, I would like to speak with Danny Chong. He is the Chief of Inspectors with the Tacoma Police Department, and is very familiar with this case. I will be happy to make a statement with him, and in the meantime, is it possible one of your officers could transport Miss Jensen back to her compound in University place? She is very fragile, and I know she would appreciate being home and away from all of this commotion."

"Well, our Chief of Police is on the way, and he will have to make that call."

Alton was getting impatient, and started back toward the patrol car to see if Penny might be able to track Danny Chong down. "Sir," one of the officers said, "I need you to remain in the immediate area."

"Oh, for Christ's sake," Alton blurted in frustration. "Listen you wanker, I'm the bloke who found her. I work for the LPGA. That's Chrissy Jensen who has been missing for the last week, in case you missed it. Now get on your damn phone and get your Chief over here, or get Inspector Chong on the tellie, so we can get something done. We've got a sick girl on our hands back there, and she needs to go home. This case is a lot bigger than you are, mate, and if I were you, I would be very careful what I was doing. Now get on it, please."

"What did you just call me?" the officer asked, and began to reach for his service revolver.

Alton's annoyance was relieved when the Gig Harbor Chief of Police arrived on the scene and asked what was going on. They were able to connect with Danny Chong, who inquired about Chrissy's wellbeing, then authorized her immediate relocation back to her residence in Tacoma.

"As a matter of fact, I believe I have a couple of personnel over there, who will be happy to transport her. In the meantime, continue to secure the scene. I am coming over the bridge right now, and will be there in five minutes."

Alton and the Gig Harbor Police Chief walked back to the patrol car, transferred Chrissy and Penny to the detective's cruiser, and they were getting ready to take off, when Danny Chong rolled up, his siren blaring loudly and his hazard lights flashing. He came over and checked in on Chrissy, who was cradling her water bottle like it was a newborn baby, had stretched the cramps out of her legs, and looked disheveled, but in somewhat satisfactory condition. Alton remembered to get their car keys from Penny before the girls took off, and went back to the Corolla and began to give his statement to Inspector Chong.

With Chrissy's departure, the crowd started to dissipate and head back into the Seven Seas, or where ever else they were going. Alton chatted with the senior officer for half an hour, and asked if they could continue their conversation the next morning. Local news people and the Tacoma regional reporters were now gathering, and Alton knew if he didn't get out of there soon, it would take him all night.

"Feel free to go Mr. Walker. But you are under direct orders not to leave greater Tacoma until we can sit down again. If you leave town, I will put out a warrant for your arrest. I would also like to speak with Ms. Brown, so please ring me in the morning at this number (he handed Alton his card). I will be expecting your call, and we can set up a meeting."

"Yes sir." Alton turned to leave, but not before glaring at the wanking policeman who had been ready to cuff him fifteen minutes ago. The cop glared back. He made a quick detour back into the brewery to thank the duty manager who had been so helpful. She was delighted at his thoughtfulness, and offered him a beer for the road.

"I would love one, dearie," he said, "but I better not."

He went out the side door of the brewery, and walked back around to the Tides, and couldn't see the harm in a little nightcap there in the bar to staunch his new six hundred thousand-dollar nerves. He walked in, bellied up, and ordered a double shot of Jose Cuervo. He took a slug of his liquor, and shook his head in near disbelief. Vincent had come through for him.

Betty had her back to the front door when he came in, as she was engaged in conversation with a gentleman she had just met, but she recognized Alton's voice when he ordered his drink, and peeked over her shoulder at the tall, redhead Aussie. He seemed preoccupied, and she was not sure he would have recognized her so out of context like this and with her hair down, but she couldn't help but think how odd it was to see him here. Maybe the little perv is following me around, she thought, and turned back to her conversation.

CHAPTER THIRTY-SEVEN

With sirens screaming, it didn't take fifteen minutes to get Chrissy back home. She thanked the officers profusely, and Will, Bob, Charlie, Bobby, Steve Reed, all of the womenfolk--the whole family-- were in the driveway to usher, carry, escort, or whatever was necessary to get her into the house. Chrissy waved to the assembled press corps while their cameras flashed, and then the family whisked her away. Bob, Ginny and the guys took care of Chrissy, while Will, Tina and Penny stayed outside to deal with the media. They felt a strong obligation to them, as all of the reporters and stations had been so helpful, and for the most part respectful of their privacy boundaries. Of course, the press was on high alert, and clamoring for information while the cameramen's shutters continued snapping.

And it certainly wouldn't hurt to have an eyewitness like Penny Brown there to answer a few questions for them. Penny needed to be careful what she said, as Danny Chong had cautioned her before they left Gig Harbor to guard her words, so she opened the dialogue with a brief statement of what had happened in the Seven Seas parking lot, answered a few questions and tried to call it a night.

"A friend and I were in Gig Harbor this evening, and he noticed some unusual circumstances surrounding a certain vehicle in the parking lot of a restaurant we were planning to attend. Upon further investigation, it appeared as if there might be some foul play involved, and we were able to gain access to the vehicle. When we opened the trunk of the car, miraculously there was a body in there, the very weakened body of a distraught young woman, who turned out to be our own Chrissy Jensen. I am so elated to have helped in some small way to bring her back home safe and sound. Thank you."

Now the questioning began in earnest. Turns out the queries in the Seven Seas Parking lot were child's play compared to what came next:

"Where exactly did you find her?"

"How long had she been there?"

"Will, has the ransom been paid?"

"How much was the ransom?"

"When will we be able to speak to Chrissy?"

"How was the ransom paid."

"Do the police know who did it yet?"

"How is Chrissy's health?"

"Was she abused or mistreated?"

"Why aren't we getting more details here?"

"What are the police doing as we speak?"

"Where was she being kept for the last week?"

"Was it in Gig Harbor?"

"How long will Chrissy stay in Tacoma?"

"How did Chrissy look when she was found?"

"Who were you dining with this evening Ms. Brown?"

"Where were you going to dinner?"

"Why Gig Harbor?"

"Has the LPGA been notified of Chrissy's recovery?

"Will you be getting the reward money?"

Finally, after answering questions for twenty-five minutes, Will held up his hands to quiet the reporters.

"Ladies and gentlemen, please be aware that we have just gotten our Chrissy back. We have as many questions as y'all do, probably more, and as Penny said, Chrissy was very weak when she was found, and therefore, we will need to let her rest and recuperate before we can offer you any personal access to her. I'm able to tell you that a substantial ransom has been paid, and that precipitated the release of our sister. The payment of the ransom was aided greatly by your coverage of this event, and the response of the general public to the Go Fund Me Campaign was overwhelming. Your compassion, generosity and financial support will never be forgotten by this family. We are so very grateful, and we ask at this time for you to allow us to go and spend a few moments with Chrissy. She will need some time to regain her strength, but she is under the care of her parents and our family physician, and as soon as we have more information for you, we will be happy to share it. I will also be delighted to meet with all of you again in a couple of hours for a final update. I can answer one final question."

"Will, how much was the ransom?" someone shouted.

"It was ten million dollars."

With that the Jensen family media management team left the makeshift dais, and were safely back in the compound which had become a fortress to them.

Inside the house, Chrissy was resting easily on the couch in the den, sipping on a bottle of Evian spring water. The Jensen's family doctor, was happy to have driven over that afternoon from Yakima, and had checked Chrissy's vitals, which he declared to be somewhat depressed, but not dangerously so. Her blood pressure was down, but he didn't consider anything to be unusual or abnormal under the circumstances. Everyone had had their hugs, and Chrissy was lounging on the couch with her feet in Steve Reed's lap, and her mom at her side.

The Doctor had prescribed plenty of rest and fluid intake, and Bob Jensen was almost ready to pop a couple of bottles of Moet White Star to hydrate the rest of the family with some French champagne. Chrissy was relating the story of her captivity to the family, and Ginny was monitoring her wellbeing with laser like concentration. But Chrissy seemed like herself, a little weak perhaps, but with no permanent damage apparent. No one was pressing her for minute details, they were all just happy to have her back home, and she could fill in the gaps tomorrow or whenever.

When Will, Tina and Penny came back inside, Chrissy sat up, and asked for quiet so she could say a few words.

"I would just like to say thank you from the very bottom of my heart, for all you have done for me during my absence. I was not mistreated for the most part while I was away, and was not physically or emotionally abused, except for being isolated and alone for the last week. Things could have been so much worse than they were, but the opportunity to be reunited with all of you again was my life preserver. You were there with me the whole time I was gone, I could literally feel you with me and I am so thankful to be back safely.

When that trunk opened, and that was by far the worst experience of the week by the way, and I looked up and saw Alton and Penny, it was nirvana for me. I am feeling a little weak, but I'm sure a few days of rest will take care of that. I would like to go up and take a shower now, and if one of my brothers would please take these clothes, once I am out of them, and burn them for me, I would greatly appreciate it." That got a laugh. "I would also like to thank you for welcoming Steve into this family while I was away. I wanted so much to be here with you all during our special week together, and win the tournament for all of us ....." As Chrissy started to cry, she picked Steve's hand up, kissed it, and leaned over into his arms.

The family gathered around and put a hand on Chrissy, as a means of sharing their deep thankfulness at her safe return. One by one they filed out of the den, and left Chrissy there in Steve's arms. When they were alone, Steve dabbed at her tears with his fingertips, and carried her up to their room.

She wasn't lying when she had said she wanted to get out of the outfit Monica had bought for her. She ripped off her tainted clothes in a flash, while Steve was drawing some hot water. She wouldn't go in the shower however, until she had stripped him down so she could lead him in with her.

"Just hold me," Chrissy whispered in Steve's ear. She put her arms around his neck, and he wrapped himself around her body, and they just slowly twirled under the bracing stream of water for what seemed like an hour.

Will received a call about nine thirty that evening from Detective Chong. "Will, the FBI and I would like to meet with Chrissy tomorrow morning as soon as it is convenient for her."

"Is that completely necessary, Detective?"

"What do you mean, Will?"

"Danny, she is home safely, she seems to be intact physically and emotionally, and our family is willing to call it good. Her return means the world to us, and to meet with you, she will have to relive the whole terrible experience all over again."

"That is true, Will, but you should know an exit interview is completely SOP in these cases. Please let me remind you, that our investigation has co-operated with your family's requests throughout this ordeal. We have backed off because of Chrissy's celebrity status, and done so to try and do our part to insure her safe return. Now, that she is home, it is vital for us to try and apprehend these criminals. Not only to bring justice to our community, but this is maybe the highest profile case we have ever dealt with here in Tacoma, and we want to close it up properly. But also, how would you feel if another young woman of Chrissy's age and/or profile was abducted, and didn't fare as well as Chrissy has? It happens all the time, Will."

"I understand your position, Inspector, but I am not sure if anything can be done anyway. From what information she has shared with us since her return, which is decidedly not too much, I am not sure how much if anything she knows about her captors."

"Will, that is for us to evaluate. What time would we be able to meet with Chrissy tomorrow? You are welcome to sit in with us."

"Detective, she has retired for the evening, and her doctor has recommended rest and a few days of convalescence. What she will be up for tomorrow, I do not at this point in time know for sure."

"Will, I will call you around ten in the morning, and I can only hope you understand the importance of our visit, and that we will have your support tomorrow."

"I don't know what tomorrow will bring, Lieutenant."

By now, Danny Chong was getting a little exasperated by Will's attitude. "Will, I am sorry to have to inform you that I can detain both you and your sister if need be, in order to attempt to have some communication and closure here. That would be extremely uncomfortable for both of us, so please reconsider your position for me overnight."

"We'll see what tomorrow brings, and don't you dare threaten myself or my family, Chief Investigator."

"I am not threatening anyone Will, I am merely trying to get a little co-operation is all."

"Good-night sir."

Will went into the kitchen, where the men had moved on to stronger drink. He was agitated, and Tina could feel his annoyance immediately. "What's wrong?" she asked.

"Goddamn cops and the FBI want to sit down and interview Chrissy tomorrow morning. As if she hasn't been through enough already."

"That is probably standard procedure, Will," Bob Jensen intoned.

"I agree," said Tina.

"Yeah, well they haven't done anything at all to help us, have they? They couldn't find out anything about her abduction. They certainly didn't find her. I think they are just trying to cover their own backsides now, and make it look as if they were players in Chrissy's rescue. I particularly asked, no demanded, they stay away from the whole operation today, so they wouldn't screw anything up. You heard me Tina."

Alton, who had returned by now from Gig Harbor, and was welcomed as a hero, had joined the group in the kitchen. Never one to turn down a proffered glass of grog, Alton sat, and let his head continue to spin. With some prodding he outlined the rescue in his own colorful style, and mentioned the fact of his near confrontation with the Gig Harbor policeman. "He was more of a hindrance than a help," Alton said.

"That's what I'm talking about," Will reiterated.

"Can we all keep calm here?" Bob asked. "Let's see how Chrissy feels in the morning. I don't see the harm in her talking to Detective Chong for an hour or so, if she's up to it."

"I'm with you, Bob," Tina replied. "Surely, they have been through this kind of thing before, and are trained on how to handle it. Especially the FBI. She just might have some information which would be of help to them, and they will surely use kid gloves and respect with her, considering what she has been through. Besides, it's her decision to make, not ours. Also, didn't they say you could be there with her, Will?" Tina could see with more unbiased eyes, just how protective of Chrissy Will was becoming.

Penny gave Alton a head jerk motion towards the door, and they began to say their goodbyes. She had to talk to Alton, and get more details of his incredible discovery. It all came down only hours ago, and she was still flabbergasted by what had happened.

"You and Penny better be here tomorrow when the cops come. I think they will want to talk to you too," Will told her.

"Thanks, buddy. Call me in the morning when you hear anything." Penny began to edge towards the door, but Charlie Jensen wasn't having any of that.

"How in the living hell did you do it? Tell us about it again," he asked Alton.

"Well, like I said earlier, Penny and I had dinner up in Gig Harbor, and....," Alton again spun the story his heroic rescue. It was his official version, and he was sticking to it.

"How did she look when you found her, Penny?" Tina asked.

"She was very weak and dehydrated. Alton lifted her out of the trunk, and she couldn't stand up by herself. He had to carry her into the pub to go to the restroom."

Penny had so much to share, she didn't know where to begin. "Once she got back from the pub, and we got put into the back one of the police cars, someone gave us a couple bottles of water, and she started to release some of her emotions. All she wanted was for me to hold her while she had a good cry. I don't think it'll dawn on her that she's home safe for a couple of days."

Ginny immediately chimed in her perspective. "Thank God you were the ones who found her. Can you imagine some strangers discovering her, or worse yet some punks or bad people or something?"

"Yep," Bob agreed. "I think it was a very good thing you were there. She knew immediately she was back in friendly hands, and I think she felt a lot safer right away. As the head of this bunch, we have never had a red headed Aussie for a family member, but I am recommending right now that we adopt Alton, and change that Walker last name to Jensen!"

"Dilly, dilly," the family crowed, and everyone cheered.

"I am just so glad we were the ones to find her, and were able to help out. She is such a strong and brave young Sheila. She is fantastic, and Penny and I are so extremely happy to have happened to be in the right place at the right time."

"Alton, we have to go, hon. I still have to call Cynthia, and update her. She has called me twice already."

Alton and Penny eased on out, and the rest of the Jensen's finished their cups, and began to dissipate. Although it was relatively early, everyone, while feeling elation at Chrissy's return, were emotionally spent after the long week of anguished separation and jangled nerves.

Penny and Alton were able to slip out the back way of the compound, ala Danny Chong, and avoid what was left of the remaining media. Immediately on their way home, Penny's cell began ringing. She picked up, and it was Marcus Rollins from KSEA TV, and now he wanted some payback for all the airtime he had donated to Chrissy's cause. Penny felt obliged to co-operate with him as best she could.

"Listen Marcus, we're in the car driving back to our hotel, so it's going to have to be brief. I was out to dinner with a friend, and we happened to be walking into a brew pub, when my friend noticed something odd," and Penny gave him the story of Chrissy's recovery. Omitting only that her friend was her lover and fellow LPGA staffer.

"Who were you with Penny, and will you be splitting the six hundred-thousand-dollar reward money with him?" Marcus asked.

Penny's was in a quandary. She was aware that her story was incredible, but she realized she might as well disclose all of the facts, because Marcus could easily retrieve Alton's name and identity from the Gig Harbor police reports. Plus, she still felt that she owed Marcus a scoop. "It was an associate of mine, named Alton Walker."

"Will you and Mr. Walker be willing to appear with me in the morning on a special report we are going to air at ten am?"

"Please let me confirm anything like that with you in the morning, Marcus. There is so much going right now, I may be flying back to LPGA headquarters tomorrow morning for all I know."

"Okay, Penny. I'll call you at eight."

"They keep asking about the reward, Alton. What are we going to do?"

"We can talk about that later, luv. The most important thing now is Chrissy is home."

"We need to talk about that when we get home, Alton."

"What's to talk about, luv? We found her, and we get the reward."

The entrance to the Tacoma Narrows Marina access passage is marked on the left by tall, skinny vertical pilings, and segues into covered boat sheds on the right, and floating docks to the left and rear. Chet easily found the entrance to the channel, and took the left-hand turn coming down from the northeast side of the waterway. He looked over and saw Stuart signaling that he was getting low on his air supply, but he motioned that they only had a little way to go, and let his sea scooter tow him the last fifty yards into their berth on the right.

Chet surfaced under the covered roof of their sheltered slip, but Stuart didn't quite make it. With Chet already in the berth, and no longer visible, Stuart accidentally goosed the throttle of his sea scooter, and instead of slowing, he was pulled another ten yards past the entry to the slip. His air supply was virtually exhausted, which required him to surface, and he navigated himself the rest of the way to their dock. What the hay. At least now he could check things out, and make sure all was well up top. Stuart reached up and turned off his lighted headgear, and cruised into the slip alongside the hull of their sailboat. In another half minute, the two divers were at the back of the enclosed berth, holding on to the edge of the floating moorage dock. It was not easy treading water and trying to struggle out of the bulky harnesses that were heavy with found money, so Tommy came over to help as did Monica. Both Chet and Stuart were shocked to see her, no one more so than Stuart. She was smiling broadly at the guys, and simply said "change of plans" to them.

They got the heavy plastic bags onto the narrow decking, and then clomped clumsily up the four-foot deck ladder in their diving fins. By the time they wriggled out of their wet suits, Tommy had one of the cash bags open, and was inspecting the cargo. It seemed to be legit. No indelible ink sprayed on his face, the electronic bug detector he was waving over both of the tote bags was quiet as a church mouse. He couldn't feel any oiliness, slickness or foreign matter of any kind on the money. Monica was watching his every move, and had her right hand inside of her untucked outer shirt, and behind her back on the grip of her Glock 9 mm revolver.

"Everything go all right down there?" Tommy asked.

"Couldn't have gone any better. They were right on time, and as long as the money is clean, we are good to go. Vincent got word that the Jensen's made sure that the cops stood down all day, so I think we are about as spotless as we can be going forward. Nice working with you."

"Whatever. You want me to scan your bags for you?"

"Sure, man. Thanks."

Tommy cut their doubled plastic bags open, unzipped the Nike bags, and scanned the contents. When the other two tote bags were exposed, they also seemed to be in order, bug free, and untampered with. Monica was still watching Tommy closely. Stuart was glad they had had Amazon handle the money, and kept it out of the cop's hands.

"I am out of here then," Tommy said as he began loading his and Vincent's five mil into the trash can he had brought along.

"Wait a minute," Stuart interrupted him. "Can you please take these trash bags with you for us?"

That annoyed Tommy who had to stop and remove one of the bags of cash and put all the empty industrial trash bags on the bottom of the can, then reload.

"There's one more thing, kid."

"Yeah, what's that?"

"You know those files you stole from Vincent's computer?"

Stuart froze and Monica tensed at Tommy's words. Her right hand returned to the Glock stuck under her belt. "Ah, that was nothing personal Tommy. Just a little insurance is all." Monica's hand stayed on her pistol, and she eased the handgun out of her waist band, then down to the side of her leg.

"You shouldn't do shit like that. And if those files ever get into the wrong hands, we will find you, where ever you are, and we will make bait out of all three of you, starting with her. You understand me? I will personally kill both of you."

"Tommy, I will destroy the files. As a matter of fact, I've got them here onboard. Let me get'em for you." Stuart went below, retrieved the zip files from his computer carry bag, returned upside and handed them to Tommy.

Tommy put the two files in his pocket, and said, "You mark my words, boy. This better be all of it, or you are dead." With that Tommy tightened his old grey hoodie up around his face, spun the trash can onto the hand truck, turned right, and strode out of their berth. He began zigzagging his way through the crowded maze of mooring slips for the steel ramp which led out of the marina and up into the parking lot. It was a good five hundred yards away, and he tried to be as inconspicuous as he could.

Tommy made it back to his Lincoln Navigator, threw the whole trash can, then the hand cart into the back of the SUV, and drove smoothly out of the crowded parking lot.

Stuart, Monica and Chet stood stunned for a minute, digesting Tommy's departing salvo. Then they slowly started stowing their diving gear in a couple of the storage hatches on the stern deck, and prepared to cast off. They could dry out the wet suits later.

Chet went into the galley, and pulled out the large, rectangular, starboard drawer that would later on hold all of their cooking equipment. Behind the cupboard was a secret compartment running along the side of the hull. It was dead space on the boat, as the curve of the line of the sailboat arced out away from the straight lines of the interior galley cabinetry and was the perfect size for their needs. Chet had fitted the compact space as a clever stash site for their goods.

"What the hell are you doing here?" Stuart asked Monica.

"Ah, I didn't want you guys to have all of the fun. Besides, I brought extra groceries, and I pull a mean watch shift."

Plus, she likes to cook, and she carries a Glock, crossed Stuart's mind. "Welcome aboard, baby," he said, and Monica jumped into his arms.

"We are good to get out of here," Chet announced.

Stuart went back to the helm. "You okay with her coming along?" he asked Chet.

"Happy to have her, as long as she pulls her weight. Probably make it easier on all of us."

With that settled, Stuart jumped over the rail guides and began releasing the tie lines. Chet fired up the diesel engine, Stuart hopped back onboard, and Chet eased out of the slip. Spirits were sky high, and the three amigos couldn't have been more excited about their very well-financed, real life adventure

They exited the marina, and Chet laid the sleek sail boat on a northern course for the Strait of Juan de Fuca, where they would ultimately exit Puget Sound and head straight for the Hawaiian Islands. Starting the voyage, Chet navigated towards the west side of Vashon Island and the Colvos Passage, and they were off. The setting sun still lingered in the northwestern sky, and the happy sailors basked in its warmth.

Monica produced a bottle of bubbles from Domaine Chandon, and popped the cork. They all just stood around the helm and drank a salute to each other right out of the bottle.

"Here's to freedom," Stuart toasted.

This was going to be the trip of a lifetime!

CHAPTER THIRTY-EIGHT

The next call Penny picked up was from her boss. Cynthia said hello, and then commented on Chrissy's safe return. "It's simply freaking amazing that is was our own Alton who actually found Chrissy Jensen. And you were with him. I mean, how is that even possible? What're the odds?" Cynthia said.

"I don't know myself, but I was there, and saw it all. Everyone is so glad we found her. She felt so much safer with us than some strangers. As a matter of fact, it was a good thing we came along when we did, she was in a pretty bad way when Alton opened the trunk of that car. Another hour in there, and she could easily have died."

"I guess he's in for some pretty big reward money, eh?" Cynthia could just see the look on Mac Tenderson's face when he had to sign off on a $100,000. check made out from the LPGA accounts to Alton Walker.

"Wow Cynthia, that is another whole matter to deal with."

"You've got that right, Penny. We need to handle this very carefully. It is going to cause a media splash, believe me."

Penny was so overwhelmed by all that had happened in the last three hours, she had just barely begun to consider the long-term consequences of the situation. "Where shall I go with this?" she asked.

"Well, hon, why don't you just hang tight until I talk to Mac and our attorneys."

"This is getting crazy, Cynthia."

"I know, Penny. The chances of you and Alton finding Chrissy Jensen were probably over a million to one."

Penny head was spinning, and she said, "Talk to our people, and let me know what to do. I have already spoken with a couple of the local news directors, but I won't answer my phone anymore."

"Good call. We just need to be ready is all, I think a tsunami is coming our way. I've got the meeting scheduled with them in twenty minutes, so don't talk to anyone, until you hear from me again. I'll be able to give you their recommendations in an hour or so, and then I will wait to chat with the national media people first thing in the morning."

"Okay," Penny said. "Alton and I are headed back to our hotel right now. I just need to lay low and wrap my head around everything. Trust me, I am still in shock over what has happened."

After their enchanted shower Steve and Chrissy, dried off and went to bed, again in each other's arms. They had to be close, because they didn't have anything else on to keep them warm.

"You don't have to go into detail, but are you okay? We were all so worried about you. Your poor mother was tormented the whole time you were gone."

"I'm okay. I was alone in this f'ing basement the whole time, with no natural light or fresh air, no TV, no nothing. They gave me a radio for a while, and I got some updates on what was going on in the world, but I tried to escape, and they took that away."

"You tried to escape? Are you crazy?"

"Heck no I'm not crazy. I almost made it. Get this, I knocked out one of the bad guys, the worst one really, with a vibrator I had clenched in my fist, and I was out the front door of the big house, when two other guys, I think they were the two guys who originally snatched me, just happened to be coming onto the front porch. I could hardly see, because the sun was shining right in my eyes, and I hadn't been out in any natural light for four days. So, they were able to grab me, and brought me back in the house. I got one of them pretty good though. He wasn't looking when I came running out of the house. My head was down, and I was going for it, when I ran into him and head butted him good."

"Where in the world did you get a vibrator, babe?"

"Talked my caretake into getting it for me. I knew I needed a weapon of some kind and didn't think they would give me the brass knuckles I wanted. So I thought of this, and it worked pretty good."

"You're nutzo, babe."

"I was just trying to get back to you, you goose."

They had pillow talk for another hour, and finally Chrissy rolled Steve over on his side, slid over as close to him as she could get, then pulled him back on top of her. They began to sway in each other's arms.

"Stay right there," she whispered in his ear. "Take your time. Take all night if you want to." She wrapped her legs around him, and looped her arms around his neck. There was no doubt in Chrissy's mind that she had been in some miserable purgatory for the last week, and now she had a lot of catching up to do. Starting with Steve Reed.

Danny Chong called at ten the next morning, and Will apologized for being obtuse the night before. "Danny, we're just so happy to have her back, that now we're being a little over protective. I guess I over reacted."

"No problem, Will. And thank you very much for your apology. We only need to speak with her for an hour or so max. We will be as sensitive as is humanly possible. Like I said, you are welcome to sit in with us if you like."

"That might not be a bad idea." And I didn't really apologize ole buddy.

"When can we meet, Will?"

"She's not up yet Danny, after she comes down, I can talk to her, and see how she feels. I'll call you then."

"Will, I am going to head over now with Special Agent McDonough of the FBI Hostage Recovery Team. We will wait outside in my car until you give us the go ahead."

Chrissy and Steve stirred around ten thirty, but Chrissy wasn't about to get out of bed before noon. Why should she? She had everything she wanted right there. They talked some more, got it on again, and finally Chrissy rolled out of bed and took another extended shower. Subconsciously or not, she was cleansing the frustrations and bad memories of the last week away in the steamy water. She modeled the new lingerie she had bought at Nordstrom's for Steve, it seemed like ages to her since she and Ginny had been shopping together, and then the happy couple walked downstairs together holding hands. They were starving.

Ginny was waiting for them, and had cooked up some corned beef hash, ranch style potatoes, fried eggs, bacon, fresh fruit, biscuits and country gravy. A bona fide farmhouse breakfast. Both of them grabbed a mug of coffee, when Will came in, and he asked her about meeting with the Police and the FBI.

"Sure, I can meet with them. I hope it won't go on all afternoon. I want to get outside; I have been cooped up in a basement and then a stupid car trunk for the last week."

"He said it would only take about an hour."

"That's fine. Let us eat our breakfast first."

Will called Danny Chong's cell and they arranged to meet at one thirty. Danny readily agreed to sit out on the back deck so Chrissy could enjoy the nice weather.

Chrissy and Steve inhaled Ginny's cooking. For her part, this could have been the happiest meal Ginny had ever prepared, or Chrissy had ever eaten for that matter.

At one thirty they met with the two law enforcement officers, and Will and Steve sat by her side. Will introduced everyone, and Danny Chong opened the meeting.

"Chrissy, thank you so much for sitting down with us. We will keep this as focused and concise as we can, but we would like you to relate your experience to us to the best of your ability, and in your own words."

"Well, I had stayed late at the course last Friday afternoon to work on a few things, which I often do, and which seems like so long ago to me. We had a houseful of guests for a dinner party, close friends and family who were coming to our compound that night, and I finally decided it was time to head home and socialize a little bit."

"Around what time was that Chrissy? Do you recall?"

"It was about six thirty. No, more like seven. I was toting my golf bag, and had just gotten to our Jeep Cherokee in the players parking lot. I opened the back hatch, and put the clubs in the car, and was reaching for my phone, when a car pulled up behind me and stopped. The next thing I knew, a man was pointing a gun at me, and telling me to get in his car. I froze for a minute, it just all seemed very surreal. I argued with the gunman, told him several times that they had the wrong person, and the next thing I knew, the driver of the car was standing behind me. He grabbed my ponytail, jerked my head back, put a knife to my throat and told me in no uncertain terms to get into their car."

"Can you remember his exact words?"

"Of course, how could I ever forget? He told me to get my fucking ass in the car, or he would cut my throat." Steve reached over and took Chrissy's hand, and gave it a squeeze.

"Do you remember what kind of car it was?"

"Yeah. It was black. I think it was a Lincoln Town car."

"What happened then?"

Chrissy teared up a bit, but continued on. "The first man pushed me down onto the floor of the car, and put a blanket over me. I couldn't see anything, but I could feel his gun jammed into the back of my head. Then they closed the back lid on our car down, and we took off. They told me to be quiet, and I wouldn't get hurt, and we drove for about twenty minutes or half an hour. I think actually, they must have driven to Gig Harbor, because that is where Penny and Alton found me, and when I left the house where they kept me yesterday, I wasn't driven very far."

"Did you get a decent look at either of the two men who abducted you?"

"Not at first, I think they were in some kind disguise. The guy in the back with me was about five foot nine or ten, and had a strong Italian accent. The other guy was pretty quiet, and I got the feeling you didn't want to mess around or do anything to get him upset. So, they took me to a house, and put the blanket over my head then they took me inside, and down into this basement. They told me they wouldn't hurt me if I didn't cause any trouble. There was a woman they called Florence who was supposed to take care of me. She had clothes for me to wear, and there was a small bathroom with a shower and toilet to bathe and change in. Florence would bring food down for me around ten in the morning and five in the evening. Otherwise, I had a small bed to sleep on, and there was not much else of anything in the room, except a bean bag a few magazines."

"Did you get a look at this woman?"

"She wore a niqab the whole time they kept me down there. She did have brown eyes, only she didn't seem to be middle eastern. I never did see her face, but the last day when she took me out, her sleeves were shorter, and I saw some tattoos on her arms. I saw what looked like a name tatted on her right wrist. I think it said Molly, or something like that."

Chrissy told them about her attempted escape, and the fact she was then able to get a look at the little guy.

"Would you be willing to sit down with a sketch artist and see if we could get a decent composite drawing of him?" the FBI agent asked.

"Sure. He was wearing aviators, but I did get a fleeting glimpse of his face. He kind of looked like Eugene Levy, that famous actor, comedian guy."

Chrissy told them about bashing and kicking the hulky guy, and then not seeing him again. Of the other two people who seemed to be in the house all of the time, and it appeared to Chrissy how they were a couple. The officers, particularly the FBI agent, thought her weapon of choice was hysterical and very creative. "You are some kind of a standup gal," he told her. "What you did was way over the top."

"All I had to do down there was work out and do yoga, so I was feeling pretty strong when I made my break. I think the big guy might have gotten a concussion, because I whacked him good, then I saw him fall down the steps face first as I was starting to run away."

"Did you hear him speaking in a foreign language of any kind?"

"What little he did say, was with a very heavy accent. He sounded Russian or Eastern European. He was a mean man, a really ugly mobster type guy, and he got very angry with Florence for talking to me one time. He said the head guy, they called him Jack, told Florence she couldn't yak with me at all. But Jack had said if I didn't cause any trouble, I could have anything I wanted within reason. I just asked her to talk to me, and this guy pitched a fit. So, even Florence got mad at him, and fixed me a salmon dinner, and brought me my vibrator."

"Anything else you can think of Chrissy?"

"Not really. I tried to be as mindful of details as I could, but they kept me pretty isolated. I could probably recognize the house again if there were pictures. I got a pretty good look at the great room during the time of my attempted escape. Also, I left lots of fingerprints around in the bathroom for you."

"Thank you so much. You have been very helpful. We don't want to bother you any more now, but would it be possible to have you spend an hour with our sketch artist later on this afternoon?"

"Just a word, gentlemen, to let you know that Chrissy will be very busy in the near future. Good Morning America has already called, and wants to send a crew out. Jimmy Fallon and Ellen DeGeneres are in touch," Will reported.

"Oh, they can wait, Will. Sure, I can meet for an hour later on. But right here, I am not leaving this deck today. I will be spending some time with Steve and the family for a few days, before we start with any interviews. I feel so lucky to be home and have Steve with me. He is already supposed be at camp." Chrissy looked over at the FBI agent, "he plays in the NFL for the Chicago Bears you know." Officer McDonough could hear the pride in her voice and see the love in her eyes.

"Let us get out of your hair, Chrissy. You have been so helpful. What time would be convenient for you to meet the artist?"

"About four?"

"Four it is, and we are so happy to have you back safely with us."

"Thank you," Chrissy said.

"Well, I'm glad that is over with. I don't know what those guys are going be able to accomplish, if anything."

"Oh Will, don't be that way. You don't know what might come of our getting together. Especially if we can get a good drawing of this guy down. And I will tell you for a fact, bro, that I will do anything possible to see these jerks behind bars."

"Well, I'm just saying that I doubt if much of anything can come of this, because the cops have done next to nothing the whole time you were gone. And if this was pulled off by organized crime, that guy is now long gone. I am just worried that rehashing all of this over and over is going to upset you."

"Not at all, Willy boy. If anything, it reinforces to me that I am home. C'mon Steve, let's go take a dip." Chrissy was mildly irritated with her brother. She wondered why he was concerned with her talking to the police, but it would be okay to blab with the media and the TV people all day? She hoped he was not getting to be all about the money.

"Okay, okay. Tina, and I are meeting with the press this afternoon. Everyone is clamoring to hear the details, details. Whenever you are ready to go, there is no shortage of people I can sign up."

"Jeez, William, I haven't even been home for a day yet. Can you please chill out?"

Vincent used his last burner phone late Friday evening to phone Tommy.

"How's tricks, partner?"

"Good, good. How's Vegas?"

"It's great. Nice and hot down here. How did everything go?""

"Couldn't have gone better. The Mariner's game was a win, win tonight. We kicked ass, and took names. There was absolutely no problem dealing with these chumps, and by the way, your package came in right on time tonight. Plus, I retrieved some old files of yours. Files from your computer that you had misplaced."

"Wow, that is fantastic. The package wasn't damaged in shipment or anything was it?"

"Hell no. It came in just like you ordered it. Tidy as could be."

"And no Postal Inspectors nosing around?"

"Are you kiddin' me? Like I told ya, that package is safe as a Brink's truck."

"Well, we'll be back Sunday afternoon, and I'll come right over and pick up everything as soon as I drop Angela off."

"Oh, that could be a problem. I'm leaving for Thailand tomorrow morning."

"Whaaaat?"

"Just kiddin' around, pal. See you Sunday."

"Who you talking to at this hour, Vincent? It's very late."

"Oh, that was old Tommy boy. We been workin' on dis nice little project, and everything come together good just dis evening."

"That's nice, Vinnie. What kind of a project?"

"Oh, just a little piece of business. But you know how them environmentalists want everything to be all green and everything now?"

"Yeah."

"Well, we is gonna be all green from now on too, baby. But a different kinda green. The kinda green we can fold over and put in our pockets, or sent over there to a bank in Switzerland."

"Wow, that sounds very nice, Vinnie." Angela's wifely antennae began to activate in anticipation of this new, greener day. "Come to bed, baby, come over here to momma."

CHAPTER THIRTY-NINE

Tacoma Chief of Police Lawrence Mills was seated in his office on Sunday morning, waiting for Inspector Chong and their eight o'clock meeting. The duty Sargent brought him a cup of coffee.

Danny Chong brought his own coffee mug along and sat down across the large walnut desk from Chief Mills. He was on time to the minute.

"How is your investigation going, Danny?"

"Very well sir."

"Tell me about it."

"Well, things are falling into place very nicely. We backed off quite a bit in this high-profile case, as discussed. But while Chrissy was confined, the FBI's behind the scenes assistance was invaluable. We were able to break down the second call from the kidnappers to Will Jensen very effectively. With the help of the Air Traffic Control people at SeaTac, and some sophisticated aeronautical equipment over at Boeing Tech Support, we pinpointed the exact position of the callers."

"How did you do that?"

"During the second cellular conversation, an airplane flew overhead right in the middle of the call. We almost couldn't hear what the perp was saying because of it. Due to the time of day, the ATC people identified the airplane, found out the flight number, its' origin and ETA. Using their cutting-edge Echo Technology, the Boeing people marked the exact time and location from where the call was made in relation to the sound waves they analyzed radiating from the incoming commercial jet. The perps were phoning from, of all places, the parking lot of the Lenny's Restaurant on International Boulevard."

"That is outstanding work, Detective."

"Wait Chief, it gets even better. The restaurant has surveillance cameras mounted outside their building. They had footage up to ten days back, and we got a make on two vehicles."

"When did this happen?"

"The report came back Friday morning."

"Was this the same vehicle Chrissy was found in there in Gig Harbor?"

"Yes sir. Chrissy Jensen had been transported in the trunk of one of those cars."

"And I'm sure you have tracked the vehicle."

"Right on, Chief. It's a rental and the information on the contract is all bogus. It was a long-term lease in the name of some guy from Iowa. But he doesn't check out at all. Then the lab went over the vehicle with a fine-toothed comb after Chrissy's recovery. It was cleaned of prints very thoroughly, and it seems like there is definitely a level of professionalism with these guys."

"Go on."

"After continuing to evaluate the tapes of the ransom calls, we noticed a pretty significant change in the negotiating pattern. Suddenly by the second incoming, the kidnappers seemed to know the money was in. Not just from TV reports, but a more in depth, classified kind of knowledge. They changed their dialogue from haranguing us about money and threatening Ms. Jensen's life. Suddenly it was all about packaging and processing the ten mil. Also, there was a critical blunder at the end of the call."

"Yes?"

"We had Will Jensen be a bit more strident with them. He wasn't happy about it, but we wanted him to be more confrontational. He did a great job demanding to talk to Chrissy again, stressing about getting the money, that type of stuff, and then he insisted on more time to complete processing his tasks. He said, and I quote, "we need more time to get things together." And the perp responded, "not from what I hear." That combination of factors led our Hostage Release Team personnel to believe the kidnappers might be getting inside information somehow. We analyzed who was in the Jensen Compound, and who had access to that privileged circle, and the data that could possibly be leaking from their group. We all concurred it might be the tall, red headed gentleman from Australia. He's the guy who ultimately found Chrissy Jensen."

"Keep going. I like it."

"He goes by the name of Alton Walker, and works for the LPGA. He is sleeping with Penny Brown, who is the Marketing and Information Director for the LPGA. He seems to have a bit of an alcohol problem, from what we can gather. We have been surveilling him for the last three days, with some very interesting results. He's been in communication with a small-time hoodlum who owns a bar and restaurant up near SeaTac on Highway 99. We think the hood is running numbers and appears to have a prostitution ring working out of his bar. He has been around for a long time and is pretty well connected. He may be buying some protection, to insure the ongoing operation of his illegal activities."

"Buying protection from who?"

"Apparently there are some cops up there who are willing to look the other way sometimes."

"Who is this restaurant guy?"

"His name is Vincent DeGrassi. He's a native Seattleite from over in Garlic Gulch. Learned his chops, and came up under old man Santini. Pulled a one to three for auto theft some time ago."

"What else do you have?" asked Chief Mills.

"The FBI was convinced the kidnappers were going to recover the ransom money from underwater. Even though the crooks tried to lead us to believe they were going to return to the crab pots by boat, and retrieve it by hauling it back up. That would be too easy to detect, so the FBI was certain they had to have underwater access. We just didn't know where Will was going to be instructed to drop the cash. They didn't make that critical call until the very last minute, so we couldn't get any bodies under water in a timely manner. Plus, we didn't want to do something to jeopardize

Chrissy. Because of the visibility of the case, the FBI was willing to send up a recon drone."

"I thought we weren't going to do anything like that."

"Chief, the FBI's technology is so sophisticated, no one even had a clue it was up there. Their high-resolution surveillance equipment can focus on an aluminum can floating on the water from five thousand feet. The drone was basically invisible. It was able to pick up a diver who emerged heading down the entrance to the Tacoma Narrows Marina. We could see his headlamp coming in and while he surfaced. He apparently missed the entrance to his berth. As he turned around, and found his way back on the surface, it seemed like he was towing some heavy cargo. Cargo that was very similar to one of the two large trash bag packages of ransom money we dropped off at Point Defiance. And the swashes of infrared paint on the outer drop bag--the FBI actually spelled out their name--showed right up on the blue light monitors."

"Whose idea was that anyway?"

"The agents from the Bureau guaranteed it could never be detected without special equipment."

"Wow. Did you investigate further at the Marina?"

"Yes sir. But before we were finished processing the surveillance information and could get a team over there, the perps had already set sail on a yacht. There were three of them, and they even appeared to be having a celebratory drink of champagne at the helm of the boat as they motored off. We checked their direction, and it looked like they were heading north for the Strait of Juan de Fuca. We alerted the Coast Guard stations in Seattle and throughout the Puget Sound region. They won't get by us, Chief."

"Don't let them slip into Canada. Then we will have to deal with extradition."

"No sir. There was actually a message from one of the Seattle outstations early this morning, and I think the yacht and its' three passengers has been detained up in Port Townsend. I just haven't had time to check it out yet."

"Then, there was another individual observed leaving the slip at the Narrows Marina. He was toting a trash can on a hand truck. We made his vehicle, and the FBI also have filed him in their facial recognition system."

"Who is he?"

"Another professional hoodlum named Tommy Thurston. He's a muscle guy, and apparently, a golfing buddy of DeGrazzi. Lives up in Normandy Park. We have both himself and his residence under twenty-four-hour surveillance.

Finally, we got a very good likeness from Chrissy and the composite artist yesterday. In spite of him wearing sunglasses, the drawing bears a striking resemblance to this Vincent DeGrazzi. If Chrissy can pick him out of a line-up, we should be in business there. Plus, DeGrazzi's Escalade was the other vehicle in Lenny's parking lot at the time of the second phone call to Will Jensen."

"Have you sat down with Alton Walker yet? That should be interesting as hell."

"I told him not to leave town last Friday evening, and made an appointment with him yesterday for twelve noon today to get a statement. He is chomping at the bit to get out of here, but I think he might be our guest downtown in the county slammer for a while. We don't believe he was involved in the actual abduction, but somehow, he seems to have gotten access to the alleged kidnappers. Since he didn't share his information with us, we can get him on felony abetting and withholding evidence. He thinks he is coming in today so we can verify him as having rescued Chrissy, which would make him eligible to claim the reward money. We will break him down as far as we can, Chief."

"Seems like there is a lot of sorting out to do, Danny. Walker won't be able to claim any reward money if the rescue was conducted illegally, correct? And what about Penny Brown?"

"Correct Chief, he won't be able to claim any money if his information on the rescue came to him through unlawful channels. And we don't feel like Penny Brown had anything to do with any criminal activities. We can talk to her, but I'm pretty sure she is buried trying to deal with all media firestorm that's going on."

"So, when are we going to proceed on the rest of this, Danny?"

"Later this afternoon, sir. Walker is in here at noon. Once he is processed, we'll need an hour or two to make sure the rest of our ducks are in a row, then we can go on it.

The FBI pulled DeGrazzi's tax returns for the last three years, and since there is some suspicion of multiple felonies and money laundering, plus weapons, gambling, and vice violations, in addition to armed kidnapping one, they are getting federal warrants for both DeGrazzi's home and business. They wanna have a look in his safe, at any bank deposit boxes, his residence, grab all his computer records, and will also round up as many of his employees as possible for preliminary statements and background checks. There is also a warrant for Thurston's residence, and we have been coordinating with King County on that."

"You have managed a fantastic piece of police work here Danny, congratulations. It looks like we can not only nab the kidnappers, but recover the ten million dollars in ransom money as well. The District Attorney is up to speed on everything?"

"Absolutely, Chief. Thanks, and yes, the District Attorney and his DDA are ready to go."

"After you wrap this up, call me, and I will notify our Media Relations Officer. She'll have a press conference set up for tomorrow mid-morning with our people and the FBI, eh?"

"You got it, Chief, and thanks for all of your support."

THE END

Acknowledgements

My sincere thanks to the following people for their timely assistance in helping assemble the material for this book, and for the seemingly endless work of editing and self-publishing a manuscript:

To the hard working, under paid ladies of the LPGA tour, and also the team that is the LPGA as an organization.

To our friend Linda Collins for her time spent not only as an early reader but for her significant contribution as a copy editor as well. Jennifer Hager, Marianne Hamilton, and Kevin Dwyer also contributed editorial input, and to Marguerite Kondrake who was an early reader with extensive experience in LPGA matters.

To former Under Sheriff of Los Angeles County Robert Edmonds, for sharing his expertise on daily Police Department operations, and their interaction with other law enforcement Bureaus. To Pete Stock, a neighbor and Washington State Trooper on his advice concerning questions of local jurisdictions.

A huge thanks to my daughter and her husband, Lauren and Devin Jensen, for their cover design work and help in navigating the self-publishing computer maze. Also, Geoffrey Jackson, Steven Kinsman and the computer wizards at AngelComputer in Tacoma, Washington.

To my good buddy and back cover model, Meryl Craft, who with her husband Brad, are expecting their first child. Godspeed there. To my niece, Deborah Hadrych and her son Steve for their time spend helping to develop a cover design. To John Petrek, whose design and content advise and observations were much appreciated.

To my good friends Craig Ross, Mike Gastineau, Paul O'Dowd, Ross McElfresh, Mike Buford and my son Jarett Jorgenson for their support and encouragement. You help keep the machine rolling guys.

Finally, I would like to thank my wife and partner, Marianne, for her patience and support. She was an early reader and also contributed computer skills and copy-editing expertise. Writing a book is a time consuming and solitary effort, and I thank you for donating the many days we would have otherwise spent exploring something fun together, while I was sitting in our office pecking away at the laptop. And now that we are wrapping things up, yes, I will as promised, take you back to Ireland in the near future.

Lee Jorgenson was born and raised in Southern California. He has lived in the Pacific Northwest for the last thirty-seven years, and is a current resident of Gig Harbor, Washington.

Jorgenson attended Orange Coast College and Northern Arizona University. He took up the game of golf in college. Lee is a Veteran of the US Army, and served a tour of duty in the Ben Hoa area of South Vietnam.

He has worked in various hotel and private club management positions, and operated his family's restaurant and catering business for over thirty years.

This is Lee's second novel in the golf genre. His first work, *Welcome to the Club* chronicles the sordid misadventures of a dysfunctional golf club in Vancouver, Washington.

Lee's hobbies are fishing and golf. He loves to play a round just about anywhere, and eats or shares every bite of salmon he is lucky enough to catch.

Should you wish to contact him, his email address: leejorgo12@gmail.com.

Made in the USA
San Bernardino, CA
19 March 2020